A NOVEL

STEALING JAKE

PAM HILLMAN

Tyndale House Publishers, Inc.
Carol Stream, Illinois

Visit Tyndale online at www.tyndale.com.

Visit Pam Hillman's website at www.pamhillman.com.

TYNDALE and Tyndale's quill logo are registered trademarks of Tyndale House Publishers, Inc.

Stealing Jake

Cover and title page designed by Erik M. Peterson

Edited by Erin E. Smith

Published in association with the literary agency of The Steve Laube Agency.

Scripture quotations are taken from the *Holy Bible*, King James Version.

Stealing Jake is a work of fiction. Where real people, events, establishments, organizations, or locales appear, they are used fictitiously. All other elements of the novel are drawn from the author's imagination.

Library of Congress Cataloging-in-Publication Data

Hillman, Pam.
  Stealing Jake / Pam Hillman.
    pages ; cm
    ISBN 978-1-4964-0126-7 (sc) — ISBN 9781414366609 (e-book)
    I. Title.
    PS3608.I448S74 2015
    813'.6—dc23   2015008436

Printed in the United States of America

21   20   19   18   17   16   15
 7   6   5   4   3   2   1

PROLOGUE

CHICAGO
OCTOBER 1874

"Where's my little brother?" Luke glared at the man with the jagged scar on his right cheek.

"You do as I say, kid, and he'll be along shortly." Pale-blue eyes, harder than the cobblestone streets of Chicago, bored into his. "Otherwise, I'll kill him. Understand?"

Luke stood his ground, memorizing the face of the man who'd paid off the coppers.

"Get in." The man motioned to a wooden crate not much bigger than an overturned outhouse.

Luke crammed in, the three other boys squeezing together, making room. Nobody said a word. Nobody cried. They didn't dare. Scarface would kill them if they disobeyed.

Luke knew he'd been stupid. He'd tried to teach Mark the art of picking pockets, and they'd gotten caught. But instead of going to jail as expected, money had changed hands, and they'd been handed off to the man with the scar.

And now Luke would be shipped out of Chicago. Without Mark.

He pulled his thin coat tight around him and curled into a ball for warmth.

Bam! Bam! Bam!

Luke shuddered with every slam of the hammer against the nails. He drew his knees to his chest, shivering. This time not from the cold.

Bam! Bam!

He pinched his eyes closed, fighting the urge to throw up.

His heart raced faster than the first time he'd picked a pocket.

Where was Mark?

CHAPTER ONE

CHESTNUT, ILLINOIS
NOVEMBER 1874

The ill-dressed, grimy child jostled a broad-shouldered cowboy, palming the man's pocket watch. Gold flashed as the thief discreetly handed his prize to another youngster shuffling along the boardwalk toward Livy O'Brien.

Livy didn't miss a thing—not the slick movements, not the tag-team approach. None of it.

Neither boy paid her any attention. And why should they? To them she was no more than a farmer's wife on her way home from the mercantile or maybe one of the workers over at the new glove factory.

If they only knew.

Her gaze cut to the man's back. When he patted down his pockets and his stride faltered, she made a split-second decision. As the thin boy with the timepiece passed, she knocked him into a pile of snow shoveled to the side of the wooden walkway. She reached out, pulled the child to his feet, and dusted him off so fast he didn't have time to move, let alone squirm away. She straightened his threadbare coat, two sizes too big and much too thin for an icebound Illinois winter. "Oh, I'm so sorry. Did I hurt you?"

Fathomless dark eyes stared at her from a hollow face. Eyes that reminded her of her own in the not-so-distant past. She wanted to hug him, take him home with her.

"No, ma'am." The words came out high-pitched and breathless.

"Hey, you!" The man hurried toward them.

Fear shuddered across the boy's face, and he jerked free of her grasp and darted down a nearby alley.

Livy let him go and stepped into the man's path, bracing herself as he slammed into her. The impact sent both of them hurtling toward the snowbank. The stranger wrapped his arms around her and took the brunt of the fall, expelling a soft grunt as Livy landed on top of him. Her gaze tripped off the end of her gloved fingers and collided with a pair of intense jade-green eyes. She stared, mesmerized by long, dark lashes and tiny lines that fanned out from the corners of his eyes. A hint of a smile lifted one corner of his mouth.

A slamming door jerked Livy back to reality.

Heat rushed to her face, and she rolled sideways, scrambling to untangle herself. What would Mrs. Brooks think of such an unladylike display?

"Ma'am?" Large, gloved hands grabbed her shoulders and pulled her to her feet. "Are you all right?"

"I'm fine."

"Those kids stole my watch." A muscle jumped in his jaw.

"Are you sure?" Remorse smote her with the same force as that of the stranger's body knocking her into the snow. She'd reacted, making a split-second decision that could have resulted in catastrophe.

"Yes, ma'am." He patted his sheepskin coat again. Suddenly he stilled and removed the watch from his pocket. "Well, I'll be. I could've sworn . . ." He gave her a sheepish look. "Sorry for running into you like that, ma'am."

Livy breathed a sigh and pulled her cloak tight against the cold. Disaster averted. *Forgive me, Lord. I hope I did the right thing.* "That's all right. No harm done."

The stranger pushed his hat back, releasing a tuft of dark, wavy hair over his forehead. "I don't believe we've met. Jake Russell."

Her gaze flickered toward the alley that had swallowed up the boy. She didn't make a habit of introducing herself to strangers, but revealing her name might keep Mr. Russell's mind off the boys who'd waylaid him. "Livy O'Brien."

"It's a pleasure to meet you, Mrs. O'Brien."

"*Miss* O'Brien," she said. At least the gathering twilight masked the flush she could feel stealing across her cheeks.

Was it her imagination, or did the grin on Jake Russell's face grow wider?

"Pleased to meet you, Miss O'Brien. May I escort you to wherever you're going?" His eyes twinkled. "It'll be dark soon, and a lady shouldn't be out alone after dark."

Livy sobered. She'd never claimed to be a lady. The tiny glow inside her faded with the setting sun. Mr. Russell would never be interested in Light-Fingered Livy O'Brien. "No thank you, Mr. Russell. I'm not going far. I'll be fine."

"I'd feel better, ma'am." He gestured toward the alley. "Especially after what happened."

He held out his arm, one eyebrow cocked in invitation. Her emotions warred with her head. She shouldn't allow such liberties, but what harm would it do to let him escort her home?

Just once.

She placed her hand in the crook of his arm. "Very well. Thank you, Mr. Russell."

"Call me Jake."

Livy's heart gave a nervous flutter. Did Mr. Russell mask his intentions behind a gentlemanly face and kindly words? A common enough practice where she came from. "I'm afraid using your given name would be a little too familiar. I don't know anything about you."

"Well, I can remedy that. What do you want to know?"

Livy shook her head, softening her refusal with a smile. It wouldn't do to ask the man questions about himself. If she did, then he'd feel at liberty to ask questions of his own. Questions she didn't want to answer.

He chuckled. "You sure are a shy little thing, Miss O'Brien."

Better to let him think her bashful than know the truth. A couple of years ago, she might have spun a yarn or two to keep him entertained, but no longer. If she couldn't speak the truth, she'd say nothing at all.

Her silence didn't stop him. "You must be new around here. I don't remember seeing you before."

"I arrived in Chestnut about two months ago."

"That explains it. I've only been back in town a few weeks myself."

Livy darted a glance from the corner of her eye to study him. Discreetly, of course—she'd at least learned *something* from Mrs. Brooks. The top of her head barely reached his chin, and broad shoulders filled out his coat. A late-afternoon shadow dusted his firm jawline.

He stepped off the boardwalk and helped her across a patch of ice. Her stomach flopped when his green eyes connected with hers, and she blurted out the first thing that popped into her mind. "Oh? Where've you been?"

She could've bitten her tongue. She shouldn't have asked, but curiosity had gotten the best of her. What made her want to know more about Jake Russell? Mercy, why should she even wonder about the man? He wasn't anyone she should worry with.

If only her foolish girl's heart would listen to reason.

"Taking care of some business in Missouri. It's good to be home, though."

They ambled in silence past the Misses Huff Millinery Shop and the recently opened Chinese laundry. The scent of green lumber tickled Livy's nose, bringing forth the image of the fresh sprig of mistletoe hung over the door of the orphanage.

The boardwalk ended just past the laundry. Livy gestured into the gathering darkness. "It's a little farther down this way."

"I don't mind."

The snow-covered ground lay frozen, Livy's footprints

from when she'd trekked into town the only evidence of anyone being out and about on this frigid day.

They rounded the bend, and Livy eased her hand from the warmth of Jake's arm when they came within sight of the rambling two-story house nestled under a grove of cottonwoods. "Thank you, Mr. Russell. This is where I live."

*　　*　　*

Jake studied the building before returning his attention to the petite lady at his side. He'd known the moment he laid eyes on her that they hadn't met. He would have remembered. "This is the new orphanage, isn't it?"

"Yes. That's right."

"I heard someone opened one up. 'Bout time. Lots of young'uns needing a place to stay these days."

"We already have five children in our care."

They stepped onto the porch, and she pushed the hood of her cape back. Light from inside the house shot fire through reddish-brown curls and revealed a smattering of freckles across a pert nose.

She'd knocked the wind out of him earlier, and the feeling came back full force now.

Whoa.

Jake stepped back, putting some distance between them. He didn't have the time or the energy to be thinking about a girl, no matter how pretty she might be. His days and nights were chock-full as it was. He tipped his hat. "Good night, Miss O'Brien."

Her smile lit up the dreary winter landscape. "Thank you for escorting me home, Mr. Russell. Good night."

He headed back toward town, rehashing the brief conversation he'd had with Livy O'Brien. She'd sure seemed reluctant to talk about herself. Come to think of it, she hadn't told him much of anything.

Did he make her nervous? He should have told her who he was, but the thought hadn't crossed his mind. Knowing he was a sheriff's deputy would have put her at ease, but she hadn't seemed the least bit interested in who he was or what he did for a living.

He continued his rounds, confident he'd find out more about Miss Livy O'Brien soon enough. It was part of his job, plain and simple. He chuckled. He didn't remember anything in his job description that said he needed to investigate every beautiful lady he ran across. Still, it was his job to protect the town, and the more he knew about its inhabitants, the better.

Not that Chestnut needed protection from Livy O'Brien. A pretty little filly like her wouldn't hurt a fly.

His steps faltered when he stuffed his hands in his pockets and his fingers slid over the cool, polished surface of his father's gold watch. Not prone to jump to conclusions or get easily flustered, he'd been certain those kids had lifted his timepiece. How could he have been so mistaken?

Good thing he'd bumped into Miss O'Brien, or he would have had a hard time explaining why he'd chased an innocent kid down the street.

Still, he had reason to be suspicious. There'd been reports of scruffy young boys like the two tonight roaming the streets of Chestnut. Urchins from back East, Sheriff Carter said. Run out of Chicago, they rode the train to the nearest town large enough to provide easy pickings.

He settled his hat more firmly on his head. Those raga-muffins didn't know it yet, but they shouldn't have stopped in Chestnut. The town wasn't big enough for thieves and robbers to hide out for long.

Jake clomped along the boardwalk, part of his thoughts on the youngsters, part on the girl he'd left at the orphanage, and part registering the sights and sounds of merchants shutting down for the night.

He hesitated as he spied Paul Stillman locking up the bank. An urge to turn down the nearest alley assaulted him, but he doggedly stayed his course.

The banker lifted a hand. "Jake. Wait up a minute."

A knot twisted in Jake's gut. Would Stillman call in his loan today?

The portly man hurried toward him, his hand outstretched, a wide smile on his florid face. "Jake. How're things going?"

"Fine." Jake shook the banker's hand, the knot intensifying. Mr. Stillman's continued grace made him feel worse than if the banker had demanded payment on the spot.

"And your mother?" His concern poured salt on Jake's unease.

"She's doing well."

"That's good. I should be going, then. I just wanted to check on the family."

Jake rubbed his jaw. "Look, Mr. Stillman, I appreciate all you've done for my family, but I'm going to pay off that loan. Every penny of it."

The banker sobered. "I know you will, Jake. I never doubted it for a minute. The last couple of years have been tough for you and Mrs. Russell."

"Pa wouldn't have borrowed money against the farm if he'd known. . . ." Jake's throat closed. "If the crops hadn't failed the last two summers, I could've made the payments."

The banker took off his glasses and rubbed them with a white handkerchief. His eyes pinned Jake, razor sharp in intensity. "That investor is still interested in buying your father's share of the Black Gold mine, you know."

"The answer is no. I'm not selling." Jake clenched his jaw. He wouldn't be party to more death and destruction.

"That's what I thought you'd say." Stillman sighed. "I admire your determination to protect miners by not selling, but as much as I'd like to, I can't carry that loan forever."

Jake shifted his weight, forcing his muscles to relax. It wasn't the banker's fault that life had dealt him a losing hand. "I know. This summer will be better."

"We'll see." Mr. Stillman stuffed the cloth in his pocket, settled his glasses on his nose, and tugged his coat close against the biting wind. "I'd better get on home. This weather is going to be the death of me. Say hello to your mother for me, will you?"

"I'll do that. Good night."

The banker waved a hand over his shoulder and hurried away. Jake stared after him. Would this summer be any different from last year? It would take a miracle to bring in enough from the farm to pay off the loan against the defunct mine.

A sharp blast rent the air, signaling the evening shift change at the mines. Jake turned northward. The low hills sat shrouded in a blanket of pure, white snow. Peaceful.

An illusion. The mines beneath the ground held anything but purity. Coal dust, death, and destruction existed there.

Along with enough coal to pay off the loan.
Jake turned his back on the mine and walked away.

* * *

Mrs. Brooks glanced up from the coal-burning stove when Livy entered the kitchen. "How'd it go?"

Livy took off her cloak and hung it on a nail along with several threadbare coats in varying sizes before moving to warm her hands over the stovetop. She closed her eyes and breathed deep. The aroma of vegetable soup simmering on the stove and baking bread welcomed her home. "Nobody's hiring. Not even the glove factory."

Mrs. Brooks sank into an old rocker. The runners creaked as she set the chair in motion. "What are we going to do?"

Worry lines knit the older woman's brow, and Livy turned away. She rubbed the tips of her fingers together. How easy it would be to obtain the money needed to keep them afloat. Livy had visited half a dozen shops today, all of them easy pickings.

She slammed a lid on the shameful images. Those thoughts should be long gone, but they snuck up on her when she was most vulnerable. When Mrs. Brooks's faith wavered, Livy's hit rock bottom.

She balled her hands into fists and squeezed her eyes shut. *Lord, I don't want to go back to that life. Ever.*

Livy forced herself to relax and turned to face Mrs. Brooks. "Maybe the citizens of Chestnut will help."

"I've tried, Livy. A few have helped us out, mostly by donating clothes their own children have outgrown. And I'm more than thankful. But money to keep up with the payments on this old place? And food?" Her gaze strayed toward the bucket of coal. "Except for our guardian angel who keeps the coal bin full, most everybody is in about as bad a shape as we are. They don't have much of anything to give."

"Don't worry, ma'am." Livy patted the older woman's shoulder, desperate to hear the ironclad faith ring in her voice. "You keep telling me the Lord will provide."

Mrs. Brooks smiled. "You're right, dear. He will. I've told you time and again that we should pray for what we need, and here I am, doubting the goodness of God. Let's pray, child. The Lord hasn't let me down yet, and I'm confident He never will."

The rocker stopped, and Mrs. Brooks took Livy's hand in hers and closed her eyes. "Lord, You know the situation here. We've got a lot of mouths to feed and not much in the pantry. Livy is doing all she can, and I thank You for her every day. We're asking You to look down on us and see our need. These children are Yours, Lord, and we need help in providing food for them and keeping a roof over their heads. In Jesus' name we pray. Amen." She heaved herself out of the rocker and headed to the stove, a new resolve in her step. "Call the children, Livy. It's almost time for supper."

Livy trudged down the hall to the parlor. The short prayer had cheered Mrs. Brooks but hadn't done much to ease Livy's worry. She'd have to find some way to bring in a few extra dollars if they were to make it to spring. Otherwise, she and Mrs. Brooks and the small brood of children they'd taken in would be on the streets of Chestnut before winter's end. The elderly woman would never survive if that happened.

A wave of panic washed over her like fire sweeping through the slums of Chicago. Livy couldn't have another life on her conscience. She took a deep breath. They weren't on the streets yet. And as long as they had a roof over their heads and food on the table, there was hope.

She stepped into the parlor. Mary, the eldest child at twelve, kept the younger ones occupied on a quilt set up in the corner. The two boys, Seth and Georgie, stacked small wooden blocks, then howled with laughter when they knocked the tower down, only to start the process again.

"Libby! Libby!" a sweet voice trilled.

Livy held out her arms as Mary's little sister, Grace, toddled to her. "Hello, sweetheart."

The toddler patted her cheeks. "Libby's home! Libby's home!"

Livy nuzzled the child's neck, inhaling her sweet baby scent. Grace giggled.

"Yes, Libby's home." Livy glanced at Mary and the other children. "It's almost time for supper. Go wash up now."

Against her better judgment, Livy's mind conjured up flashing green eyes as she wiped Grace's face and hands. Would Jake Russell call on her? Why would such a thought even occur to her? What man who could have his pick of women would call on a girl who lived in an orphanage, a girl who came from a questionable background and didn't have a penny to her name?

And one who'd sprawled all over him like a strumpet.

Mercy! What if Miss Maisie or Miss Janie, the Huff sisters, had witnessed such an unladylike display? Her reputation would be in tatters. Not that she'd brought much of a reputation with her to Chestnut, but Mrs. Brooks had insisted she could start over here. There was no need to air her past like a stained quilt on a sunny day.

Maybe she wouldn't see Jake again. Or maybe she would. Chestnut wasn't that big.

More importantly, did she want to see him?

She didn't have any interest in courting, falling in love, and certainly no interest in marriage and childbirth. She knew firsthand where that could lead. Rescuing children from the streets fulfilled her desire for a family, and she'd do well to remember that.

Georgie shoved ahead of Seth. Livy snagged the child and tucked him back in line. "Don't push. You'll have your turn."

When all hands were clean, Livy led the way to the kitchen. A scramble ensued as the children jockeyed for position at the long trestle table.

Mrs. Brooks clapped her hands. "All right, everyone, it's time to say the blessing." Her firm but gentle voice calmed the chaos, and the children settled down. "Thank You, Lord, for the food we are about to partake. Bless each one at this table, and keep us safe from harm. Amen."

The children dug in with relish, and Livy took Grace from Mary's arms. "Here; I'll feed her. Enjoy your supper."

Livy mashed a small helping of vegetables in a saucer and let them cool.

"Grace do it," the child demanded.

"All right, but be careful." Livy concentrated on helping the child feed herself without making too much of a mess.

Thwack! Thwack! Thwack!

Livy jumped as loud knocking reverberated throughout the house.

"I wonder who that could be?" Mrs. Brooks folded her napkin.

"I'll get it." Livy stepped into the foyer. Resting her hand on the knob, she called out, "Who's there?"

"Sheriff Carter, ma'am."

Livy's hands grew damp, but she resisted the urge to bolt. The sheriff didn't have reason to question her or to haul her off to jail. Jesus had washed away her sins and made her a new creature. She wasn't the person she'd been two years ago. She prayed every day she wouldn't let Him down.

Some days were harder than others.

She took a deep breath and opened the door, a smile plastered on her face. "Good evening, Sheriff. May I help you?"

The aged sheriff touched his fingers to his hat. "Evening, ma'am. Sorry to bother you, but we've got a problem."

"Yes?"

The sheriff glanced toward the street, and for the first time, Livy noticed a wagon and the silhouettes of several people.

Mrs. Brooks appeared behind her. "What is it, Livy?"

Sheriff Carter spoke up. "There's been a wagon accident. A family passing through on the outskirts of town. Their horses bolted. I'm sad to say the driver—a man—was killed, leaving three children."

Livy peered into the darkness, her heart going out to the little ones. "Are the children out there? Are they hurt?"

"They're fine. Nary a scratch as far as we can tell. We thought the orphanage might take them."

"Of course." Mrs. Brooks took charge. "Bring them in out

14

of the cold. Livy, go fetch some blankets. The poor dears are probably frozen with cold and fear."

Livy ran, her mind flying as fast as her feet. Less than an hour before, they'd prayed for help to feed the children already in their care. How could they manage three more? Of course they couldn't turn them away. They'd never do that. But would she be forced to do something drastic to feed them all?

Lord, don't make me choose. I'm not strong enough.

Heart heavy, she found three worn blankets and carried them downstairs.

Mrs. Brooks met her in the hallway. "They're in the kitchen. Mary's already taken the other children to the parlor."

Her arms laden with the blankets, Livy followed Mrs. Brooks. Two girls huddled together on the bench at the table, their eyes wide and frightened. Poor things. If only she could take them in her arms and tell them everything would be all right. It must be. She'd beg in the streets before she'd let them all starve.

She searched the room for the third child. Her gaze landed on a tall, broad-shouldered man with a tiny dark-haired child nestled snugly inside his sheepskin coat. The man lifted his head, and Livy came face-to-face with Jake Russell. She saw a fierce protectiveness in his haunted eyes.

"I don't believe you've met my deputy, Jake Russell." Sheriff Carter waved in Jake's direction.

Dread pooled in the pit of Livy's stomach, and for the space of a heartbeat, she stared.

"Pleased to meet you, Deputy Russell," Mrs. Brooks said, her attention already on the two little girls at the table. "I'm Mrs. Brooks, and this is Livy O'Brien."

Livy jerked her head in a stiff nod. For a few moments tonight she'd let her imagination run away with her, thinking maybe Jake Russell would call on her, that he might want to court her, that maybe he thought she was pretty.

And maybe he would. Maybe he did.

But it didn't matter. It *couldn't* matter.

Jake Russell was an officer of the law, and Livy had spent her entire life running from the law.

CHAPTER TWO

TWO WEEKS OF SEARCHING, and still no sign of Mark.

Luke crept forward, keeping to the dark shadows of the warehouse but edging closer and closer to the two men who'd brought three crates from the train.

"I need a shot of whiskey." The man named Butch slapped the top of a crate and growled. "These filthy little beggars ain't goin' nowhere."

The other one, Grady, laughed and threw a crowbar on top of a crate. The steel crashed like a clap of thunder in the stillness. "Sounds good to me."

The two men stomped off, taking the lantern and leaving the warehouse in total darkness.

Suspicion clouded Luke's mind. They never left the crates unattended. Could it be a trick? No, they couldn't know he was here. He shot out of his hiding place and knocked on the nearest crate, three times, a space, twice, three more. "Mark? Anybody? Knock if you're there. Hurry. We don't have much time."

No response. Not even a whisper.

He moved to the next wooden box, his heart threatening to jump out of his throat like a frog leaping off an overflowing water barrel.

Please. Please. Please answer.

Finally a faint gasp from inside the last crate made him nearly jump out of his skin. He scrambled backward. Where was that crowbar? The crate on the end, near the door. He stumbled through the darkness, counting crates as he went.

One. Two. Three. His fingers touched cold steel.

He wrapped his hand around the metal, then hurried back to the crate and pried against the lid. He gritted his teeth and hung every bit of his weight on the crowbar. The shriek of nails pulling free bounced through the warehouse. He paused, muscles aching. If Butch and Grady came back now, he'd be dead.

Better dead than leaving Mark to fend for himself.

The last nail popped free, and he reached inside. His grasping fingers met rough cotton and a bony shoulder before the kid gasped and jerked away. No time to explain who he was and what he was doing. "Mark?"

The kids in the crate didn't move, didn't speak, didn't even answer.

"Has anyone seen a boy named Mark? He's five but looks a lot younger."

"Who wants to know?" A scared voice shot back with a touch of bravado.

"My name's Luke. I'm his brother. I've got to find him."

"Don't know no Mark."

Luke's hopes shattered like the splintered boards he'd pried off the crate. What had happened to Mark? He should have been in Chestnut by now. But even if his brother wasn't here, he could pluck these kids out of Grady and Butch's clutches.

"Let's go. They'll be back any minute."

"Why should we trust you?"

Luke slammed a hand against the side of the crate. "What did they tell you? That they'd found families for you and the coppers had agreed to let you go out of the goodness of their hearts?"

His questions were met with silence.

"It's all a lie. They paid off the coppers. You'll work sixteen hours a day for a crust of bread and a pail of dirty water from the creek once a day. But if you want to stay, it's no skin off my nose."

He headed for the door.

A rustle of clothes filled the darkness as the street urchins climbed out of the wooden box. "All right. But you'd better be telling the truth."

Before they could reach the door, it burst open and slammed against the wall. Light spilled across the floor. Luke grabbed a little girl no more than five or six years old and dove between two crates. When he looked back, the other kids had disappeared from sight.

Luke hugged the girl close. He didn't have to tell her to stay quiet. She didn't utter a sound.

Eerie shadows danced against the walls. A tall man dressed

in a thick overcoat strode into Luke's line of vision, followed by the hulking forms of Butch and Grady.

Light reflected off the diamond stickpin in the man's necktie. A stickpin he'd bought from the labor of children.

The man faced Butch and Grady. "If you two ever pull a stunt like that again, you'll pay—and pay dearly."

"We didn't mean no harm, boss. And it's not like they can go anywhere."

The man stopped and held the lantern high. Brightness spilled from the globe, stretched out, and pushed the darkness away.

"Then what is this?"

The icy chill of suppressed rage in the clipped words spurred Luke to action. The girl still in his arms, he lunged for the door.

"Hey," Grady yelled, but Luke had a head start. He ducked out the door. Gaining speed, he darted around the corner of the building, down one alley, then another, finally burrowing beneath a pile of crates. He held the girl close.

Grady ran by their hiding place, cursing a blue streak.

Luke kept still, the little girl tight against him. Minutes ticked by, but Luke waited.

"There was a Mark." The little girl's voice was a whisper in the cold night air.

Luke's heart slammed hard against his rib cage. "Where?"

"In the other crate."

✳ ✳ ✳

Would he see Miss O'Brien again?

Jake hauled the wagon to a stop in front of the orphanage.

He halfway hoped Mrs. Brooks would answer the door so he could complete his mission and hoof it back to town like a scared rabbit. He didn't have time to think about a woman, but his thoughts didn't seem to understand that fact.

He set the brake and stared at the rambling old farmhouse nestled in a grove of trees, as if it had been waiting for a bunch of orphans to show up and take over. The snow had stopped for the time being, but the dark, moisture-laden clouds threatened to dump more anytime. He jumped down and crunched across the white surface to the front porch, knocked, and waited. He tugged off one glove and undid the top button of his coat before he suffocated. It might be below freezing outside, but the thought of seeing Livy again brought his temperature up a notch or two.

Livy answered the door, and he blinked. Last night's dim light hadn't done her justice. Her eyes were bluer than he remembered, her hair a deeper russet brown. She'd twisted the mass up on top of her head, but a few curls trailed down onto the starched, stand-up collar of her dress. What would her hair feel like? Would it curl around his fingers like it curled against her long, slender neck? He clamped his jaw, shoving down his distracting thoughts.

"Good afternoon, Miss O'Brien." Jake yanked off his hat and forced words past the coal-size lump in his throat.

She dipped her head, prim and proper. "Deputy Russell."

"Just Jake, ma'am."

A hint of a blush covered her cheeks. "Won't you come in?"

He entered the warmth of the foyer and unfastened the remaining buttons on his coat. To his left, a savory aroma wafted out of the kitchen, and to his right, the sounds of energetic—if off-key—singing drifted from the parlor.

Livy tracked his gaze toward the noise. "The children have finished their chores for the day, and Mrs. Brooks decided to teach them a few carols."

"They seem to be enjoying themselves."

She gave him a bright smile that seemed to come out of nowhere and sucker punch him in the gut. "Yes, they are."

He cleared his throat, trying not to stare at the way her lips tilted just so at the corners. But he couldn't help himself. The right corner tipped up slightly more than the left. His pulse ratcheted up a notch.

Whoa, Russell. Think of something else.

"Sheriff Carter and I spent the morning out at the site of the accident."

Her smile faded like the winter sun behind snow-laden clouds. "Did you find anything?"

"A Bible with the family's last name: Hays. The sheriff's trying to contact the next of kin, but it might take a while. Anyway, I've got the family's supplies in the back of the wagon. There are a couple of trunks, too. Where do you want them?"

"Supplies?" Lines knit her brow.

"Meal, flour, sugar. All kinds of provisions. Seems Mr. Hays was a careful man. Wherever they were headed, he didn't intend to run out of anything."

"But we can't take the Hayses' supplies."

"The orphanage is taking care of the children." He nodded toward the parlor. "And a lot of others from the sound of it. I'd say you're more entitled than anyone else."

She worried her bottom lip for a moment. "I suppose you're right. Pull around back while I tell Mrs. Brooks."

Jake went out into the cold and drove the wagon around to the side porch off the kitchen. Livy waited, the door open behind her. The two of them unloaded the wagon, Livy taking the smaller items and Jake wrestling with the kegs of flour and sugar and the two trunks. He shouldered the heaviest of the trunks, grunting. Finally they had everything stacked haphazardly inside the storage room.

Jake stood with his hands on his hips, breathing hard. But the expression on Livy's face made the labor worth it all. She looked like a child at the candy counter over at McIver's, her blue eyes sparkling with excitement.

"It's an answer to prayer." She ran her hand over a barrel of sugar. "I can't believe there's so much."

He removed his coat and wiped his sleeve across his brow. "Maybe Mr. Hays intended to open a store."

"Poor man. Did you ever find out what happened?"

Jake shook his head. "We really couldn't tell. Something must have spooked the horses while he was taking the harnesses off. It's a miracle the children weren't hurt."

"Yes, it is." She hesitated and looked away from him, her gaze finally landing on the stove. A blush stole over her cheeks. "Would you like some coffee before you go?"

He hesitated. He'd worked up a sweat hauling in the supplies, but a cup of coffee would be nice. "Thanks."

"I'm afraid it's been sitting on the stove awhile."

"If I can drink that stuff Sheriff Carter makes, I can drink anything."

She laughed. He liked the sound, like little silver bells.

"Do you take sugar? I'm afraid we're out of cream."

"Black is fine."

As Jake nursed his cup of coffee, Livy stirred a big pot of stew, and he tried to think of something to bring her out of her shell. She tucked a strand of hair behind her ear before glancing over her shoulder at him, a questioning look on her face.

"How long have you known Mrs. Brooks?"

Her gaze shifted, and she turned away. The ladle in her hand seemed to have become the most important thing in the world. "About two years."

"Then you're not from around here, are you? Sheriff Carter said she came from Chicago."

"Yes, that's right." She reached for the coffeepot, her smile firmly in place. Had he imagined her unease? "Would you like some more?"

Her eyes flashed like a bluebird on the wing, and his fingers itched to feel the softness of her cheek, the curve of her jaw. He blinked. What kind of spell had Livy O'Brien woven? Or was he weaving one of his own? He needed to concentrate all his energies on paying off that loan before he lost the family farm. Then, maybe, he'd think about courting, about starting a family. But not for a long, long time.

"No thank you. I'd better get back to the jail."

He gulped the rest of the bitter brew and grabbed his hat, determined to put some distance between himself and Livy O'Brien.

CHAPTER THREE

THE BOSS TURNED TOWARD the motley group of kids cowering in front of him. One gangly boy stared back at him, angry defiance on his face. Grady stood in front of the door, muscled arms crossed over his chest. The faint hum of sewing machines in the next room overrode the silence.

The boss pinned the boy with a look that meant business. "What's your name?"

"Bobby." The kid's chin lifted, and he looked him square in the face. Cheeky little bugger. The kid would bear watching.

"How'd you get out of the crate?" He reached for an apple, well aware the children hadn't eaten in days.

The boy looked away from the fruit, a mulish expression settling over his face.

"So you don't want to tell me, huh?" He sliced off a small piece of apple and stuck it in his mouth, chewing slowly. There were ways to make him talk. "Grady?"

"Yeah, boss?" Grady straightened, flexing his muscles.

He nodded toward a small, dark-eyed youngster. Grady grabbed the child and wrapped his beefy hands around the kid's arm. The kid's eyes widened.

One squeeze would crush the arm like a bug.

The boss's gaze slid back to Bobby. "When I ask a question, I expect an answer."

The kid stood rigid, watchful, eyes narrowed.

One thing he'd learned about these kids: they were street savvy to the core. Both boys knew exactly what would happen if somebody didn't give an answer.

Soon.

Bobby's gaze bounced between the boss and Grady's too-eager hold on the smaller child. Grady's free hand wrapped around the boy's neck, fingers flexing, an evil grin spreading across his face.

The boss flicked a small piece of apple peel toward Grady. "Easy. No need to get carried away."

They could use the kid in the factory, but it was more important the others knew who was in charge. "Now, Bobby, you want to tell me what happened in the warehouse?"

"A boy, an older kid, pried the lid off and let us out."

"What's his name?"

Something flickered between the two boys.

Interesting. Did they know more than they were letting on?

"Grady." The boss spoke the name quietlike, but Grady

knew what to do. His fingers tightened on the kid's neck. The dark eyes widened with fear, and a whimper gurgled up the small throat.

"He said his name was Luke. That's all I know." The words rushed out of Bobby in his haste to protect the younger boy.

The boss motioned to Grady, and the ex-prizefighter loosened his grip.

"Luke, huh?" Settling on the corner of his desk, the boss smiled at the youngsters. This little episode might turn out for the good. These kids were so afraid him and Grady, they'd do anything. Anything at all.

"Grady, take them to the back. Bobby can run one of the sewing machines. I think he's more than up to the task."

"Yes, sir." Grady opened the door. "Come on. Let's go."

The youngsters followed Grady through the door, meek as little lambs. Just the way the boss liked them. Grady slammed the door shut, locking it behind him, and the boss settled behind his desk and reached for a cigar.

Luke.

Must be one of the kids who'd gotten away the night a crate fell off the train and burst open. The four boys inside had scattered like rats down the alleys of Chestnut.

He'd watched them go. There was no way to link them to him, and they were criminals, after all. The last place they'd go was to the cops. He lit his cigar and took a puff, eyes narrowed in thought.

But why would this Luke risk his life to save the others? Now there was a question worth pondering.

* * *

Boards creaked under Jake's boots as he made his midnight rounds. A scuffling sound came from a nearby alley, and he paused. Were those street kids prowling around again? He eased into the shadows and followed the noise. Ten yards into the passageway, a familiar humming wafted toward him.

What was Gus doing out so late?

Augustus P. Jones lived in a shack outside of town. He did odd jobs for people but didn't mingle with many. The old man had risked his life to pull Jake out of a tight spot a couple years ago, and Jake made a habit of checking on him as often as he could.

"Gus?" he called out, careful not to startle him. "Augustus?"

A loud clattering and banging ensued, and Jake winced. So much for not scaring the old feller. It didn't take much to send Gus into a panic.

"Whaddaya want? I ain't got nuthin'."

"Gus, it's all right. It's me, Jake."

A nervous laugh shot out of the darkness, followed by the shadowy form of a round, little man leading a donkey hitched to a cart. "You scared the bejeebers outta me, Mr. Jake." He wiped a hand across his whiskered face.

"Sorry, Gus. I didn't mean to. What've you been doing today?"

"Nuthin' much." Gus shrugged and dropped his head, tucking his chin against his chest.

"Help McIver any?"

He shook his head. "No, sir."

Why was he being so evasive?

Gus eased away, signaling the end to the conversation.

Jake scratched the donkey behind the ears, then swiped at the snowflakes clinging to the animal's back. "It's starting to snow again. You'd better head on home before it gets real heavy."

"Yes, sir, me and Little Bit was just about to do that."

"Take care of yourself, Gus. Are you warm enough? Got enough coal to keep your fire going?"

But Gus and his donkey were already shuffling down the alley, Gus humming a tune that sounded like a Christmas carol. Jake continued his rounds, hoping the old man would be all right. He'd check on him tomorrow, just to be sure.

* * *

By the time Livy draped her heavy black cloak over her shoulders and pulled the hood over her hair, darkness covered the town. But she wasn't worried. The darkness was as familiar as the cloak she wore. She wrapped a shawl around her neck and covered half her face before picking up a basket of leftovers and two blankets. The food wasn't much, but it was better than nothing.

She glanced at the overflowing pantry. One prayer answered in abundance. How could she have doubted God? Her faith in God's provision was so weak—and her faith in herself was even weaker. She'd learn to depend on God and not take matters into her own hands if it killed her.

Hurrying back to the pie safe, she added several more slices of corn bread and the rest of the leftover ham. The food in the pantry wouldn't last forever, but she couldn't bear to let even one street kid go hungry.

The latch clicked quietly as she inched open the back door of the orphanage. She paused at the sight of more snow drifting out of the night sky. The drop in temperature from a few hours before caused her to shiver, and the temptation to abandon her mission and go back inside gripped her.

But memories of brutal nights just like this one assaulted her, and she could no more turn around and head back inside to the warmth of the orphanage than she could cease to breathe. She pulled her cloak closer, determined to see her task through.

She picked her way across the frozen ground, watching for icy spots. When the clouds parted, feeble moonlight reflected off the snow, lighting her way. She crossed in front of the laundry, headed down the alley between the livery stable and the blacksmith shop, angled across another street, and came to the edge of shantytown.

The snow was deeper here, but at least the powder kept her from slipping and sliding on ice. The grist mill lay dormant, ice clinging to the huge paddle wheel. Pausing, she peered into a narrow alley leading to the frozen creek behind the buildings.

At least the wind had died down. For now.

Thank You, Lord.

Stacks of empty crates and boxes leaned haphazardly against the outer walls of the buildings. A heavy blanket of snow covered every inch of the area, creating the illusion of softness and purity. Nothing could be further from the truth. The black mud and coal-dusted surfaces beneath the snow mimicked the bleak circumstances of many inhabitants of shantytown, especially the boys she'd come to find. She picked her way through the cluttered alley to the dilapidated cabins along the creek bank.

The gutted shanties showed evidence of fire in the recent past. Some structures still stood, leaning against each other like drunks after a long night at the saloon. Others lay collapsed upon themselves, having succumbed to the ravages of fire and decay. The first big gust of wind—or even another layer of new-fallen snow—might bring the remaining shacks crashing down.

Then it would be too late to find the boys who'd tried to steal Jake's watch. And too late to convince them to come to the orphanage, where they could have a hot meal and a warm place to sleep.

She'd caught glimpses of them around town a couple of times. Tattered clothes covered their wasted bodies, and a hungry, desperate look emanated from their eyes.

She knew that look. She'd lived it.

It would take courage for them to give up their freedom and come to the orphanage. But she'd win them over. No matter what it took, no matter how long.

Livy peered into the darkness. Would the children come forward tonight? She listened but heard nothing other than raucous laughter accompanied by the out-of-tune piano from the saloon down the street. She shoved aside a half-rotted crate and placed the basket against the wall. The kids would come for it. They always did.

Livy turned to go.

Rustling echoed behind her. She hesitated. A rat? Or the kids? She couldn't tell . . . the noise had come from the other end of the alley.

She gestured in the direction of the basket. "I brought some corn bread, fried ham, and two more blankets. I know you're there, and I understand why you won't come out. I just want you to know that—" she paused for a moment—"all of you are welcome at the orphanage. It's not much, but at least there's a fire to keep you warm and food to eat."

No response. Had she really expected any?

Livy pulled her cloak close. Unbidden, hot tears sprang to her eyes and overflowed, burning icy tracks down her cheeks.

Lord, why won't they listen? How many have to freeze to death before they realize I only want to help them? Show me what to do, where to go. Take me to them, Lord, or bring them to me. Before it's too late. No matter what it takes, please help me save these children.

She waited until the cold seeped through her cloak and into her bones; then she turned away. She'd done all she could for now. She didn't have to tell them how to find the orphanage. One of them had followed her home one night. He hadn't tried to talk to her or come inside, but he'd been curious enough to find the place. She had thought she'd have time to win him over, but the sudden drop in temperature worried her. Trust didn't come easy for kids who lived on the streets. She knew that better than anybody.

She left the alley, hurrying through the deserted town toward the warmth of home. She stepped off the boardwalk and skirted a patch of ice, concentrating on her footing. Too late, she caught a glimpse of movement seconds before colliding with a solid wall of muscle and sinew. Steel bands reached out, grasping her shoulders to keep her upright.

"Whoa."

Jake Russell.

Her heart skittered against her rib cage, and she fought the urge to wrench herself from his grasp and flee into the night.

She closed her eyes and took a deep breath. She'd done nothing wrong. Nothing. She'd been on an errand of mercy—nothing more, nothing less.

"Livy?" He gave her a gentle shake. "What in the world are you doing out here so late?"

"I had an errand to run."

"It couldn't wait until morning?" he asked. "You don't have any idea the kind of riffraff wandering the streets at night." He jerked his head in the direction of the bawdy music. "Especially this close to the saloons."

His brows drew together in a concerned frown. The man only wanted to protect her. He couldn't know she'd seen much worse than anything the small town of Chestnut offered.

She patted his arm. "It's all right. I know what I'm doing."

"I'll escort you home." He pulled her gloved hand through the crook of his arm. "Not only are drunkards and gamblers roaming the streets, we've got those street kids from Chicago to deal with."

Livy's heart skipped a beat. Had the boys done something foolish? As long as they stayed out of sight, the townspeople wouldn't give them a second thought. "What's happened?"

"Somebody broke into the laundry last night."

Oh no. "What did they take?"

"Some blankets and coats and stuff. Not much."

"They're freezing."

"Yeah, but that's no reason to break into someone's business."

Livy stopped and held out her hand. "Give me your coat."

"What?" He scowled.

"Your coat." She glared at him. "If you don't think freezing is a reason to steal a coat, you haven't had to do without one."

Jake exhaled. "I'm sorry. You have a point, but they could ask someone for help."

"They're afraid, and they're just trying to survive. They don't have any place to sleep or anything to eat. I've been—" Livy broke off.

"You've been what?" Jake stepped closer and grasped her shoulders. His hooded gaze searched her face. "That's what you were doing out here tonight. Trying to find those kids."

She went limp. He'd guessed right about her actions tonight. But she'd almost told him about her past. She should know not to open her mouth. "Not exactly."

He frowned. "What do you mean?"

"I already know where they are." *At least I have a pretty good idea.* "I've just got to convince them to come to the orphanage."

"Livy, those boys will chew you up and spit you out. They're not like the three little orphans we brought to you last night. These boys are used to lying, stealing, and cheating to get whatever they want."

She shook her head, the need to defend the street kids so strong she threw caution to the wind. If only someone had defended her. Just once. Before she'd lost Katie. If someone had, maybe her sister would be alive today instead of in a cold, dark grave.

Oh, Katie, I miss you so.

She took a deep breath. "No, they don't take what they

want, only what they *need*. That's all they dare risk. I've seen children with their feet wrapped in rags to keep from getting frostbite. I've seen them lose toes and fingers to the bitter cold. I've seen them take turns beating off rats so everyone could make it through the night. I've seen the police chase them down and whip them like dogs." She blinked to hold the tears at bay, but one slipped free to track down her cheek. "No, these children don't steal because they want to; they do it because they have to. They don't know any other way."

He reached out a gloved hand and wiped the moisture from her cheek with his thumb, his touch soft as the brush of a snowflake. His green eyes darkened. "I'm sorry. I hate that you saw things like that in Chicago, but I can't let these young hoodlums run loose."

"You don't have to." She grabbed his hand in both of hers. "If you find them, send for me. Let me talk to them. Please?"

A pained look crossed his face. "Livy . . ."

"Please, Jake? Give them a chance. Believe in them."

Just like Mrs. Brooks had believed in her on that fateful day in Chicago.

He stared at her for a moment before he glanced away. "I'll think about it."

"Thank you." She slipped her arm back through his. "You can take me home now."

＊　　＊　　＊

Luke ducked into the shack he shared with the other kids, the basket under his arm. The others dove for the hamper, grabbing the food. He made sure they shared with the younger ones. He took a small piece of ham and hunkered down in front of the fire. The girl he'd rescued from the warehouse stared at him, her eyes red and swollen from crying.

"I want Bobby."

He wrapped one of the thin blankets around her shoulders. "Is Bobby your brother? Was he in the crate with you?"

She nodded, fresh tears brimming in her green eyes. The other boys had never come out of the warehouse, so Butch and Grady must have caught them.

"I'll look for Bobby, but if I find him, I'll have to know your name so I can tell him where you are." He handed her the ham. "You gonna tell me your name?"

She gave him a look, one that said she didn't trust him any more than she'd trusted Butch and Grady but that maybe he had a point. "Jessica."

Luke tugged on a shank of matted red hair. "I'll find him if I can." He slanted his gaze at her. "You said there was a Mark in another crate. Can you tell me what he looked like? How old he is?"

She squinted at him, her face thin and gaunt in the firelight. "He looks like you."

Quick tears sprang to Luke's eyes. He blinked. Mark was here. Here in Chestnut.

In the clutches of Butch, Grady, and the man with the diamond-studded stickpin.

CHAPTER FOUR

JAKE TILTED THE SPLIT-BOTTOM CHAIR against the wall and listened to the half-dozen men gathered around the stove in McIver's Mercantile. Sam McIver leaned on the counter, throwing his two bits into the conversation in between his morning customers. Jake whittled on a small piece of wood, trying to figure out what it might turn out to be. Sometimes he came up with an idea, and sometimes he whittled a hunk of wood down to nothing while he pondered things.

"Hey, Jake, how ya like being a deputy?"

"It pays the bills." He took a swipe at the wedge in his hands. A sliver of wood fluttered on top of the pile of shavings at his feet.

"Yeah, ain't much going on around here right now other

than the coal mines. That's where the money is. They're hiring over at the Lucky Strike. You'd be a shoo-in, Jake."

He gripped the wooden block in his suddenly moist palm. Could he do it? Could he go underground again? To save the farm? Go in to darkness so thick you could cut it with a knife? The deathly silence, broken only by the shifting earth and dripping water?

And the moans of the dying.

He shoved the memories away, pushed them into the dark crevices of his mind and mentally sealed them off like a caved-in tunnel deep inside a mine. He couldn't—wouldn't—think about the mines. Not now.

Not ever.

McIver spoke up, a hint of steel and maybe anger in his normally quiet voice. "Quit filling the boy's head with nonsense. Sheriff Carter's been ailing and needs Jake in the worst way right now."

Jake focused on the block of wood in his hands. *Think about the carving.* Nothing but the knife and the smooth wood in his hands.

The conversation wandered on to the weather and how long it might be before the snow melted.

He let them talk while he worked, beginning to see the shape of a dog's snout. He nodded. A dog it would be. If he didn't chop off one of its legs or its head, that was.

The bell over the door jingled, and he glanced up. Livy entered the store. His heart skipped a beat as her gaze slid across his. She smiled, the slightly uneven corners of her mouth pulling him in like a moth to a flame.

"Good morning, Miss O'Brien. Can I help you with anything?" McIver asked.

"No thank you. I'm just looking." She nodded in the general direction of the men, skirted the gathering, and headed to the back of the store.

Jake tried to concentrate on the conversation, now about some poor fellow over in Cooperstown who'd lost his foot in a mining accident, but he found it hard to think with Livy so close by. What was it about this little slip of a woman that made him forget everything but the sound of her skirts swishing along the aisles in the back of the store?

When he chopped off the dog's ear, he closed his knife and placed the piece of wood in his pocket. He eased the chair down and slipped away from the group. The men barely noticed his departure, they were so deep in a discussion about the price of coal.

Livy stood near several bolts of bright cloth, fingering a robin's-egg-blue ribbon the color of her eyes. She glanced up, gave him a tiny smile, and focused on the ribbon again. As usual, his heart clunked against his rib cage.

"Morning." He nodded at her.

What was he doing? Hadn't he told himself he didn't have time to get mixed up with a girl?

"Good morning to you, too."

He searched for something to say. Something that wouldn't make this conversation personal. "How are the Hays children?"

He congratulated himself on finding a topic that was important to both of them. That was, until her smile drooped and her eyes filled with sadness.

"The baby's too young to know what happened, but the girls cried most of the night and into the morning. Right now they're too exhausted to cry anymore. We found out their mother died not too long ago, so this is really hard on them."

Poor tykes. To lose both parents so close together and at such a young age. Jake thought of his younger brother and sisters. When his father died, he'd been so focused on his own loss and stepping in as head of the household that he hadn't really thought about his siblings' grief. He'd make a point to spend time with them, not just rush around doing chores. *Thank You, Lord. At least we have Ma and each other.* "Have they mentioned any relatives?"

"An uncle, but I don't think they know him very well."

He should wish her a good day and leave, but something about the curve of her jaw and the soft pout of her lips kept him rooted to the spot. He wanted—no, needed—one more smile to tuck into his heart and carry away. And besides, he'd been the one to take the smile off her face with his question about the Hays children. He had to do something to bring it back again.

In desperation, he gestured at the stacks of cloth, ribbons, and thread on the shelves. "Planning on doing some sewing?"

Her lips moved. Just a tiny twitch upward. He'd succeeded. Barely.

"I'm trying to figure out something I can make the children for Christmas. I'm at my wit's end."

"How about dolls?" Had he really said that aloud? He'd wanted to take her mind off the tragedy of the day before, but where had dolls come from?

She gave him an incredulous look. "I couldn't afford one, let alone five."

Jake rested his forearms on a stack of cloth, heat creeping up his neck. "Not store-bought dolls. Corn-husk ones."

"Corn-husk?"

He shrugged, aiming for a nonchalance he didn't feel. He lowered his voice. The men up front would have a field day if they overheard him talking doll making. "They're easy enough to make, and you don't need anything but shucks and some string or yarn."

Her face fell. "I don't have any corn husks."

"I've got plenty in the crib out at my place. I'll bring you enough to make as many as you want."

"Really? And will you show me how to make them? Mary probably knows, but I want it to be a surprise. Every little girl deserves something special for Christmas."

Jake's heart twisted at the wistfulness in her voice. What had her childhood been like? "I'll bring the husks over tomorrow and show you how to do it. I've never made one, but I watched Ma make them lots of times for my sisters. See if you can find some yarn or something."

Her eyes widened. "But what about the boys? I'll have to make something for them too."

Jake fingered the disfigured dog in his pocket. "How many boys are there?"

"Only three, thank goodness."

Though he was unsure how he'd managed to rope himself into making dolls for a bunch of girls, carving a few horses and farm animals would be a piece of cake.

"Leave the boys to me."

✳   ✳   ✳

Luke hovered in the shadows of the building, melting into the darkness. According to Jessica, his little brother was in this building, working like a dog to make greedy men rich.

And it was all his fault.

He clenched his fists. He never should have let Mark pick that man's pocket. Faster than he could say, "Crackerjack pickpocket," they'd been collared, thrown in jail, and sold to the highest bidder. Luke had run at the first opportunity. But had he made the right decision? If he'd stayed, maybe he and Mark would be together by now.

Or would they both be locked in the squat building that reminded him of the stone tombs in the cemeteries in Chicago? A sick feeling settled in the pit of his stomach.

The barred windows were too high to see into and too small to shimmy through even if he could reach them. He made his way around the building, looking for an opening, an unlocked door, anything.

His desperation grew heavier with each passing moment. He backed into the shadows and hunkered down, staring at the front of the building.

As far as he could tell, there was no way in. And no way out. Except through that locked door.

✳   ✳   ✳

Noon came and went with no sign of Jake. Maybe he'd forgotten or decided that making dolls for orphaned girls wasn't high on his list of priorities. Livy tamped down her disappointment. The idea of something affordable for the girls for Christmas had lifted her spirits, not to mention the anticipation of seeing Jake again.

No matter. She'd managed fine without Jake Russell until now, and she'd carry on without him. Maybe Mrs. Brooks knew how to make corn-husk dolls. She'd ask her after supper tonight. She'd worry about finding enough husks later.

Livy helped the children with their lessons, keeping them occupied while Mrs. Brooks prepared the evening meal.

Mrs. Brooks stuck her head in the doorway. "Livy, I'll take over now. You've got a visitor."

Livy's face grew warm. "Thank you, ma'am."

Mrs. Brooks leaned close as Livy passed, her eyes twinkling. "Jake told me what you two are up to, so I'll keep the children out of your way."

Livy paused before the mirror in the hall, straightened her collar, and smoothed her hair. She jerked her hands down. How silly. Jake wasn't interested in her. He'd only offered to teach her how to make dolls because he cared about the girls. And she wasn't interested in him, either. She wasn't looking to fall in love, get married, and have children. Ever.

She trudged down the hall and found him in the kitchen with a sack of corn husks at his feet.

"Afternoon, Livy."

Her heart fluttered at the crooked smile he gave her, making it awfully hard to remember why she wasn't supposed to be interested. "Afternoon."

"Sorry I'm so late getting here, but we had another robbery last night."

"Oh no. Was anyone hurt?"

He piled dry, crackling shucks on the table. A cloud of dust hovered in the air, and Livy sneezed.

"No, but those kids are getting brave. This is the second time this week. When I get my hands on them, they're going to wish they'd never landed in Chestnut, Illinois."

"Jake, they're innocent until proven guilty."

His gaze snapped to hers. "Sorry. I know how you feel about those kids. Did you find some string?" he asked, effectively changing the subject.

Livy sighed. The discussion of the street kids might be on the back burner for now, but she'd bring it up again. Soon. She pulled a ball of bright-red yarn out of her pocket. "Will this work?"

"Yeah, that'll do." He rubbed his hands together, looking a little out of his element. "Okay, we need a pot of warm water. We've got to soak the husks to make them easier to work with. We'll need some scissors too."

Livy stepped outside and filled a black pot with snow while Jake sorted through the shucks.

When she returned, Jake glanced at her, his green eyes bright. "Did the Hays children sleep better last night?"

"Yes, they did. I think they were exhausted."

Livy put the pot on the stove and concentrated on the melting snow, her back to him. How could he feel such compassion for the Hays children but not for the street kids he wanted to run out of town? She didn't like the direction of her thoughts, but she couldn't help but compare his different reactions. Of course she wanted him to care about the orphans, but she wanted him to understand the plight of the street kids as well.

When steam rose from the water, Jake threw a handful of husks into the pot. Livy poked at them with a wooden ladle as the husks became soft and pliable.

Unlike Jake's feelings about the street kids.

There wasn't any difference between the three children who'd lost their father two days ago and the kids who made their beds in the alleyways at night. How could she make Jake see that?

He caught her studying him, and his eyes narrowed. "Is something wrong?"

Heat rushed to her face, and she shook her head. The man was giving of his time to help her, and all she could do was find fault. "No."

He watched her for a moment longer before lifting the pot from the stove and carrying it to the table. He fished the shucks out and placed them on a towel.

Livy poked the soggy-looking mess with her spoon. "How on earth do you intend to make a doll out of that?"

He laughed, more a grunt of amusement than anything. "You'll see. Just watch." He picked up a husk. "First, you shape the head." His strong hands balled up a piece of corn husk, making short work of the task. "Once you get it about the size you want, you fold two husks over the ball and tie it off at the neck with a piece of string. See? Hand me that yarn."

Livy measured off about six inches. "Is this enough?"

"Plenty."

Livy rested her chin in her hand, stewing over the street kids like a cat worrying a mouse. "Have you found any of the street kids yet?"

"No." He squinted at her, his intense stare making her squirm. "Have you?"

"No."

His brows drew together in a frown. "You been wandering around at night again?"

She shook her head, able to answer him truthfully. This time. His scrutiny made her squirm, not because of the questions he asked but because it made her aware of her everyday dress, patched and faded, and that she'd barely had time to run a brush through her hair that morning before pinning the mass up out of the way.

He turned back to the job at hand.

"Okay, now we make the arms. Here." He handed her three pieces of husk. "You'd better do this part."

"Me?" Livy sat up straighter. "What do I do?"

"Just braid 'em. Like pigtails."

She complied, and Jake threaded the braid crosswise through the layers of the bodice. Then he picked up two corn husks and fitted them over the shoulders like a shawl, crossing and gathering the pieces at the waist. "How does that look?"

"Perfect."

"Tie a piece of string here while I hold this in place."

Livy did as Jake instructed. Her fingers brushed against his, and she felt the warm, rough texture of his hands. Her eyes flew up to meet his gaze, and he gave her a lopsided smile. Her heart did a slow somersault in her chest, and for a moment, Livy thought she might not be able to draw breath again. For the first time, she noticed tiny flecks of gold in his green eyes. He had the most amazing eyes she'd ever seen.

She could stare at them for hours. His eyes flickered, shifted, focused on her mouth. She drew in a sudden breath and looked away, breaking their connection.

Unnerved, she blurted out the first thing that popped into her mind. "You won't send them back to Chicago, will you?"

He frowned. "Who?"

"The boys. You promised to let me know if you found them, remember?"

"I said I'd think about it." His expression turned almost fierce. "Why are you so worried about these boys?"

"Why shouldn't I be concerned? They're children."

Jake leaned forward. "Livy, we've been over this already. They're little hoodlums. Well, they're not so little. Mostly, they're half-grown youngsters who aren't interested in finding a job and contributing to society."

She bristled. "They are not. They're children, just like the Hays children and Mary and little Grace." Every child deserved a chance. Those boys were babies once. Toddlers. Some mother's little man. Who knew what horrific incident, what horrible sickness had torn them from their families and tossed them on the streets like leavings from a slop jar?

"You're looking at this through rose-colored glasses. You can't save every child that crosses your path."

His words pierced her heart, and tears pricked her eyes. She knew she couldn't save them all. She couldn't save the two who'd mattered the most. But he didn't understand, and the only way to make him would be to tell him the truth about her past.

And she'd left her past in Chicago.

"I can only try," she whispered.

He reached out and wiped a tear from her cheek with his thumb, then cupped her face in the palm of his hand. "I don't want to see you hurt."

She froze, the warmth of his hand caressing her cheek. His green eyes darkened, and he stared at her lips. He wanted to kiss her. She could see it in his eyes, feel it in the rough texture of his fingertips. She lowered her gaze, focused on his lips.

He moved. Or did she?

Oh, Lord. She didn't want this, did she? Not after Katie.

A burst of childish laughter came from the parlor. They jerked apart, the spell of attraction shattered. Livy sat ramrod straight and refused to look up. Her heart raced as her mind scrambled to figure out what had just happened between her and Jake.

Seconds ticked by before Jake cleared his throat and picked up the doll. "All right. Now she's beginning to look presentable, don't you think?"

"Yes." Livy barely managed to get the word out. What if he had leaned forward to kiss her? What would she have done? Would she have let him . . . or slapped his face for being so forward?

"Um . . . do you have any flour?"

She blinked, ignoring the questions banging against her brain. "Flour?"

"Yeah." He rummaged around in his sack and brought out a handful of soft, golden corn silk. "Mix some flour and water together to make a paste. This little lady needs some hair."

Thankful for something to occupy her, Livy controlled

her shaky fingers, stirred up a batch, and handed the paste to Jake. He looked so calm, as if he weren't going to kiss her moments before. She bit her lip. Maybe she'd imagined the whole thing. Her sister's words came back to haunt her.

"Stolen kisses lead to more than you need or want."

She'd do well to remember that. She clasped her hands in her lap and concentrated on the doll.

Jake dabbed a small amount of the sticky goo on the doll's head and added silk to create a halo of golden curls. Next, he made a bonnet, letting the curls peek out from underneath. Finally he trimmed the ends of the skirt and stood her up in the middle of the table.

Livy touched a finger to the doll. "Oh, she's beautiful!"

"Yes, she is."

She looked up. Jake stared at her instead of the toy, his gaze skimming lightly over her face.

Her breath caught. He meant her.

Livy's heart fluttered as her cheeks warmed. She lowered her gaze, afraid of what he'd see in her eyes —that when he said it, it made her feel beautiful in a way she never had before. She stared unseeingly at the corn-husk doll as a place deep in her heart she hadn't even known was wounded began to heal.

CHAPTER FIVE

COFFEE.

Jake needed coffee in the worst way. Skinner had kept him up all night. Singing. Or caterwauling, to be more accurate. He hadn't heard a peep from the man's cell in over an hour, so either Skinner had died or he'd fallen into a drunken stupor. And to tell the truth, it didn't matter which, so long as the drunkard kept a sock in it.

Jake had already gulped down two cups when the door opened, letting in a blast of frigid air.

"Man, it's cold out there this morning." Sheriff Carter shuffled inside and made a beeline for the stove.

Jake tilted his chair back and took a sip of the hot brew. "Looks like we got another foot of snow."

"I don't know how much more of this we can take." The older man huddled close to the firebox, his hands extended toward the warmth. "Did you have a quiet night?"

"Mostly." Jake jerked his head toward the back of the jail. "Skinner and a couple of strangers are sleeping off a drunk back there. Finally."

"Skinner?" Sheriff Carter shook his head. "Don't reckon that boy'll ever learn."

"Reckon not."

They both looked up as the door opened and Sam McIver stepped inside, a frown on his normally cheerful face.

"Morning, Sam." Sheriff Carter held up the blackened pot. "Coffee?"

"No thanks." The mercantile owner took off his hat and stomped snow from his boots. "Somebody broke into the store last night."

"Really?" Sheriff Carter's eyebrows shot up. "What all did they take?"

"A case of beans, several jars of sausages, some blankets. And a Dutch oven, of all things." McIver twisted his hat.

Jake snorted. "Nobody's going to get very far toting a Dutch oven."

"That's what I thought. It's bound to be that riffraff from Chicago."

"Now hold on, Sam," Sheriff Carter reasoned. "You don't know that for a fact."

"I told my boys to keep an eye on 'em if they came in the store. They'll steal you blind." McIver slapped his hat against his pants. "I'm telling you, it's them. Look at the stuff they took. And if we don't do something about it, they're going to take over the whole town."

"All right. I'll send Jake over to take inventory of everything that's missing, and we'll try to find the culprits."

"I'll be waiting." McIver stomped to the door and let himself out.

"Sam's mighty stirred up." Jake moved to the window. The storekeeper stormed across the street, ignoring friendly greetings from the few folks already opening up shop.

"Reckon he has a right to be."

Jake rubbed his jaw. What if McIver was right? What if the street kids had broken into the mercantile? Livy would be disappointed. She wanted to believe those boys were sweet little mama's boys, when they were well on their way to becoming faces on the wanted posters on his desk.

"You think it was those kids?" Jake topped off his coffee and took another sip.

"Who else could it be?" The sheriff eased into his chair, leather creaking as he adjusted his weight. "Chestnut's growing like a newborn Jersey calf. That's one reason I needed some help this winter, not to mention I'm getting too old for this. Why, before the railroad came through, I'd head home for some shut-eye after I let Skinner out of jail. If someone needed me, McIver'd send Gus or one of the boys to get me."

"The discovery of coal hasn't helped things either." *In more ways than one.*

If it hadn't been for the coal mines, his father would still be alive. Jake would be scratching out a living at the farm instead of fighting to keep crime off the streets of Chestnut.

He might even be married by now with a family of his own. But he'd never found a woman he wanted to settle down with.

Until now. Big blue eyes and a slightly crooked smile beckoned him.

"You're right about that. Chestnut, especially shantytown, has tripled in size in the last year."

"At least they're tearing down some of the burned-out shacks to make room for new buildings. That's good." Jake tamped down thoughts of his family, drained his coffee, and grabbed his coat. Worrying about the past—and what the future might hold—would get him nowhere fast. "I might as well go on over to Sam's and take a look. He's fit to be tied."

Sam McIver's two strapping sons were shoveling snow off the walk in front of the store when Jake arrived.

"Morning, boys."

"Morning." The eldest, Will, sported a black eye as big as a fistful of coal.

"What happened to you, Will?"

The boy, on the verge of manhood, scowled. "Nuthin'."

"You get in a fight with those boys roaming the streets?"

"No. Pa said not to have nuthin' to do with them." Will ducked his head and kept shoveling. His younger brother did the same.

"I see." Jake shrugged. He'd only asked out of curiosity. Boys got into tussles all the time.

He pushed open the door to the mercantile, a tinkling bell announcing his presence. The sound reminded him of Livy. He scowled. Everything reminded him of Livy. He couldn't seem to think of anything else.

He'd gone soft over a woman.

Sam McIver rested his palms on the counter and glared at him. People enjoyed shopping with Sam, who was usually easy-going and friendly. But not this morning. He looked like a tornado intent on destroying the town. Jake couldn't blame him. He glanced around the tidy establishment. Canned goods lined the shelves; dry goods were stacked head-high in the back. Farm tools hung from hooks on the far wall. A place for everything and everything in its place. Nothing scattered about, turned over, broken, or destroyed. The thief seemed to know his way around the store pretty well from the looks of things.

Jake turned to McIver. "Did you discover anything else missing?"

"Besides the foodstuffs I mentioned earlier, they took a bone-handled skinning knife and a gold-plated pocket watch I ordered for Mac MacKinnion. Both cost a pretty penny. I didn't realize they were gone before because I'd left them under the counter here." Sam slapped his hands against the flat surface, his eyes flashing. "I tell you, Jake, we've got to round these boys up and ship them back to Chicago. If they've taken to stealing knives, there's no telling what they might do next."

"I don't blame you for being upset, but until we have some proof, I can't go off accusing just anybody." He didn't even know where the boys were. They were slippery as the sun perch in Chestnut Creek. "And besides, what about all the folks who've showed up looking for work in the mines? It could be any one of them."

Sam huffed.

The shopkeeper's mind was made up, but Jake needed more than a gut feeling. He shoved his hat back. "How'd they get in?"

"Through the back. Come on, I'll show you."

McIver led the way through a jumbled storage room, the clutter at odds with the neatly organized store out front. Faded bolts of cloth lay on top of each other on an old steamer trunk. Stacks of overstocked crates leaned haphazardly toward the narrow aisle leading to the rear door. A keg with *PICKLED HERRING* printed in large letters sat to Jake's left.

Jake scowled. "Pickled herring?"

"Somebody accidentally shipped it here. I haven't been able to sell it to anyone. Wish that riffraff would've taken that with them."

The back door hung ajar, the bitter cold sucking the warmth right out of the room. Making his way toward it, Jake hoped he didn't knock a stack of crates over. He didn't have a hankering to be buried alive under a hundred pounds of pickled herring. His gaze swept over the doorframe, noticing the lack of splintered wood or any marks showing a forced entrance.

He hooked a thumb toward the door. "You keep this bolted, don't you?"

"Yep." McIver glanced around. "That's funny. What happened to the lock?"

Jake viewed the snow-covered landscape, unmarred by footprints or any evidence that would shed light on who'd broken into the mercantile. "You got a shovel, Sam?"

"Of course."

The shopkeeper disappeared and came back moments later, a spade in one hand and a curious glint in his eyes. "What're you gonna do?"

Jake palmed the shovel and stepped outside. "Well, it's

not much to go on, but it's all we've got right now. I figure we got about twelve inches of snow last night. If I can find that lock, I might be able to tell what time the thieves broke in."

"Good idea. A big shipment came in yesterday, and Gus and the boys brought everything up from the train station. As many trips as we made, yesterday's snow should be packed solid." McIver leaned against the doorjamb and watched for a moment. "You need any help? I can call the boys."

"Nah, too much tramping around would defeat the purpose." Jake carefully peeled an inch-thick layer off the surface of the snow and tossed it to the side.

"Right. I didn't think of that."

The tinkling of the bell drew McIver away to attend to his first customer of the day.

Jake worked in silence, carefully shoveling a narrow strip in a semicircle about eight feet from the storeroom, working his way from the outside in. As McIver suspected, the virgin snow played out about ten inches below the surface when he'd cleared the perimeter, revealing the hardpack from the day before. He moved closer to the door and started another round.

Twenty minutes later, he found the padlock. It lay cocooned about four inches below the surface. He calculated what time the robbery could have taken place. It had started snowing about dusk and snowed throughout the night.

"Find anything?" McIver asked from the doorway.

"Yep. There's the lock." He jabbed at it with the shovel. "I'd say the robbery took place around two o'clock. Not that it'll help us catch the thief, but at least it's good information to know when we have a suspect."

The bell chimed again just as Jake palmed the cold steel.

"Sam."

McIver turned back. "Yeah?"

"It's not broken." Jake pushed his hat back.

The shopkeeper swore. "Let me see that."

"Did you lock up at closing time?"

"Like I said, a big delivery came in from Chicago. You can tell by the looks of the storeroom." McIver frowned. "It was getting late and had already started snowing by the time we got it all inside. Will had been ill as a hornet and itching to go somewhere all day. I closed up the front but don't remember checking the back. But the boys and Gus know to take care of things."

The bell tinkled again.

Jake waved McIver away. "Go on. There's nothing else we can do here. I'll talk to Gus and the boys and see what I can find out."

McIver hurried in to take care of his customers.

Jake left the shovel propped against the wall and crunched around to the front of the building. The McIver boys had worked up a sweat clearing the boardwalk. All along the street, other business owners were busy doing the same.

"Will, can I talk to you and Abner?"

Jake stopped short of calling Will a boy. The young feller had shot up so much in the last year, he'd pass for a grown man except for the scraggly tuft of whiskers on his chin.

Will propped himself on his spade, as sullen as before. "I reckon."

"What do you remember about closing time yesterday?"

"Don't remember nuthin'. We helped Pa unload a whole trainload of junk; then I left."

"Did you leave the door unlatched?"

"I left before they got through." He shrugged and went back to work. "Don't know what happened after that."

Jake looked at the younger boy. "Abner, what about you?"

"I thought Will or Gus took care of everything." Abner's eyes grew wide. "Pa'll have our hides if we forgot and someone broke in."

"I'm sure it wasn't your fault." Jake slapped the boy on the back. "Besides, even if you forgot, nobody would know. They'd have to be planning to break in and get lucky. See?"

Abner frowned. "Yeah, Mr. Jake, but there ain't no need in making it easy for them, now is there?"

Jake laughed. "I reckon you're right—"

"Abner McIver, do not say *ain't*."

Jake turned to see Lavinia MacKinnion sweeping toward them, her hawkish face ensconced in a black scarf, a black cloak billowing behind her like the wings of a giant bat.

"Yes, ma'am." Abner stepped to the side of the boardwalk, giving the teacher a wide berth.

She smiled at Jake, but it only made her cheekbones more prominent. Jake winced. Lavinia made no secret she'd set her cap for him. "Good morning, Jake."

"Morning, Lavinia. How's your pa?" Jake weighed his words with care. One misstep and Lavinia would have him committed to Sunday dinner or a taffy pull or some other such nonsense in a heartbeat.

A shadow crossed her face. "Still grieving, but he's doing better. Thank you for asking."

"I don't want to keep you." He stepped aside to give her room to pass. "I'm sure you have a busy day."

He didn't mean to be rude, but he didn't want to get ensnared in Lavinia's schemes. And he didn't want to wake up to her the rest of his life either. Now, Livy O'Brien in the mornings might be a different story. Just the thought of waking up with Livy produced a wave of longing he'd never had for another woman.

"I do need to hurry. The children will be arriving soon. Abner, don't be late for school."

"Yes, ma'am." Abner hung his head and shuffled toward the store.

Jake bit back a smile. Abner looked less than thrilled about the prospect of spending the rest of the day with the teacher as well.

* * *

Livy hurried toward the mercantile, mentally reviewing the list of items Mrs. Brooks wanted. She sidestepped a patch of ice, then grabbed her skirts in one hand to ascend the steps to the boardwalk. Her heart skipped a beat when she spotted Jake talking to a tall, slender woman dressed in a black cloak. She couldn't see the woman's face, but her height complemented Jake's broad shoulders.

Jake helped the woman down the steps, his gaze following her as she crossed the street and headed toward the train station. An unexpected pang of longing caught Livy by surprise. Did Jake ever watch her out of sight like that? She shook her head, banishing the question as quickly as it surfaced. Her mind conjured up the strangest notions. She didn't want a husband or the family that came with one. She'd committed herself to saving orphans, not marrying and throwing more children on the mercy of society.

Jake started her way, his head down, hat obscuring his vision. Panic coursed through her. He'd see her if he kept on track. Should she stay on the narrow boardwalk or duck into one of the stores? Her choices were the gunsmith's or the barbershop. Not having business in either establishment, she stayed glued to the spot.

Just as he reached her, he glanced up. A slow smile filtered across his face, leaving Livy slightly weak in the knees.

"Livy."

Her name rolled off his tongue like a caress. Over his shoulder, she spotted the woman in black hurrying away in the opposite direction. She fingered her basket, irritated. He should save his smiles for the willowy woman in black. "Good morning, Jake."

"Where're you off to this early?"

"To the mercantile. Mrs. Brooks needed me to pick up a few things for her. I also want a bit more yarn."

"I don't think you're going to find McIver in his usual friendly mood." Jake glanced at the mercantile.

"Really? What makes you say that?"

"Somebody broke into the store last night and stole an expensive pocket watch and a skinning knife, among other things."

"Oh no." Livy frowned, the woman in black pushed to the back of her mind.

"Sam thinks it's that riffraff from Chicago."

Livy's heart skipped. The merchants wouldn't stand for much of this. "What do you think?"

"I don't know. But it's my job to find out."

"Be careful, Jake."

STEALING JAKE

A tiny smile quirked up one side of his mouth, and he reached out and squeezed her elbow. Such an innocent touch, but one she felt to the tips of her toes. "I will."

Jake tipped his hat and strode away, his boots loud on the boards. Livy turned toward the mercantile and frowned. Why would the children take a watch? She could understand the skinning knife, but a timepiece? They might be intending to sell the goods, but where? She thought back to the day they'd picked Jake's pocket. They'd taken a risk pilfering something that wasn't purely for survival. Street kids would filch food and clothing to stay alive, but their code of ethics demanded they not steal for profit. They had their pride, tattered though it might be. And as long as they stayed out of sight and out of mind, upstanding citizens ignored them. Most of the time, anyway.

Livy made up her mind. Until now, she'd respected the boys' fear of exposing themselves to those in authority or coming to the orphanage for help. She well understood the consequences that might befall a street urchin if he or she fell into the wrong hands.

But no more.

She'd seek out those boys and find out why they'd risk the wrath of the local merchants, and the law, by doing something so foolish.

CHAPTER SIX

TUCKED AWAY at the base of a hillside on the outskirts of town, surrounded by cedars and cocooned in several inches of snow, Gus Jones's cabin looked downright cozy. But Jake knew better. The rickety structure could collapse at any time. Sheriff Carter had tried repeatedly to get the old man to move into town, afraid they'd come out one morning and find him buried under the remains of the shack.

But Gus refused. Said the cabin with its lean-to was all he and Little Bit owned.

Jake heard the humming before he dismounted and tied his horse to a low-lying tree limb. Another Christmas carol.

"Hello, the house?"

The humming stopped, and silence descended. But Gus didn't answer his call or come to the door.

"Gus, it's me. Jake. I need to talk to you."

After what seemed like an eternity, the door creaked open, and Gus squinted out through the sliver of a crack. "Mr. Jake?"

"Morning, Gus." Jake smiled to put the old feller more at ease. A two-day-old colt couldn't be more skittish. But Gus had a right to be cautious. Not much more than five feet tall, he'd been the brunt of more than one mean-spirited joke in his sixty-odd years. "Mind if I come in?"

A look of surprise jumped across Gus's face, and Jake brought himself up short. He stopped by to check on Gus often, but he'd never once invited himself inside. A shy smile replaced Gus's confusion, and the door eased completely open.

Jake stepped inside the doorway and swept his eyes across the room, taking in every aspect of the man's abode. He didn't know what he'd expected to find inside Gus's cabin, but it wasn't this. A cheery fire burned in the fireplace, keeping the one-room dwelling toasty. A small table and single chair sat to the left of the fireplace, while a cot, neatly made up with a patched and fading quilt, took up most of the opposite wall. Rough lumber shelves held a few canned goods and other odds and ends. All in all, the place looked as clean as Jake's mother's house, if a good bit smaller.

Swinging his gaze toward Gus, Jake found the old man grinning from ear to ear, his hands on top of the straight-back chair. He pushed the chair forward. "Sit here, Mr. Jake."

Jake wanted to refuse, seeing as Gus only owned one chair, but he didn't want to offend his host. He took off his hat, placed it on the table, and eased down onto the rickety chair. Gus started humming and bustled over to the fireplace to pour a cup of coffee from a battered pot. He shuffled the few feet back to the table and offered the brew. A lump formed in Jake's throat as he accepted the mug. "Thanks, Gus."

Gus hummed as Jake sipped his coffee, surprised to find it good, if a tad weak. He didn't know how to broach the subject of the robbery. Gus seemed to be beside himself with joy over having a visitor. Jake didn't want to destroy the old man's happiness.

"How's Little Bit, Gus?"

Gus hurried over to a shuttered window between the fireplace and the bed. He opened the window and whistled. Little Bit brayed and poked her head through the opening. Gus scratched her between the ears and she butted against his chest.

Jake laughed. "Well, at least you know she's okay, since she's right here."

Gus grinned his shy smile again and pointed to the fireplace and the lean-to at the back of the cabin. "And she's warm."

"That she is." Jake eyed the setup. "That's a good idea, Gus. To use the heat from the back of the fireplace for Little Bit's lean-to. Where'd you come up with that?"

The man scratched his scraggly beard and shrugged. "I dunno. It just happened."

"Well, it's a good thing, no matter." Jake stood and scratched the donkey behind her ear. "Gus, I need to ask you something. Yesterday you helped Mr. McIver out at the mercantile, didn't you?"

Gus nodded.

"Do you remember if you locked up the storeroom at the end of the day?"

"I don't remember." Gus screwed up his face in concentration. "Maybe Will did, but he was in a bad mood yesterday."

"I know. McIver told me."

"He told you? Why would he do that?"

"Somebody robbed the mercantile last night."

Gus's face went pale, and he backed away. "I didn't do it, Mr. Jake. I didn't steal nuthin'." When the backs of his knees hit the cot, he plopped down, his gaze riveted on Jake.

Jake held out a hand, palm up. "It's okay, Gus. I don't think you did anything wrong."

Gus shook his head, his eyes big and filled with fear. "I don't want to go to jail, Mr. Jake."

"You're not going to jail. Everything's fine."

"Are you sure?" Gus eyed him as if he'd suddenly grown two heads.

"I'm sure. There's nothing to worry about. I just wondered if you'd seen anything or knew who might have locked up."

"I don't know nuthin'."

"I believe you, Gus. You're not in any trouble, okay?"

Gus nodded.

Jake placed his hat on his head and moved to the door, giving Gus some space. The poor fellow was too upset to think straight right now. "If you think of anything, you'll tell me, won't you?"

"Yes, sir."

"Good. Take care of Little Bit, okay?"

Jake let himself out, mounted his horse, and headed back to town. The road split, and he swung toward shantytown. Might as well ride that way and check things out while he was on this end of town. He rounded the bend and pulled his mare up short. Two, three, no, four new buildings—not more than shacks, really—hugged the banks of the frozen creek. A crude sign proclaimed one a saloon. Jake clenched his jaw. Just what they needed. Another one to take the coal miners' hard-earned pay.

He could see the glove factory in the distance, nestled under some trees close to the creek and away from town. The structure wasn't big, but he supposed a large workshop wasn't needed to make gloves. The new industry didn't provide many jobs, but it did offer a few people work other than in the mines. And that was always a good thing.

A young woman hurried toward him, a basket of laundry clasped against her waist. Her gaze lifted and caught his. Her steps faltered, but she gave a short nod in recognition before ducking her head and continuing on.

Johanna Thorndike.

Widowed with two small children to raise.

Jake watched her out of sight, then turned away, a tight knot forming in his chest.

God, why did I survive when Derek didn't?

Not expecting an answer to the question he'd asked a thousand times over the last two years, Jake dismounted in front of a cabin in better repair than most and pulled a burlap sack off his saddle. He knocked, and a frail voice called out for him to enter. A small amount of light from a single dingy window and the low flames of the fire illuminated the cabin. The room felt warm and cozy compared to the bitter cold outside. Jake's eyes adjusted to the dim light and the figure seated before the fire, rocking slowly back and forth. "Seamus?"

The old man smiled. "Ah, young Jake. Come in. I haven't seen you in a coon's age."

"Now, Seamus, I came over here last week." Jake left the sack on the table. He knew better than to mention he'd brought a few things with him. Seamus would find them soon enough.

Confusion lined the elderly man's face. He'd not been the same since the mine collapse a couple of years ago that had killed his two sons, Johanna's husband, and—

Jake tamped the memories down.

"You did? Oh, well, the noggin ain't what it used to be. Sit a spell, and tell me what's going on outside these four walls."

Jake straddled a chair. "Lots of new folks in town, but I guess you've noticed that."

"Hmmm."

"Snowed over two feet the other day. You been outside lately?"

Seamus cackled. "Not if I can he'p it."

They sat for a few minutes, warming by the fire. Jake made a mental note to check the coal bin on his way out. Seamus didn't have anybody else to care for him these days. "You heard anything about a bunch of street kids roaming around?"

"Ah, you know young'uns. They wander around day and night. Nobody cares what they do. I'da took a switch to mine and made 'em stay at home."

"These kids don't have a ma or a pa. They live on the streets."

Seamus shook his head. "Well, I never. What's this world coming to?"

"I don't know."

After a few minutes of silence, Seamus dozed off, rousing when Jake stood.

"I'd better get going. I'll see you next week, okay?"

"All right. Take care, and tell your pa to come see me when his shift is over. He's working too hard."

Jake's throat constricted. Sometimes Seamus could carry on a conversation for hours without slipping into the past, but today didn't seem to be one of those days. He'd learned to humor the old man rather than explain things.

But inside, he felt not an ounce of humor.

He placed a hand on the old man's bony shoulder and gave it a gentle squeeze. "I'll do that, Seamus."

✳   ✳   ✳

Church bells pealed throughout town, calling everyone to Sunday morning services. Livy bit back a grin as Mrs. Brooks marched down the street, the children following like a brood of little chicks. Livy brought up the rear, keeping an eye on Seth and Georgie. She'd promised them a treat if they stayed away from the iced-over mud puddles. So far, the promise of a sliver of carefully horded peppermint outweighed their desire to see if they could crack through the ice.

They arrived at the small church to a flurry of townsfolk entering the front door. Reverend Warren smiled and shook hands with Mrs. Brooks. "I'm delighted you and the children could make it out today."

"We're very happy to be here, Reverend." Mrs. Brooks hurried her charges inside. "Come along, children; let's find a seat."

Livy glanced at the children, making sure the boys hadn't managed to splatter mud on their pants. She pulled Seth aside, extracted a moistened hankie from her reticule, and scrubbed a spot of mud off his pants. She gave him a quick hug and a smile. "There you go. You look very handsome this morning."

Seth squirmed away and joined the others. The girls looked as well as they could, considering their worn and threadbare clothes. The patched clothing didn't concern Livy. Many of the townspeople didn't have much better. But she did want the children to behave and represent Mrs. Brooks well.

As they filed into the church, Livy caught a glimpse of a couple of matronly women standing with Miss MacKinnion, the teacher, eyeing them and whispering behind their gloved hands. She glanced at Mrs. Brooks, who didn't seem to notice the women. Georgie glared at the teacher, and Livy stepped between them, giving him a frown.

She sighed. Some people would always look down on destitute children who didn't have much chance to better themselves. She'd learned that lesson firsthand. No matter. She and Mrs. Brooks would have to do everything they could to make sure the children earned the respect of the townspeople . . . starting with Georgie's attitude toward Miss MacKinnion.

If only she could do something about Miss MacKinnion's attitude toward the children. More than once the orphans had spoken of how the teacher treated them in front of the other students.

They settled on a bench close to the back as more people filed in, the men stomping snow off their boots, the women chattering among themselves about the past week, the cold, and the upcoming Christmas holiday.

Georgie grinned before pointing. "Miss Livy, look. It's Mr. Jake."

Livy's face warmed even as she gently tugged his arm down. "It's not nice to point, Georgie."

She gave Jake a timid smile.

He shook Georgie's hand. "Good morning, Georgie. How're you today?"

"I'm fine." He pushed his shoes against the bench in front of him. "Look—I got new shoes."

Livy cringed. Georgie's hand-me-down boots barely had enough remaining leather to protect the soles of his feet. But at least he wore shoes, polished to a high shine late last night.

Jake eyed the boots. "And they're very nice shoes too."

Livy noticed a middle-aged woman at his side, watching the exchange with a friendly smile. Jake turned. "I'd like to introduce you to my mother. Ma, this is Livy O'Brien. She and Mrs. Brooks are the ones I told you about. And this young man beside her is Georgie. Livy, my mother, Claudia Russell."

Livy stood and made an awkward curtsy within the confines of the benches. "Pleased to meet you, ma'am."

Mrs. Russell reached out and gave her a quick squeeze. "You, too, dear. Jake told me all about the good work you and Mrs. Brooks are doing. You are a godsend to this town, I'll tell you that."

"Thank you, ma'am." Livy blushed at the praise, not daring to look at Jake. He'd been talking about her? And to his mother? Had he said anything else about her? Anything at all? And did she want him to?

Mrs. Russell shook Georgie's hand. "And how are you, young man?"

"I'm fine, ma'am."

Livy stared at Georgie in amazement. Where had this polite youngster come from? And what had he done with Georgie?

"Jake?"

He and his mother turned to face Miss MacKinnion and another woman. The other woman's thin, hawkish face resembled the teacher's, only a few years older. Probably her sister. The two women ignored Livy. Embarrassed, she sat down. She didn't always understand the proper social mores of when she should be included in a conversation or not. But she couldn't help but feel she'd been snubbed by the two women. She kept her eyes glued to the pulpit, unable to tune out the conversation going on in the aisle.

"Good morning, Lavinia. Mrs. Johansen."

"Good morning, Jake. I'd be honored if you'd join us for Sunday dinner," Mrs. Johansen said. "Lavinia made a brown sugar cake, and I know it's one of your favorites."

"Thank you for the invitation, ma'am, but Ma's got dinner waiting for me at home." He cleared his throat. "Maybe some other time?"

Livy chanced a glance out of the corner of her eye. The teacher's lips thinned into a straight line before she relaxed, revealing a pretty smile for such an austere woman. A black cloak was draped over her arm. Livy's eyes widened and she jerked her gaze away, a sick feeling in the pit of her stomach. Was Miss MacKinnion the woman she'd seen with Jake? Her stomach threatened to reject the meager breakfast she'd eaten earlier.

Lots of women had black cloaks, didn't they?

But few were as tall as Miss MacKinnion.

The thought did little to calm her stomach.

"Another time, then." Mrs. Johansen and Miss MacKinnion moved away.

The organ music started, signaling the beginning of the service, and Jake put his hand on his mother's elbow. "We'd better find a seat."

Mrs. Russell touched Livy on the arm as she passed and whispered, "It was nice to meet you, Livy."

"Likewise, ma'am."

Jake escorted his mother up the aisle to a seat near the front. Two neatly dressed young girls and a towheaded boy moved over to allow room for them. The congregation stood to sing the opening hymn, and Livy's gaze fell on Jake, head and shoulders taller than those around him.

What had Jake told his mother about her and the orphanage?

And what kind of relationship did Jake and Miss MacKinnion have?

And more importantly, why did Livy care so much about the answer to either question?

*　　*　　*

He needed some fresh air.

Three women with daughters of marriageable age had asked him over for Sunday dinner, and so had Lavinia MacKinnion's sister. Since she hadn't been able to snag the deputy for dinner, she'd set her sights on him.

He shuddered.

Playing the part of a devout Christian turned his stomach in more ways than one. Adjusting his diamond stickpin, he moved past the knot of men congregated at the back of the church, but McIver motioned him over.

"We've got to put a stop to these hooligans running around, or they're going to steal us blind. Don't you agree?"

"Yes, but what can we do?" He'd just as soon stay out of local problems, but as a businessman, it was expected that he'd have a strong opinion about thievery.

"Well, for starters, Sheriff Carter and Jake can start combing shantytown for these youngsters and get them off the streets." McIver clamped his hat on his head.

The circle of men nodded. He nodded along with them because it was the thing to do. But inside, a slow anger bubbled below the surface, kept in check by sheer willpower.

Just what he needed, the sheriff and his deputy snooping around, making trouble. He'd lost half a dozen youngsters to Butch and Grady's incompetence the last couple of weeks, and now the ungrateful strays—ones that he'd bought and paid for—were bringing attention to themselves.

And as a result, to him.

He'd do something about them, all right.

But he doubted if McIver or anybody else in this town would approve of his methods.

✳　✳　✳

Jake blocked the tackle and grabbed his assailant around the waist, hoisting him over his shoulder with a primal growl. Gut-busting giggles filled the kitchen.

"That's enough, Jake."

He lowered Tommy to the floor, then glanced toward his

mother, who was putting the finishing touches on Sunday dinner. The indulgent smile on her face belied her reprimand.

"Go wash up now, Tommy. Dinner'll be ready in no time."

"Aw, Ma."

"Do what Ma says," Jake ordered.

"And tell your sisters to come on too," she called out as he skidded into the hallway.

"Yes, ma'am."

"How're things in town?" she asked, busy setting the table.

Jake hesitated. His mother knew enough about the goings-on in Chestnut that he couldn't make light of his duties as deputy. "Not bad."

She spared him a glance, lines of worry and grief etched on her once-youthful face. "I heard about the robbery the other night."

"It was nothing. Just some kids trying to get a little spending money."

"Spending money? Youngsters haul coal and pull corn in the summer for things they want. They don't break into the mercantile and steal things, let alone expensive knives and pocket watches."

She sat across from him and clasped his hands in hers. "Jake, I wish you'd give up this foolish notion of being a deputy. I worry about you staying up all night, then coming out here four or five times a week and helping me with chores. I can't imagine how you'll manage this summer."

"Ma, we need the money, and Sheriff Carter needs the help."

"I'm afraid something's going to happen." Tears swam in her eyes. "I don't think I could stand it if . . . if something happened to you, too. It's as dangerous as working in the mines, maybe even more so. Your father—"

The sound of Jake's two sisters and Tommy pounding down the stairs interrupted her. His mother sniffed and jumped to her feet, wiping her eyes with her apron.

Jake sipped his coffee and listened to the chatter as his brother and sisters told of their adventures the previous week. He couldn't blame his mother for worrying, but what else could he do? He needed to work through the winter, and the job of deputy had been the only thing available other than working the mines.

And contrary to what his mother believed, his job as deputy wasn't nearly as dangerous as working in the mines. He'd rather face down a drunken outlaw any day than be trapped in a mine.

A wagon rattled into the yard.

"There's Charlie and Susie." His mother pulled a pone of hot corn bread from the oven. "Just in time."

Jake's oldest sister and her husband entered the kitchen a few minutes later. Jake pumped Charlie's hand and gaped at his expectant sister. "What happened to you, Sis? You look like a maypop with four sticks stuck in it."

Where his sister once would have thrown a skillet at him, she simply smiled and hugged him. "Nice to see you, too, little brother."

Jake looked down at her. "And who are you to be calling me little?"

She nudged him aside and sat in the chair he'd vacated. "Just because you're bigger in size does not mean you're bigger in brains."

Jake laughed and claimed another chair. "How much longer before I'm an uncle?"

"Doc Valentine says not for another month, at least."

"Another month?" He couldn't believe Susie had a whole month to go. He wasn't joking about the maypop.

"Babies come when they're good and ready," his mother said. "Okay, everybody, sit down, and let's eat while it's hot. Charlie, would you say the blessing please?"

Charlie's ruddy cheeks stained red, but he cleared his throat. "Lord, bless this food and the hands that prepared it. Protect each and every person in this household as we go forward into this next week. Amen."

Jake's younger sisters started pestering Susie to tell them all about the clothes she'd made for the baby. While Susie described the baby's outfits in detail, Jake turned to Tommy. "How's school, squirt?"

"Fine."

"Tommy, don't talk with your mouth full," his mother said.

His brother swallowed. "Georgie and I have snowball fights every day."

"And they've been throwing them at us, too, Ma, even though Miss MacKinnion told them not to."

Tommy stuck out his tongue at his sister. "Did not."

"Did too."

"Did—"

"Quit arguing, you two."

"Georgie?" Jake asked. "From the orphanage?"

Tommy frowned. "What's an orphanage?"

"It's a place where children who don't have any parents live."

"Oh." Tommy poked another spoonful of peas in his mouth. "Then I must be half an orphan." Without giving them a chance to respond, he piped up, "Georgie's my bestest friend, 'cept he's always hungry."

Jake suspected Georgie wasn't too hungry now that he lived at the orphanage. He slathered butter on a piece of corn bread. "I met Georgie the other night."

Tommy's eyes grew round. "You did?"

"Yeah. I had to go to the orphanage."

"I heard the lady who runs it is from Chicago," Charlie said.

"Yeah. A Mrs. Brooks. She's seems to be a good woman, and the girl that helps her is right nice, too."

"Right nice?" Susie grinned. "Do tell."

Jake's ears started burning like someone had doused them in kerosene and stuck a match to them. He wished he'd never mentioned Livy around Susie.

He'd never hear the end of it.

CHAPTER SEVEN

THE FACTORY DREW Luke like a gnat to a syrup jar. If caught, he'd be snuffed out just as quickly. No, not quick. Gnats didn't die instantly when they got stuck in the sticky goo.

They became prisoners. Then they died slowly.

And that's what drew him. Not the thought of what might happen to him if caught, but of what Mark was going through.

Dying, a little at a time.

He'd take his brother's place with the snap of two fingers if he thought he could get away with it.

But the man with the stickpin didn't work like that. He'd lock them both up and not even blink an eye.

Thump-thump. Thump-thump. Thump-thump.

Luke flattened himself against the snowy ground behind some bushes. Butch rounded the bend, carrying a sack. As he passed, the smell of fried chicken hit Luke square in his empty stomach. A rumble gurgled up inside him, and he clenched his stomach muscles to stop the sound.

If Butch heard, he'd snatch Luke up like a rat catcher in an alley full of garbage.

But Butch hurried through the door, apparently too intent on his own meal to worry about anyone watching the factory.

Luke inched forward, getting close to the door, watching for an opportunity to sneak in. The door slammed in his face, the sound of something heavy falling into place on the other side.

"'Bout time you got back. I'm starving."

That sounded like Grady. Luke pressed his ear to the door.

"The boss stopped by." Grady's words were muffled as if he'd stuffed a piece of chicken in his mouth. Luke's mouth watered, but he ignored his hunger. Wishing wouldn't change anything. His empty stomach twisted with a new worry. What about Mark? Did he have anything to eat?

"What'd he want? Got more beggar lice on the way? We're busting the traces as it is."

"No. He's throwing a fit 'cause somebody's stirring up a stink around town, breaking into businesses, stealing stuff. People are getting mad, and he's afraid the sheriff's gonna start sniffing around."

"What's that got to do with us?"

"He thinks it's those boys that got away when that crate got busted. He wants us to find 'em and get rid of 'em."

Luke's eyes closed, and he took a deep breath. Not only did they have to hide from the law, but now Butch and Grady would be on the lookout for them. He was so tired. Tired of worrying, tired of fighting to stay alive, just plain tired. He wanted his brother, he wanted to be warm, and he wanted food to fill his empty belly. Why couldn't everybody just leave them alone?

Butch snorted. "Kids raised on the streets can't be found iffen they don't wanna be."

"No matter. That's what the boss wants."

A shuffling noise had Luke scrambling away from the door. After one final glance at the building that held his brother prisoner, he hurried back to shantytown, to the shack he shared with the others.

Luke tried to think of ways to keep his little group safe from Butch and Grady. For one wild, crazy moment, he thought about going to the lady at the orphanage. The pretty woman who'd knocked into him the day he stole the watch had left food and blankets for them more than once.

And she'd begged them to come to the orphanage. She made it sound so easy. Was she really as good and kind as she sounded?

Luke shook his head, banishing the warm, fuzzy feeling stealing through him. He couldn't risk it.

He'd never met an adult he could trust; why would she be different?

✳   ✳   ✳

Livy waited until Mrs. Brooks and the children were all sound asleep before she slipped out of the orphanage. She hurried down the street, keeping to the shadows, uneasy that there weren't many back alleys for her to cut through.

In Chicago, she could lose herself—or her pursuers—in the maze of streets and thoroughfares crisscrossing the city. But there weren't enough side streets in Chestnut to hide a cat, let alone a grown woman. And besides that, she didn't want Jake to see her. She might not be able to explain herself as easily as the first time he'd caught her out late at night.

She cut down the alley between McIver's and Baker's Boardinghouse, sidestepping a pile of garbage that smelled to high heaven. She ran low and light on her feet, not lingering and not making any noise. A dog barked up ahead, and she froze. Wonderful.

The back door to the boardinghouse opened. "What'chere hollering about, dog?"

Livy didn't linger. She took off in the opposite direction, the dog's frenzied barking following. She made note of the house with the dog. She wouldn't make the mistake of going that route again. Not if she wanted to avoid answering questions at the wrong end of a shotgun.

Another thing about Chicago. Dogs were as plentiful as street children. Nobody thought twice if a pack of snarling, fighting dogs careened down a refuse-strewn street. In Chestnut, if a dog so much as sneezed in someone's yard, a double-barrel shotgun came out from under the bed.

She backtracked, cut across Main Street, hurried two blocks down, then eased into a darkened alley leading to shantytown. Tinny piano music drifted to the street. The saloons were in full swing and would go on into the wee hours of the morning.

Wedging herself between a stack of crates and a rain barrel, she set in to wait. If she didn't miss her guess, her prey would be out in full force tonight. They'd waylay the patrons of the saloons as they came out, hoping to relieve them of any change they might have left. Many times it wasn't much, but it didn't take much to buy a stale loaf of bread. As she waited, she pondered the various places the boys might buy food in Chestnut. There weren't many. She bit her lip. Maybe she'd found another way to track them down. Tomorrow, she'd ask around.

A bump came from the building behind her. Livy pressed her cheek against the wall and listened again. A scrape and another bump sounded from within, followed by a muffled curse. Frowning, Livy tried to remember what the building housed. Her eyes widened—it was the gunsmith shop. Surely the boys wouldn't . . .

She almost jumped clear out of her hiding place when a window no more than six feet away screeched open. Livy shrank against the wall, hoping the stack of crates hid her from view.

Why had she thought she could do this? Hadn't she left her past behind?

Or was that why she *had* to do this?

A bag lowered to the ground; metal striking metal clanked loud in the silence. Next, the intruder let himself out the window, dangled by his fingertips for a moment, then lightly dropped to the ground, crouching as he took stock of his surroundings.

She peered from the crates, eyes glued to the thief. The very lack of moonlight that hid her from view kept her from seeing his features enough to recognize him if she saw him again. But he looked a sight bigger than the boys she'd seen on the streets. He turned, and she caught a glint of a pistol tucked into his waistband.

Livy didn't move, didn't breathe. She'd learned to be self-sufficient and not afraid of much of anything, but she feared a man—or anybody for that matter—with a gun. When he gathered up the sack and skulked to the end of the alley-way, she breathed a sigh. Just a few more minutes, and he'd be gone.

Thank You, Jesus.

"Hey, you. Stop!"

She started at the shout. Someone had spotted the thief. Not daring to linger, she took off in the opposite direction. Footsteps echoed off the dingy walls as the thief raced back down the alley, then crashed headlong into the stacked crates where she'd been hiding.

"Sheriff Carter. That way, toward Emma's!"

Was that Jake? If he spotted her, he'd never understand.

She gathered her skirts and lit out, hoping and praying the ruckus would allow her to get away unscathed. Shots rang out, and she kept running. The thief raced after her, followed by his pursuers. They were gaining. On her? On him? No matter.

She had to hide.

Now.

Praying for guidance, she skidded to a stop, dropped, and rolled, wedging herself in the darkness cast by the rear porch of the nearest building. She lay there, willing her pounding heart to slow, her ragged breathing to quiet.

The thief raced by, the burlap bag bouncing over his shoulder. Thirty feet away, he slipped on a patch of ice and went sprawling, so close she felt the thud as his body slammed against the ground. She heard the metallic rattle of the contents of the bag as it tumbled from the thief's grasp.

Livy shrank into the dark shadow of the porch and lay still. *Please, Lord. Please.*

The thief paid her no mind but scrambled up on one knee and faced his pursuers, gun pointed in the air above their heads. He squeezed off two shots, then jumped up and sprinted down an alley, leaving the sack behind.

His pursuers' heavy boots shook the ground as they neared her hiding place. If possible, she drew into herself even more. A tall, broad-shouldered man rushed past, followed more slowly by a stockier man gasping for breath.

Jake and Sheriff Carter.

She willed her breathing to slow so that they wouldn't hear her or see any movement. Her gaze narrowed to slits, keeping them in her sights, hoping and praying they'd never notice the dark lump huddled beside the building. Jake kept after the thief, but Sheriff Carter slowed to a walk as he neared the bag, leaning over and propping his hands on his knees.

He stayed like that for a long time, gulping in shuddering breaths. He groaned and clutched his chest. Had he been shot in the melee? Should she help him? She started to her feet but shrank back when Jake returned. The sheriff straightened, his breathing starting to return to normal.

"I lost him." Jake hardly sounded winded.

Livy groaned inwardly, not daring to move a muscle. What would she do if Jake and Sheriff Carter discovered her? They'd never believe she didn't have anything to do with the robbery.

Please, Lord. Please.

The sheriff reached for the sack, grunting with the effort. "Jake, these are guns. He must've broken into the gunsmith shop. If we don't stop them, those young hoodlums are going to do something dangerous. They're liable to hurt someone."

Livy bit her tongue. It wasn't the boys, but she couldn't defend them. Not here. Not now.

"We'll catch them soon. It won't be long until one of them slips up. We almost caught this one tonight."

Sheriff Carter sighed. "I wonder what he got away with."

"We'll find out in the morning. If you'll take these on to the jail, I'll look around some more. I don't think they'll try again tonight, but just in case. Are you all right?"

"I'm not as young as I used to be." The sheriff took a shaky breath. "That short chase about did me in. We're going to have to talk seriously about getting more help."

The sheriff shouldered the sack and trudged off. Jake stood still, his gaze raking the surroundings. How could he not see her? Other than lying in the shadows of the porch, covered in black from head to toe, she hid in plain sight.

She squeezed her eyes shut. *Hide me, Lord.*

After what seemed like an eternity, he moved off in the direction the thief had gone, taking his time. Livy released the breath she'd been holding.

She waited a good five minutes before she moved. She rolled over, put both hands in the snow, and scrambled to her knees. The sound of tearing cloth rent the air, and she groaned. Just one more thing to go wrong tonight. Reaching around, she grabbed her skirt where it was caught on a splintered piece of wood, tugging until she freed the material. She resisted the urge to examine the damage. There'd be time enough for that later.

Gathering her ripped skirt and her wits about her, she made a beeline for home. With Jake roaming the streets looking for the thief, she couldn't very well search for the boys.

But she would find them, and she'd gain their trust.

One way or another.

✳   ✳   ✳

Jake canvassed the town and didn't see anything out of place. From the looks of things, he'd run the thief to ground, at least for tonight. He headed toward the saloons. If they were good for anything, it was information. A couple of them were closed, but light spilled from the Golden Nugget. He stepped inside.

"Lucky, you 'bout ready to shut down for the night?" He nodded at the bartender, his narrowed gaze studying the half-dozen customers nursing their drinks.

"I reckon so. But not necessarily because you say so." The saloon keeper rested well-manicured hands on the bar. "The boys are mostly out of money."

Jake eyed him, not in any mood for Lucky's shenanigans. It didn't matter to him why the man closed up shop, as long as he did it. "Heard any commotion tonight?"

Lucky wiped the counter, squinting through the smoke. "Like what?"

"Somebody stole some guns from the gunsmith."

"I haven't heard a thing, but I'll keep my ears open."

"Thanks." Jake turned away.

"Take that Skinner with you." Lucky motioned across the saloon. "He'll freeze to death if I throw him out in the street."

Skinner lay passed out at a table. Jake lifted him to his feet. "Come on. Let's go sleep it off." Would the man never learn? What was it about some men who couldn't say no to a bottle of whiskey?

Jake propelled the drunk out the door, the blast of cold air reviving him long enough to keep upright until they reached the jail. Skinner sprawled on a cot and passed out again before Jake could even lock the cell door.

Stepping into the front room again, he stared at the two rifles and the shotgun spread out on Sheriff Carter's desk. "Those boys sure have upped the ante."

"Looks like we've got ourselves a mess of trouble. It was one thing when we thought we were after a bunch of little fellers looking for a square meal and a warm blanket. But this is a whole 'nuther bucket of coal. I wonder where they planned to get rid of this stuff."

"Probably Cooperstown or Brownsville. I'll scout around as soon as it's daylight and see if I can find anything."

Sheriff Carter leaned his elbows on his desk and smothered a yawn.

Jake studied his father's old friend. The sheriff didn't want anyone to know about his weakness, but Jake saw more than he let on. The man's shortness of breath grew more worrisome with each passing day. "Go on and get some rest."

"You sure you'll be all right?"

"I'll be fine. I doubt we'll have any more trouble tonight."

The sheriff shuffled out the door. Hopefully a good night's rest would take care of the worn, haggard look on his face.

Jake leaned his chair against the wall, intending to close his eyes for a minute before he made rounds again.

But worries kept his mind from resting.

It seemed like the whole world wanted to cave in on him at once. What should he do? About the farm, about these kids running wild, and about Sheriff Carter?

❋　　❋　　❋

The whistle blew for the six o'clock shift change at the mine, jerking Jake out of a deep sleep. Sheriff Carter sat at his desk, and the smell of fresh coffee filled the room.

Jake rubbed a hand down his face. "I must have been dead to the world. Didn't even hear you come in."

"Looked like you needed a bit of a rest." The sheriff handed him a steaming cup.

"Both of us did."

They discussed the events of the night as the sun crept over the horizon.

Jake sipped his coffee, letting the bitter brew wipe the cobwebs from his mind. "I want to look around before anyone disturbs the tracks. Will you be all right for a while?"

"Yeah." Sheriff Carter relaxed into his chair. "Pick up our breakfast on the way back. Might as well bring Skinner some too."

"Will do."

Only a light dusting of snow covered the boardwalks, so the tracks from the robbery would still be visible. The shopkeepers would be happy, too. They wouldn't have to shovel snow for the first time in days.

A few people were already stirring, sweeping the walks in front of their businesses, lighting potbellied stoves to knock off the chill. Jake crossed the street to where Sam McIver was unlocking the mercantile. Paul Stillman stepped onto the boardwalk on his way to the bank.

"Morning, Jake. Paul." McIver greeted them.

The banker took a deep breath and grinned. "Beautiful morning, isn't it?"

McIver scowled. "The sooner I can get a fire blazing inside, the better I'll like it." He glanced at Jake. "You're out and about early. Something wrong?"

"Another robbery last night."

Stillman paled. McIver's eyes flickered to his store and his lips thinned. "Who'd they hit this time?"

"J. G.'s."

"They stole guns?"

"I don't think they got away with much of anything. Sheriff Carter and I were making rounds about that time and almost caught one of them."

McIver shook his head. "I'm thinking of sleeping in my store until these thieves are behind bars."

"It might not be a bad idea."

"You know—" Mr. Stillman rubbed his jaw—"I haven't been too worried about these kids breaking into the bank, but they're getting more daring every day. You don't suppose they'd try it, do you?"

"Surely not. That's the last thing we need." McIver

motioned to the store. "You gentlemen want to come inside? I'll have a fire and a pot of coffee going in no time."

"Thanks, Sam, but I'd better get on over to the bank."

"Another time. Thanks." Jake headed down the boardwalk.

Mr. Stillman fell into step beside him. "Glad I ran into you this morning, Jake. Sturgis stopped by yesterday. He wants to have a meeting."

Jake's stomach clenched. "You think he's ready to sell?"

The banker shrugged. "He wouldn't say. Said he wanted us all together. He's been adamant about keeping that mine sealed. What about Seamus?"

"He has his good days and bad, but he's a shareholder, so he'll have to be there if we take a vote."

Mr. Stillman paused in front of the bank. "I'll let you know as soon as we set up a date and time."

Jake nodded and continued on. If Sturgis sold, they'd have a new shareholder in the mix, and who knew what would happen then. None of them could afford to buy Sturgis out. If Jake could, he'd buy every single share and seal that mine forever, or at least for his lifetime.

He turned down the alley between the gunsmith shop and the bakery, where he'd spotted the thief last night. He didn't even bother trying to sort out the jumbled footprints. The stack of crates and wooden boxes the thief had crashed into lay scattered halfway across the alley.

An open window above the crates showed where the thief had broken into the shop. J. G. wouldn't even discover the break-in until noon. The elderly proprietor opened up shop late and closed early, putting in a few hours a day.

Jake pulled the window closed. He'd drop by J. G.'s this

morning and give him the news before he heard it from someone else. He edged past the crates and followed the prints they'd made the night before. A tamped-down spot indicated the dropped sack of guns.

Farther on, he distinguished the running steps of the thief versus his. He squatted and pushed his hat back, studying the prints. They looked too large to be a child's, but the snow didn't leave any real clear prints to go on. Could someone else be breaking into the stores, trying to make it look like the street kids? Could they have stolen the blankets and the beans just to throw him off track? The information was worth thinking about, so he tucked it away and retraced his steps.

A scrap of dark cloth snagged on a porch caught his eye. He stopped a few yards from where he and Sheriff Carter had stood last night. A wallowed-out spot snugged against the edge of the building. He plucked the scrap of black cloth from the nail. Had someone else been out here last night? His gaze canvassed the area and landed on a handprint embedded in the snow.

A handprint the size of a young boy's. He fingered the black material and frowned.

Or that of a woman.

CHAPTER EIGHT

JAKE SAT ON HIS HORSE in the pine thicket, branches around him sagging beneath the weight of snow. The rumble of a locomotive straining up the steep incline reached his ears. If anybody jumped the train, he'd spot them as the brakeman slowed for the last bend before Chestnut.

The train huffed into view, and Jake pulled farther back into the trees. Black smoke marred the pristine whiteness of the snowy landscape; creaking cars shattered the stillness. Jake saw neither hide nor hair of any freeloaders bailing out, adult or otherwise.

The engine lumbered past, smoke belching, brakes squealing, slowing for the daily two o'clock stop. Jake eased out of the thicket, hat pulled low against the bitter wind. His mare plowed her way through the deep drifts, keeping to the trail she'd cut earlier.

He'd spent the last week combing the area, looking for signs of stowaways.

Nothing suspicious so far. But those kids were coming into town somehow, and the most likely transportation was the train. Chicago was too far away and the weather too fierce for them to attempt to walk the distance. The train had to be their ticket out of the city.

He rounded a bend, and the station came into view. The train was pulled onto a side track, engine idling as passengers got off and others prepared to board for the next leg of the journey. He crossed the tracks, dismounted, and looped his horse's reins over a hitching rail.

Stomping the slush off his boots, he clomped up the steps and scrutinized the passengers as they hurried into the warmth of the tiny café built onto the side of the building. Most would grab a bite to eat, maybe buy a copy of the *Chestnut Gazette*, climb back aboard, and be on their way. Only a handful ever stayed, mostly locals returning after a short trip to Chicago or men looking for work in the mines. He saw two children, their hands clasped tightly in their mother's gloved hands.

Jake nodded at a tall man with a mean-looking scar on his right check, probably a coal speculator, and strode the length of the train. Two men unhooked the caboose. A metal car with its door ajar caught his eye, and he peered inside. Empty. And no evidence of anyone being inside recently. He inspected the next and the next, found nothing, then watched as rail workers unhooked the last freighter.

"Afternoon, Deputy."

Jake turned to find the conductor studying him. "Afternoon."

"Can I help you?"

Pushing his hat back, Jake glanced at the empty railcar, then squinted at the man. "As a matter of fact, you can. We're getting a lot of street kids out of Chicago. Have you had any trouble with stowaways?"

The conductor's chest puffed out, the brass buttons on his blue coat threatening to pop off any minute now. "I do a thorough check before we leave Chicago and again at every stop along the way. No stowaways on my watch. No sir."

"Glad to hear it. Since you're checking anyway, I'll follow along, just to set my mind at ease."

The man's face flushed. "That's not necessary. Like I said, nobody's in any of them—except the passenger cars, of course."

Jake could take the man at his word, but those boys had come from somewhere. "I'd like to have a look myself, if you don't mind."

"All right. If you insist. Sounds like a lot of bother to me, though." The conductor turned sharply and hurried toward the engine, stopping three car lengths up the line. He picked up the whistle around his neck, then gave four short bursts. Without missing a beat, he unlocked the padlock and slid the heavy door back. "Nothing in here."

He unlocked the next one. A fancy carriage sat inside, gleaming in the faint sunlight streaming through the open door. "Some rancher over in St. Louis special-ordered that. It's a beauty, ain't it?"

"Sure is." Jake climbed inside and made a thorough inspection of the storage space. "It's clear."

"Told you." The conductor shrugged and heaved the door closed. The padlock clicked into place. "Hope you're satisfied. I need to get the passengers loaded up."

"Hold on." He pointed to a freshly painted padlocked freighter. "Let's check this one out."

The conductor jerked his watch out of his vest pocket. "I've got a schedule to keep, and that's been locked since we left Chicago."

Jake stilled, his gaze steady on the conductor, trying to determine if the man might have something to hide or if he just didn't like to have his authority brought into question. "And I've got a town to run. Mister, if you know what's good for you, you'll open that door and let me look inside."

The man's jaw tensed. After a moment's hesitation, he stuffed the watch back in his pocket and crunched through the snow.

"Conductor."

Jake turned to find a well-dressed man in his midforties striding toward them. He recognized Mr. Gibbons, the owner of the glove factory. "Afternoon, gentlemen."

Jake nodded in reply.

Gibbons turned to the conductor. "I'm expecting a shipment of machinery today. Very expensive machinery. Has it arrived? No one came to inform me."

"I'm sorry, Mr. Gibbons." The conductor threw Jake a flustered look. "I was detained. We're unhooking your private freighter right now. We'll leave it on the side track as usual."

"Good. My men are on their way over to unload it."

Jake stepped forward. "Sir, I'd like to take a look inside."

Pale-gray eyes rested on the badge pinned to Jake's coat before shifting to meet his gaze. A bemused expression blanketed Gibbons's face. "What for, Deputy?"

Jake hesitated. How much did he want to share? The influx of homeless children on their streets wasn't a secret, but he didn't want one of the town's newest and most influential citizens to get the wrong idea. "Looking for stowaways. We're getting more than our fair share, it seems."

"Well, I don't think you have to worry about that with my private cars." Mr. Gibbons's gaze raked him from head to toe. "I'm sorry, Deputy; I didn't catch your name."

"Jake Russell." Jake clenched his jaw. Gibbons hailed from Chicago, and word had it that he came from old money. The man couldn't be more than ten years older than himself, but he looked at Jake like he'd smelled something unpleasant.

"Ah. Deputy Russell." A slight smile played over the man's face. "Like I said, my freighters are locked tight as a drum all the way from Chicago. No one can get inside. I've got a lot of money invested in that machinery, and I'd hate for vandals to have access to it." He nodded. "Good day to you, Deputy."

He turned away. Jake eyed the business owner's retreating back. What did Gibbons have to hide? Seemed like he'd appreciate the local law looking out for his interests. Only one way to find out. "Conductor, open that door."

"What did you say?" Gibbons whirled around, his eyes colder than the wind blowing out of the north.

Jake faced him, feet apart, legs braced. He jerked his head toward the lone car at the end of the line. "I told the conductor to open her up so I can have a look inside. If everything is as you say, you don't have anything to worry about, do you?"

"It's not me who has anything to worry about. It'll be you if you keep on with this foolishness." His gaze shifted, and Jake glanced around. Three burly men spread out behind him.

"Trouble, boss?"

"Nothing I can't handle, boys." Gibbons palmed a set of keys and moved closer to Jake. "Listen, Deputy, I'm going to let you have your look-see to prove there's nothing in that shipment other than what I said. I'm a man of my word, and the sooner you get that through your thick head, the better off you'll be."

Gibbons turned the key with jerky motions, and one of his men slid the heavy door open, revealing two large crates. Other than that, the container stood empty.

"Satisfied?"

Jake searched the shadows of the car and found nothing, other than the crates. He stepped back and tipped his hat. "Just doing my job."

He strode to his horse as the whistle blew. Mounted, he reined away, but not before he caught Gibbons's hard-eyed gaze following his every move. Jake headed toward the jail. He'd just made an enemy out of one of the richest men in town, someone Chestnut's founding fathers had wooed to help grow the city. With a few well-placed comments, Gibbons could have Jake's tin star pinned to the nearest Christmas tree before he could say, "Merry Christmas."

*　　*　　*

Victor glared at Jimmy Sharp and threw a set of keys on the desk, the clatter a pale imitation of the clamoring anger in his gut. "So my brother sent you in his place, huh?"

"He's busy." Sharp stared him down, his ice-blue gaze cutting in its intensity.

Scowling, Victor turned away and poured a shot of whiskey. Busy. Like he'd been for the past ten years. Their father had passed the reins on to his older brother and left Victor with nothing except the crumbs from his brother's table.

Part of that inheritance should have been his. But his brother didn't think he was capable of taking over any of the family businesses and always gave the jobs to people like Sharp. And their father agreed with him.

Sharp opened the door between the office and the factory floor, revealing a room crowded with sewing machines and small workers scurrying about. Doing their master's bidding. Shouldn't that count for something? Victor operated a tight ship, and the local law didn't suspect a thing. His jaw tightened. At least they hadn't until those boys had stirred up trouble.

"Nice little operation you've got going here." Sharp's scar stood out in stark relief.

Victor downed the shot of whiskey. *Little?*

Just like his father's lawyer to dub his endeavor *little*.

"Your brother thinks you're running a big risk setting up shop in a small town like this."

"And my father?"

Sharp shrugged. "I'm sure he agrees."

No matter what he did, he could never please any of them.

Unlike the rest of his family, Victor had moved out of the big city, out from under the watchful eye of the Chicago police. Here there were no cops to buy off. No bribes to pay. The Chestnut sheriff didn't even know the meaning of the word, and his deputy couldn't find his way out of a mine lit by a hundred lanterns with exit signs posted every three feet.

Doing business in Chestnut had turned out to be easier than expected. With the exception of the street kids horning in on his territory. But Butch and Grady would take care of them in short order.

Opening the locked drawer on his desk, he hefted a leather pouch filled with money. "Go back to Chicago and tell my brother that I'll be running this town in a few months. Wait and see."

Long after Sharp left, Victor sat at his desk, staring at nothing. What would it take to prove himself worthy in his family's eyes?

✳ ✳ ✳

Livy slipped into the schoolhouse, hoping not to draw attention to herself. A meeting had been called to talk about the rash of robberies in the last week. It looked like half the town had turned out.

Jake spotted her, worry lines creasing his brow. He moved toward her. "What are you doing here? Things could get pretty nasty."

"I'm here to see after the welfare of the children."

Jake shook his head. "Livy, they're thieves and robbers."

"They're innocent until proven guilty." She crossed her

arms, holding in the words that might exonerate the boys. The thief was too big, too well fed, and too well dressed to be one of the street kids.

Why didn't she have the courage to tell Jake she'd been there that night?

Because she was a coward, plain and simple.

"All right, but if these men start a ruckus, promise me you'll leave. A town meeting with a bunch of riled-up men is no place for a lady."

"I promise." She didn't have any desire to be involved in a shouting match or a brawl, but she wanted to know if the town decided to do anything drastic about the homeless children. They weren't responsible for the robberies, but none of the townspeople would believe her.

And how could she convince them without casting suspicion on herself?

She looked around. Mr. McIver's wife and the elderly Huff sisters, who owned a millinery shop, sat on the end of a row. At least she wasn't the only woman in attendance. She moved to stand next to the ladies. Miss Janie gave her a smile and a hug.

Mr. McIver stepped behind the teacher's desk and brought the meeting to order. "We're here because we've got a problem on our hands. Some young hoodlums have taken to stealing, and we've got to put a stop to it."

Livy bit her lip to keep from refuting his claim. Without proof, she couldn't clear the boys, just as the shop owners shouldn't be able to lay blame on them without the same kind of proof.

But that wouldn't stop them from doing that very thing.

An elderly man, the gunsmith, stood. "Those boys stole

several expensive guns out of my shop, and I want to know what the sheriff and his deputy are doing about it."

Shouts of agreement rose around the room. Livy took in each hard-faced man in the crowd, and her heart sank. These men were out for blood. They wouldn't listen to reason, and they certainly wouldn't listen to her.

Even if she could tell them the truth.

Sheriff Carter stepped forward, his stance commanding, his gaze steely. "We're handling it to the best of our ability. So far, the perpetuators haven't hurt anyone—"

"It's just a matter of time," someone called out.

The sheriff gave the man a withering stare. "Maybe, maybe not. Looks like they're stealing for extra money. It's stuff that can be sold off easily. I sent Jake over to Cooperstown yesterday to see if he could find out if any of the guns or stuff from Sam's had shown up over there. I'll let him tell you what he found out."

All eyes turned to Jake. "The livery stable bought a couple of bridles off a man the day before, but the description of the man didn't fit anyone I know. The same man offered the gunsmith two handguns, but he declined. We'll keep an eye out. But their description of a tall, bearded cowboy who smelled like a whiskey distillery set in a pigpen is a far cry from the boys we've been suspecting around here."

"Well, of course it is," the gunsmith said. "Do you think those youngsters would be dumb enough to steal the stuff and then try to pawn it off in another town? They've got sense enough to pass it off to a stranger first. We need to round up all these kids off the street and put them in jail. Ship 'em back to Chicago, where they came from."

Murmurs of agreement came from the crowd.

Livy clenched her fists, fighting the urge to wade into the fray. How could he say such things about a bunch of kids no one but her seemed to care about?

"Hold on now." Jake's eyes panned the room and, for the briefest of moments, lingered on Livy. "They're just kids, like you said. They don't have anything: no place to sleep, no food, not even warm clothes. They're doing what they can to survive."

Warmth that had nothing to do with the overheated room flooded through her. Jake had defended the boys in front of half the town. True, he hadn't said they weren't guilty, but he'd given these people something to think about. She prayed they'd listen to him.

Mr. McIver pounded his fist on the teacher's desk. "Yeah, but stealing's against the law no matter how hungry they are. If they're hungry and cold, why don't they go over to that orphanage Mrs. Brooks opened up?" He sought out Livy. "Right, Miss O'Brien? Mrs. Brooks would take them in, wouldn't she?"

Her cheeks grew warm. She'd wanted to stay on the fringe of things, but with Mr. McIver's question, everyone looked her way. And they expected an answer. "Yes, of course; we'd love for the children to come to us. But—" She glanced at the expectant crowd hanging on her every word as if they thought she could solve the problem of the street kids. The gunsmith's gold watch fob caught and reflected the light. Sweat rolled off the man next to him as heat from the coal-burning stove ratcheted up the temperature in the crowded room.

These men were toasty warm, and children were freezing in the streets.

And that made her blood boil.

She clenched her jaw and plunged in. "But these children have been used and abused until they're afraid to trust adults. They won't come to the orphanage because they don't know we won't ship them back to Chicago to work in a sweatshop sixteen hours a day for a little bit of bread and water." She paused, her gaze sweeping the crowd.

This might be her chance to open their eyes to the plight of the street children. But doing so might rip her heart from her chest. Still, she didn't have a choice. She had to try. For the children. "They don't dare trust anybody because they've never been able to trust anyone. Even the police in Chicago—"

"Well, little lady, let's not be too hasty here."

Livy blinked as Mr. Gibbons, the owner of the glove factory, stepped forward. She took a deep breath. She'd let the whole town have it with both barrels.

Not that they didn't deserve it . . .

But how much would she have revealed if Mr. Gibbons hadn't stopped her when he did?

Mr. Gibbons tucked his thumbs into the waistband of his trousers and smiled at the crowd, his dark hair gleaming in the lamplight. "I'm not sure we have as big a problem as you men think we do. I realize I'm new around these parts, but I've seen precious little evidence of street urchins roaming around here."

One is too many. Livy held her tongue.

"As far as who's breaking into our businesses, I imagine it's one or two rogue youngsters with nothing better to do. Why, it might even be one of our own, not a homeless child at all."

Angry murmurs rose from the crowd. These people didn't want the truth. They wanted a scapegoat.

The children.

Mr. Gibbons lifted a placating hand, a smile still on his handsome face. "I know that seems far-fetched, but I just thought I'd mention it. We don't want to cast all the blame on the street kids if they're not guilty, you know."

Sheriff Carter stepped forward. "All right, everyone has offered suggestions, and we still haven't resolved matters. I don't suppose we will until we catch the perpetrators. I suggest you men start keeping an eye on your businesses at night." He looked toward the sisters who owned the millinery shop. "Jake and I will watch your store, ladies, so you don't have to worry about that."

"Ain't no thief in his right mind gonna break into a hat shop," someone called out from the back of the room. The men snickered, lightening the tense atmosphere.

Mr. McIver tried to hide his smile. "All right, if that's all, then this meeting is adjourned. If you see anything, report it to Sheriff Carter or Deputy Russell immediately."

The meeting broke up, and men started talking all at once. Livy eased to the side to stay out of the way. Mr. Gibbons stepped up to her. "Evening, ma'am."

"Mr. Gibbons."

"It's Miss O'Brien, correct?" he asked, looking down his nose at her.

"Yes, that's right." Livy lifted her chin. She wouldn't be intimidated.

"Your description of the street kids seemed a little over-wrought. You can't believe everything you hear, you know." Cold eyes raked her, belying the well-meaning tone of his voice.

"Really?" What part of her speech did he think so out of

bounds with the reality of the children's lives? Did he know how they lived? Did he care?

"Yes, ma'am. You'd do better to stay over at the orphanage and take care of the poor little orphans who come your way than to try to get mixed up with these older boys from Chicago. I can assure you, they can take care of themselves."

Some might say the smile he gave her was charming. But not Livy.

"They can be quite dangerous, and I would hate for a pretty little thing like you to get hurt. Good night, ma'am." He tipped his hat and disappeared into the crowd.

Livy narrowed her gaze and stared after the man. On one side, he'd tried to convince the townspeople they had nothing to fear while at the same time warning her to stay away from the lads roaming the streets. Had he offered a friendly warning to keep her safe, or threatened her?

All her senses warned of the latter.

"Miss O'Brien."

Livy turned to find the Huff sisters bearing down on her, Jake following in their wake. Miss Maisie and Miss Janie were dressed snugly in head-to-toe black cloaks and woolen scarves wrapped securely around their ears. In contrast to their all-black attire, Miss Maisie's dazzling multicolored scarf rivaled Joseph's coat of many colors.

"Good evening, ladies."

"Good evening, dear. Jake has offered to escort us all home." Miss Maisie smiled at him. "He's such a gentleman."

"And so handsome, don't you think?" Miss Janie chimed in. She held out a gloved hand, palm level with the floor.

"I remember him as a little fellow in knee britches. Cute as a button, even way back then."

Jake met her gaze, a sheepish look on his face. "Ladies?"

A blast of cold buffeted them when he swung the door open. The sun hung low over the horizon, barely peeking through heavy clouds. Livy wrapped her woolen scarf around her ears and the lower part of her face, already longing for the warmth of the parlor at the orphanage. Instead of letting the children sleep in their bedrooms upstairs, she and Mrs. Brooks were bedding everyone down on the first floor. They'd continue to do so until this severe cold snap lifted. They couldn't afford to heat the whole house in this kind of weather.

"Watch your step now, Miss Maisie." Jake helped the sisters down the steps and across the street, his hat angled to keep the wind off his exposed face and neck. Livy clutched her scarf close to her face.

"I'll be fine, dear. Make sure Janie doesn't fall. She's been feeling poorly lately."

"Really? I'm sorry to hear that."

Livy shuddered. How could he stand the wind biting against his face? What about his scarf? Or maybe he didn't think he needed one. She shook her head. *Men.*

"Oh, it's nothing really. Just a few aches and pains."

Miss Janie did look frail. Being out in this weather couldn't be good for her. The sisters weren't in the best of health, and Jake took his time making sure they arrived home safely. Livy positioned herself close behind Miss Janie so she could keep an eye on her. The sisters should have stayed inside tonight. They could have found out all they needed to know later.

Other than those hurrying home from the meeting, the

streets were deserted. She spotted only a few merchants closing up shop. Sane people, or at least those fortunate enough
to have a home, knew to stay in the warmth of their homes
when the temperature dropped.

They neared the millinery shop, where the sisters lived
and worked, and Miss Maisie asked, "How's your mother
doing these days, Jake?"

"She's fine."

"The poor dear. I know she misses your father. How long
has it been?"

How long since what? Livy strained to hear the conversation over the gusting wind.

"Two years, ma'am."

"Such a shame to lose him so young."

"Yes, ma'am."

What had happened to Jake's father? The question begged
to be asked, but Livy held her tongue. Jake's clipped response
indicated he didn't want to elaborate.

Jake stopped in front of the shop. "Here you go, ladies."

Miss Maisie fiddled with the door. "Confounded locks. In
the old days we didn't have to worry with such contraptions.
No one would dare break in and steal something from their
neighbors."

Jake reached for the key and unlocked the door. "It's a
different world we live in, Miss Maisie."

"It sure is."

The sisters gave Livy a quick hug and a peck on the cheek.
"Get this poor girl home, young man, before she freezes
to death."

"Yes, ma'am."

Jake offered Livy his arm, and they continued down the street at a much faster clip. He sidestepped a film of ice and held out his hand to help her across. "Be careful. It's slippery."

The wind picked up, and he hustled her the last few yards to the orphanage. Livy hurried around to the kitchen door to keep from tracking slush into the entryway. "Would you like a cup of coffee? It's a long walk back to the jail."

"Don't mind if I do."

Jake hung his hat on a peg, then warmed himself by the stove while she poured. After removing his gloves, Jake took the cup, his hands dwarfing it.

"I hope it's not too strong."

"It's hot." He closed his eyes and took a sip. "That's good."

She cradled hers, barely sipping the aromatic brew. "It's awful, and you know it."

He laughed. "It's not that bad. You've never drunk Sheriff Carter's."

Livy shook her head, laughing. They sipped in silence for a moment. "Would you like some more?"

"Thank you."

Jake held out his cup, and Livy's fingers brushed against his as she took it. Her eyes flew up to his, and heat suffused her face. Livy jumped up and grabbed the coffeepot and poured. She slid the brew across the table, not wanting to risk touching him again.

"Do I make you nervous, Livy?"

"No." She forced her voice to remain calm despite the pounding of her heart.

"Liar."

Her gaze collided with his, filled with an amused glint.

He was teasing, flirting. Still, she didn't want to be teased. The thought frightened her. She looked away and took a sip of her coffee, her heart fluttering like a caged bird against her rib cage.

Keep it light. Don't let him know what his green eyes and crooked smile do to you.

"You shouldn't say that. It's not polite to call someone a liar. Didn't your mother ever tell you that?"

He laughed. "Yeah. All the time. Oh, I meant to tell you that my little brother met one of the boys from the orphanage at school. They're best friends already."

"Really. Who?"

"Georgie. My brother's name is Tommy. They're about the same age."

Livy pounced on the topic of his family, relieved to have something safe to talk about. "How many brothers and sisters do you have?"

"Four. One older sister who's married, two younger sisters, and a brother. They're a real handful for my mother since Pa died."

"I heard Miss Maisie mention he'd died. I'm sure it's been hard on all of you." She kept her tone neutral even though she was dying to know everything about Jake Russell.

One corner of his lips turned up in a sad smile. "We'll be all right. We're making it fine—all of us except Ma, that is. She took his death hard, and now she worries about me. She worries about all of us, actually."

"That's what mothers do."

At least that's what she supposed a mother would do. The closest thing she'd ever had to a mother had been Katie—and now Mrs. Brooks. She couldn't even remember her mother and father. Her earliest memories were of the streets.

And Katie.

"Livy?"

She started and looked at Jake.

"You all right?"

She smiled. "Yes. I'm sorry. Just thinking."

Jake's gaze lingered on her face a moment before he looked away. "Well, I'd better go. I need to make some rounds and check on things."

"Be careful." Why did his leaving do strange things to her?

"I will. Good night, Livy." He jammed his hat on his head and tugged on his gloves. "Thanks for the coffee."

"You're welcome."

He moved to the door, his boots loud on the hardwood floor.

She fingered the scarf around her neck. "Jake?"

He turned.

"It's really cold out there." Livy removed the muffler, glad it wasn't as colorful as Miss Maisie's. She held it out to him. "Take this."

✳   ✳   ✳

"Hurry up. Get them out and inside before someone comes along."

Luke watched as Butch pried the lid off the crate. The boss's horse pranced in the snow.

Butch lifted out two girls and a boy about Mark's size. One of the girls held a smaller kid on her hip. They looked half-starved and didn't have coats. The boy was barefoot. They stared at Butch without making a sound.

"Get rid of that one." The boss jabbed a finger toward the toddler.

The girl's eyes widened, and she tightened her frail grip on the child in her arms. "No. Please." She shook her head and backed away, holding the child tight against her.

"Boss, maybe it could wait until morning?" Butch eyed the kid and rubbed his hands across his chest.

"See to it, Butch. Now. And keep the rest of them out of sight and quiet. The town's all riled up as it is. The sheriff and that deputy of his are sniffing around all over the place."

"Yes, sir."

The boss reined his horse around and rode away. The *swish, swish, swish* of the horse's hooves through the snow faded, and the girl's harsh breathing was all that remained.

Butch plucked the child from the girl's arms and held her under one arm like a sack of potatoes. Silent tears ran down the older girl's cheeks. "Please, mister. Don't take my sister. She won't be any trouble—I promise."

"Shut up, kid. I got my orders, see?"

Luke's heart ached for her, but there was nothing he could do.

Grady herded the three children through the door into the factory, dragging the girl who'd given up her sister. Luke caught a final glimpse of her face, white as death. He swallowed the helplessness that rose in his throat. He knew the feeling of being separated from his only kin, of not knowing if Mark was dead or alive.

Grady left the door open.

A surge of hope coursed through Luke. He glanced toward Butch, but the hulking man's attention stayed focused on the toddler he carried. He lumbered off, a scowl on his face.

Luke crouched in the bushes next to the building, torn between slipping inside the factory and following Butch. This might be his only chance to get inside. But what about the little girl? Would Butch kill her?

Tearing himself away from the building, he followed Butch, staying far enough behind not to get caught but close enough not to lose him.

For a big man, Butch moved awful fast. He looked back, and Luke ducked behind a broken-down wagon covered in snow. When he looked again, Butch and the child were nowhere to be seen.

Where had they gone? Taking a chance, Luke ran toward the street, heart pounding. He'd missed his chance at getting to Mark, and now he'd lost Butch and the little girl. He couldn't do anything right.

He caught a glimpse of movement two blocks over. Butch? He darted down a parallel alley, then another, before he saw him again.

Empty-handed.

Butch hurried off into the night.

Luke stood still, gulping in air.

Horror crawled across his skin and down his throat, spread through his chest, and settled like a raging inferno in his belly. He wanted to walk away, run. Go to the small, safe place he and the others had carved out of a burned-out shack and pretend this had never happened. But he couldn't. He couldn't leave her, even if Butch had killed her.

He moved forward, unable to feel his legs. He'd gone numb.

He found the small form tucked under a stack of crates in the alley. With shaking fingers, he reached out and touched her, only to find her alive and breathing. He took off his thin coat and wrapped her in it, hoping to bring warmth to the tiny child left to die in the freezing cold.

Tears he'd held back ever since he and his brother had found themselves alone on the streets of Chicago gathered in his eyes.

Clutching the small child to his chest, he wept.

CHAPTER NINE

WHAT NOW?

Livy clutched the slip of paper in her gloved hand and hurried across town. Miss MacKinnion's scrawled note requested a meeting with her as soon as school let out. She'd left Seth and Georgie at the orphanage, one with a split lip, the other sporting a black eye.

Seth had looked scared to death when he'd handed her the note. But try as she might, she couldn't get a word out of either of them. And when tears welled up in Georgie's eyes and spilled over, she'd simply hugged him. Livy quickened her steps, anxious to find out what the boys had done but afraid at the same time.

She stepped inside the church that doubled as a schoolhouse

and paused to peel off her gloves. Miss MacKinnion stood at her desk, flanked by Mrs. Johansen and another woman.

Livy started to back out. "I'm sorry, Miss MacKinnion. I'll come back later."

"No, that's all right, Miss O'Brien." Miss MacKinnion stepped toward her, expression solemn. "You've met my sister, Martha Johansen, and Mrs. Benson, haven't you? They're here to talk about what happened today as well."

"Mrs. Johansen. Mrs. Benson." Livy hadn't talked much with Mrs. Benson, but she recognized the woman from church. She focused on Miss MacKinnion. "May I ask what this is all about?"

"Of course." Miss MacKinnion looked down her nose, her hawkish expression and somber manner giving her the appearance of a vulture.

Mrs. Johansen moved forward, her tall, sparse form a slightly older version of her sister's. "I'll tell you what happened. Those two little hoodlums attacked my Billy today. They aren't fit to associate with decent children."

Livy went on the defensive, hackles rising. "Georgie and Seth are not hoodlums, ma'am, and I'm sure they didn't attack anyone."

The color in Mrs. Benson's plump cheeks rose. "Now, Martha, don't you think *attacked* is too harsh a word to use?"

Mrs. Johansen shot her friend a sharp glance. "No, I don't. That's exactly what happened."

Hogwash.

Five or six years older than Seth, Billy could pound the smaller boy into the ground if he wanted to. He'd make two of Seth any day. Mrs. Johansen had an ax to grind, but for the life of her, Livy couldn't figure out what the woman was after. "I can't imagine a five-year-old and an eight-year-old getting the best of Billy."

"That's neither here nor there, Miss O'Brien. The fact remains that they bloodied his nose and that littlest one— what's his name? George? He bit Billy!"

Georgie wouldn't have latched his teeth onto the older boy without a good reason. "I'm sorry, Mrs. Johansen, I'll see what I can do to keep Georgie from biting Billy in the future."

Mrs. Johansen crossed her arms at her waist. "Well, it shouldn't be too hard. seeing as he won't be attending school in the foreseeable future."

Livy stiffened, her gaze riveted on Miss MacKinnion. "I beg your pardon?"

Miss MacKinnion plucked a piece of paper from her desk and held it out. "Under the circumstances, Miss O'Brien, I've taken the liberty of suspending both Georgie and Seth from school for the rest of the term."

"You can't do that."

"I can and I will." The teacher's tone brooked no argument.

Livy glared at the teacher, who gave her a tight smile that smacked of triumph. Mrs. Johansen gloated while Mrs. Benson looked on, eyes as big as a lump of coal.

Miss MacKinnion edged closer. "We don't want you and your kind here, Miss O'Brien."

Livy's gut twisted. So that's what this was all about. They felt threatened by the orphanage, as if those defenseless children could do them any harm. Livy tried to think what would be best for the children, for Mrs. Brooks. Bewildered, she stood there. She'd never faced an adversary like this. If the woman hit or threatened her, she could show her a thing or two that would make Billy's bloody nose seem like a scratch. But this verbal assault out of nowhere took her completely off guard.

"Those orphans aren't fit to associate with our children. And that Mary, batting her eyes at the boys. Why, it's a crying shame the way she carries on!" Miss MacKinnion exchanged a glance with her sister, then slid her gaze back to rake over Livy. "I do wonder where she gets it from."

Livy clenched her fists in the folds of her skirt and stepped forward, crowding the teacher. "I don't know what you're talking about, but Mary's one of the sweetest, most pure girls I know, and I won't have you casting slurs on her."

She lowered her voice to a harsh whisper, contrasting the pounding of her heart. "And if I hear one word about her character from anyone else in this town, I'll know *exactly* where it started."

Miss MacKinnion's eyes widened before she regained her haughty composure. "Are you threatening me, Miss O'Brien?"

Livy plucked the suspension slip from the teacher's fingers. "Only so far as you've threatened me, Miss MacKinnion."

✳   ✳   ✳

Livy stomped into the kitchen, resisting the urge to slam the door behind her.

Mrs. Brooks and Mary stood in the center of the room, the older woman's arms wrapped around the girl. As soon as Mary saw Livy, fresh tears tracked the girl's cheeks. "It's all my fault, Livy. I'm sorry."

Livy's heart sank. Surely Miss MacKinnion hadn't been right about Mary. Not dear, sweet Mary. Livy smoothed the girl's hair back from her forehead. "Mary, I want you to tell me what happened."

"Billy asked me to walk with him, but I told him no, and he got mad." Mary sniffed, a tinge of red creeping into her cheeks. "He called me some names, and Seth and Georgie heard him." Her tear-filled eyes met Livy's. "I tried to stop them, but they wouldn't listen. Before I knew it, Billy, Seth, and Georgie were fighting. Billy's a big old bully!"

So Livy had been right to assume there was more to the story. Billy didn't look like the type to let two little kids get the best of him. "Shh, it's all right, Mary. You didn't do anything wrong. And the boys were just trying to defend your honor. That was mighty sweet of them, don't you think?"

Mary sniffed one last time and smiled. "For a little squirt, Georgie fights like a wildcat."

"I imagine he's been forced to. Now, go get cleaned up. Supper'll be ready in no time."

"Yes, ma'am."

Mrs. Brooks turned to stir the brown gravy on the stove. "Well, I'm glad that's all cleared up. The poor girl has been beside herself with worry."

Livy fingered the note in her pocket from Miss MacKinnion. "I'm afraid it's not that easily cleared up."

*　　*　　*

Jake ducked into the back of the jail the moment he saw Lavinia's sparse frame sweeping toward the door, a basket under one arm. "Tell her I'm not here."

"Tell her yourself." Sheriff Carter leaned back in his chair, a grin on his face.

"Good morning, Sheriff. Is Jake here?"

"He sure is." Sheriff Carter laughed, and Jake wanted to strangle the man. "Jake, get out here. Miss Lavinia's here to see you."

With no way out of the situation, Jake sauntered into the office, feeling foolish for trying to avoid her in the first place. "Morning, Lavinia."

Lavinia pulled a cake out of her basket. "Jake, I brought you a brown sugar cake since you missed Sunday dinner."

"You shouldn't have gone to so much trouble, but we appreciate it, don't we, Sheriff Carter?" Lavinia was a passable cook, but he didn't want to encourage her. Including the sheriff just might get him off the hook.

"We sure do, Miss Lavinia." Sheriff Carter bent down and sniffed the cake. "Hmm-mmm. That sure does smell good. Thank you kindly, ma'am."

"You're welcome." Her gaze swung between the two of them, then settled on Jake like a hawk eyeing its prey. "I'd better run. I'll drop by later and pick up the plate."

She left, closing the door with a firm click.

"That woman's sweet on you."

Jake cringed and tossed an out-of-date wanted poster into the potbellied stove.

"That's why she turned those orphans out of school. And the fact that Billy's her nephew and her sister ain't got the sense God gave a goat is beside the point."

If Sheriff Carter didn't shut his trap, he'd have the whole town convinced Lavinia MacKinnion wanted to marry Jake.

Jake shuddered. He'd gone to school with her, and no way on God's green earth would he be saddled with that woman. Half the time she looked like a mule eating persimmons. She wasn't plain-out unattractive, but the way she acted made her seem that way.

"I'm telling you, she wants to get her hooks into you like nobody's business. She's got her eye on your farm, especially since Johansen's land butts up against yours. That would make her and Martha neighbors, and nothing would suit her better."

Jake groaned. Bad enough he knew Lavinia's intentions, but for Sheriff Carter to put into words what Jake had only suspected turned his stomach, souring the coffee he'd been choking down all morning.

"What I can't figure out is why she became a school-teacher." Sheriff Carter grabbed a mop and a bucket and headed to the jail cells. "She don't even like young'uns, near's I can tell."

Jake wadded another poster and tossed it into the stove. "I'm sure she enjoys teaching a lot better than you realize, Sheriff. She's been at it three years now."

"Well, it's still a mystery to me."

The door opened, and a blast of cold air swept into the room. Mrs. Brooks, bundled head to foot in scarves and a woolen cloak, hurried in. Snow flurries followed in her wake.

"Morning, ma'am."

"Good morning, Deputy."

"Call me Jake." He pulled up a chair for her. "Would you like a seat?"

"Thank you."

Sheriff Carter bumbled out of the back, a once-white apron tied around his waist. His eyes widened. "Mrs. Brooks. I didn't know you were here."

"I just arrived."

The sheriff turned red as a beet, then made an about-face, retreating. Jake frowned in the man's direction, hoping he didn't have another weak spell coming on. He glanced at Mrs. Brooks. "Uh, ma'am, would you like some coffee?"

"No thank you. I'm here to see Sheriff Carter. I'll wait." She sat ramrod straight, her gloves clasped in her ample lap, looking like she didn't have a care in the world.

Sheriff Carter returned, minus the apron and looking more composed than moments before. "Mrs. Brooks. What can I do for you?"

She held up a slip of paper. "Miss MacKinnion has suspended Georgie and Seth for fighting and suspended the rest of the children 'by association.' My boys didn't do anything but defend Mary's good name, and I demand they *all* be allowed back in school."

Sheriff Carter rubbed the back of his neck. "I'm sorry, Mrs. Brooks. I'm afraid there's nothing I can do."

"You are on the school board, aren't you?"

"Yes, ma'am."

Jake lifted his coffee cup to hide the grin spreading across his face. The woman had the sheriff dancing faster than a drunk outlaw with a six-shooter full of bullets.

"Then I suggest the school board have a meeting and resolve this immediately, or I'll be forced to take drastic measures."

"Drastic measures, ma'am?"

"If the board doesn't reinstate the children's rights to attend school, I'll bring them here to the jail for instruction every day. If they're unfit for public school, maybe tutelage at the hand of the law will teach them some manners."

The color drained from Sheriff Carter's face. "Ma'am, you can't do that."

"I can and I will." Mrs. Brooks stood and looked him right in the eye. "I'll expect a verdict from the school board by the end of the week."

"I'm sorry, Mrs. Brooks, but that's impossible. Two of the five board members live out of town, and with the snow and all, there's no way we can set up a meeting that quickly. As soon as the snow melts . . ."

"Very well, then. I'm willing to wait a few more days under the circumstances." She nodded at Jake. "Good day, gentlemen."

Mrs. Brooks swept out of the office as fast as her girth would allow.

Sheriff Carter sank into the chair behind his desk, his gaze glued to the door.

Jake picked up his whittling knife. "Do you think she means it?"

"Oh, she means it, all right."

CHAPTER TEN

"Of course I didn't mean it."

Livy breathed a sigh. She'd worried over nothing.

Mrs. Brooks bustled about the kitchen, her movements quick and efficient. Livy finished cutting the potatoes, scooped them up, and dumped them in the soup pot. Next she gathered the fixings for two pans of corn bread. The aroma of vegetable soup filled the kitchen, making her mouth water.

"Unless he doesn't get the children admitted back in school."

Livy gasped. The older woman's eyes twinkled, and she shrugged her shoulders. "Well, the threat worked. Let's hope the board can get something done. That woman doesn't have the right to turn our children out of school. Her nephew should be punished if anyone should."

"You and I know that, but since we're new in town, I imagine folks won't believe us over Mrs. Johansen." She reached for the empty coal bucket. "Be right back."

Mrs. Brooks eyed the pail. "The coal bin was almost empty last night. We'll have to see Mr. McIver about buying some on credit."

Livy's gaze met the older woman's. "Unless our guardian angel fills it up again."

"I wish I knew who's been providing us with coal. I've been so grateful, but I don't like not being able to thank someone for their kindness."

"Maybe they have a good reason for not wanting us to know."

"Maybe so."

Livy trudged outside to the small porch and grabbed the shovel. When she opened the lid, a full load of coal lay nestled inside. *Thank You, Lord, and bless the generous person who sees to our needs.*

Shivering in the bitter cold, Livy hurried to fill the container. Before she could head back inside, a sound came from around the corner of the house.

Then whispers. And giggles.

Livy frowned. Seth and Georgie were up to something. Again. She set the bucket down and hurried to the edge of the porch. Leaning over the railing, she caught a glimpse of the two boys huddled against the side of the house. "Seth, what are you doing?"

Seth's wide-eyed stare met hers. Georgie's eyes grew

round. Seth cradled something inside his coat. Livy crossed her arms. "Seth? What have you got there?"

"Please, Miss Livy, can we keep her? Please? She's cold and hungry."

"Please," Georgie echoed.

"Keep who?"

Seth tugged the flap of his coat back, and out popped the bewhiskered face of a scrawny cat.

"Seth—"

"She won't eat much, Miss Livy. I'll share my biscuit with her. Pleeeaaasse."

"Pleeeaaasse."

Livy sighed. "I don't know, boys. You'll have to ask Mrs. Brooks. But come on, let's go in. It's too cold to stand out here talking about it."

She moved aside, and the boys filed past her. She picked up the bucket and hustled them inside, smiling as they immediately begged Mrs. Brooks to let them keep the cat. Livy didn't doubt the outcome as soon as she saw the woman's face.

"Boys, boys. Hush now. I can't hear a word you're saying."

"Can we keep her? Miss Livy said we could."

"Seth, I never said any such thing. I said you'd have to ask Mrs. Brooks."

The cat jumped from Seth's arms, made a beeline to the stack of old newspapers piled in the corner beside the stove, completed three turns, and bedded down as if she'd found a home at last. The scrawny cat looked ready to drop a litter of kittens any minute. Apparently Mrs. Brooks noticed the cat's predicament too.

"Well, I guess we can let her stay at least until the weather clears up. It's too cold for man or beast out there."

The boys whooped and raced out of the kitchen.

"Poor thing. Looks like she's in a bad way." Mrs. Brooks looked a mite sheepish. "I just couldn't say no."

Livy hugged her. "Of course you couldn't. And she won't eat much. We should have plenty of scraps to keep her fed. And we could use a good mouser anyway."

"You're right."

Livy reached for the bucket. "Oh, I forgot to tell you—the coal bin is full again."

"Thank You, Jesus." Mrs. Brooks raised her hands heavenward. "God is so good to us, isn't He?"

"Yes, ma'am."

The two put the finishing touches on supper, and Livy smiled when Mrs. Brooks replaced the old newspapers with a pile of rags she'd saved to make a string quilt. The woman's heart was softer than butter left too close to the stove.

Half an hour later, Livy called the children. Over the meal, they named the cat. Or at least they tried to. Seth and Georgie insisted on calling her Tiger. The girls settled on Ginger, except for Grace, who could only be induced to say kitty.

"Well, we don't have to name the cat today. Once we get to know her a little better, one of the names will stick, and that's what she'll be." Mrs. Brooks leveled a stern look at all the children. "I don't want her upstairs in your bedrooms, do you hear?"

"Yes, ma'am," they chorused.

A knock silenced everyone. Livy hurried to answer the

door. Jake stood on the porch, her black scarf covering most of his face. His green eyes sparkled beneath the brim of his hat. "Evening, Livy. Can I come in?"

"Of course."

Georgie hopped up and ran over to him. "Hey, Mr. Jake."

Jake took off his gloves and unwound the scarf, revealing a day's growth of stubble on his cheeks. He ruffled Georgie's hair. "How you doing, pardner?"

"Look, we've got a cat." Georgie took him by the hand and led him over to the stove. The cat dozed on her bed of multicolored rags, seemingly unaware of the attention.

Jake hunkered down and dutifully admired the cat. Livy's heart squeezed as he squinted at Georgie and asked with all seriousness, "What's her name?"

"I want to name her Tiger, but the *girls* all like Ginger."

Livy laughed at the disgusted expression on the little boy's face as she motioned to the stove. "Would you like a cup of coffee?"

"Thanks." His gaze slid to hers, and a lopsided smile tilted up a corner of his mouth. He leaned closer, and Livy's stomach somersaulted. "I need to talk to you. Can we go somewhere a little more private?"

She nodded, then turned to fix his coffee.

"Jake, I think someone likes you," Mrs. Brooks said, her voice filled with laughter.

Livy sloshed coffee over the rim of the cup, and she made a pretense of wiping it up. What was Mrs. Brooks thinking, saying such a thing?

Jake laughed. "I think you're right."

Livy glanced at him out of the corner of her eye. Grace

stood at his feet, gazing straight up at him. Jake held out his arms, and the toddler let him lift her high, her eyes never leaving his face.

Jake quirked an eyebrow at Livy. "That talk?"

She rubbed her hands down her apron, relieved that Mrs. Brooks hadn't taken leave of her senses. "Mrs. Brooks, I'll be in the parlor if you need me."

"Take your time, dear." The woman winked at her. Actually winked!

A heated flush swooshed into Livy's face, and she pivoted, leading Jake out of the kitchen.

Mrs. Brooks acted as if Jake wanted to *court*, when there could be any number of reasons he needed to speak with her. Although she couldn't imagine what they might be. She led the way, balancing Jake's coffee cup. Jake carried Grace, her head resting snugly on his shoulder.

Once seated, Jake juggled his coffee cup and the child. Livy reached for her. "Come here, Grace, and let Mr. Jake enjoy his coffee."

Grace shook her head, her dark curls bobbing with the movement.

He smiled. "She's all right."

"What did you need to talk about?" Livy fidgeted.

"Remember those carvings I promised you?"

"Yes."

"I've finished two or three horses—"

"Horsie!" Grace said, clapping her hands.

Jake raised an eyebrow and lifted the coffee cup high to keep the child from knocking it out of his hands. "Uh, maybe I shouldn't have mentioned that in front of her."

Livy shook her head. "She won't know exactly what we're talking about, so she can't really spill the beans."

"Good. I'll bring them by later this week. Maybe I can make a couple more in the meantime."

"Thank you. Don't try to make them a whole stable. They'll be happy with a couple of pieces, you know."

"I know, but I enjoy doing it. But there's something else."

Grace squirmed, and he let the child down. She toddled toward the door leading to the hallway. Livy followed her and called out, "Mary, watch Grace; she's headed to the kitchen."

"I've got her," the older girl called back.

Turning, Livy sat on the settee and clasped her hands in her lap. "You were saying . . . ?"

Jake leaned forward, resting his forearms on his knees. "I reckon you know about Mrs. Brooks's visit to the jail this morning?"

"Yes." Only the grim look on Jake's face kept Livy from breaking out into a grin. Jake and Sheriff Carter must have taken Mrs. Brooks's threat much more seriously than she'd imagined.

He squinted at her. "Do you think she meant it? I mean, a jailhouse is no place for a passel of youngsters, you know."

Livy bit the inside of her lip, trying to keep a straight face. Mrs. Brooks would never intentionally abandon her charges, but Jake and Sheriff Carter didn't have to know that. "I really don't think it will come to that, do you?"

"Other than Sheriff Carter, do you know who the other school board members are?"

"No."

"Me, Sam McIver, a man named Jesse Tatum, and Mac MacKinnion. Mac is Lavinia and Martha's father."

"Oh." Livy's heart sank. "I see. Mr. MacKinnion will have to side with his daughters, won't he?"

"Probably." Jake nodded, his gaze steady.

Livy smoothed her skirt. "I can't understand why Miss MacKinnion insisted on suspending the children. They really didn't do anything wrong. Certainly nothing worse than Billy."

Jake took a sip of coffee, a flush darkening his cheeks.

Livy crossed her arms. "You're not telling me something."

"Like what?" He eyed her over his coffee cup, a guilty look on his face.

"Something. I don't know what. But I can tell."

He stood and turned his back to her, rubbing his neck with his hand. Looking over his shoulder, he scowled. "You really want to know?"

"Of course I do." Livy stood, placing her hands on her hips. "We're talking about these children being denied schooling because . . . because of some woman's prejudice against . . ." She flailed her arms. ". . . against orphans."

"Well, that's part of it, but it's not all."

"What else could she have against the children?" Livy asked, casting about for anything that could make the teacher despise not only Seth and Georgie but the girls too. Enough to suspend them indefinitely.

"You."

"Me?" Livy gasped. "Why me?"

Jake looked downright miserable. "She's . . . uh . . . jealous. There aren't many eligible men in Chestnut, and she's hoping to get her hooks into any one of them. And to tell you the truth, you're competition for her."

"Competition?" Livy sputtered.

Jake downed his coffee and grabbed his hat. "Look, Livy, I shouldn't have said anything. Forget it, okay? I'll let myself out."

And with that, he bolted for the door.

Livy stared after him, amazed anyone could be jealous of her. Livy never intended to marry, so Lavinia could set her mind at ease. She bit her lip, trying to think of bachelors she'd met at church or at the mercantile whom Lavinia might have her heart set on.

There was Victor Gibbons, but he wasn't exactly young. He was wealthy, though. Or so she'd heard. Maybe Lavinia had her heart set on him. She could have him, as far as Livy was concerned. There was something about him that Livy didn't quite trust. And then there was Jake.

Livy's heart somersaulted.

"Oh."

Jake.

CHAPTER ELEVEN

JAKE STOMPED THE SNOW off his boots and entered the bank. Mr. Stillman motioned him toward his office in the back. All the shareholders would be there except Seamus. The weather was too bad for the old man to get out. If it came to a vote whether to reopen the mine, Jake could only pray that Seamus would be lucid enough to make the right decision.

Jake squeezed Alton Brown's hand. "Alton."

The older man met his gaze briefly, then looked away. Jake didn't ask about his family. What could he say? *Have you gotten over losing your only son in that mine accident? How many days go by that you don't think of him?*

None, just like when you lose your father in the same accident.

No, it was better to keep the meeting all business and not ask questions.

Mr. Stillman ushered in Ike Sturgis and shut his office door. "Gentleman, glad you could make it."

"What's this all about, Stillman?" Alton asked, hands fisted tight against his hips. "It looks like it's gonna snow again, and I need to get on home."

Stillman cleared his throat and glanced at Ike. "May I?"

Ike stood near the door, arms folded across his chest, face like granite. "Go ahead."

Dread pooled in Jake's gut. Was Ike selling out? Had the man who'd contacted Stillman about buying the Black Gold mine gotten to Ike?

"Ike has agreed to sell his shares of the mine."

"He can't do that!" Alton Brown shot to his feet. "We all agreed not to sell."

"There's nothing in writing." Stillman shuffled some papers on his desk. "I'm sorry, Alton."

Alton grabbed his hat and stalked out of the bank.

Jake studied Ike. He hadn't lost family in the mine, and he'd worked the day shift himself. Two years had passed, and he was ready to recoup his losses and move on. Jake could read the truth in his face like a deposit of coal in bedrock.

Ike Sturgis could sell, and he would.

And there was nothing Jake or the others could do about it.

✳   ✳   ✳

When Luke touched the toddler's forehead, heat burned the backs of his fingers. Freezing wind slammed against the cracks of the tumbledown shack, the drafts forcing out the small amount of heat from the fire.

He wrapped a tattered blanket around the child and held her close, trying to share his body heat with her. Paper-thin eyelids fluttered against her cheekbones. He'd risked his life to save her and lost his chance to rescue Mark.

And now she lay in his arms dying.

The other children gathered around the fire, sharing their warmth. Gradually they dozed off, one by one, huddled together like a litter of puppies.

Fresh tears burned his eyes. She didn't deserve this. None of them did. But what could he do? They had no one, nothing. Except themselves.

Had he saved her life only to let her die because he didn't know how to take care of her? He didn't have food, water, medicine. Even if he had those things, he was just a kid. He didn't know how to take care of a child in diapers.

The woman from the orphanage would help. Wouldn't she? Or did she want them to come to the orphanage so she could sell them to men like Grady and Butch and the man they called the boss?

Luke stared at the fire, frowning. She wouldn't give the child back to Butch, would she? He'd watched the children who lived at the orphanage on their way to and from school. He'd watched the two little boys playing in the snow. They'd looked full and happy, not like children forced to do work in a sweatshop.

The child in his arms drew in a shuddering breath, then grew still. Luke clutched her against him, pressing his ear against her tiny chest, his heart pounding. He heard a sound like a tiny mouse squeaking. Then nothing. Then again. He jostled her in his arms, relieved when she drew another raspy breath.

How long before the faint movement of her chest stopped?

He couldn't let her die. Not if there was a chance she could live.

*　　*　　*

Jake grabbed his coat and hat and left the bank. Ike's decision didn't change a thing. He only owned 25 percent of the mine. As long as the others didn't sell, the new owner couldn't do a thing with his shares. And they'd all adamantly refused to sell.

He headed across town and stepped inside Emma's Place just in case Seamus had stopped in. The old man was nowhere to be seen, but Jake didn't really expect him to be out and about. He dreaded sharing the news that Ike had sold out.

His eyes met Emma's across the crowded café, and she called out a greeting.

"Find a spot if you can, Jake. How about a bowl of stew?"

"Don't mind if I do." Maybe something hot to eat would ease the frustration gnawing at his insides. He plopped down at the end of a table filled with miners.

She hurried over, a piping hot bowl in one hand and a pone of corn bread in the other. She slid the platter to the center of the table. "Help yourselves, boys."

"Thank ye, Emma." A grizzled miner winked at Jake and grabbed a hunk of bread. "If I wasn't already married, I'd hitch up with that woman for her cooking alone."

"Oh, hush up, Roger Perkins." Emma placed a hand on Jake's shoulder and sobered. "How're things going, Jake?"

"Pretty good. And you?"

Emma smoothed back graying hair, the tired circles under her eyes showing fatigue. "I can't complain."

Jake nodded. Emma's husband had died along with Jake's father, but she'd been better off than most. She owned this little café and made a few extra dollars feeding miners. "Glad to hear it."

She patted his shoulder before hurrying away to tend the rest of her customers. Jake dug in, listening to the talk about the mines.

"Discovered a new deposit in the Copper Penny today. We'll be busy for another six months at least. Don't know what we'll do after that. Reckon the coal's about petered out 'round here?"

"Hope not."

Perkins shot Jake a glance. "You thought about opening up the Black Gold mine again, Russell?"

All eyes focused on Jake. "Reckon not."

"Lots of pure coal in that mine, son."

Jake pushed his food away, appetite gone. "I know, but it's too dangerous. Perkins, you of all people should know that."

Perkins's son-in-law had died in the disaster, leaving a wife and a couple of kids. Jake knew it wasn't easy for Johanna to make ends meet, even with her family around.

The old miner leaned both elbows on the table. "Not for the right managers. Jake, you and your pa, Seamus, and the others had the right idea, having the workers own shares in the mine. I wish you'd reconsider. I heard Sturgis already sold out. That true?"

"News sure travels fast." Jake took a sip of coffee.

"It's only a matter of time before everyone agrees to sell. No telling what kind of feller will be in charge then. I'd rather see you, Brown, and Seamus running the show than some money-hungry yahoo from Chicago who don't care about nuthin' but making a dollar."

The rest of the men nodded in agreement.

"I'd go to work in the Black Gold mine, given the right men opened 'er back up." Perkins tapped him on the arm with his spoon. "Think about it."

Jake sighed. These men risked their lives day in and day out, and he couldn't bring himself to take one step underground. How could they respect him and the other owners enough to consider working for them again?

He pushed away from the table, then carried his bowl to where Emma stood, elbow-deep in sudsy water. "Food's good as always, Emma."

She looked him in the eye. "Don't let Perkins get to you, Jake. You do what you think's right."

"The problem comes in knowing what's right."

"I'll pray for you. I always do, you know."

"Thanks, Emma. I appreciate it."

The door flung open. "Russell, you here?"

Jake squinted at the dark figure outlined against the night sky. "Yeah?"

"It's Seamus. He's calling for you. I think he's about to kick the bucket."

Jake rushed for the door, his heart in his throat. He'd known this day would come, but not now. Not this soon. He wasn't ready.

*　*　*

Seamus passed on kind of peaceful-like. Doc Valentine told Jake his heart just plain gave out. When the six o'clock whistle blew, the old man smiled, took a deep breath, and went home to rest.

Forever.

*　*　*

Livy put away the last of the supper dishes and wiped down the table. Mrs. Brooks puttered around in the other room, getting ready for bed. The children were settled in for the night, so Livy banked the stove. She yawned, ready for a good night's sleep.

A pounding on the door startled her. She wiped her hands and hurried to the door. "Who is it?"

Nobody answered, but a soft groan came from the other side. Without thinking, she undid the latch and jerked open the door. A small child, eyelashes feathered against pale cheeks, lay wrapped in a ragged blanket at her feet. Livy scooped up the slight form and held it close. She could feel heat radiating from the listless child. She scanned the side yard and grove of trees that buffered the orphanage against the sound of the train but didn't see anyone. She didn't waste any more time looking. Whoever had left the child didn't plan to show themselves.

She shut the door and gazed at the bundle in her arms. Who would leave a child, barely a year old, on their doorstep? Then she noticed the blanket. It looked like one she'd left for the boys over in shantytown. She unwrapped the child, checking for injuries.

Mrs. Brooks stepped into the kitchen, tying the sash of her robe around her ample waist. "I thought I heard the door."

"You did."

When she saw the child, the older woman hurried to Livy's side. "Oh, my. What happened?"

"I found her on the porch a few minutes ago."

"It's a girl, then?"

Livy nodded.

Mrs. Brooks cupped the child's face in her hand. "She's burning up."

"I know." Tears pricked Livy's eyes. *Dear Lord, save this little one.*

Mrs. Brooks took the child. "Stir the fire up again. Looks like we're going to have a long night."

"Yes, ma'am." Livy's heart ached. *Lord, we need a miracle if this child is to survive.*

Her tears overflowed as she thought of her sister's baby. She would have been three by now. But Katie's child had never seen the light of day, and Katie had died with the babe. Livy swiped at her tears and hurried to the stove. She didn't have time to mourn a sister who'd lived on the streets and thought the young dockworker who'd professed love for her would take care of her and her child. He'd taken off as soon as he found out Katie carried his baby. Katie never heard from him again, and his abandonment sucked the life from her.

Livy didn't blame her sister for the choices she'd made. More than once, Katie had held her close and whispered that as soon as she married, they'd have a real house to live in, with real beds and food to eat.

They'd enjoyed a pipe dream.

One Katie never woke from.

*   *   *

Livy, Mrs. Brooks, and Mary spent two days and nights taking care of the little girl and the other children. Two others came down with colds, making the entire lot of them grumpy.

On the third afternoon, Livy stood in the kitchen and surveyed the mess, hands on her hips. Dirty pots and pans from Mrs. Brooks's steeped poultices littered every surface along with the dishes from breakfast and the noon meal. They were all exhausted from caring for a houseful of sick children. Even Seth seemed listless. Livy frowned. Could he be getting sick too? The last thing they needed was another sick child to deal with. She closed her eyes.

Forgive me, Lord. I didn't mean it. We'll take it one day at a time and take care of every last one of these children as long as we have strength in our bodies.

She turned to Mary. "Come on. Let's get this kitchen cleaned up while the others are busy with their lessons."

"Yes, ma'am."

"Thanks, Mary." Livy gave the girl a quick hug. "You're always willing to do whatever I ask."

The girl ducked her head at the praise.

Livy washed while Mary dried, and soon they were down to scrubbing pots. "Do you miss going to school?"

Mary shrugged. "Some. But Mrs. Brooks teaches us just as much as Miss MacKinnion."

"Really?" Livy scrubbed at a baked-on spot. "That's good."

"I miss seeing some of the girls, though."

"Well, as soon as Sheriff Carter and the rest of the school board have their meeting, you should be back in school."

"Yes, ma'am."

When they were done, Livy put Mary to work peeling vegetables. Livy chopped up the leftover ham from breakfast and dumped it in the pot. Later, she'd bake some corn bread, and they'd have a warm, filling supper tonight.

The jingle of a harness drew her attention. She dried her hands and hurried to open the door.

Jake's mother and the preacher's wife picked their way across the frozen ground, both bundled against the cold. A wagon sat in the alley, a man reaching into the back for something. Livy smiled as she recognized the set of Jake's shoulders. A tingle of pleasure skittered down her spine when she spotted her black scarf wrapped around his neck. She shifted her gaze to the two women and realized she'd kept them standing outside.

"I'm sorry, Mrs. Russell, Mrs. Warren. Please come in." She held the door wide, and the women stepped across the threshold.

"Thank you."

They looked around the spotless kitchen, appreciation on their faces. Livy sent up a prayer of thanksgiving. How embarrassing if these ladies had seen such a mess.

"Can I take your coats?"

"Thank you, dear."

The women placed large baskets on the table and unbuttoned their heavy outerwear. Jake's mother smiled at her. "I hope you don't mind, but we've brought a few things over from the church for the children."

"Of course we don't mind." Livy could barely keep her eyes off the bounty. "We're very grateful."

"Jake has a couple more things to bring in."

As if on cue, a knock sounded at the door. Jake lugged in two large hampers filled with clothes and what looked like blankets. Livy itched to go through everything right there on the spot.

His gaze caressed her. "Afternoon, Livy."

"Jake." Her cheeks burned.

Livy turned to Mary, who stood silently by. "Ladies, this is Mary Gregory. She's a huge help around here. I don't know what we'd do without her."

The ladies murmured greetings.

"My girls have really missed you at school." Mrs. Russell smiled.

"I've missed them, too, ma'am." Mary lowered her gaze, blushing.

"Mary, why don't you tell Mrs. Brooks we have visitors?"

"Yes, ma'am."

Mary left the room, and a few moments later Mrs. Brooks hurried into the kitchen, her hair and clothes in disarray, a tired smile creasing her face. She embraced both women. "Mrs. Warren, it's so good to see you. You, too, Mrs. Russell. And Jake. I'm sorry we're in such a dither around here, but someone dropped another little one off a few days ago. A darling child. She's been at death's door ever since."

Mrs. Warren gasped. "Oh! Is there anything we can do to help? Did you send for the doctor?"

Mrs. Brooks looked pained. "I'm afraid there's no money for a doctor."

Livy moved to the stove and started brewing a fresh pot of coffee.

"May I see her?" Mrs. Warren said. "And I'd dearly love to see the rest of the children."

"Of course." Mrs. Brooks glanced at Livy. "Bless you, Livy. I could use a fresh cup. Are there any of those tea cakes left?"

"Yes, ma'am."

"Wonderful. I hope you all will have a cup of coffee with us."

"We'd love to."

"Come along, then. I'll introduce you to our latest addition. Mary's sitting with her now."

The women filed out, leaving Jake and Livy alone. Livy busied herself with the baskets, remembering the last time he'd stopped by and his insinuation that Lavinia might be jealous of her. With Livy's past hanging over her head and Jake's distrust of the street kids, Lavinia didn't have a thing to worry about.

Jake leaned over and scratched the cat behind the ears. She purred in satisfaction. "Looks like she's made herself at home. Ever settle on a name?"

Livy sorted the clothes into piles. "The girls insist on Ginger. Georgie and Seth are sticking to their guns with Tiger. I'm not sure which group will hold out the longest."

Jake chuckled and leaned against the table, arms crossed over his chest, his gaze lingering on her face. "You look tired."

Livy tucked a strand of hair behind her ear, trying to ignore the way his presence filled the kitchen. "You, too. Has something happened?"

"An old friend died."

He looked so pained that Livy longed to soothe the frown from his brow. Instead, she reached for a child's shirt and smoothed its wrinkles. "I'm sorry."

"He lived a long life, but it's still hard to see him go. He was a good man." He cleared his throat. "But what about you? Looks like you and Mrs. Brooks have your hands full."

"The little girl isn't the only sick one. Georgie and Grace have the sniffles. We're hoping and praying they don't get any worse."

"Ma and Mrs. Warren would be glad to help out. If you and Mrs. Brooks work yourselves to the bone and get sick, who'll take care of the children?"

Livy smiled. "From what I remember, you and Sheriff Carter will get your turn."

He shook his head. "Uh-uh. The sheriff's going to get that mess with Lavinia sorted out as soon as they have a board meeting. We're not going to have a bunch of young'uns running around the jail."

"We'll see. Mrs. Brooks doesn't back down easily."

Jake eyed her. She turned away and swallowed a smile. He and Sheriff Carter were too easy to tease when it came to dumping the children on their doorstep.

She put the tea cakes on a platter and carried them to the table. "So how's Lavinia?"

"She's fine as far as I know. Why do you ask?"

She shrugged. "Just wondering."

A horrified look crossed his face. "What's that battle-ax said now?"

Livy shook her head. "Nothing."

Jake grunted, his face screwed up, looking like a horse

chewing on a sour apple. Tingles spread out from Livy's spine. If Jake felt anything at all for Lavinia, he sure didn't act like it. Not that she wanted him to care about her. But what if he did? The thought sent an unexpected thrill through her, shocking her with its intensity.

Mrs. Brooks ushered their guests into the kitchen. The pastor's wife put a hand on her arm. "Now listen, if she doesn't get better by nightfall, you send for the doctor. We'll figure out some way to pay the man. She's such a little tyke. Please, Mrs. Brooks. I'd never forgive myself if she . . . if she died."

Mrs. Brooks sniffed and wiped her eyes with her apron. The tender hug the preacher's wife bestowed on her brought tears to Livy's eyes as well. These women were kindhearted Christians, a lot like Mrs. Brooks. Everyone wasn't like Mrs. Johansen and Lavinia MacKinnion.

Thank You, Lord, for sending someone our way who loves and cares for the orphans as much as we do.

Livy wiped her eyes and placed some saucers on the table with the tea cakes, along with several mugs and the pot of coffee she'd brewed. They sat, and Mrs. Brooks asked Mrs. Warren to say grace. Livy noticed the ladies took the smallest cookies on the platter, only one each, and nibbled daintily at them.

After pouring coffee for everyone, she placed a hand on Mrs. Brooks's shoulder. "I need to go check on the children. They've been awfully quiet the last hour or so."

"Oh, Livy, I'll do that and you visit with our guests." Mrs. Brooks folded her napkin and threw a glance at Jake. "I'm sure Jake would much prefer your company to mine."

Livy resisted the urge to look at him. "That's all right, ma'am. I'll get the younger ones down for naps, and the older ones can color with some of that charcoal and old paper we salvaged from the newspaper."

"All right. Thank you, dear."

✳   ✳   ✳

With effort, Jake forced his attention away from Livy's retreating form and found Mrs. Warren eyeing him with speculation.

"That girl is going to make some lucky man a good wife one day," she said, smirking.

Heat climbed the back of his neck. Mrs. Warren might be a godly woman, but she could spill a bucket of coal faster than anybody he'd ever seen. Mrs. Brooks needed Livy here. She didn't have any business gallivanting off somewhere and marrying some sodbuster or coal miner.

"She's been a godsend, I tell you. I don't know what I would have done without her." Mrs. Brooks sighed. "My husband died several years ago, and my health isn't what it used to be. But there are always little ones who need care. I reckon as long as I have breath in my body and older girls like Livy and Mary to come alongside me and help, I'll keep taking in strays."

"What a blessing," Jake's mother said.

Jake agreed. Even in the midst of taking care of a houseful of children, Livy took the time to think of Mrs. Brooks, make a pot of coffee, and offer their guests tea cakes. Something simmered on the stove for the evening meal, the aroma making his mouth water. Probably Livy's handiwork as well. She reminded him of that woman in the Bible, the one who always worked in the kitchen to feed Jesus and the rest of the disciples. Which one? Martha? Mary? He always got those two mixed up but figured Livy must be the one always cooking and cleaning. Never still.

"Both girls have worked awful hard the last few days. They haven't enjoyed a minute's rest. Poor Mary is looking a mite peaked."

Jake's mother laid a hand on Mrs. Brooks's arm. "I have a wonderful idea. Sunday is Jake's birthday, and I'm cooking dinner for him. I'd love for Livy and Mary to come visit. They can ride out with Jake. My girls have missed Mary at school, and the fresh air will do them good." She glanced at him. "You don't mind, do you, Jake?"

"I reckon—"

"Oh, I don't know—" Mrs. Brooks shook her head.

"Don't worry about a thing," Mrs. Warren chimed in. "I'll come over and help you with the children. We'll have a regular little Sunday school since Reverend Warren will be away preaching on the circuit."

"Thank you both. I'm sure the girls will enjoy a break."

The ladies sat back, looking extremely pleased with themselves.

Jake eyed his mother and Mrs. Warren. What were those two up to? Seemed like they were determined to throw him and Livy together. Not that he intended to complain, but he could find ways to see Livy without the two of them sticking their noses into his business.

That was, if he wanted to.

CHAPTER TWELVE

"Mary's too sick to go. I'd better stay here too."

"Stuff and nonsense. It's just a little cold. A day or two and she'll be fit as a fiddle. Besides, Mrs. Warren will be here any minute. We'll be fine."

Livy twisted her hands in her apron. "Mrs. Brooks—"

"Hush, child. Mrs. Russell is looking forward to your visit. You can't disappoint her." The woman gave her a little shove. "Now, go get dressed."

Livy trudged down the hall to the bedroom she shared with Mary. Butterflies fluttered in her stomach at the thought of riding alone all the way to the Russell homestead with Jake, spending the day with his family, and making the return trip.

She couldn't let herself get close to him. She couldn't let

herself care or entertain thoughts of a future with him. She was a nobody from Chicago, a former pickpocket. He was a good Christian man, raised in Chestnut, where everybody knew and respected him and his family. They'd never accept her as one of their own.

She closed her eyes.

God, forgive me for such thoughts, but people would reject me if they learned the truth. I can't bear to get close to Jake or his family only to have them spurn me because of my past.

The butterflies magnified, their wings beating so fast Livy thought she'd be sick right there on the spot. But she didn't have time to calm herself or figure out some way not to go.

Jake arrived at that moment.

Livy wished him a happy birthday, blushing slightly with the familiarity, and accepted his hand as he helped her into the wagon. She appreciated his running commentary on his family all the way to the farm. As long as he talked, she didn't have to.

"My parents were some of the first to settle this part of the country. They came in the forties, a few years after the incident with Black Hawk." Jake paused and glanced at her. "Are you cold?"

She burrowed deeper into the thick coat Mrs. Brooks had insisted she wear under her threadbare cloak. "No."

"I don't believe you."

"Well, it's a nice kind of cold if that makes you feel better." She smiled, gritting her teeth to keep them from chattering. Surrounded by buildings all her life, she hadn't realized how the wind could slice through even the thickest of coats out in the open countryside.

He laughed. "Okay, I'll accept that. Am I boring you with tales of my family? I figured you'd want to know a little about them before you met everybody."

"I enjoy hearing about your family. You were telling me about your parents."

Jake rested his boot against the footboard on the wagon, looking relaxed and not the least bit cold. "My father died two years ago. I think Miss Maisie mentioned it the other night, didn't she?"

Livy nodded, not wanting to interrupt him.

Jake told her a little more about each of his siblings. "My oldest sister and her husband are expecting their first child any day now."

A pang hit Livy in the stomach. Why did the mention of an impending birth bring the memories back so suddenly? Thoughts of the tattered rags she'd used, the filthy water, the screams of pain and terror, then silence as her sister and the babe both perished. She bit her lip to keep from crying out.

"Are you all right?" Jake placed a gloved hand on her arm. "What'd I say?"

Livy shook her head. How much could she tell him without dredging up more memories? Without revealing the utter horror of her life in Chicago?

"I . . . I lost a sister in childbirth." She looked away.

He squeezed her arm just enough that she felt the pressure through the sheepskin coat. "I'm sorry. You must have been close."

"She was my only family."

"I should have mentioned it sooner." He slapped the reins

against the horse's backs and cleared his throat. "My sister and her husband will be at Ma's today. Will you be okay?"

"I'll be fine." Livy attempted a smile.

But would she?

✳   ✳   ✳

"I wonder where they are." Jake's mother busied herself at the stove, then peered out the kitchen window for the umpteenth time. She threw an apologetic look at Livy. "I'm sorry to be such a worrywart, Livy, but when you have children of your own, you'll understand."

"Oh, Mrs. Russell, I understand. I worry plenty about the younger children at the orphanage."

Jake took a sip of coffee and grinned at Livy. "Ma takes the art of worrying to a higher level. There's nothing she can't worry to the bone. Like whether or not Tommy's socks match, or if one braid is higher than the other one, or—"

"Oh, hush, Jake."

He laughed and dodged the kitchen towel his mother snapped at him, happy he'd brought a smile to her face. Livy's wide-eyed gaze had him wondering if she and Mrs. Brooks ever teased each other.

"Let's eat." His mother turned to the stove. "They'll be here soon enough, I guess."

Jake sat at the head of the table in his father's place, his mother at the other end, close to the stove, where she could hop up and grab the coffeepot or dessert. He sniffed. Peach cobbler if he didn't miss his guess. One of his favorites. Next to brown sugar cake.

He groaned as a familiar face came to mind. Not the best

thing to be thinking right now. He glanced at Livy. Now if she could bake a brown sugar cake, he'd be a happy man.

"I'm sorry Mary couldn't come today, Mrs. Russell. She really wanted to but didn't feel up to getting out in the cold."

"I understand. We'll do this again, as soon as she can come." Mrs. Russell glanced at Tommy and the girls. "When everyone's feeling better, all the children could come out, and we could enjoy a day of sledding. You'd like that, wouldn't you, Tommy?"

Tommy shoved a spoonful of peas in his mouth and grinned. "Yes, ma'am. I ain't seen Georgie in *forever*." He chewed and swallowed before muttering, "It's all that ol' Vulture 'Vinia's fault."

Jake almost spewed coffee across the entire table but managed to swallow it instead. Livy hid a snicker behind her hand. Her eyes met his, and they were filled with hysterical laughter.

"Tommy!" His mother frowned. "I won't have that kind of talk at my table. Hear me?"

"Sorry," Tommy mumbled around his next mouthful, not sounding the least bit repentant.

Jake's mother cast him a beseeching look. He turned to his little brother, wincing at the bulge in the child's jaw. "Tommy, quit talking with your mouth full or Ma's going to make you leave the table. And if she doesn't, I will. Is that understood?"

Tommy's eyes grew wide and he opened his mouth. Jake shook his head, and Tommy remembered to swallow before answering. "Yes, sir."

"Good." Jake nodded.

"Livy, would you like some more pota—" His mother's eyes grew wide at the sound of pounding hooves and a jingling harness careening into the side yard. "What in the world?"

"Mrs. Russell! Mrs. Russell!"

At the sound of his brother-in-law's frantic voice, Jake jumped up, his chair crashing to the floor behind him. The door flew open, and Charlie rushed inside, eyes terrified, hair wild. "It's Susie. She's . . . she's having the baby. I don't know what to do."

Jake's gaze locked with Livy's. She looked like she'd seen a ghost. Her hands gripped the table, turning her knuckles white. Her sister had died in childbirth. Suddenly, birthing babies didn't seem so simple after all. A full-fledged panic hit him square in the chest. What were they going to do? Both girls started crying, and even Tommy looked like he might burst into tears. Jake turned to his mother. "Ma?"

"How far apart are her pains, Charlie?" His mother, who made worry into an art, calmly took off her apron and reached for her coat, looking as if she didn't have a care in the world.

"Uh, five minutes. No. Ten." Charlie ran both hands through his hair, making it stand up on end. The man, crazy with fear, didn't even have a hat. "I don't know. They're close, though. It's too soon, isn't it?"

"No. This baby is right on time." She hugged the girls. "Hush, now. It'll be fine. Remember what I told you? Clean up the kitchen and keep Tommy occupied. Before you know it, you'll have a little niece or nephew. Charlie will come and tell you as soon as he can, okay?"

The girls sniffed and wiped their tears. "Yes, ma'am."

"Mrs. Russell?" Charlie stood in the open doorway, letting in the bitter cold, but nobody seemed to pay him any attention, least of all Jake's mother.

She turned to Livy and gave her a quick hug and a tremulous smile. "I'm sorry to leave like this, Livy, but I'm sure you understand."

"Yes, ma'am. I'll . . . I'll be praying," Livy whispered.

"Livy?" Jake moved to her side, reaching out to hold her upright. Her face looked as pale as his mother's biscuit dough rising in the morning. She gripped his forearm and leaned against him.

Shell-shocked blue eyes met his before ricocheting toward his mother. She shook her head. "I'll be okay. Take care of everybody else."

One last hug and his mother hurried out the door.

Livy insisted on helping the girls clean up the kitchen, but Jake knew her heart wasn't in it. She tried to act cheerful, but he could tell the news of the baby's impending birth upset her.

An hour later he bundled her up and headed to town, promising the girls he'd be back as soon as he could to help them with evening chores.

Halfway to town, he cleared his throat and addressed the matter at hand. "Susie and the baby will be fine; you'll see."

"How can you be sure?" Her hands fluttered until she clasped them tight in her lap.

"I'm not." He squeezed her fingers. "I just have to believe."

"I believed, but it didn't do any good."

His heart lurched at the anguish on her face. Tears shimmered on her lashes. He stopped the team and pulled her into his arms, tucking her head under his chin.

"I did everything I could for my sister, and she still died. The baby was so tiny. A little girl. She . . . she never even took her first breath. There was nothing I could do."

Jake held her at arm's length and searched her face. "You attended her? Alone?"

She nodded. Her blue gaze searched his; her tears spilled over. "I must have done something wrong. What if it was my fault they died?"

"Shh." Jake used his gloved thumbs to wipe her tears away and pulled her to him again, cradling her against him. "Please don't cry. I know you did everything humanly possible to save her. It wasn't your fault."

Jake held her as she cried. He closed his eyes and breathed in the flowery scent of her hair, relishing the way she fit perfectly in his arms as if she was made for him and him only.

Never anyone else.

The intensity of his raw emotion shocked him, and he tightened his hold.

A long while later, she pulled away, her cheeks blooming. "I'm all right now." She took a deep, shuddering breath and reached to smooth her hair back. "I shouldn't have gotten so upset."

"Don't worry." Jake tilted her chin up. "I'll let you know how they're doing as soon as I can, okay?"

"Thank you." She bit her lip and her chin trembled.

"Now don't get all teary-eyed on me again."

She sniffed, a faint smile brightening her face. "I won't."

He kissed her on the forehead and gave her one last hug, then picked up the reins. "Giddyap."

They rode the rest of the way in silence. The streets were

practically deserted on this cold Sunday afternoon. Jake stopped the team in front of the orphanage and helped Livy down. He held her by the shoulders, willing her to look at him.

She lifted her eyes, a questioning look on her face.

His gaze went to her lips before rising to capture her misty blue eyes again. He pulled her toward him. "Livy, I—"

"Not yet. Please."

She touched his face, the tips of her fingers featherlight against his shadowed jaw. Then she drew out of his arms, turned, and hurried toward the front porch.

Jake watched her go, his heart heavy. Did she feel *anything* for him? She'd said, "Not yet." That meant something, didn't it? She opened the door and glanced back at him, wiggling her fingers in farewell, a soft smile on her lips. Jake jumped into the wagon, slapped the reins against the horses' backs, and filled his lungs with a gulp of fresh, cold air.

A wave, a smile, and a "Not yet."

That left a lot of hope for the future.

CHAPTER THIRTEEN

LUKE WRUNG OUT the heavy mop one last time for the night.

Mr. Wong nodded his approval and carefully counted out a small handful of pennies.

The coins clinked against each other as he handed them over. Luke grabbed the change. It wasn't much, but it would be enough for a loaf of bread. They would eat tonight.

"Wait." The Chinese shopkeeper held up a crooked finger.

He shuffled to the little stove in the corner of the shop, right next to a neatly made cot. He wrapped something in several layers of oil paper and tied it with string. "Rice."

"Thank you." Luke saluted the old man.

"Tomorrow? Same time?"

"Yes, sir."

Luke hurried through the darkened town, the bundle of rice clutched under his arm. He had to get to Emma's before she closed and buy some bread. It would cost more than he had, but she'd let him have day-old bread for half price.

A movement caught his eye and he darted into the shadows of a barn. Two men came down the street about a block away, bundled against the cold. They laughed, and the bigger guy gave the smaller one a shove into the snow. Luke caught a glimpse of the smaller one's face. Billy Johansen.

He didn't get a good look at the other guy as they came by, but he knew he didn't want Billy catching sight of him. Luke had seen Billy around the schoolhouse with the other children. Billy bullied people for fun. It was his way. Luke gripped the rice. He had more important things on his mind than matching wits—or fists—with that one.

Especially since Billy's friend looked like he could wipe the floor with both Luke and Billy if he took a mind to.

As soon as they were out of sight, Luke took off in the opposite direction.

✳   ✳   ✳

Monday night, the miners were broke, and the saloons quiet.

Which suited Jake just fine.

Chestnut lay cloaked in snow, the scent of smoldering coal hovering on the air. Jake patrolled past the street leading to the orphanage. Light spilled from the kitchen window onto the snow-blanketed yard. Livy and Mrs. Brooks would be cleaning up after supper and getting the children ready for bed, so he decided to stop in and ease Livy's mind about Susie's baby.

He stepped onto the porch, the boards creaking under his weight.

Mrs. Brooks opened the door on his first knock. Her eyes lit up with a welcoming smile. "Good evening, Jake. Come in out of the cold. How are you?"

"I'm fine, thank you." He took off his hat and stood close to the door, careful not to muddy her floor.

"Would you like a cup of coffee to warm you?"

"Thank you, but I can't stay." He looked around the empty kitchen. "How's the little girl?"

"Much better. I think she's on the mend."

"Is Livy here? I wanted to give her the good news."

"Oh?" Mrs. Brooks arched a brow.

"My sister had her baby." Jake grinned, proud as punch to be an uncle.

"That's wonderful." Her smile widened. "I'll get Livy. She's been mighty worried."

Moments later Livy came into the kitchen, an armload of blankets in her arms, a worried look on her face. "How are your sister and the baby?"

"They're both fine. A healthy boy."

She smiled, the relief on her face evident. "Oh, I'm so glad."

Jake's eyes took in the damp splotches dotting her dress. She caught his gaze and shrugged. "Sorry I'm such a mess. Grace managed to spill her supper. I just gave her a bath, and she enjoyed splashing water all over us both."

Shadows danced across her face, softening features framed by wispy curls. Jake reached out and tucked a loose strand of hair behind her ear, his fingers brushing her cheek. "You look fine."

Jake wanted to take back the husky words as soon as the rose tint flooded her cheeks. He remembered her parting comment from the night before, and with an effort, he let her go and stepped back. He didn't want to rush her, but if he didn't put some distance between them soon, he'd give in and kiss her, and she'd as much as told him she wasn't ready for that, even though the look in her eyes told him otherwise.

She glanced away. "Thank you for stopping by."

"Good night, Livy."

"Good night."

He opened the door.

"Jake?" She took a step toward him, her eyes luminous in the lamplight, the blankets clasped like a shield in front of her. "Take care."

He touched her cheek, wanting to take her in his arms, to feel her close for just one second. Instead, he let his fingers slide down her jaw and backed away. "I will."

Jake headed toward shantytown, thinking of Livy's face, soft and pretty in the glow of the lantern. She'd drawn him in, then held him at arm's length. Why? Could there be a man in her past? Could that be why she'd said she wasn't ready?

His long legs ate up the distance as he stomped out his rounds, the thoughts in his head swirling faster than the snow flurries from the week before. Surely that couldn't be the reason she seemed hesitant.

His stride faltered.

What else could it be?

He stepped into the Golden Nugget, not in the mood to face the smoky room and deal with the drunks and coal miners who wanted to prove how tough they were. Out of habit, he took in the room as soon as the door shut behind him.

Four old-timers played cards, a friendly game that wouldn't get out of hand. A couple of strangers stood at the bar, and the corner table boasted another card game in full swing. The greenbacks in the center of the table screamed that this was a group of gamblers intent on taking that pile of money home. Jake didn't know two of the players, and the third sat with his back to the door. His tall, lanky form looked familiar even through the haze, but Jake couldn't place him.

The fellow slumped over the table, bracing himself with his elbows, looking like a good stiff wind might knock him down. He tried to play a card, and it fluttered to the floor. Jake shook his head. Anybody with one eye and half sense ought to know not to mix whiskey and gambling.

"Evening, Lucky. Quiet night?"

"Pretty much."

He jerked his head toward the card game. "Who's that in the corner?"

"Those two fellows? New in town, I guess. Never seen 'em. The big one looks like he might work in the coal mines." Lucky wiped down the bar and threw him a glance. "Don't you recognize the other one?"

Jake peered over his shoulder, trying to figure out where he'd seen the slender fellow. "Sorry—can't say as I do."

"That's Will McIver."

"Will McIver?" Jake jerked around to stare at Sam's kid. He swung his gaze back to Lucky. "He's just a kid, barely sixteen."

Lucky shrugged. "No law against letting him in here,

I reckon. And besides, I didn't know how old he was. He looks grown to me."

Jake straightened and headed over to the table. He placed a booted foot in the empty chair beside Will and leaned his forearm on his knee. A glance at the winnings revealed Will wasn't faring too well. "Evening, gentlemen."

The big man scowled and didn't reply.

The other man nodded a cautious greeting. "Evening, Deputy."

Will never acknowledged him in the slightest. Jake nudged his shoulder. "Will?"

The youth looked up, eyes bloodshot, face red. He grinned, found Jake; then his eyes focused somewhere over Jake's shoulder.

Jake turned to Lucky. "He's drunk."

"I told you, Jake, he looks a lot older than he is. And his money's as good as anybody's. What else was I supposed to do?"

Jake placed a hand on the boy's shoulder. "Will, time for you to cash out. I'm taking you home."

"Can't."

Jake sighed and thumbed his hat back. "Why not?"

Will waved a handful of cards in his face. "I got a winnin' hand here. I can't lose."

"Leave the kid alone."

Jake eyed the big man seated across from Will. "Sorry, mister. I can't do that. Will here isn't old enough to drink, let alone gamble. I'm taking him home. You got any objections?"

"Well, I reckon I do. We've got a friendly game of cards going here, and contrary to what he thinks, I've got the winning hand. I don't take lightly to not getting to play it."

Jake straightened and hauled Will out of his chair. "If that's how you feel, make sure you pick someone older than this to swindle next time."

He heard the slide of metal against leather when the stranger drew. He pushed Will out of the way and rolled left. The roar of the man's pistol filled the room. The old-timers hit the floor and covered their heads with their hands. Jake came up with his gun in his hand, keeping the bar between him and Lucky. He hit the floor again when a shotgun blasted inches above his head, buckshot peppering the wall in the corner.

"Hands up," Lucky roared. "I don't take kindly to people shooting up my saloon. The next shot won't be over your head, mister."

With Jake and Lucky drawing a bead on him, the stranger dropped his pistol and lifted his hands.

"Good thing I know to keep my head down, Lucky, or you would've blown it off!" Jake glared at the saloon keeper through the metal-gray swirl of spent gunpowder and cigarette smoke.

Two spots of color blazed on Lucky's cheeks. Nothing riled him up more than folks shooting up his saloon, even though he always did more damage with his shotgun than the rowdy crowd ever did with their six-shooters. Jake sighed. He'd stay mad for a month over this, and Jake would end up with a jail full of unfortunate souls who'd faced Lucky's wrath. At least Lucky never shot anybody.

Yet. Jake could be thankful for that.

"I told them when they came in here that I wouldn't put up with no trouble." Lucky waved the shotgun in the general direction of the corner, and everybody ducked again. "Look at that wall."

"He's loco." The gambler's eyes widened, and his hands shot up another notch.

Lucky stalked around the end of the bar and rested his shotgun on the card table, the barrel pointed at the gambler's midsection. Lucky's cold, black eyes eased from the gambler to the pile of money and back again. "You gonna pay for all this damage?"

The gambler's gaze shifted to Jake.

Jake shrugged. "It's up to you, pardner."

"Looks like I don't have any choice in the matter."

Lucky scooped up the cash and stuffed it down his shirt. "Remember that the next time you decide to pull a gun in the Golden Nugget. I don't put up with such foolishness. Get him out of here, Jake."

Will clambered to his feet looking bewildered by all the commotion. Jake collared him and hauled him and the stranger outside, taking a gulp of the brisk winter air. There'd be time enough later to send someone to fetch Sam McIver.

✳   ✳   ✳

Gibbons stood beside the livery stable and watched Jake haul the McIver boy off to jail.

What a shame. McIver's kid going to jail and all that. That plowboy turned deputy could've cut the youngster some slack. His gaze followed Jake as he half carried, half dragged the youngster toward the jail.

They'd all be better off if the deputy would do his job and catch those street kids, instead of spending all his time sparking that li'l gal over at the orphanage and hauling drunks who didn't mean anybody any harm off to jail.

Gibbons walked away, pondering the situation.

If Sheriff Carter and his deputy didn't show some progress in catching those street kids soon, he'd demand some changes.

After all, he had a business to run.

* * *

Once all the children were in bed and the kitchen was cleaned up, Livy eased into the bedroom. She donned her nightgown and slipped under the covers, shivering against the chill. Mary rolled over, the covers sliding to her waist. Livy pulled the blanket up around both of them and scooted closer to Mary's back. Warmth seeped into her bones as she lay there thinking about Jake's visit.

She relived the moment he'd touched her hair. He'd wanted to kiss her. She'd felt the tension in the air and wanted it too, but the very thought of falling in love terrified her. Marriage, childbirth—the whole idea made her break out in a cold sweat.

Livy had been spared from working the streets only because her sister had protected her as long as she could. By the time Livy grew old enough to attract the attention of men who preyed on pretty young street girls, Katie had insisted she dress like a boy and keep her hair lopped off. Since they didn't have much more than baggy rags scrounged out of the garbage, the ruse hadn't been hard to pull off.

Yes, Livy had been spared the attentions of men, but as

her skills as a pickpocket and a crackerjack lock picker gained notoriety, they'd preyed on her in other ways. At first, she and Katie had hoped her skills would take them off the streets. But the more she stole, the more indebted she became to the ones who could turn on her like snarling dogs fighting over a piece of rotting meat.

Mary sighed and rolled over on her back. Livy stared at Mary's sweet, innocent profile in the pale moonlight. Mary wouldn't have lasted a week on the streets of Chicago.

She squeezed her eyes shut. *Oh, Lord, help me. Help me forget.* Tears sprang to the surface, and she blinked them back.

No, Lord, I didn't mean it. I don't ever want to forget. Help me remember so I can show girls like my sister that there is a better way, that You stand with open arms, ready to forgive and forget, to offer a new and better life.

Livy's heart pounded, and she breathed deep to calm herself. A pang of sorrow hit her. If they'd only met Mrs. Brooks years earlier. Mrs. Brooks would have taught Katie that succumbing to the pleadings of her beau would be her undoing.

Katie had been wrong. Like so many young girls before her. Livy didn't want to see more girls fall into that trap. If what she'd learned on the streets of Chicago helped her save ten girls, five, or even one, Katie wouldn't have died in vain.

And Livy was desperate to not let that happen.

Even if it meant staying away from Jake and the feelings he stirred within her. She'd do it if it killed her. She'd live her life at the orphanage, rescuing boys and girls thrown to the streets like yesterday's garbage, showing them Christ's love and His plan for their lives.

✳   ✳   ✳

Livy skirted the gathering of men around the potbellied stove, disappointed not to see Jake among them. She lifted her chin and tamped down the feeling. She'd made a promise to herself last night to keep doing the work she felt called to do.

And a pair of twinkling green eyes and a crooked smile would not sway her from her purpose.

She didn't see McIver, so she took the time to look at the cloth while she waited. She fingered a piece of dark-brown wool, daydreaming of the warm clothes she could make for the children if she had the funds to buy the material. She'd never match Mrs. Brooks's skills as a seamstress, but she'd learned to sew tolerably well. Her fingers stilled when someone mentioned Jake's name. The storyteller's voice, tinged with excitement, wafted toward her.

"I was right there in Lucky's—saw it with my own eyes. The gambler—somebody said he works in the Copper Penny mine—drew a bead on Jake, but Jake pushed young Will out of the way and dove for cover."

Livy's heart lurched in her chest. She grasped the shelf full of cloth, willing her head to stop spinning.

A shoot-out? No. Not Jake.

She forced her numb legs to move, to carry her toward the front of the store. She had to know if—

"If it hadn't been for Lucky's shotgun, we'd probably be burying ol' Jake today."

Livy stopped, hand clutched against her pounding heart. He was alive. She closed her eyes and breathed a prayer of thankfulness.

A lifetime passed before her shaking limbs gathered strength again.

Someone almost shot Jake? When? It must have happened last night after he'd come by the orphanage. She'd determined not to talk to him or to even think about him. If she ignored him, then he'd lose interest in her, and . . . well, maybe he'd court Lavinia MacKinnion.

The thought made her heart ache even more.

She didn't *want* him to court Lavinia MacKinnion. But on the other hand, she didn't want him to court her either.

Did she?

"May I help you, ma'am?" Mr. McIver's younger son, Abner, looked like he'd lost his best friend.

Livy stared back, struggling to remember what she'd come to town for. Gathering her wits, she gave him her order. Without a word, he collected the items and wrapped them up, and she realized why he looked so sad. The man had said Will was involved in the trouble last night.

She touched the boy's arm. "Is Will all right?"

"Yes, ma'am. The deputy brought him home early this morning." Tears filled the boy's eyes, and he blinked, his face crumpling.

"I'm glad."

"Thank you, ma'am," he mumbled before bolting for the storeroom.

She left McIver's, her heart heavy. What had happened last night? Abner couldn't—or wouldn't—tell her anything. Feeble sunlight reflected off the windows of the jail across the street. Would Jake be there or at the boardinghouse? Should she check on him? She hesitated, her heart and head warring with each other.

Her head won, and she pulled her coat tight against the chill and headed toward the orphanage, her steps slow. He'd be fine. He had his mother and Miss Nellie from the boardinghouse to look after him.

And . . . and Lavinia.

She made it to the millinery shop before her heart pulled rank. She'd just make sure he was all right; then she'd go home. That was it. Nothing more. It was the Christian thing to do, after all. And besides, Mrs. Brooks and the children would worry when they heard. She could give a more accurate report on his condition if she'd seen him firsthand.

As she neared the jail, her heart lodged in her throat, and her palms grew sweaty. And it didn't have a thing to do with Jake. She'd never entered a police station willingly. She almost backed out on the spot, but what did she have to fear? She wanted to check on Jake, not turn herself in. Besides, she'd been washed clean of her past sins. She took a deep breath, reached out, and touched the knob. Best get it over with.

The room lay quiet and empty, so unlike the stations in Chicago. They'd been filled to the gills every time she'd been hauled inside, kicking and screaming. Chestnut's jail, with its sparkling windows and clean-swept floors, didn't resemble any she'd seen in Chicago. She moved to stand in the center of the room, pivoting in place.

Two battered desks, both littered with papers and wanted posters, sat across from each other with a half-open door between them leading to the back room. Disappointed not to find Jake, she turned to go but froze when a groan came from the back.

She eased toward the door and peered around it. As she'd suspected, all the cell doors stood ajar, and like the front, the barred cubicles were neat and tidy, the cots made. A soft snoring sounded to her left and she almost jumped out of her skin. Her gaze darted to the corner behind the door, housing a cot.

And Jake.

He lay on his side, head pillowed in the crook of his arm. Dark lashes curved against his cheekbones, and his lips parted slightly in sleep. He breathed in a deep, shuddering breath. Her heart turned over. He'd probably been up all night patrolling the streets of Chestnut while she slept—or at least tried to.

She sighed. She'd never cared if a copper might be tired from his job or in danger. She'd never pondered what they did when they weren't working. Staying out of their way kept her more than occupied. There'd been way too many bad apples to trust the few good that were thrown in. But she'd learned some law officers were cut from a different cloth.

Like Jake.

When Jesus had filled her heart, He had helped her see the good in people where she'd never looked for it before. Back then, she'd been suspicious of Mrs. Brooks's motives for helping her, but by the time she'd recovered enough to leave, she realized the woman was as good as her word, and she'd stayed. The girl she'd been two years ago wouldn't have trusted Jake's mother or Mrs. Warren or their reasons for being kind and generous.

But now she understood. Their actions mirrored Christ in their lives. They could do nothing else but be mothers to the motherless and fathers to the fatherless, much the same way Jesus had reached out to everyone He came into contact with.

Her gaze caressed Jake's face one last time. She wouldn't wake him. That would be too awkward. She only wanted to make sure he hadn't been hurt, and he looked fine. She didn't even know why she'd worried. If he'd been in grave danger, she would have heard at the mercantile. She turned to go and the hem of her cloak snagged on a mop propped against the wall. It clattered to the floor, making enough noise to wake the dead.

Or at least Jake.

He jumped to his feet like he'd been shot out of a cannon, his eyes wide. His hand slapped his empty holster for his gun.

Livy giggled. She couldn't help it. She covered her mouth, trying unsuccessfully to stop her laugher. "I'm sorry. I came by to see you, and you were asleep. Then . . ." She trailed off, motioning at the mop. "I really am sorry. I didn't mean to wake you."

"That's all right." Jake raked his fingers through his hair, making it stand on end. "I dozed off for a bit."

He looked all male with his dark hair mussed and his eyes heavy from sleep. Livy's fingers itched to smooth the wayward strands into place. She swallowed and edged toward the door, reining in her thoughts and her runaway heart.

She needed to leave. Now.

"What did you want to see me about?" Jake cocked his head to one side and gave her a puzzled frown.

"Oh. That."

Heat flooded her cheeks. Coming to check on him had been a dim-witted idea, but she hadn't been able to stop herself. She'd given in to worry, and now she'd gotten herself into a pickle. How could she explain?

He took a step toward her, all hint of sleep gone. "What's wrong? Has something happened?"

"No, nothing's wrong." She bit her lip, looked away, then glanced back at him. The best thing would be to spit it out. "I heard over at the mercantile that you'd been shot at last night, and I was . . . uh . . . worried."

"You were worried?" A slow grin spread across his face. He narrowed the gap between them, a teasing look in his eyes. "About me?"

"A little." She sidestepped and waved a hand in dismissal. "You know, as a friend."

"A friend?" He lifted a brow.

"Yes, a friend."

He moved closer, so close she could see the gold flecks in his green eyes. The teasing look on his face disappeared as his gaze flickered to her lips. "Livy, I'm not sure I want to be your friend." His voice sounded low and husky.

She wanted to turn and run but felt she couldn't move if her life depended on it. "Well, I—"

He reached out and pulled her toward him, lowering his face to hers. His lips covered hers, and she drank in the taste of his kiss. He wrapped his arms around her and drew her closer before slanting his lips against hers, deepening the kiss. As if of their own volition, her arms twined themselves around his neck and pulled him closer still. He pulled back and kissed the corner of her mouth, then lifted his head, his hooded gaze moving over her face.

"Just friends?" he whispered, his breathing as ragged as hers.

Tears sprang to Livy's eyes, and she put a trembling hand to his lips. "Just friends."

Then she disentangled herself, turned, and ran from the jail, struggling to keep the gathering tears from falling.

CHAPTER FOURTEEN

LIVY LOST THE BATTLE LONG before she reached the orphanage. She cut through the alley behind Miss Janie and Miss Maisie's shop, hoping to avoid questions if the two elderly ladies saw her.

She slowed when she reached the orphanage. She never planned to fall in love, ever. She placed a hand on her quivering stomach. Jake would want children, wouldn't he? She'd seen him with Gracie and his brother and sisters. He'd want a houseful. Images of her sister pleading with her to do something swam before her eyes. She just couldn't. She wasn't brave enough.

No matter what she felt for Jake Russell.

Slipping into the lean-to attached to the kitchen, Livy

smoothed her skirt and patted her hair. Long before she wanted to, she went inside.

Mrs. Brooks smiled at her from the stove. "I was beginning to worry."

Livy took off her coat and her gloves and tried not to look at the older woman.

"Livy?"

"Yes, ma'am?" Her voice cracked, the result of her tears.

"Did you bring the nutmeg and salt?"

Livy's face burned, and fresh tears sprouted. "Oh, I'm sorry. I left it in the lean-to." She darted outside and retrieved the package. How could she have been so careless to leave it outside? Mrs. Brooks would know something was wrong for sure. She trudged back inside and handed the parcel over.

Mrs. Brooks dried her hands, tilted Livy's chin up, and searched her eyes. Concern filled her face. "You've been crying. What is it?" Her gaze hardened and she looked like a mother hen about to fly into a rage. "Is it that MacKinnion woman again? What's she gone and done now?"

"No, it's not her." Livy shook her head.

"Then what is it?"

"I—it's Jake." Tears fell from her eyes. "He almost got shot last night."

"Oh no. Is he all right?"

"Yes, ma'am." Livy swiped at the tears that refused to stop, no matter how hard she willed them to. Mrs. Brooks took Livy in her arms and let her cry. When she could cry no more, the woman held her at arm's length and searched her face. "There's something else, isn't there?"

Livy pulled away and folded her arms tight against her stomach. "I think he cares for me, but . . ."

"But what?"

"He won't feel the same when he finds out about my past."

And did she want him to care? No, because she could never return his feelings. Not after what happened to Katie. If Jake stayed out of her life, she could forget about him, and life would be so much simpler.

Wouldn't it?

"Oh, Livy, I don't think you're giving him enough credit. As he gets to know you, he'll see that you're not the same girl you were in Chicago." A slight smile creased Mrs. Brooks's face. "Even I can attest to that. You care for him too, don't you?"

"I don't know. I can't ever be a . . . a wife." Livy's heart pounded. "I—I just can't."

"Because of what happened to your sister and the babe?"

Livy nodded, unable to talk past the lump in her throat. Mrs. Brooks didn't know the full story. Nobody did. Livy broke out in a cold sweat. How long had Katie suffered? Livy wasn't even sure herself. She'd blocked it out to save her sanity.

"Livy, my mother died in childbirth when I was a girl, probably about the same age you were when your sister passed. I know the circumstances weren't the same, but for a long, long time, I didn't want to marry and have children. Then I met my dear Horace. God never saw fit to give us children of our own, but I wanted them. We both did. As you get to know Jake—and fall in love with him, God willing—you'll feel the same."

Livy nodded, blinking back tears, aching for her mentor's loss as she ached for her own.

"I need to check on the children." Mrs. Brooks hugged her. "Why don't you set the table while I'm gone?"

"Yes, ma'am."

Livy reached for a stack of plates, thinking about Mrs. Brooks's words. The woman always saw the best in people. She couldn't know that if Jake had his way, every street kid in Chestnut would be rounded up and shipped right back to Chicago.

Would he still care if he knew about her past?

A tear trailed down her cheek.

And if he did, would she be able to forget the horror of her sister's death and embrace the hope a future with Jake would bring?

Did she dare try?

Was it worth the risk? The risk of her heart?

❋   ❋   ❋

Jake splashed water on his face and stared in the chipped mirror over the washbasin, droplets dripping off his chin. What did Livy want from him? She'd enjoyed his kisses. No, she'd not only enjoyed them, she'd responded, giving as good as she got.

Then why did she insist she wanted to be friends and nothing more? What made her run like a scared rabbit every time she felt ensnared by the possibility of a relationship with him? Her past? What was she hiding?

He toweled his face, rubbing hard. He hadn't been searching for love, hadn't even thought about it. The last two years since his father's death had been chaotic enough without adding a woman to the mix. His duties as deputy and riding out to the farm to help his ma with the chores barely left time to eat, let alone sleep.

Why did he even want to see more of Livy?

Because the thought of not seeing her turned his stomach into knots.

Thoughts of her filled his every waking moment. He saw her eyes in the blue ribbons bedecking the hats in the millinery shop, her reddish-brown curls in the sunset, heard her laughter in the birds' singing.

And God help him, since Susie had presented the family with a brand-spanking-new baby boy, he'd even started thinking about a family of his own.

With Livy O'Brien smack-dab in the center of it.

CHAPTER FIFTEEN

MIDAFTERNOON, Gibbons leaned against a post in Ed McIver's blacksmith shop, his horse dozing while the blacksmith shaped a pair of horseshoes. "Heard anything else from the sheriff about those street kids running loose?"

"Nope." The blacksmith pounded the horseshoe, the sound of metal striking metal ringing throughout the open area of the shop.

"Don't look like they're doing much to find them."

"You heard 'em in that meeting. Kinda hard to catch them if they don't want to be found."

"If Jake would spend more time doing his job instead of out at the family farm and making eyes at that girl from the orphanage, he'd get a lot more work done."

"You think he's sweet on her?"

"As sweet as honey." Gibbons chewed on his cigar. "I just don't think he's doing much to find those kids."

"You might be right about that." Ed dropped the horseshoe into a bucket of water. The hot metal hissed and steam rose from the bucket.

Half an hour later, Gibbons rode away from the blacksmith shop, satisfied with the morning's work. He'd planted seeds of doubt in Ed's mind. With a little prodding, the hotheaded blacksmith could be depended on to do the rest.

❋　　❋　　❋

The school board gathered at McIver's Mercantile after closing time on Wednesday night. Sheriff Carter, Jake, Jesse Tatum, Mac MacKinnion, and Sam McIver sat around the potbellied stove, nursing hot cups of coffee strong enough to pass for liquid coal.

Jake eyed the rest of the men, his stomach growling. He'd missed the noon meal and could already taste the chicken and dumplings Miss Nellie'd promised him for supper. He scowled. If MacKinnion had put a stop to this nonsense when it started, there wouldn't have been any need for discussion. And they could have saved Livy and Mrs. Brooks a lot of worry.

Livy.

Just the thought of her energized him, made him want to go out and conquer the world and lay it at her feet. Or at the very least sample the taste of her lips once again. He tapped his foot, impatient for Sam to get on with it. If this meeting went as planned, he might skip supper and stop by the orphanage instead.

Sam brought the meeting to order. "We all know why we're here. Tom, you want to tell us what happened?"

Sheriff Carter stood. "Well, it was like this. Two of the boys from the orphanage got in a fight with Mac's grandson, Billy. Seeing as how Billy is Lavinia's nephew, she kicked all the orphans out of school."

"Now hold on a minute." Mac's ruddy face turned as red as the glow from the coals in the stove. "The fact that Billy is Lavinia's nephew didn't have a thing to do with her turning those orphans out of school."

"Then why didn't she suspend Billy as well?"

"Well, he didn't do nothing. They jumped him."

"I saw the two boys. They'd definitely been in a scrape."

"Anybody could have done that. It wasn't Billy." Mac shook his head. "Lavinia wouldn't have played favorites."

Jake barely held back a snort. Mac wore blinders concerning his daughter and grandson.

Jesse Tatum spoke up. "Mac, I hate to tell you, but Billy is the biggest bully at school. He runs roughshod over the other children, and Lavinia lets him."

A fair man, Jesse Tatum wouldn't have said anything unless he felt strongly about it, Jake knew. Mac caught Jake's eye. "That true, Jake?"

Jake nodded. Mac probably didn't even know how Billy's ma had lorded it over the rest of them when they'd been kids. "Yep, that's about the way it is. It's gotten worse as Billy's gotten older."

Sheriff Carter leaned forward. "Mac, school's going to be out from now on until after Christmas. Why don't you talk to Lavinia and see if she'll reconsider? I'd rather she take all the children back willingly, but if she doesn't, then she'll have to suspend Billy, too."

Mac sighed. "All right. I'll talk to her. Maybe the whole thing will blow over after Christmas."

Thankful they'd made some headway in solving the school suspension, Jake couldn't wait to tell Livy the good news. Halfway there, he spotted Gus and Little Bit, pulling a small cart filled with coal. The old man stopped at the millinery shop and shoveled the coal bin full for the spinster ladies, then whispered something in Little Bit's long ear. The two of them set off again. Out of curiosity, Jake followed. Gus made a beeline for the widow Peterson's house.

Jake moved into his line of vision.

Gus stopped dead still, gripping Little Bit's lead rope like a lifeline. "Who's there?"

"It's Jake." No matter how hard he tried not to startle Gus, it seemed he always did. He moved closer. "You need some help?"

When Gus didn't say anything, Jake picked up a shovel.

"You gotta be real quiet," Gus whispered.

Jake nodded slowly. "Okay. I will."

Why did the old codger seem so intent on keeping his good deed a secret? Jake did as he was told and filled the bin, keeping the noise to a minimum. When they moved out of earshot of the building, Jake asked, "Where do you get the coal, Gus?"

"Here and there."

"You're not stealing it, are you?"

Gus's eyes grew round. "No, sir, Mr. Jake. I'd never do that."

"All right. Then where you getting it?"

"You promise not to tell?" The old man squinted at him.

"As long as you're not stealing it, I promise."

"I've got my own coal mine."

"You do? Well, I'll be."

"But don't tell. If the other miners knew about it, they'd come steal it; then I couldn't give Miss Maisie and Miss Janie and the others enough coal to keep 'em warm."

"All right. I won't tell." Gus must have found a small deposit, or he'd be selling coal to the speculators shipping it to Chicago. "Do the ladies know you're filling their coal bins for them?"

Gus shrugged.

Jake took that to mean no.

Gus and Little Bit kept plodding toward their cabin on the outskirts of town. Jake watched him for a minute, noticing the way Gus's britches hung on him.

"Hey, Gus." Jake loped after him. "Can you spare some coal for the jail?"

Gus studied him, considering. "I reckon."

"Good. Bring some over in the morning, and I'll have Miss Nellie fix up an extra breakfast. You like bacon or sausage?"

A shy smile lit Gus's face. "Both."

Jake laughed. "Both it is."

He headed over to the orphanage and was disappointed to find Livy wasn't home. Jake relayed the message to Mrs. Brooks that Mac planned to have a talk with Lavinia, then left for the boardinghouse.

When had Livy's happiness become so important to him? His stride faltered. No other woman had ever made him feel like she did. Was it her smile, the tilt of her chin when she laughed, her hair, her eyes, her compassion for children?

Jake didn't have a clue, but one thing he did know.
He wanted to see her again. Soon.

*   *   *

Livy held her skirt high enough to keep it out of the mud. She'd been to every decrepit shop in town today, asking about the street kids. Nobody knew their whereabouts or what, if anything, they might be eating. One kind woman admitted to giving them some food but couldn't tell Livy anything else.

She stepped inside a ramshackle building touting itself as a café. Not much more than a shack, but the interior looked clean as a freshly laundered shirt. Rough tables and benches crowded the room, waiting for customers. A middle-aged woman, gray hair pulled into a tight bun, labored over the stove, her movements quick and sure.

Ham sizzled, and the aroma of brewed coffee lay like a soothing blanket over the room. The woman pulled a pan of hot biscuits, glowing golden brown, from the oven. If her food tasted as good as it smelled, she'd have all the customers she could handle.

"Good evening."

The woman glanced up, barely taking a moment to acknowledge her. "Evening."

"I'm Livy O'Brien, from the orphanage on the other side of town."

"Name's Emma. I heard about the new orphanage." She smiled. "God bless you for taking care of the little ones."

"You're a Christian, then?" Livy didn't remember seeing Emma in church, but she'd been busy helping Mrs. Brooks with the children. When she could take her eyes off Jake, that was.

"Yes, I am. God's been good to me. I can't complain." She kept working, not wasting a moment. "What can I do for you?"

"I'm looking for some boys who've been living on the streets."

"You and everybody else, it seems."

"Excuse me?"

"Oh, don't mind me. But everybody's looking for those youngsters, thinking they're stealing stuff. Maybe they are, and maybe they ain't, but I feel sorry for them just the same."

"So you know them? You know where they are?"

"I don't know about that, but one of the boys comes by every few days and buys a loaf of bread or two."

"Is he one of them?" Livy stepped closer, a hitch of breathless excitement fluttering through her.

"He doesn't say much except to ask for bread. And the few times I've asked questions, he clams up right quick and takes off."

Seeing Emma's harried movements, Livy blurted out, "I'm looking for work."

The woman paused and pushed strands of hair back from her forehead. "The pay's not much."

"That's okay."

Emma jerked her head toward the back. "Well, come on, girl. Those miners'll be here any minute. You know how to make ham gravy?"

"Yes, ma'am." Livy grinned and took off her gloves and cloak.

"Here you go, then." Emma handed Livy a bowl of flour and pointed at the stove.

Three hours later, Livy hurried into the orphanage, her first wages in her pocket. She passed through the empty kitchen and found Mrs. Brooks and the others in the parlor, getting ready for bed.

Mrs. Brooks looked relieved. "Livy, I was getting worried. It's been dark for hours. Where have you been?"

Giddy with excitement, Livy pressed the small amount of cash into Mrs. Brooks's hand. "I got a job. My first job."

Mrs. Brooks's eyes widened. "Oh, my. Where?"

"Emma's Place."

The wide smile left Mrs. Brooks face. "What exactly is Emma's Place?"

Livy hugged her, her excitement overflowing. "Oh, don't worry. Emma cooks breakfast and supper for some of the miners. I can work a few hours in the morning and a few in the evenings and still be able to help out here during the day. And she said Mary could work too."

Mrs. Brooks shook her head. "Mary's too young. She needs to keep up with her lessons."

"Oh, mornings aren't as busy as the evening meal. She said she'd just need Mary in the evenings."

"Oh, could I, Mrs. Brooks?" Mary asked, her face glowing. "We could use the money."

Mrs. Brooks pursed her lips. "I suppose."

Mary squealed and hugged her. Gracie ran to Livy, tripping over the hem of a too-long hand-me-down nightgown. Livy picked her up and swung her around. Soon, all the children were jumping up and down laughing, most of them not even knowing or caring about the reason for the excitement.

Livy laughed, happier than she'd ever been. She was making an honest wage doing honest work for a God-fearing woman.

She laughed and twirled with Gracie again. It felt good to be able to hand Mrs. Brooks a few dollars to help keep a roof over their heads and food on the table.

Even better than when she'd fingered a mark and scored big.

✳   ✳   ✳

Jake eyed the uneven spindles he'd made, wondering where he'd gone wrong. Old man Jacobson had let him use his shop to make a chair for Gus. Jake assured him he didn't need any help, and Jacobson had gone home for the evening. Now he wished he'd agreed to the old man's instruction. He'd be here until Easter at this rate.

The door opened, and Sam McIver walked in. "Evening, Jake. Sheriff Carter said I'd find you here." He eyed the pieces of the chair Jake planned to make. "What's that supposed to be?"

"Spindles for the back of a chair." Jake scratched his head. "Maybe I should stick to carving."

"Nah. We can fix this." Sam rolled up his sleeves and set to work.

Jake watched as Sam made all his spindles the same length, then planed them down where they were all equal diameter. They worked on the chair for a few minutes in silence, Jake watching Sam's every move.

"I didn't know you could make furniture." Jake handed him a saw.

Sam shrugged. "I can put together a decent chair and table, but nothing to compare with what Jacobson can do."

He marked the places for holes in the seat and handed Jake the hand drill. "Here, this should make holes small enough. We can whittle them out a bit if we have to."

They were sanding the pieces when Sam spoke up, his voice low and thoughtful. "Amazing how you knew what you wanted when you started this chair and yet each piece turned out so differently."

Jake glanced at him, noticing the somber expression on the man's face. Jake concentrated on a rough spot on a spindle, buffing it smooth. He ran his hand down the wood, pleased with the texture. "What's on your mind, Sam?"

"Where'd I go wrong, Jake?"

"With Will?"

Sam hung his head. "His mother and I tried to teach him right from wrong, but he's bound and determined to do everything we've ever told him not to do. I'm grateful to you for bringing him home the other day, but it hasn't done any good. If anything, he's worse than he was before."

"I'm sorry, Sam. I don't know what to tell you."

Sam started fitting the chair together, sanding the legs down just enough that they'd fit tight into the seat. Soon, the chair took shape. Sam talked and Jake listened, knowing the man needed an understanding ear.

"He's come in drunk a couple of nights this week, and he says he's tired of working for me in the mercantile. He keeps threatening to go to work in the mines." Sam gave a nervous laugh, sounding anything but amused. "He doesn't realize how easy he's got it."

"None of us ever do."

"I could take it if he just wanted to work in the mines, but this drinking and gambling is killing his mother."

Jake handed Sam another piece of the chair. "I reckon raising kids is like making this chair. It didn't turn out like I expected, but I didn't give up on it either." Jake clapped Sam on the shoulder. "Well, I might have if you hadn't come along. Don't give up on him. He'll come around."

Sam smiled. "I hope you're right, Jake. We've done a sight of praying for him, and I don't want to see him going down the wrong road."

Jake thought back to his early years, when he'd been ready and willing to try everything that came his way. He hadn't had any money to blow on whiskey or gambling, but he'd given his mother grief in more ways than one. Young Will faced so much more temptation these days. But he still deserved a chance.

Just like the street kids.

Jake stopped sanding. He swiped at the wood again. If the kids were stealing from the merchants, there wouldn't be much he could do to help them, but maybe Livy was right. Didn't they deserve the opportunity to prove themselves just like anyone else?

He turned to Sam. "I'll keep an eye out for Will around town. Maybe the next time, I'll throw him in jail and let him stay a couple of days. That ought to cool his heels a bit."

"It might."

"You'd better square it with the missus first. I don't want Mrs. McIver breathing down my neck."

"I'll see what I can do."

Sam sanded a couple of spindles and tapped them into place with a mallet. He lifted the chair and gave it a steady thump on the floor. "Well, looky there. Just what the doctor ordered."

✻   ✻   ✻

Luke waited until the miners left before knocking on Emma's back door.

"Back again?" Emma smiled.

He stepped inside, skittish about revealing too much to the woman, but she never asked questions, just smiled and gave him the bread for his handful of pennies.

"I've got a pone of leftover corn bread. Will that do?"

"Yes, ma'am."

He handed her the coins, and she wrapped the corn bread in a piece of old newspaper. He noticed movement through a split in the curtain separating the kitchen from the dining area. Someone else was here. He sidled closer to the door, ready to take off at the least sign of trouble.

Emma glanced at him. "By the way, Miss O'Brien from the orphanage started working here yesterday. She was asking about you and the others. I think she'd be willing to help if you'd let her."

His heart pounded, and his gaze darted toward the dining room.

"She's here, if you'd like to meet her."

"No, ma'am." Luke shook his head and backed toward the door.

"Emma, did you say something?"

At the sound of the familiar voice, he turned and ran. When he'd put enough distance between himself and

Emma's, he slowed, glancing over his shoulder to make sure he hadn't been followed.

Did she really want to help? He'd seen her with the deputy several times and that didn't sit well. Even though she'd brought them food more than once, he still didn't trust her. Anytime somebody went out of her way to befriend him, he grew suspicious.

He didn't dare trust anybody, not until he found Mark.

And maybe not ever.

* * *

Things didn't look good.

"It's taking too long." Livy hunkered down and eyed Ginger. Almond-shaped emerald eyes stared back at her, unblinking. Livy stood and paced the kitchen, her arms hugging her waist.

Mrs. Brooks sat at the table, calmly peeling potatoes. "Don't worry, Livy. She'll be fine."

"Supper will be ready within the hour. What will we do then? We don't want the children to see her giving birth, especially if something goes wrong."

Mrs. Brooks pushed the bowl of potatoes toward Livy and handed her the knife. "Here. You take care of this."

Mrs. Brooks took Ginger and her bedding to the storeroom and closed the door. She moved to the washbasin and washed her hands. "Now that's taken care of. She can have her babies in privacy, and the children won't have to watch. Does that make you feel better?"

"Yes." Livy bit her lip, her gaze lingering on the storeroom. "But now I'll worry about her all through supper."

"We'll check on her after we put the children to bed. There'll be plenty of time for them to see the kittens tomorrow."

Livy peeled potatoes, worrying about Ginger the whole time. She'd never thought she would be so concerned about a cat having kittens, but it couldn't be helped. She'd never seen newborn kittens before. She'd found a half-grown cat once in Chicago. Katie hadn't wanted her to keep the cat, but Livy had cried until her sister gave in. After a while, even Katie had accepted the mouser, since he kept the rats at bay. Then one night, he disappeared and never came back. Livy cried for days, worrying herself sick.

"Mrs. Brooks?" Livy finished the potatoes and carried the bowl to the stove.

"Hmmm?"

"How many children have you taken in over the years?"

The older woman looked up, a thoughtful frown on her round face. "Oh, I don't know. Dozens, I guess. Why do you ask?"

She dumped the potatoes in boiling water, thinking of the children she'd known on the streets of Chicago. After she'd recovered from her sickness, she'd gone back to her old stomping grounds, hoping to convince the younger children to come with her to Mrs. Brooks's orphanage. But she couldn't find a single one of her friends. They'd simply disappeared. Probably been hauled in and carted off to sweatshops throughout the city. Or worse.

She bit her lip and prayed the prayer that was never far from her heart and mind. *Lord, send someone to care for the children still on the streets in Chicago. Send food and clothes and a warm place to stay. Send someone like Mrs. Brooks.*

"How do you stand knowing they'll leave you someday and you'll never see them again?"

Mrs. Brooks eyed her. "I don't know. I guess the good Lord just put it in me to let them go. It's not easy, mind you, but if a family comes along wanting to adopt a child, who am I to say no? There's always another needy child to fill the vacancy."

"I don't think I could stand it for one of the children to be taken away."

"Livy, if and when it happens, the Lord will help you get through it. I promise you that."

All through supper, Livy thought about Mrs. Brooks's words while worrying about Ginger. She hadn't known the Lord when Katie died, and she hadn't met Mrs. Brooks for almost a year after that fateful day. There'd been no one to depend on, no one to turn to except the other street kids, and all they knew was heartache and despair and living hand to mouth every day, barely surviving.

Her life since she'd met Mrs. Brooks had been so different from her life on the streets. Not just because she had food to eat every day and lived in a warm house but because of caring for others and their needs. Life these days revolved around the children, not herself. What made the difference? Because Jesus lived in her heart or because He lived in Mrs. Brooks's heart?

Or maybe a little bit of both?

*   *   *

As soon as the children were all in bed, Livy slipped back into the kitchen to check on Ginger. She turned the lamp up and left it on the kitchen table before easing the store-room door open. Ginger popped out, a multicolored kitten in her mouth.

"Oh, my." Livy didn't get much of a look at the tiny crea-ture as Ginger shot past her. The new mother made a beeline for her spot by the stove, where she placed her baby and nuzzled it with her nose. The kitten looked none the worse for having been carried around by the scruff of its neck.

"Ginger," she whispered, pointing to the storeroom, "you're supposed to be in there."

The cat didn't pay her any attention. *What now?* Should she move the mama cat and the kitten back into the store-room? Maybe that would be best. She tried to pick Ginger up, but the cat squirmed away like a greased pig, settling next to her baby on the floor.

Livy rocked back on her heels. *Okay. Think.* Maybe if she took the kitten back, Ginger would follow. She scooped up the bundle of wet fur, marveling at its tiny perfection. Ginger jumped to her feet and followed, meowing. Pleased with her progress, Livy hurried to the storeroom and found another kitten on the bed of old clothes and blankets Mrs. Brooks had left on the floor. Ginger sniffed at the kitten, grabbed it, and trotted back toward the stove.

Livy sighed. *So much for that.*

She cradled the kitten, gazing into its pinched little face, the tiny pink nose with tufts of soft hair for ears. She fingered paws smaller than the tip of her pinkie. The kitten sneezed, and her heart turned over. Helpless didn't begin to describe the tiny living thing.

Since Ginger seemed determined to make a home beside

the stove, Livy took the kitten back to the kitchen. Then she put the blankets back where they'd been all along. Ginger nuzzled her babies, then stood and circled them. She stretched out on her side, and Livy watched her, pleased with the turn of events. The children would be so happy when they got up in the morning and found two kittens.

Ginger stood and made another circle. Livy frowned at the cat's still-distended belly. Her heart started pounding. Ginger was *not* through having babies. She jumped up and turned away. What now? She closed her eyes.

Okay; do not panic. Ginger managed to have two babies just fine on her own. She's capable of doing this.

She headed toward Mrs. Brooks's room, then changed her mind. The elderly woman would be asleep already. It would be silly to wake her because Ginger might need help. She went back to the kitchen and peeked at the cat, relieved to find another kitten on the pallet. She pulled out a kitchen chair and cradled her head in her hands.

How long had Ginger been in labor? It had taken her almost four hours to have three tiny kittens. Were there more? Livy gently rubbed her hand over Ginger's stomach. From the lumps and bumps, she felt sure there were. "How many babies you got in there, girl?"

An hour later, Ginger delivered another kitten. Livy had never dreamed it would take this long or that Ginger would have so *many*.

By one o'clock in the morning, five little bundles of fur nestled close to Ginger. Livy had all but worn a hole in the kitchen floor. She wasn't sure, but she thought Ginger might be done having babies now.

Livy cradled the firstborn kitten against her cheek, marveling at the miracle of birth she'd witnessed. She had never been so proud, even if Ginger was only a cat.

＊　　＊　　＊

Jake scowled at the paperwork on his desk. If there was one thing he hated about being a deputy, it was the mountain of wanted posters and letters asking if they'd seen so-and-so. He picked up a letter from a Mrs. Goldstein, looking for her son who'd fought with his father and declared he'd find a job in the mining towns in Illinois. Brown hair, brown eyes, medium height, no discernible scars.

He sighed. That description could fit a couple hundred miners in Chestnut alone. He tossed the letter aside, feeling sorry for the frantic mother but not knowing how he could help her.

The door opened, and Paul Stillman stepped inside, stomping snow off his boots. "Afternoon, Jake. Got a minute?"

"Yes, sir. What is it?" Jake's stomach churned. The look on the banker's face told him this wasn't a social call.

Stillman pulled a chair close to the stove and settled his heavyset frame into it. He took his time cleaning his glasses before spearing Jake with a concerned look. "Don't know how to tell you this, Jake, so I'll just come right on out and say it. You're Seamus O'Leary's sole heir. Besides his personal effects, you own his shares of the Black Gold mine."

Jake stared at him, the wind nearly knocked out of his chest. "There was no next of kin?"

"None."

"But why? Seamus knew none of us planned to open the mine back up."

"Seamus came to see me not long after the mine explosion. He knew his health wasn't the best, and he asked me to prepare a will and keep it at the bank."

"So you've known all this time?"

Stillman nodded. "He asked me not to say anything until he died. He wasn't a talkative man, but of all the shareholders, he knew he could count on you to do the right thing. He said when the chips were down, you'd do what needed to be done."

Jake placed his palms on the paper-strewn desk and leaned back. "Mr. Stillman, I appreciate you telling me all this, but it doesn't change a thing."

"Other than the fact that you own 50 percent of the mine now."

"That's 50 percent I don't want or need."

CHAPTER SIXTEEN

JAKE PATTED MISS NELLIE on the shoulder and surveyed the damage to the boardinghouse's café. "Don't worry, Miss Nellie. Harvey will have everything set to rights in no time."

"But why would someone break into my café?" She dabbed her eyes with a lacy handkerchief. "We don't have anything of value."

"They're looking for money, food, or anything they can sell for cash."

Miss Nellie gazed at him with red-rimmed eyes. "If they're hungry, all they've got to do is ask. There wasn't any need to tear things apart."

Jake nodded. Miss Nellie would never turn a hungry child away. And neither would the orphanage. Which was why he couldn't understand why these children wouldn't go there.

Livy insisted they were afraid. Afraid of what? Livy? Mrs. Brooks? Nothing to fear there. Unless he counted the way Livy made his heart pound. And the longer she held him at arm's length, the worse the feeling got.

"Jake? Are you all right?"

Jake blinked and saw Miss Nellie staring at him, confusion lining her eyes.

"I'm fine. Just thinking."

"Look at this mess." Miss Nellie wiped her eyes again, then stuffed her hankie into an apron pocket.

Tables and chairs lay topsy-turvy, scattered across the floor as if an angry bull had rampaged through. Miss Nellie's prized checkerboard tablecloths dotted the carnage. She trudged across the room, reached down and picked up a tablecloth, shook it out, and started folding it into a small, neat square, sniffling as she went.

Jake set the tables and chairs to rights in no time and stepped into the kitchen. He spotted Harvey trying to tilt a corner pie safe upright. "Here, let me help you with that."

The two righted the cabinet and pushed the furniture into the corner where it had sat as long as Jake could remember. Many a night since he'd started boarding with the Bakers', he'd raided that pie safe for a piece of Miss Nellie's chocolate cake or apple pie.

Too bad he hadn't been around last night. Maybe he would have heard the commotion. Nobody else had. Harvey couldn't hear spit, and Miss Nellie slept like the dead.

Harvey grabbed a bucket and tossed a pie in. Jake hunkered down and salvaged two loaves of bread wrapped in cheesecloth. "Harvey, do you know what's missing?"

"Huh?"

Jake raised his voice. "Anything missing?"

"The money from the cash box."

"The one Miss Nellie kept in the pie safe?"

"Yeah. Been telling her for years not to leave it there. But she wouldn't listen. Said if somebody needed it more than she did, they were welcome to it."

"Well, I guess somebody took her at her word." Jake sat back on his heels, elbows resting on his knees, and surveyed the damage. Harvey dumped another ruined pie in the bucket.

Miss Nellie stepped into the kitchen, still dabbing at her eyes.

Jake stood, tossed an arm around her shoulders, and gave her a hug. "Everything will be fine, Miss Nellie. We'll find out who did this."

"I'm sure they had a good reason." She patted his shirt-front with a gnarled hand. "Now, don't you be too rough on them youngsters when you find 'em. They're just children, after all. If we could get 'em in church, that'd do them a sight more good than jail."

Jake sighed as he looked into her kind face, lined with age and wisdom. He was probably looking at Livy O'Brien sixty years from now. Almost too tenderhearted for her own good.

She glanced around her kitchen, looking a bit confused. "I'm sorry you missed breakfast, Jake, but when I came down and saw this mess, I got so upset, I didn't know what to do."

"Tell you what. When Harvey and I get everything straightened up, we'll let you treat us to some fried ham, biscuits, and gravy." He raised his voice. "How's that sound, Harvey?"

Harvey swiped at some gooey apple pie filling on the floor. "Best news I've had all day."

* * *

Livy finished sweeping the spiderwebs from the upstairs bedrooms, then cleaned the washroom. The harsh Illinois winters kept the inhabitants of the orphanage confined close to the warmth of the kitchen, but they'd had a few days of sunshine to chase a bit of the cold away. The children would start sleeping upstairs as soon as the weather allowed.

A door slammed, followed by the boys' raucous laughter. Seth and Georgie must have come in from the cold. Moments later, they raced upstairs, grinning from ear to ear. "Tommy's here."

Livy's heart rate spiked. Jake as well? Tommy's dark hair and freckled face popped up on the stairwell a few steps below Seth. She smiled at him. "Hello, Tommy."

The boy grinned, looking like a kid version of Jake. "Morning, Miss Livy."

The three boys tore down the stairwell, rattling the walls. Seth hollered over his shoulder, "Mrs. Brooks said to come downstairs. We've got visitors."

Livy hurried into the washroom and smoothed her flyaway curls. Frowning, she eyed the cobwebs sticking to her brown dress. She shouldn't have worn the brown to clean in, but it was too late now. She swiped at the gossamer threads to no avail. "Oh, drat it." Cobwebs or no, she didn't have time to change.

She hurried down the stairs, passed the parlor, and saw Jake's sisters with Mary and the other girls. Mrs. Brooks and

Mrs. Russell were in the kitchen digging through a box of clothes. Livy tamped down a twinge of disappointment when she didn't see Jake. Mrs. Brooks smiled, her face beaming. "Look, Livy, Mrs. Russell brought some clothes Tommy and the girls have outgrown."

Livy peeked in the box and pulled out a pair of twill pants. "Oh, these should be perfect for Georgie."

"And look." Mrs. Brooks held up a tiny smocked dress. "This should fit Grace. Isn't it darling?"

A shriek sounded from outside, and Mrs. Russell pressed a hand to her heart. "My word, what was that?"

Livy glanced out the window. "Seth fell out of the tree, but he's fine. The snow cushioned his fall." She laughed. "Looks like they've discovered a new game. That should keep them busy for a while."

"If it doesn't give me a heart attack in the process."

The shared laughter felt good.

Mrs. Brooks poured coffee, and Livy carried the cups to the table. "Do you take cream? Sugar?"

"Just a little sugar, thank you."

"How are Susie and the baby?"

"Both are fit as a fiddle. I'm having a hard time keeping Susie from overdoing it, but other than that, they're doing fine."

"We're so glad you stopped by. The children will be thrilled with the clothes."

"It's the least I could do." Jake's mother sipped her coffee and smiled at Livy. "Actually, I wanted to invite you and Mary over again. The girls have been pestering me all week." She covered her mouth as her eyes grew wide. Then she laughed, her eyes twinkling. "Oh, my goodness. That sounded like I was only inviting you two because of the girls. The truth is, I'd love to have you visit again. And, Mrs. Brooks, when the weather clears, you'll have to bring all the children out to the farm. We'll make a day of it."

"That's too much trouble for you, Mrs. Russell."

"Oh, it's no trouble. Jake always comes for Sunday dinner, and he'll be more than happy to bring the girls with him. By the way, have you seen him lately? I've been so busy helping Susie with the baby that I've missed seeing him when he comes out to the farm."

Sudden heat filled Livy's face. The last time she'd seen Jake, he'd kissed her. And to her shame, she'd kissed him back. Then told him she only wanted to be friends. Had he taken her at her word and given up so easily? Did she want him to honor her wishes or see through her fear and listen to her heart?

She mumbled something about having seen him on Tuesday.

Mrs. Russell sighed. "Since his father died, he's taken on a huge load of responsibility for all of us. I keep telling him we can manage fine without the extra income from his job as deputy, but we suffered a terrible crop this past year. He's afraid if we have another bad year, we might lose the farm."

Mrs. Brooks reached out and clasped her hand. "Surely it's not that bad, is it?"

Tears filled Mrs. Russell's eyes, and she blinked them away. "We can only pray that it won't be."

CHAPTER SEVENTEEN

JAKE HANDED LIVY UP into the wagon and placed a quilt over her knees. Her gaze met his. "Thank you."

"You're welcome." He winked, and her breath caught in her throat.

His mother was standing right behind him. To cover her embarrassment, she smiled at Mrs. Russell. "Thank you for inviting us to Sunday dinner again. I enjoyed every minute of it. And thank you for the recipe for potato dumplings. A new way to cook potatoes is always a good thing with all the children at the orphanage."

"Think nothing of it, dear." Jake's mother placed a basket in the wagon bed. "Now, girls, don't turn this over. You don't want potato dumplings and fried chicken all over the place."

Jake hurried around to the other side while Tommy clambered into the back with the girls. "Are you sure you don't want to go with us, Ma?"

"I've been over at Susie's most of the week, Jake. A nice quiet afternoon—" she glanced pointedly at the girls, now squabbling with Tommy—"sounds heavenly."

Jake laughed. "All right, then. We'll be home in a little while."

"Take care."

Livy glanced into the back of the wagon and smiled. Jake's two sisters sat with Mary sandwiched between them, the three of them giggling. Whatever they laughed about didn't even have to be funny. They were just being girls. She and Katie had had precious little to laugh about, but sometimes they'd get tickled about the silliest things, like how the German butcher down the street got mad at the stray dogs that hung around his shop every day. He'd yell at them to not come back as if the dogs understood him.

At night, Katie mimicked his thick accent until Livy cried from laughing so hard. She sighed. They'd had nothing, but in some ways they'd had everything. They'd had each other.

Tears pricked her eyes. She missed Katie so.

They pulled out of the yard, the wagon creaking and the harness jingling. Tommy hung over the seat. "Can I take the reins, Jake? I've been practicing, just like you told me."

Jake threw Livy a grin and scooted toward her. "All right, squirt. Hop up here."

Tommy scrambled forward and plopped down. Jake handed him the reins. "Don't drop them."

Livy peeked around Jake. Could Tommy keep still long

enough to guide the horses and keep the wagon on the road? The boy tucked his bottom lip between his teeth, a ferocious look of concentration on his freckled face. She covered her mouth with her hand.

Jake leaned over and whispered, his breath tickling the hair at her temple. "What?"

She glanced at him, his green eyes inches from hers. A warm feeling engulfed her. "Nothing. He's just so cute like that."

He shook his head. "Too bad it won't last very long."

She giggled. She probably sounded as silly as the girls in the back of the wagon. Jake sobered, his gaze turning serious as it dipped to her lips, then returned to her eyes. The half wink and lopsided smile told her that he would've kissed her again had they been alone. Just knowing he wanted to turned her insides to jelly.

But what would she do this time if he tried?

The quilt slid off her knees into a puddle at her feet. Jake grabbed it and spread it over her lap and across his knees. In the process, he snagged her gloved hand and twined his fingers through hers. Livy sat ramrod straight, aware of how close he sat. His thumb rubbed the back of her hand in slow, lazy circles that tied her insides in knots.

"You okay with going to see Susie's baby?" Jake asked, his voice laced with concern.

"I'll be fine."

Babies were a fact of life, and the sooner she accepted that, the better off she'd be.

All too soon they arrived at Susie's small farmhouse. The girls hurried to the door, chattering like magpies, anxious to see the baby. Tommy followed right behind them, although he'd said he didn't want to see any ol' baby. Jake came around the wagon to help Livy down.

His hand lingered on hers, and although she enjoyed the sensation, she didn't want Susie and Charlie to get the wrong idea. She pulled away and turned to the back of the wagon. "Oh, don't forget the food your mother sent over."

"I've got it." Jake snagged the hamper.

Charlie met them at the door, barely acknowledging them, his hungry eyes on the basket. "What you got there, old man?"

Jake laughed and handed over the prize. "Leftovers. Ma said you were probably hungry."

"Starving." Charlie led the way inside. "Susie and the baby are in the kitchen, where it's warm."

The girls were kneeling around Susie, who sat in a rocker, the infant nestled in her arms. Susie loosened the blanket so the girls could get a good look at the baby. The girls oohed and aahed, while Tommy helped Charlie empty the bounty onto the table. Jake sat on the bench and pulled Livy down beside him.

"What's his name?" Mary asked.

"Charlie Andrew Benson III," Susie said, sounding like any proud parent.

"But we're going to call him Andy," Tommy piped up, his mouth full. Livy shook her head. They'd just gotten up from the dinner table. Surely the boy couldn't be hungry already.

Susie's gaze met Livy's. She smiled. "You must be Livy."

"Oh, sorry, Sis. This is Livy O'Brien and that pretty little filly over there is Mary Gregory. Ladies, meet my sister Susie, her husband, Charlie, and little Andy."

"It's a pleasure, Mrs. Benson. Your baby is adorable."

Susie laughed. "Oh, please call me Susie."

"If you'll call me Livy."

Little Andy opened his eyes and yawned. Livy smiled. The adorable baby had a thatch of dark hair and a little rose-bud of a mouth.

A pang at what might have been hit her. Memories of a tiny baby girl with dark hair and perfect fingers and toes but no life surged through her mind. *Help me, Lord.*

She took a deep breath and looked around, taking in the cozy kitchen and the warmth of the fire, thankful baby Andy lived in a warm home with a loving mother and father and aunts and uncles to take care of him.

What if Katie's baby *had* lived? What kind of life would the child have had on the streets of Chicago? What if Katie had died and Livy'd been left to care for the baby? What would she have done then? Everything in her power to save Katie's child, of course. But would it have been enough? As Mrs. Brooks always said, maybe it was for the best, because God didn't make mistakes.

Susie unwrapped the baby. "Look at his fingers. They're so tiny. Can you imagine him ever being big enough to hold a hammer or a hoe?"

"Or the reins of a horse." Tommy pointed to the baby's hands. "They look like a coon's paw."

Amid the laughter, Jake leaned over and let the baby grasp his index finger. The contrast of the baby's tiny hand clasping Jake's tugged on Livy's heartstrings. He rubbed his thumb against the back of the baby's hand, much as he had done to hers on the ride over, and she remembered how he would have kissed her if they'd been alone.

Had his feelings for her changed? Developed into more? Maybe she'd been wrong to tell him she wasn't interested.

Jake lifted his finger slightly. "For such a little fellow, he's got a good grip."

"And he eats like a horse too." Susie's eyes grew moist. "I'm so thankful he's healthy."

Jake chucked his sister under the chin. "You did good, Sis."

Livy marveled at the resemblance between Jake and his sister. Jake's babies would probably look like Andy. The Russell family all had dark hair and bronzed skin. She glanced at Charlie, busy making a dent in the provisions from Mrs. Russell's kitchen. Charlie sported dishwater-blond hair and skin that freckled rather than tanned. Livy's gaze swept over Tommy, Susie, and the two younger girls, wondering what they'd looked like as babies. Had Jake looked like Tommy as a child? And been as mischievous? She smothered a tender smile.

Probably.

Livy sat there, feeling strangely comfortable. In this peaceful scene with Susie and her little family, she could almost forget the past.

Almost.

Mrs. Brooks's words came rushing back. Could her feelings for Jake and the longing for children—dark-haired babies like little Andy—overcome the worst of her fears?

✳   ✳   ✳

The day flew by way too fast to suit Jake.

At the orphanage, Mary hurried inside to tell Mrs. Brooks all about the baby. Livy stepped up on the porch, but Jake snagged her hand before she could go farther. "Hey."

She dipped her head and gave him a shy smile. What he wouldn't do to keep that smile on her face. He tugged her closer.

"You've been quiet today." He grinned. "'Course, it's hard to get a word in edgewise with Tommy and those girls yakking nonstop."

"I didn't mind."

He studied the bemused expression on her face, unable to ignore the soft allure of her lips, the curve of her cheek. He took a deep breath as if he'd been slugged in the stomach. He'd never wanted to cherish and protect anyone as much as he did Livy. She made him wish for things he'd never dreamed possible. But she'd told him to wait. And wait he would. He didn't want to rush things and scare her off.

No matter how much he wanted to taste her kisses again.

He rubbed her arms through the thick cloak she wore. "Cold?"

She shook her head, her reddish-brown hair glistening in the winter sun. "I'm fine."

"I'm sorry the girls insisted on going to see the baby."

Livy placed a hand on the front of his coat, close to his heart. "It's all right. Seeing your sister's baby today helped me let go of a lot of the fear I've had since losing my sister and her child." She smiled, a tender look on her face, tears in her eyes. "Maybe . . . maybe I can move forward now."

"Now?" he whispered as he drew her closer.

"Yes," she whispered before his lips claimed hers.

CHAPTER EIGHTEEN

☩☩☩☩☩☩☩☩☩☩☩☩☩☩☩☩☩
....

SOMETHING WAS WRONG.

"Gus?" Jake dismounted and crunched through the snow to the door and knocked. He listened for any sounds, but Gus's ever-present humming was noticeably absent.

Gus hadn't shown up to fill the coal bin at the jail today, and he always arrived before daylight. No smoke curled from the old man's chimney, which struck Jake as odd. Gus hadn't said anything yesterday about being away from home today. And where would he go, anyway?

When nobody answered, Jake pushed open the door to the dark cabin. The coals in the fireplace lay cold. Little Bit poked her head through the opening between the cabin and the lean-to and brayed. One thing was for sure. No matter where he went, Gus wouldn't leave Little Bit behind.

In the gloom, Jake spotted Gus on his cot, a blanket draped over him.

"Gus?"

The old man didn't move or acknowledge his presence. Jake hurried to his side, worried that his worst fears had materialized and that Gus had died in his sleep. *First Seamus and now Gus.* He reached out a trembling hand and laid it on Gus's forehead. His skin felt hot to the touch.

Thank You, Lord. He's alive.

"Gus? Can you hear me?"

Gus mumbled something, but Jake couldn't make out what he said. He grabbed a couple of ragged blankets and piled them on. He glanced at the cold fireplace and frowned. Making a quick decision, he hurried outside and hooked Little Bit to the cart. They'd be snug in town before he could get the fire going and bring the doctor.

He lined the bed of the cart with half of Gus's tattered blankets, hefted him into the little wagon, then covered him with the rest of the blankets and quilts. He mounted his horse, leading Little Bit behind. He hurried Little Bit as fast as he dared. The game donkey's short legs kept pace with Jake's long-legged mare as if she knew Gus needed help.

Jake decided against taking Gus to the boardinghouse, the orphanage, or even to Doc Valentine's. Miss Nellie didn't have time to see after a sick man, and neither did Mrs. Brooks and Livy, although none of the women would turn him away. But Gus wouldn't want to wake up at either place.

Instead, he headed straight for the jail. Either Jake or Sheriff Carter were there around the clock. They probably couldn't take care of the old man as good as the women, but they'd do the best they could.

Abner came out of the mercantile as Jake halted his mare at the jail. "Hey, Abner, run and get Doc Valentine. Hurry."

"Yes, sir." Abner darted away.

Jake settled Gus on a cot in one of the cells. He groaned and muttered a couple of times but didn't wake up.

Lord, help Gus. Forgive me for not doing more for him, for not encouraging him to go to church and to learn more about You. I don't even know if he's a Christian.

He worked to make the old man comfortable, sending prayers heavenward for his life and his soul. Relief coursed through him when the door opened. "In here, Doc."

"What's the matter?"

"It's Gus." Jake stepped back. "He's burning up with fever."

Doc Valentine pulled up a chair and checked Gus over. He mumbled as he worked.

Jake gritted his teeth. "What's wrong with him?"

"A touch of pneumonia." The doctor muttered under his breath, stood, and snapped his black bag shut. He handed Jake a bottle of medicine. Jake leaned in so he didn't miss any of the garbled instructions. "Keep his fever down. . . . Give him a dose of this three times a day. Hmmm . . . I'll be back later."

And with that, Doc Valentine mumbled himself right out of the jail.

Jake spent the rest of the day sponging Gus. His fever would go down, and he'd rest for fifteen minutes or so; then he'd get restless again. Around noon, Gus looked at him, his eyes glazed with fever. "Mr. Jake?"

"I'm here, Gus."

Gus reached out a feeble hand. "Take care of the kids."

"The kids? What kids, Gus?"

"Cold."

"You're cold? I'll get another blanket."

"No." Gus gripped his hand. A spasm of coughing hit him. When he could speak again, he rasped, "Kids. Cold."

Jake frowned. "The kids are cold?"

Confusion clouded the old man's eyes, but he held up a trembling hand, focused on it a moment. "Gloves."

"I know they need gloves, Gus." Jake patted Gus's shoulder, trying to comfort him. "I'll see what I can do."

Gus babbled on, but Jake couldn't make anything else out. After a while, he lapsed into a fitful sleep. Jake spooned a dose of Doc's medicine into him and tried to keep his fever down.

Sometime midafternoon, Reverend Warren stopped by. "I just heard. How is he?"

"About the same."

"Mrs. Warren insists we move Gus to the parsonage."

Jake raked a hand through his hair. "He'd better stay here. You know he'd be mighty uncomfortable to wake up with Mrs. Warren fussing over him."

The preacher nodded. "You're probably right. He'd high-tail it out of there so fast, he'd forget his britches. We'll leave him here for now." He thumbed over his shoulder toward the front room. "The wife sent over a pot of chicken stew. Eat something and get some rest. I'll watch Gus for a while."

"Thanks, Reverend."

Jake wolfed down two bowls of Mrs. Warren's soup, stumbled out of the jail, and crossed the street. He'd never been so thankful that Baker's Boardinghouse faced the jail, right next door to McIver's. He mounted the stairs to his room and closed the door, falling asleep as soon as his head hit the pillow.

* * *

The six o'clock whistle pierced the evening stillness, echoing through the whole town. The sound galvanized Livy, Emma, and Mary into action. The miners would flood the small café in fifteen minutes. The men would be starving, as usual. Livy rushed around, cutting corn bread and ladling up bowls of beef stew.

Emma took another pone of corn bread out of the oven and dumped it on a platter. "Go ahead and put those bowls on the tables. All we've got is stew and corn bread. If they don't like that, they'll have to go someplace else."

There wasn't anywhere else to go. Miss Nellie only served her boarders. And most of the men who stopped in at Emma's didn't have a wife to cook for them. But the miners would be more than satisfied with Emma's cooking. They wanted something hot and filling, and Emma's cooking met both requirements.

Livy started pouring coffee the minute the first wave of men hit the door.

And didn't stop for the next hour.

Over the last few days, the three women had developed a system. As soon as the diners arrived, Livy filled plates and bowls and coffee cups, refilling as needed. Mary washed dishes, and Emma kept cooking more food until she ran out or the crowd thinned, whichever came first.

Tired after a twelve-hour shift, the men rarely lingered.

They thanked Emma for a hearty meal and left as soon as they finished. Some would go home to sleep, while others chose to drop by the nearest saloon.

When the café cleared, the women went to work washing up and restoring order. The same crew would want breakfast in the morning.

Livy wiped down the tables, then started washing pans. "Emma, why don't you serve a noon meal?"

"I can't hold out for sixteen hours a day. Besides, the miners who work nights are usually asleep during the noon meal, so I don't think it would be very busy anyway."

"You never know."

"I'll think about it. I'd have to have some more help, though. I'm not as young as I used to be."

"Have you always lived in Chestnut?"

"No. When my husband came to work in the coal mines, I opened the café to bring in a few extra dollars." A shadow passed over Emma's face. "He died in the Black Gold mine collapse in '72."

Livy touched Emma's shoulder. "I'm sorry. I didn't mean to bring up bad memories."

Emma smiled. "That's all right. There were a lot of other women in worse shape than me. I had the café and didn't have any children to support. Twenty-nine men died that day, and a lot of them left wives and young children behind. Only mine disaster around these parts so far, thank the Lord. I cringe every time I hear one of those whistles if it's not time for a shift change."

"A lot's changed since you've been here, hasn't it?"

"When my husband and I came, everybody knew everybody. We didn't have the riffraff we have now. All these bums from Chicago who ride in on the trains looking for an easy mark. And the children—that's the worst."

Livy stopped scrubbing. "The street kids?"

"Yep. Remember that boy I told you about? He stopped by the other night but took off as soon as I mentioned that you wanted to talk to him. He's a skittish one, he is."

"Has he caused trouble?"

"No, not that. But it's sad to know they're roaming the streets and nobody cares anything about them."

"I've taken them some food," Livy said.

"Do you know where they're staying?"

"No. But I know where to leave the food, and they pick it up."

"To tell you the truth, I always cook an extra pone of corn bread or biscuits. The boy brings a few pennies, and we both pretend it's enough."

"I know they appreciate your help." Good Samaritans like Emma were few and far between.

"There's some leftover ham and corn bread. You can take it to them if you've a mind to."

"Thank you. I'll do that." She called to Mary, who'd been busy sweeping up, "Mary, are you ready to head home?"

"Yes, ma'am. I'm finished."

The door opened and Emma called out, "We're closed."

"I'm not looking for a meal, Emma." Jake pushed back the curtain. "I'm looking for Livy and Mary."

Livy blushed.

Emma looked from one to the other. "I didn't know you knew Jake." Then she laughed. "Well, I guess everybody knows Jake, since he's a deputy and all."

Jake's gaze met Livy's. "I told Mrs. Brooks I'd walk you two home. I'm making rounds anyway, so it's no trouble."

"We're almost done here." A wave of pleasure wafted over Livy. He cared enough to see that they made it home safely.

Emma waved her away. "You girls go on now. All I've got to do is lock up. I'll see you in the morning, Livy."

"Yes, ma'am." Livy picked up the parcel of food Emma had wrapped for her. She'd better wait until later to deliver it. She didn't want to expose Mary to the burned-out shantytown, and she didn't want Jake to worry either.

"Ladies." Jake held out both arms. Livy slipped her hand through the crook of his arm, while Mary giggled.

"How's Gus? We heard he's been sick." Livy lifted her skirt and stepped around a patch of snow turning to icy slush.

"Better. His fever broke this afternoon, and we're having trouble keeping him in bed."

"Mrs. Brooks will be so glad to hear that. We've been praying for him."

They walked two blocks down, cut across behind McIver's, crossed Main Street, and turned left toward home. Jake kept up a brisk pace along the boardwalk until they reached the orphanage.

Once out of the cold, Livy took off her gloves and coat. She picked up the tin coffeepot. "Would you like a cup?"

Jake leaned against the doorjamb, staring. The dim lamplight cast shadows over his sculpted features. Livy bit her lip. What would it be like if he were her husband and this their kitchen? If the children asleep in the parlor were theirs?

"I wish I could stay, but I've got a few more rounds to make before I head back to the jail."

"What time do you get off?"

"Sheriff Carter relieves me around daylight."

"You'll be up all night?"

"Yes. I'll make a couple rounds around town. Helps pass the time." He leaned in close and whispered, "Want to come over to the jail and keep me company?"

"Jake!" Livy glanced at Mary, but the girl sat cross-legged in front of Ginger, engrossed in the three kittens in her lap.

"I was just kidding." He winked at her. "Night, Livy. See you tomorrow."

Livy wrapped her arms around her waist and watched him walk away until the darkness swallowed him up.

What *would* it be like to keep Jake company all the time? Her heart tumbled through her rib cage at the very thought.

✳   ✳   ✳

Luke spotted the same guy he'd seen with Billy Johansen sneaking around the blacksmith's house. If he could get a good look at the man's face, he could prove his and the rest of the street kids' innocence.

But who could he tell?

The sheriff and the deputy wouldn't believe him. And neither would the man who had Mark locked up in his factory. Maybe he could bargain with the man. If he knew who the thief was, then he could convince the man to trade Mark for the information.

It was a risk. The man might just kill him, but what other choice did he have? He needed to save his brother.

Luke watched the man slip into the blacksmith's house. He ignored the cold and settled in to wait.

The thief would come out, and Luke would be watching and waiting.

∗   ∗   ∗

Chestnut lay still and quiet, blanketed in snow. Livy pulled her cloak closer, paused at the edge of a building, and let her eyes become accustomed to the darkness. She listened but didn't hear anything other than the bark of a dog in the distance and the usual sounds from the saloons several blocks away.

Hopefully, she wouldn't run into Jake tonight, not after he'd taken the time to escort her and Mary home. He wouldn't like the idea of her venturing out, so she'd kept quiet about her errand. It wouldn't take long to dart across town and back. She'd be snug in her bed in less than an hour, and he'd be none the wiser.

The thought of his teasing warmed her even in the chill night. He would come around to her way of thinking regarding the boys. She believed he cared, and with time, she could convince him they weren't the outlaws he thought they were.

She crossed the street and hurried down another alley, cutting across behind the barbershop. Since the night of the break-in at the gunsmith's, she'd taken the time to explore the alleys and dead-end streets all over town. She didn't intend to get caught in a bind again if she could help it.

A few minutes later, she reached the spot where she left food.

A sliver of moon cast light over the snow-covered ground, illuminating the alley. Livy picked her steps so she didn't trip over the boxes and crates scattered about. She moved to the rear of the alley, placed the basket under the edge of the building, and shoved it back. The children would know where to find it.

She looked around, not sensing anyone near. Sighing, she turned away and headed home again. She'd hoped they would eventually trust her enough to come out and talk to her and maybe even come to the orphanage to get out of the cold, but they couldn't put their faith in her . . . yet. How long would it take, and what would she have to do before they realized she only wanted to help them?

A movement, just the flicker of a shadow, caught her eye, and she flattened herself against the nearest building. A dog looking for scraps? A cat, maybe? Either way, she waited. She'd learned to be patient after years on the streets of Chicago.

The shadow moved and became a man—or maybe a boy. He crouched and ran from one building to the next, focusing on something ahead of him. He never noticed her. Was the thief out and about again? She darted forward, staying low and to the shadows but keeping him in sight.

She ducked behind a rain barrel when he stopped, keeping her eyes on his back. Maybe she should just go to the jail and warn Jake. But if she did, this fellow would be long gone. No, she'd try to get a look at his face or at least track him to wherever he stopped. Then she'd go get Jake.

She took stock of her surroundings, didn't see or hear anything, and hurried to keep up with her quarry. All she wanted was one good look at his face. He took off again and cut down an alley. Livy followed, amazed that he didn't watch his back.

The closer she got, the more concerned she became that maybe this was one of the boys who lived on the streets after all. He didn't look as big as the thief she'd seen the other night.

Uncertainty filled her. Had she been wrong about them all this time? She'd defended those boys because she'd been convinced they would steal only for food and clothing, to keep from freezing to death. Maybe Jake had been right and she'd been duped.

All of a sudden, he flattened himself against the nearest wall. Livy crouched behind a wagon, her narrowed gaze watching. Then it dawned on her. He was following someone else. No wonder he hadn't been concerned about checking behind him. He moved forward again, this time darting away as if his prey hurried on ahead.

Livy gave chase, not wanting to lose sight of him. This must be one of the boys she'd been trying to talk to. But whom could *he* be following? Moments later, she reached the edge of a building and peered around it. Ahead, the boy hunkered down against a corral fence beside a ramshackle barn a hundred yards away. She followed his line of vision. Someone slipped into the barn. She hurried forward, determined to talk to him.

The boy was so focused on watching the barn, she could reach out and touch him before he realized she was there. "Don't move," she whispered.

The boy jumped but didn't run. "Who are you?"

"You should know who I am." Hopefully, he wouldn't bolt until she got some answers out of him.

He glanced at her. She could barely make out his features in the darkness, but he couldn't be more than ten or twelve. His eyes widened. "You're the woman from the orphanage."

"Yes."

"How'd you sneak up on me?"

"You were so busy watching whoever you're trailing that it

wasn't too much trouble. I followed you halfway across town," she whispered. "Now, who are you following and why?"

He turned and focused on the barn, not answering.

"My name's Livy O'Brien. What's yours?"

Still no answer.

"After all I've done for you and the others, you can at least tell me your name."

He threw her a look. "You took the watch."

"You stole it off Mr. Russell. It wasn't yours to keep."

For a moment, he didn't answer her; then he uttered one word. "Luke."

"Nice to meet you, Luke."

"How'd you know?"

"Know what?"

"That we tag-teamed the deputy and stole his watch." He laughed, a soft sound. "We didn't know he was a deputy at the time, or we wouldn't have done it. So how could you tell?"

"I can do that maneuver in my sleep."

He looked at her then, really looked at her. "You're joshing."

"I'm not." She grinned. "How long before you realized the watch was missing?"

He squirmed. "Long enough. For a while, I thought I'd dropped it somewhere along the way, but it was too risky to go back and look for it."

"You're right. It was too risky. And it was even riskier for you to steal the thing in the first place. What I can't figure out is why. Why steal something like that? And why steal a watch from McIver's and those guns from the gunsmith?"

"We—I never stole nothing else since we took the watch from the deputy."

"That's not what the townspeople think."

"I know." He cut his eyes at her. "Do you believe me?"

"I do. I lived on the streets of Chicago, and I know the last thing you want is for people to suspect you of stealing and come after you."

He nodded, seeming to realize that she really did know the kind of life he lived. "How'd you, uh . . . how'd you get off the streets?"

Livy put her hand on his coat sleeve. "I learned to trust someone. We all have to do that at some point."

He shrugged her hand off and focused on the barn. "I done that once, and it almost cost my brother his life."

"I'm sorry, Luke." Livy's heart broke. Not even a man but old in the ways of the world. "I know there are people who only want to use you, but there are some who can be trusted. Mrs. Brooks is a good woman, and she has a heart of gold. Remember that."

The barn door creaked open, and they ducked down, not speaking. Two men stepped outside, one clean-shaven, one bearded. The bearded man slapped the other one on the shoulder and sent him on his way before stepping back inside.

Livy made to rise.

Luke put a hand on her arm. "Wait."

Moments later, the bearded man led out two horses, one saddled, one with a pack strapped across its back. He shut the doors, mounted, and rode toward the outskirts of town, leading the pack horse.

"Do you know who they are?" Livy asked.

"No. That's why I followed him."

"Luke, these men could be dangerous. Why don't you tell the sheriff what you've seen?"

"Without a name or a face, it won't do any good."

"Then we can tell Sheriff Carter and Jake to come here and wait. They can catch them the next time."

Luke shook his head. "He never takes the loot to the same place twice."

Livy shook her head, exasperated. "You've followed him before, haven't you? What's going to happen to the others if you get yourself killed? Your friends are depending on you. You need to stop taking risks or at least tell the sheriff what you know to keep from being railroaded out of town or put in jail. I want to help, but you're not making it easy."

"I don't know . . ."

Livy tried another tactic, hoping she'd broken the ice with him. "I'd like to meet the others. I think you know by now you can trust me."

"Maybe."

A noise from behind them drew Livy's attention.

Jake, making his late-night rounds, headed straight toward them.

She whispered, "Now's a good time for us to tell Jake what happened."

"I—I can't," Luke said. Then he took off like cannon shot. Not more than thirty feet away, he sprawled on a patch of ice.

"Hey, you. Stop." Jake rushed forward as Luke scrambled to his feet.

Livy did the only thing she could to protect the terrified boy. She walked out in plain sight and found herself staring down the barrel of a Colt .45.

CHAPTER NINETEEN

"LIVY?"

Jake's hand shook, and he lowered the gun, feeling sick. He'd almost shot her. He stared at her, dressed head to toe in black, hair covered with a thick scarf. "What are you doing out here? It's two in the morning."

"I—"

"Who were you with?" He grabbed her by the arm, not giving her a chance to answer. "Come on, we're going somewhere warm where we can talk."

He pulled her down the boardwalk toward the jail. He wanted answers, and he wanted them now. And he wanted to see Livy's face when he got them.

Ten minutes later, he shut the door of the jail, turned up

the lantern, and swung around to face her. He crossed his arms and glared at her. "I left you at the orphanage hours ago. What are you doing out here at this time of night?"

"You got any coffee?" she asked, pinching the tips of her gloves and pulling them off one finger at a time as if she didn't have a care in the world.

His temper spiked a notch. She didn't even like coffee. What was she trying to hide? "There." He jabbed a finger at the coffeepot, filled with hours-old black slush.

She took her time removing her cloak and the black coat underneath it. Mud covered the patched hemline of her black dress. He waited until she'd taken a sip of the bitter brew. She winced, more reaction than he'd gotten when he asked her to explain herself.

"Livy, I'm sorry I yelled at you, but you scared the living daylights out of me. What were you doing?"

She tossed her head. "I took some food to the street kids, if you must know."

Just like that? She'd been out delivering food to some kids at two in the morning? He raked a hand through his hair, his heartbeat just now returning to something akin to normal. She wasn't like any other woman he'd ever known. His mother and Mrs. Warren and any other number of women wouldn't be caught dead wandering the streets alone after dark—especially in shantytown. "Who were you with? I saw someone take off in the opposite direction."

She didn't answer, just took another sip of coffee.

Her nonchalance kicked his temper up another notch. What was going on underneath that mass of curls? "You don't have to tell me who it was. It was one of the street kids, wasn't it? Livy,

I want you to stop sneaking around at night. These young boys are stealing guns, and they won't hesitate to shoot someone. If their aim had been better, they might have hit Sheriff Carter or myself when we were chasing them the other night."

Her eyes flashed. "It wasn't one of the boys."

Jake stared at her, her words taking a moment to sink in. "How do you know?"

She looked away, the first time he'd seen uncertainty in her eyes since he'd gotten the drop on her.

His gaze traveled the length of her dress. Suddenly the pieces clicked into place, like getting four consecutive jumps in a game of checkers. The thief, the guns, the scrap of black cloth, and the woman-size handprint in the snow. His gaze ricocheted back to her face. "You were there, weren't you? That was a piece of your dress I found."

The look on her face answered his question. He felt sick to his stomach. Had Livy been in league with the thieves the entire time?

No. He wouldn't—couldn't believe such a thing.

Not the woman he dreamed of a future with. Not the woman who claimed to be a Christian, who lived and worked at the orphanage, who had defended the children's rights in a room full of storekeepers.

"Do you have anything to say?" *Please, Livy, say something. Prove me wrong.*

Her chin hitched up a notch, her silence deafening.

His hope and his temper snapped. Why hadn't he seen it earlier? "You wormed your way into Mrs. Brooks's good graces in Chicago, then moved here to Chestnut, bringing your little gang of street urchins with you."

Her eyes widened and two splotches of color graced her cheeks. Jake grunted. Good. At least he'd finally gotten a reaction out of her. "Maybe Mrs. Brooks is in on the scheme as well." He crossed his arms over his chest. How far could he push her before she lost it and started talking to him? "I should have thought of that sooner. An orphanage would be a good cover for a couple of women intent on fleecing a town, now wouldn't it?"

She slammed the coffee cup on the desk and marched up to him, eyes flashing blue fire. "You leave Mrs. Brooks out of this. She's a godly woman and would never steal a thing from anybody."

Finally.

Jake stared her down, his nose inches from hers. "And you, Livy O'Brien? Would you ever steal anything from anybody?"

A stubborn expression settled on her face, and Jake knew he'd won this round.

Or had he?

*   *   *

Livy's heart ached with wanting to tell Jake everything. But she pressed her lips together, determined not to say another word, afraid he would just twist anything she said to suit his purposes. She hadn't wanted to mislead him or anybody else, but she could only say so much without revealing her whole sordid past.

He stared at her, disappointment overlaid with anger in his green eyes. As if he cared. But he wouldn't care, not if he found out the truth. There'd been no one to care what she did until Mrs. Brooks came along, and she'd known about

Livy's previous life when she befriended her. Livy hadn't wanted her past to follow her to Chestnut, but now it had caught up with her full force, and there wasn't a thing she could do about it.

"I could arrest you." He spoke low and dangerous.

Her heart plummeted to her toes. "On what grounds?" she asked, mustering a bravado she didn't feel.

"Aiding and abetting."

She sighed inwardly. "You don't have any proof."

"I have reasonable suspicion."

She'd bluffed her way out of tighter situations than this, but that was before she'd become a Christian. She couldn't outright lie to Jake, but she didn't want to get Luke in trouble either. If he'd spoken the truth, he hadn't done anything wrong.

"I haven't aided or abetted anyone, but I'll tell you what I know, okay? Your thief is six feet tall, weighs about two hundred pounds, and has the gangly gait of a dim-witted pup. His accomplice—or at least one of them—is middle-aged, bearded, and scraggly."

Jake crossed his arms and stared at her. "What else?" he asked, sounding as if he didn't believe a word she'd said.

"They have at least one meeting place on the west side of town, an old barn with a broken-down corral. Close to where we were earlier."

"I'll keep a watch on it."

"Won't do any good. Luke says they rarely use the same meeting place."

"Luke? Is that the street kid you were talking to?" Jake lifted an eyebrow. "How does he know?"

She hesitated, hoping and praying she didn't say anything that might implicate Luke. "He . . . he's been following the thief, trying to find out who it is, because he knows it's the only way to convince everyone that he's not the real thief."

"And you've been keeping this from me?"

"No. I just found out tonight."

"If he really wants to convince me he's not a thief, he needs to turn himself in and tell me what he knows."

Livy wrapped her arms around her waist, feeling chilled at the harsh tone of Jake's words. "You don't have a clue, do you? In Chicago, the law would chew him up and spit him out before they'd believe him. Then they'd sell his half-dead carcass to a sweatshop for a few dollars. There's no way he's going to turn himself in that easily. He's got half a dozen, if not more, mouths to feed, and he'll die trying to protect them from the law."

"You were one of them, weren't you? A street kid in Chicago?" Jake stared at her.

All her defenses were broken. She couldn't lie in the face of an outright question about her past. She lowered her gaze and took a deep breath.

"Yes."

* * *

Jake tilted his chair against the wall and took out his whittling knife. Whittling settled his mind and helped him think through problems. He'd escorted Livy to the orphanage and left her there. No one had reported a crime, and as far as he could tell, she didn't have any stolen goods on her, so there'd been no reason to arrest her.

And the last thing he wanted to do was put Livy behind bars.

He wanted to take back his harsh words and tell her he was sorry. He wanted to believe that she was good and perfect and only concerned about the welfare of the boys on the streets.

But the facts were stacked against her. He attacked the block of wood with a vengeance. She'd been on the streets of Chicago. He'd assumed she'd lived with Mrs. Brooks all her life and had decided to help the older lady instead of marrying. Fresh hurt stabbed at his chest. Why hadn't she told him?

Because she knew how you felt about street kids.

Jake scraped his blade across the soft wood. A curled sliver fell to the floor at his feet. He scowled. He didn't have anything against the boys themselves, but somebody was stealing from the merchants. It was his job to be suspicious, especially of folks wandering around in the middle of the night.

He didn't know what to do. Tell Sheriff Carter? Tell him what? That Livy had been delivering food to the street kids?

A thought niggled at the back of his mind. Maybe he should telegraph Chicago and ask for information on Mrs. Brooks and Livy. Sheriff Carter knew some detectives in Chicago. He'd see what the older man thought when he showed up first thing in the morning.

Jake stared at the flickering lantern on Sheriff Carter's desk, his knife hovering over the block of wood, the long night catching up with him. He rested his head against the wall and closed his eyes.

What if they took off in the night, leaving all those kids at the orphanage? He shook his head, disgusted at the crazy thoughts ricocheting around in his brain. Mrs. Brooks and

Livy wouldn't abandon the orphans. No matter what they might be, they loved those kids. That much he knew.

Nobody could put on that good of an act, could they? They couldn't be guilty of wrongdoing. He'd just keep a closer eye on the orphanage, and if Livy snuck out again, he'd be watching. After all, if she was as innocent as she'd claimed, she'd need his help if she ran into trouble, wouldn't she?

A clamor woke Jake, and he slammed both legs of his chair to the floor and shot to his feet. Gus lugged two buckets of coal in the door, banging the pails against the wooden facing.

Jake grabbed one of the buckets. "Gus, Doc told you to take it easy for a few days."

"I'm all right, Mr. Jake." Gus smothered a cough and lumbered out again. Minutes later, he came back with another bucket of coal, making just as much noise as before.

Jake slid a hand down his whiskered jaw and squinted out the window into the still-dark street. The whistle for the morning shift change hadn't even blown. But the night was over as far as he was concerned. Jake stretched and fired up the stove to make a fresh pot of coffee.

An hour later, Gus was mopping the cells, still muttering and singing. Jake kept an eye on him. As soon as his fever had broken, Gus had insisted on heading back to his cabin. Lately, he'd taken it on himself to clean the jail, and he didn't want any help from Jake or Sheriff Carter. Gus kept the place as spick-and-span as his cabin in exchange for three squares a day.

When Gus finished, Jake gestured to the coffeepot. "Have a cup, Gus. Miss Nellie'll send Harvey along shortly with some breakfast."

Gus poured a cup of coffee and retreated to a chair in the

corner. He'd move a chair rather than sit in the open. And if there wasn't one available, he'd stand with his back to the wall to keep someone from catching him unawares.

Jake propped his feet up on his desk and sipped his coffee. "You get out and about a lot at night, don't you?"

Gus cut a glance at him, then concentrated on his cup.

"You ever see much comings and goings behind the orphanage or over in shantytown?"

Gus squirmed. Wouldn't be long before he'd thank Jake politely for the coffee and shuffle out into the cold. It didn't take much for him to get nervous and skedaddle like a scared jackrabbit. But Jake had to take the risk in case Gus knew anything. He dropped his feet to the floor and leaned forward. "I need your help."

A frown of concentration marred Gus's forehead.

"There've been some robberies here in town, and we've got a bunch of street kids here from Chicago. If you see or hear anything that might help me find those kids and stop the robberies, you'll tell me, won't you?"

Gus fidgeted, then gave a short nod. In some ways, Gus was smart as a whip, and Jake figured he knew more than he was letting on, but he didn't know how to get him to talk without scaring the daylights out of him. Jake took another sip. He'd leave well enough alone for now. He'd planted the seeds that something wasn't right, so maybe Gus would come to him if he saw anything.

The door opened and Sam McIver's brother, Ed, limped inside, his injuries from the war ten years ago still plaguing him. Ed's face, always flushed from the whiskey he drank to dull the pain, looked worse than usual. For brothers, Sam and Ed were as different as night and day. Sam spent his days laughing and talking with folks in the mercantile while Ed hammered out his pain in his blacksmith shop.

"Morning, Ed. Something the matter?"

"Someone broke in my house last night and stole my wife's emerald brooch and her pearl necklace. Her mother gave her that necklace."

Remorse slammed into Jake. Could Luke be to blame? Or maybe Livy? Jake shook his head. It couldn't be. "What can you tell me about the robbery? What time did it happen?"

"The wife noticed her jewelry missing this morning. They came right into the house and stole us blind." The veins in McIver's neck popped out until Jake thought the man might have an apoplexy. "It's them thieving street urchins. I want to know why you haven't arrested them."

Jake held out his palm in a calming gesture. "Now hold on, Ed. We're looking into every robbery. But it's a little hard to put the culprits behind bars if we can't catch them."

Ed glared at him, his meaty hands balled into fists. "Jake, we all know they're living in that burned-out shantytown behind the livery stable. Come spring when the river thaws, we oughta burn the lot of 'em out."

"Ed, they're kids. And we're not sure if it's them doing the stealing or not."

"Well, I've had enough of it. I can't watch the blacksmith shop and my house at the same time, but I'll tell you what I can and will do." McIver jammed his hat on his head and stabbed a finger in Jake's face. "The next person that so much as pokes his head out of the shadows around my house or my shop is going to get his head blowed off."

McIver slammed out of the jail and stomped down the street.

Jake stared after him, wanting to hit something or someone. Had Livy pulled the wool over his eyes? Maybe skipped town in the middle of the night? If she'd made up the story about Luke trailing the thief to the old barn on the outskirts of town, then she'd know that the jig would be up come morning. He rubbed a hand over his face. She'd be long gone by now, so there was no need to rush over to the orphanage to question her again.

The sick feeling in the pit of his stomach reminded him of how much he wanted her to still be in Chestnut, how much he longed for her to be telling the truth.

CHAPTER TWENTY

"Luke, where are we going?"

"You'll see." He looked away from Jessica's accusing gaze. He'd made the decision to take her to the orphanage late last night. Butch and Grady had been combing shantytown for them, and he couldn't risk them nabbing the little girl. Miss Livy would take care of her.

He halted a couple of blocks away from the jail and looked both ways. As he stepped out into the street, the blacksmith came stomping down the boardwalk from the direction of the jail, muttering to himself. Luke jerked back and pushed Jessica into the alley behind him.

"Shhh."

After the blacksmith passed by, Luke grabbed Jessica's

hand. They'd take the long way around to get to the orphanage. Better that than get caught close to the jail.

"Ouch." Jessica tugged against his grip.

"Sorry." He loosened his hold on the little girl's hand and pulled the blanket tighter around her shoulders. "Come on."

Movement in front of the mercantile caught his eye, and he stopped.

Will McIver swept the boardwalk in front of his father's store. Luke stared at the tall, lanky young man. Will reminded him of the thief, but he couldn't be sure. What if it wasn't Will? What if it was somebody else, and he got Will in trouble for no reason?

He slipped away, towing Jessica behind him. Who should he tell? Miss Livy wanted to help, but what could she do? She'd just tell the deputy. What good would it do for the sheriff and his deputy to know? They'd simply arrest him, and Luke's brother would still be locked up in that factory along with a bunch of other kids nobody cared about.

Luke frowned. He had information that might free his brother.

And he intended to use it as soon as he got Jessica to safety.

✳   ✳   ✳

At least Jake had given her the benefit of the doubt last night. And Livy knew how much trusting her cost him. The first light of dawn split the sky as she slid a pan of biscuits out of the oven. Then she turned the ham, sniffing at the enticing aroma wafting from the pan. She'd bought the ham with her earnings from Emma's. *Thank You, Lord, for extra income to feed the children.* Ginger rubbed against her skirt, purring in contentment. The kittens lay snuggled together in a tangled wad, sound asleep.

A soft knock sounded on the kitchen door. Livy frowned and glanced at Ginger. "Wonder who that could be so early?"

She wiped her hands and hurried to the door. Luke stood there, a little redheaded child wrapped in a tattered blanket clutching his hand.

Livy blinked. "Luke. What a nice surprise." She stepped back. "Won't you come in?"

Luke nodded at the girl and tugged her inside. Both looked like they might bolt at any minute, and Livy figured the girl would have if Luke hadn't held fast to her hand.

Pushing the child forward, Luke cleared his throat. "This is Jessica. Jessica, Miss Livy here will take good care of you."

Big eyes stared at Livy from a gaunt face. Livy knelt in front of her. "What is it, sweetheart?"

"I want Bobby," she whispered.

Livy glanced at Luke. "Who's Bobby?"

"Her brother." Luke touched Jessica's shoulder. "Jessica, Bobby's got to work. He'll come see you as soon as he can. All right?"

Livy smiled at the girl. "Are you hungry?"

She didn't respond, so Livy cut her eyes at Luke. "I bet Luke's hungry. How about I fix you both a ham biscuit?"

Jessica sniffed and looked at Luke. He nodded and urged her to sit at the table. Livy sliced open two biscuits and placed a piece of ham inside. After pouring two glasses of milk, she set the offering on the table. Jessica started eating immediately. Luke ate his slowly, seeming to savor every bite.

When he finished, Luke stood. "Jessica, I've got to go. Be good for Miss Livy, you hear?"

Jessica's lip trembled.

Livy followed him to the door and touched his sleeve. "Luke, why don't you come to the orphanage? Please. Bring the others."

Luke shook his head. "We can't."

She glanced at Jessica and lowered her voice. "Are they wanted back in Chicago?"

He threw her a surprised look.

"Luke, I lived on the streets of Chicago as far back as I can remember. I know what it's like."

"Some of them."

"Where is Bobby working?"

Luke pressed his lips together.

Livy grabbed him by the arm. "He's working in a sweatshop, right? Here in Chestnut? Where is it? Tell me." She glanced over her shoulder at Jessica, but Ginger and her kittens had entranced the little girl.

"I can't tell you. He'll kill me."

"Luke, if you don't tell me, he's going to kill you. I know what those places are like."

Luke met her gaze head-on, his eyes older and wiser than his years. "He brings the kids here to work for him for six months, or longer, depending on how much they cost him."

"And what makes you think he'll just let them walk out of there in six months or a year?" Livy whispered.

Luke hung his head. "I don't know, but there's nothing else I can do." His gaze strayed to Jessica. "Except bring kids like Jessica to you before he gets his hands on them."

"Tell me where the sweatshop is."

A mulish expression thinned his lips. "No. I've got to go."

Livy sighed. "All right. Just a minute." She sliced open the rest of the biscuits, filled each with a slice of ham, and wrapped the food in used newspapers. She'd cook a pot of corn bread mush and open a can of syrup for breakfast this morning.

She held out the food. "Do you know the man's name? The one who runs the place?"

"No. They just call him the boss."

"Please, Luke, please stay."

His eyes filled with tears as he glanced around the warm, homey kitchen. "I can't."

He slipped out the kitchen door while Jessica kept herself occupied with the kittens. Livy pressed a hand to her mouth to keep from sobbing.

✳　✳　✳

The mercantile buzzed with tension when Jake walked in. Several shopkeepers stood around in addition to the regulars, their attention focused on Ed McIver, who was wound tighter than a Swiss clock.

"I'm telling you, if we don't do something soon, those kids are going to take over our town."

"What are we supposed to do, Ed?" Jesse Tatum said. "Them young'uns are slippery. I've only seen a couple of them on the streets late at night, and they scatter like rats before anybody can get a good look at 'em. I wonder how many there are. Jake, you have any clue?"

"Don't know. Like you said, they make themselves pretty scarce." Jake leaned against the counter and shrugged.

"I heard they're living over in the burned-out shantytown." Sam spoke up, busy restocking a shelf with canned beans.

"That's a fire hazard waiting to happen. Gibbons bought all the land along the creek when he built the glove factory. Said he was going to clean it up and try to get more business in here."

Jesse aimed for the spittoon and wiped his mouth with the back of his hand. "It'll take some work to clean all that up. Half the buildings were gutted by that fire last winter. But Gibbons has the right idea. We could use some more businesses."

"Jake, have you been over there to see if you could find 'em?" Ed asked, his jaw jutting forward. The thief taking off with his wife's jewelry clearly had Ed's blood boiling.

"I go through shantytown almost every day," Jake said. "If you've been over there, you should know it's like looking for a needle in a haystack. With all the squatters and ramshackle buildings popping up, it's hard to keep track of who's where at any given time."

"We ought to burn the whole place down."

Jake shook his head. "It belongs to Gibbons now, Ed. You can't just go in there and burn down a man's property, no matter how dangerous it is."

Ed slammed a meaty fist into his palm. "First it was a little food and some blankets from Sam, then guns; now they're breaking into our homes. They've already shot at Sheriff Carter and Jake. What're we going to do when someone gets killed?"

Jake straightened. Ed seemed determined to stir up the townspeople to the point where someone did something reckless. He'd always been one to go off half-cocked, but his anger had worsened over the years. "That's going a little too far, Ed. Nobody's going to get killed."

Ed jerked to his feet, the sudden movement knocking his seat over. The chair popped the wooden floor like a gunshot. "Seems to me you aren't all that interested in putting these fellers behind bars. You're much too busy courting that little gal over at the orphanage, ain't ya?" He sneered at Jake. "Maybe we need a new deputy around here."

Jake's jaw tightened. He wasn't courting Livy, but if he were, it wouldn't be anybody's business but his.

"Ed." Sam's warning tone sliced through the thick air. Sam's mild manner kept Ed from digging himself in too deep sometimes. "No need to get hot under the collar."

Jake fingered the broken strand of pearls he'd found in the abandoned barn. The same barn Luke and Livy had tracked the thieves to. He'd looked around, put two and two together, and come up with the notion that Livy had to be telling the truth.

At least he hoped so.

"Ed, I received some information last night pointing to someone other than the street kids. I can't be sure, of course, but I believe my source is telling me the truth."

"So who is it?"

"I don't know." Jake pulled the necklace from his pocket and held it out to Ed. "But my source told me where to find this."

Ed stared for a moment, then held out his hand. Jake dropped the pearls into his palm, the milky-white orbs clinking against each other. Ed closed his fist over the necklace, turned on his heel, and stomped out of the mercantile.

Sam threw Jake an apologetic look. "Sorry. Ed's a little riled up this morning."

"I don't blame him. I reckon I would be too if someone broke into my house."

Jesse spoke up. "Ed lets his temper get the best of him, but he's a good man at heart and a hard worker."

Heads nodded all around. They sat for a moment in silence, thinking about Ed's sacrifice in the war. Half the men seated around the stove had fought in the war, so they knew the horrors he'd seen. Ed's shattered knee had almost cost him his life, and he'd live with the pain until he died. They could forgive him a little rage now and then.

"Reckon somebody else is doing the stealing?" Jesse speculated. "Remember Gibbons mentioned that at the meeting, but nobody wanted to hear it."

Jake pulled out his knife and listened to the men talk. Livy had tried to tell him several times before last night that she didn't think the street kids were to blame for the thefts. She'd also told him about the barn, and he'd found the pearls wedged between a trough and a horse's stall. Surely she wouldn't have told him all that if she thought the street kids were responsible.

"Nah. We didn't have a problem with thieves until those kids from Chicago showed up. It's gotta be them."

Sam came out from behind the counter, righted Ed's empty chair, and straddled it. "Well, I don't know. Chestnut's growing like a bad weed. Don't get me wrong—more people means more business for me, but we're seeing more and more gamblers and drunks showing up." A pained expression crossed his face. "They're having a bad influence on our kids."

Nobody said a word. Everyone knew about Will's troubles.

"Sam's right. Those kids might be the least of our problems. Chicago's bursting at the seams, and we're getting the dregs of society. Why, ten years ago we had one saloon, and if you stopped in, you knew almost everybody there. Now we're got three or four, maybe more."

Everybody nodded, murmuring agreement.

"Remember that little gal from the orphanage who came to the meeting? She mentioned those sweatshops in Chicago where they work some of those kids twelve and fifteen hours a day. Anybody who'd do that to a kid needs a good horse-whipping. I don't blame 'em for heading to Chestnut."

"But that don't give them the right to steal," Jesse replied.

"I'm agin stealing as much as the next man, but what if your girls were starving or freezing to death, Jesse? Would you steal to keep them alive? It's something to think about."

Sam leaned his forearms on his knees. "Maybe we're not doing enough to help 'em. I mean, how can we say we're Christians if we don't feed and clothe the hungry? Maybe give them a leg up so they can better themselves."

"There are some people who are never going to better themselves. If you give 'em a piece of bread, they'll stick their feet under your table three times a day and never offer to do a lick of work in return."

"Yeah, but you can't refuse to help everybody because of the few who'll take advantage of you."

While the men pondered this, Jake thought about Livy and Mrs. Brooks. They'd taken in every orphan who'd darkened their door, and he figured they'd take in every one that came their way until children spilled out of the orphanage like an overflowing ore cart. Livy roamed the streets at night trying to find more kids to save. They were doing their part to help those who couldn't help themselves. Jake hung his head, suddenly ashamed. What had he done lately to help someone in need?

He'd been so focused on saving his town, he'd lost sight of the fact that saving the people came first.

✳︎ ✳︎ ✳︎

Livy hurried down the boardwalk, avoiding the muddy splotches left by melting snow. The warmer weather brought out farmers by the dozens, and wagons and buggies filled the streets with people making last-minute preparations for Christmas. She hastened past the laundry and waved at Mr. Wong. He bobbed his head and smiled back. They'd exchanged no more than a dozen words in the couple of months since she'd met him, mainly because he didn't know enough English to carry on a conversation, and she couldn't afford to have any clothes laundered.

She spotted the sisters Huff in their hat shop, chatting with a couple of customers. Livy passed on by. She'd stop in later and check on Miss Janie, but right now she needed to find Jake. Mud covered the side street running between the hat shop and the butcher's, but a couple of boards made passage easier. Livy lifted her heavy cloak and skirt and headed across the shaky walkway, making it to the other side without mishap.

From this distance, she could see the jail. She took a deep breath. Would Jake be there, or Sheriff Carter? She hadn't spoken much with the sheriff. Maybe she should talk to him. That would be better than talking to Jake, wouldn't it? Her steps faltered and her hands turned clammy as she eyed the jail. Maybe she should just go back to the orphanage. She clenched her jaw. She couldn't. No matter what Jake thought of her, Luke and the other boys' lives depended on her.

She found the jail empty. The cells mocked her. Livy pivoted, her heart pounding. She didn't have to be afraid. She'd been forgiven of everything she'd done wrong. Her sins had been cast into the depths of the sea, just as God promised. If He had forgiven her, then why couldn't she forgive herself?

She bowed her head. *Lord, forgive me for doubting You. I know I'm forgiven, and I don't intend to slip back into my old ways ever again. Thank You for sending Mrs. Brooks my way.*

The door opened, and she whirled around. Jake stepped inside and removed his hat. A surprised glint lit his eyes when he saw her. Then his face hardened, and he turned away, taking his time placing his hat on a peg and shrugging out of his coat. "Morning, Livy."

She shivered at his cold, impassive tone. Whatever feelings he'd felt for her had died when he'd found out she'd roamed the streets of Chicago. Ice coated her heart, and she shrugged. She had nothing to lose now, so what did it matter what he thought about her? "Luke came to see me this morning."

He faced her, his eyes narrowed. "He did? Is he ready to turn himself in?"

Livy glared at him. "Why should he turn himself in? He's done nothing wrong. For your information, he brought another orphan to us. Then he told me . . ."

Jake took a step toward her. "What? What did he tell you?"

She plunged in. "You know what a sweatshop is, don't you?"

"I've heard the term."

"Well, according to Luke, there's a sweatshop here."

"In Chestnut?"

"Yes."

Jake's brow creased, and he sat on the edge of Sheriff Carter's desk. His green eyes probed hers. "Why are you telling me this now? Last night you said you didn't know anything about the robberies."

"I still don't know anything about the robberies, except that I don't believe it's Luke who's doing it." She met his gaze head-on, wishing she could've talked to Sheriff Carter instead. Suspicion about her motives seemed to cloud Jake's opinion of everything she said. Sheriff Carter would've listened without second-guessing. She tilted her chin up. "I'm here because if we don't find out who bought these kids, they'll probably end up dead."

Jake held up a hand. "Whoa. What do you mean by 'bought' them?"

"From what Luke said, the owner of the sweatshop—"

"Who?"

She shook her head. "He didn't know the man's name. Called him the boss. From what Luke said, the owner gets them out of Chicago if they'll work for him for six months to a year. There's only one reason I can think of that would make the kids agree to that."

Jake's eyes narrowed. "If they'd been arrested?"

"I think so. What if the Chicago police are involved? I wouldn't be a bit surprised. I've seen my fair share of corrupt officers."

Jake stood and paced the length of the jail. "Let me get this straight. A kid is arrested in Chicago. The police contact the sweatshop owners and make a deal. The city gets rid of the boy, and the sweatshop gets free labor for six months to a year. The kid isn't charged with a crime, he gets out of Chicago, and everybody's happy."

"Pretty much." Livy crossed her arms. "Except for one thing."

"What's that?"

"The sweatshop owner has no intention of letting the kids go after six months. Do you think anybody who's buying children will let them walk away when the specified term is up? Hardly. He can't afford to."

Jake took a deep breath. "Where are all these kids coming from?"

Livy shook her head. "Who knows? Some lose their parents to sickness, and some are abandoned. Other families lost their farms and got split up by the war."

*   *   *

Jake raked a hand through his hair. Having a bunch of older boys preying on the citizens of Chestnut was one thing, but knowing that someone might be shipping in children to work in a sweatshop was a different matter altogether. Where to begin looking? The logical place would be shantytown. "All right. Looks like I've got my work cut out for me. You'll let me know if you hear anything else, won't you?"

Livy crossed her arms. "You're not getting rid of me that easily. You need my help, and you know it."

"Uh-uh." Jake mirrored her stance. "You're going right back to the orphanage, where you belong."

She glared at him, blue eyes spitting fire. "Make me."

He glared right back, wanting to shake her and take her

in his arms and kiss her all at the same time. He did none of the above. "I could lock you up."

She laughed. "We've been over that before. You don't have any grounds. If you won't accept my help, then leave me alone. I'll look around, and if I find out anything important, I'll let you know." She turned toward the door.

Jake took three strides and grabbed her arm. "Hold on a minute. You're not going to find out anything."

She shrugged him off. "Jake, you have a choice. You can take me with you when you start looking for the sweat-shop—there may be more than one—or . . ." Her gaze slid to the cells at the back of the jail. "Or you can lock me up. I won't see these kids dead."

Jake watched her face; she meant every word. She'd just get in the way if he let her tag along. But on the other hand, he'd be able to keep her out of trouble. He let loose a grim smile. "All right; you win. I'll stop by the orphanage about ten tonight."

"I'll be ready."

He leaned against the doorjamb and watched her pick her way down the boardwalk, daintily holding her cloak above the icy slush. His gaze narrowed. After one night of trying to keep up with him in this weather, she'd have enough of this foolishness and be ready to leave everything up to him.

CHAPTER TWENTY-ONE

"Douse the light. Somebody's coming."

The mine plunged into darkness, and Luke and the other boys waited. Just his luck that the new hiding place he'd been scouting for himself and the other street kids was so quickly discovered. He wouldn't be coming back here anytime soon. A dim light flickered along the walls, leading the way for whoever had entered the abandoned mine.

"Be still, you little beggar."

Luke's mouth went dry as he recognized Grady's voice. Shadows, long against the moisture-slick walls, drew closer as Grady appeared. He held a lantern in one hand and a child in the other.

"Let me go." The boy jerked against Grady's hold.

Grady didn't reply, just kept moving deeper into the mine,

the child struggling against his grip. Grady cursed as the boy kicked out, making contact with his leg.

Luke strained to hear more. Was it Mark? He couldn't decide if they should rush Grady and grab the boy or wait and see what Grady intended to do. Before he could make up his mind, Grady slipped on a piece of loose shale, and the boy jerked out of his grasp and scrambled away.

"Hey, get back here." Grady lunged for the boy.

The boy stepped back, his eyes widening as he teetered on the edge of a drop-off. Luke bit back a gasp as the boy tumbled down the steep incline, his scream mixed with the sounds of falling rock and dirt. When the rocks stopped falling, there was dead silence.

"Hey, kid?" Grady held the lantern high. "Answer me, boy."

There was no reply. Grady cursed under his breath as he stumbled along the ledge. After several minutes, he stopped, peering into the darkness below.

"Good riddance. Saves me the trouble of knocking you off like the boss wanted." Grady turned and walked out of the mine, the flickering light fading to complete darkness as he disappeared.

Luke crouched in silence, horrified at what he'd just witnessed. Was the boy dead? If he hadn't fallen, would Grady have killed him right before their eyes? Grady hadn't even bothered to see if he was still alive.

Suddenly one thing became clear. He couldn't bargain with these people for Mark's freedom.

*   *   *

Darkness cloaked the orphanage.

Jake rapped his knuckles on the kitchen door, just loud

enough for Livy to hear. He waited about two seconds before turning away. After all her brave talk, she'd probably decided she'd rather sleep than wander around shantytown in the cold. He eased off the porch, being careful not to cause the boards to creak. He didn't want to wake Mrs. Brooks and have to explain why he was here. A dark shadow, covered head to foot in a black cloak, slipped away from an oak tree a few feet away. He stopped and stared.

Livy? She moved silently, coming right up to him. Blue eyes, sparkling in the moonlight, peered out from underneath the hood covering her hair. "You ready?" she breathed, so low he barely heard her.

He nodded and headed toward the center of town, setting a bruising pace. If she wanted to play detective, she'd need to keep up. He crossed the street and cut down the alley between the blacksmith shop and the livery stable. Livy fell behind. Jake slowed his pace and let her catch up with him. "Too fast for you?"

She jutted out her chin. "I'll manage."

He zigzagged across town, avoiding houses whose dogs tended to bark if a shadow came within a hundred yards of their space. They were both winded by the time he paused at the edge of shantytown and canvassed the area. The grist mill lay to their right, shrouded in the grove of cottonwoods nestled against the frozen creek. Shantytown ran the length of the creek between the mill and the coal mines north of town.

Early Chestnut settlers had raised families and started businesses along the creek, but when the railroad came through, people moved closer to the train station, abandoning the buildings. Squatters, indigent coal miners, and now a gang of street kids had taken up residence. If they could cobble together a place to live for free, they would.

Jake panned the area, not seeing anything out of place. He padded across an alley to a jumble of dilapidated buildings, intending to skirt them. Livy followed. Moments later, she tugged at his coat sleeve. Then she leaned close and whispered in his ear. "Follow me."

Curious, he let her lead the way. She ducked low and entered a ramshackle building that looked in danger of falling down on their heads. He started to call out for her to wait, but she'd already darted through the opening. Jake squeezed through. No wonder the street kids were so elusive. They were able to get into much smaller spaces than he could. The shack, leaning against another building, acted almost like a hallway. The rear wall had collapsed, and Livy eased through that as well, glancing over her shoulder to make sure he still followed.

She wove her way in and out of close places. "This is the type of place the street kids would stay in. Buildings most people wouldn't think twice about looking into."

"It's a fire hazard waiting to happen."

Coming out into the open again, they passed half a dozen tar-paper shacks thrown up in the last week. But a building with a lock and boarded-up windows caught Jake's attention. Apparently Livy noticed it as well. She pulled out a couple of long wires.

Jake reached out to stop her. "What do you think you're doing?"

Her gaze met his. "Don't you want to see what's inside?"

Jake eyed the wires in her hand, doubting she could get inside even if she wanted to. "We can't just break in."

"Even if something illegal's going on in there?" She turned to the lock.

"Livy—"

To his surprise, the lock popped open a few seconds later, and Livy slipped inside the building. He gritted his teeth and followed her, intent on dragging her outside and raking her over the coals.

He took one look inside the empty building, grabbed Livy by the arm, and pulled her outside. He snapped the lock into place and stuck his nose within inches of hers. "I oughta haul you in for breaking and entering."

"But what if it had been a sweatshop? You have to admit it looked suspicious. Windows boarded up, locked up tight as a drum."

"Doesn't matter. You can't go around breaking into buildings just because they look suspicious."

She huffed away, and he followed, shaking his head.

They checked out several more buildings, small shops making candles and such, but none of them looked like they were trying to hide their enterprises. Everything seemed on the up-and-up.

"Come on, let's call it a night," Jake said. "We're not likely to find anything else."

Livy turned down the nearest alley.

"Where you going?"

She glanced at him. "Back to the orphanage."

"That way?"

"It's the shortest route I know of."

"But not the safest. We'll go the long way if you don't

mind." Jake snagged her wrist and pulled her along with him. "How do you know your way around shantytown?"

"When I moved here, I spent a couple of hours every day exploring Chestnut. There's not much of the town I don't know. Except that it's growing so fast. There's a whole new section of shacks close to the coal mines that I haven't explored yet."

Jake scowled. He knew the place. She was determined to get herself killed. "Livy, you know better than to wander around a place like that. It's dangerous."

"No more dangerous than wandering around with you." She smiled, a cheeky grin that showed she wasn't afraid of anything. "Besides, I can take care of myself."

Jake shook his head. How had she survived all those years in Chicago? Who knew when a drunk would stagger out of an alley intent on knifing someone for a few dollars? His heart lurched.

He stopped and turned her to face him. "Livy, maybe you can, but promise me you won't keep wandering around town after dark." He rubbed his hands up and down her arms and pulled her close so there would be no mistaking his intent. "I don't want to find you in an alley or floating in the creek some morning. Promise me?"

Clear blue eyes stared at him, letting him look into her soul. Fear clutched his stomach. He might not understand her, and he wasn't sure he could trust her, but he couldn't lose her, not when he'd just found her.

She tucked her head down, her hood covering her face. "No one's ever cared where I was or what I did, except for Katie and Mrs. Brooks."

Jake tipped her head up, the pale moonlight revealing a sheen of tears glistening in her eyes. He slid his hand to the nape of her neck and drew her toward him, wanting to taste the sweet nectar of her lips once again. She melted against him. Her hood fell back as Jake wrapped his arms around her.

He slanted his lips over hers and savored the taste of her, drawing her closer until he thought his chest would burst with wanting. He lifted his head and stared into her heavy-lidded eyes.

A loud clatter sounded from the other end of the alley. Jake reacted instantly, pushing Livy behind a stack of crates. Three men dressed in miners' garb held on to each other and staggered down the alley, passing within a few feet of where Jake squatted with Livy pressed in the corner behind him.

The men passed on by, and Jake relaxed but waited. As soon as the alley cleared, he stood and pulled Livy to her feet. "You all right?"

"I'm fine."

"Good. Let's get out of here."

He held on to her hand and led the way out of the alley, crossed another street, and retraced their steps toward the orphanage. As the building came into sight, he paused. Someone crouched on the porch next to the kitchen. "Wait here," Jake whispered.

"No. It's Luke." Livy hurried forward. "Luke? What's happened?"

Two boys stood there, looking like they'd rolled in a coal bin. Jake didn't know which one was Luke. A bundle lay on the porch between them.

"Somebody's hurt, Miss Livy." One boy's gaze darted to Jake, but he stood his ground.

He must be Luke. Both boys wore worn-out coats that were too small for them. Their faces, what little he could see beneath the coal dust, looked thin and haggard.

Livy dropped to her knees beside the child, wrapped in a stained and tattered blanket. "Bad?"

"Yes, ma'am." Luke's voice trembled.

"What happened?" Jake asked.

"Not now, Jake. Please." Livy looked up, her eyes pleading with him to be patient. "Help me get him inside."

She was right. There would be time enough for questions later. Jake lifted the unconscious boy into his arms and followed Livy. She lit some lanterns and led the way. Luke and the other boy followed.

"What's his name?" Livy asked

"I don't know," Luke responded.

Jake gently placed the boy on the bed and took stock of the situation. Filthy rags wrapped his left hand. Jake could only imagine what his body looked like beneath the torn clothes, black soot, and filth that covered him from head to toe.

He looked around. Luke stood inside the bedroom, his eyes glued to the youngster on the bed. The other boy had disappeared. "Do you know what happened?"

"No. We went to the mines tonight to get some coal, and—" his gaze dropped to the floor—"found him in a mine shaft."

He wasn't telling the whole truth, but Jake let it slide. For now. He unwrapped the boy's hand, growing more concerned by the minute. With the mangled fingers fully exposed, he drew in a sharp breath. They needed Doc Valentine if they were going to save this child's hand, maybe even his life. He stood. "I'll go for the doctor."

Livy reached out, her gaze imploring. "We can't pay him." She bit her lip and looked at the boy on the bed. Tears shone in her eyes. "I'll wake Mrs. Brooks. She'll know what to do."

"He needs a doctor." Jake took her by the shoulders. "That injury is several days old, and it's starting to fester. Mrs. Brooks can't fix this one."

She sniffed and nodded, and he pulled her to him, kissing her on the forehead.

"I'll be back soon." He glanced at Luke. He wanted to talk to him, but right now he needed to get help for the child at death's door. Obviously Luke cared enough about the younger boy to bring him to the orphanage, and he hadn't taken off when he'd seen Jake. "Luke, will you stay here with Miss Livy until I get back?"

The boy swallowed. "Yes . . . yes, sir."

"Good. I'm glad I can count on you."

✻   ✻   ✻

True to his promise, Luke stayed by Livy's side until Jake returned with the doctor. Now, he looked ready to bolt. Jake stoked the fire in the kitchen and made coffee while Doc Valentine, Livy, and Mrs. Brooks tended the injured boy.

He eyed Luke, trying to gauge his age. Maybe ten or twelve, but it was hard to tell. His small stature gave one impression, but his face spoke of something entirely different. He was whipcord thin and probably just as tough. The kid would have to be to live on the streets and take care of himself and, from what Livy said, a bunch of other youngsters too.

A month ago, Jake would have collared him and hauled him off to jail, but after seeing the way he'd risked his safety for the hurt boy, he hesitated. Could he have been so wrong? For now Jake would give him the benefit of the doubt.

"How about a cup of coffee to warm you up?"

Luke didn't respond, his gaze locked on the bedroom door across the hall where they could hear Doc Valentine and Mrs. Brooks speaking in low tones.

Jake poured a cup, unsure if the boy would drink it, but he figured it didn't matter. He needed something to warm him up. He added milk and sugar and found some corn bread and butter in the pantry and brought that to the table as well. "Here. You hungry?"

Luke shook his head no, but Jake placed the food in front of him anyway.

A low moan sounded from the bedroom across the hall. Luke shot out of his chair, panic in his eyes.

Jake grabbed his arm and eased him back down. "It's okay. Doc Valentine will take good care of him."

Luke's knowing gaze locked on Jake's. "His hand's hurt bad."

"Yeah, it's bad." Jake sipped his coffee. "We'll just pray that the doctor can save it."

"Pray?" Luke snorted. "Where I come from, prayer is a long way down the list, mister."

Jake didn't doubt it. "Luke, you know who I am, don't you?"

"Yes, sir." His defiant tone reminded Jake of Livy's when she'd insisted she'd done nothing wrong and he couldn't arrest her. "You gonna take me in?"

"Why do you think I'm going to arrest you?"

"I'm not crazy." Luke looked at him like he'd gone off his

rocker. "I know what everybody's been saying. They say that me and the other kids are the ones who've been stealing stuff, but it ain't true. We ain't done nothing."

"Do you know who it is, then?"

The boy didn't answer. Instead, he took a huge bite of corn bread. A diversion if Jake had ever seen one. If things hadn't been so serious, he would have laughed.

"Luke, if I can catch the thief, it'll go a long way toward keeping the townspeople from coming after you and your friends."

"I don't know who it is, but Billy Johansen knows something. I saw him and the thief together the night you almost caught Miss Livy and me."

"Billy Johansen?" In a way, Jake wasn't surprised. In Martha's eyes, Billy could do no wrong, and her husband, Clarence, was as henpecked as they came. If his parents didn't rein him in, he'd cause some sheriff many a headache down the road. "You think Billy's doing the stealing?"

"He didn't that night."

"Is that all you've got?"

"That's all I know."

"I need something else."

Luke stared at him.

"You going to tell me how you kids ended up in Chestnut?"

Luke lowered his gaze and stared into his coffee cup.

"I want to help you, but I can't if I don't have something to go on."

The boy jumped to his feet, knocking his chair over backward. "I've got to go."

Jake stood as well. "You've got to trust me."

Luke shook his head. "I . . . I can't. The others . . ."

"What? What about the others? Who are you afraid of? Luke, what is it you're not telling me?"

"Nothing."

Livy walked into the kitchen, and Luke glanced at her, then at Jake.

"Don't go back. Stay here and let me help you." Frustrated, Jake didn't know how to get through to the boy.

Luke's eyes filled with tears, and he shook his head. "I can't."

"Why not?"

"He's got my brother."

CHAPTER TWENTY-TWO

"Where?" Desperate for answers, Livy placed her hands on Luke's thin shoulders. "Please, Luke, where is the sweatshop? Where are the kids working? Is it in the mines? Jake and I want to help."

Luke pulled away and dashed at the tears on his face. "He'll send them all back to Chicago. They'll go to jail. For good, this time."

"Luke, the cops lied to you, and so did the man who brought you here. Nobody has the right to barter your life like that. Look at what happened to that child with the mangled hand. He's not going to let any of them go. Ever."

"I don't know anything." He backed away. "I've got to go. I've got to check on the others."

Jake held out his hand. Luke stared at it, his fearful gaze flickering to meet Jake's. He reached out, his movements slow and unsure. Jake shook the boy's hand, then released him.

Livy swallowed the lump in her throat. It took a lot for both of them to trust each other. "Thank you for everything you've told me, Luke. You've been very brave. I wish you'd stay here so you could be safe, but I understand why you can't."

Luke sniffed and dashed his sleeve across his eyes. He glanced at the now-quiet bedroom. "How is he?" he asked Livy. "Is he going to lose his hand?"

"The doctor says it's going to be close for a while. You'll come check on him, won't you?"

"Maybe." He shrugged.

He slipped out the door, and Livy wrapped her arms around her waist, sick with worry for him—for all the street kids. Jake placed his hands on her shoulders. "There's nothing you can do."

"I know, but it's so hard. What if . . . what if something happens to him? If this man finds out he's talked to us, he'll—"

Jake stopped the flow of her words with a finger to her lips. "Shhh. He'll be fine." He pulled her to him, wrapping her in strong arms.

Livy wanted to resist. She was no good for Jake. But she didn't. She closed her eyes and let him hold her. She rested her hands against his shirt, feeling the solid warmth of him through the fabric and drinking in the strong comfort of his arms.

"I sure could . . . hmmm . . . use a cup of coffee," Doc Valentine interrupted.

Livy jumped away from Jake, heat blistering her face. She hurried to the stove, not daring to look at the doctor.

"How's the boy?" Jake asked.

Livy concentrated on the coffee, glad he could ask a coherent question while she gathered her wits. Hopefully the absentminded doctor hadn't noticed a thing.

"Hmmm . . . resting," the doctor mumbled while sipping his coffee.

"Is anything broken?"

The doctor shrugged, and Livy strained to hear his almost-unintelligible words. "A broken arm, a knot . . . head . . . cracked ribs. Hmmm . . . touch and go . . . next week or so. And . . . uh . . . bruises. Bruises head to toe."

Livy winced. "What do you think happened?"

The doctor took a sip of coffee before answering. "Looks like he fell down . . . a mine shaft."

✳   ✳   ✳

"Doc thinks he fell down a mine shaft."

The six miners seated at one of Emma's tables stared hard at Jake.

"What are you getting at, Jake?"

Jake took a sip of coffee. "If anybody's using child labor in the mines, you guys would know about it."

Perkins shook his head. "There are a couple of twelve-, thirteen-year-old boys working as trappers up at the Copper Penny, but they're being treated as fair as anybody else. Maybe even better. Everybody looks after those two youngsters."

"That's what I thought."

"There's a new bunch near Cooperstown that might be doing such a thing. But I haven't heard any rumors."

After talking with the men, Jake saddled up and headed

out to the mine Perkins had mentioned. The discovery of coal in the area had brought more business to Chestnut than even the railroad. The prospect of more people meant more business for everyone, but for every decent, hardworking coal miner who came to work, there were twice as many hard-drinking, lazy bums right alongside.

And as many greedy businessmen who didn't care who got hurt or killed in the process.

A hastily assembled shack squatted at the entrance to the mine, smoke curling in lazy circles around the shingled roof. Jake dismounted and tied his horse to a hitching post. He started toward the shack, rubbing his hands together. It was a mite cooler here, and the snow hadn't melted as much as in town.

The door opened, and a stranger stepped out. Tall, lean, and tough-looking, he had the look of a miner himself. Their eyes met, and the man removed a fat cigar from his mouth. "Deputy. How can I help you?"

"Morning." Jake took a step toward the shack. "I'm here to see the owner of the mine. He inside?"

"I'm the owner. Carpenter's the name. What can I do for you?"

"A kid showed up at the orphanage the other night. Hurt pretty bad."

"What does that have to do with me?"

"Doc Valentine says he might have gotten hurt while working in a mine."

A bark of laughter escaped Carpenter. "Deputy, do you realize how many kids pass themselves off as adults to get work in the mines? They'll be ten or twelve and insist they're four or five years older. Even their parents will vouch for them, saying they're just small for their age."

"There was no way to mistake this kid for an adult. Doc says he might not make it."

"What happened to him?"

"We don't know for sure, but he might have fallen down a shaft. He's black and blue, got some broken ribs, and he might lose his hand. It's in pretty bad shape."

Carpenter swore, his face hardening. "I treat my workers fair, and if one of them was injured, I'd call on Doc to take care of them. You ever work in a mine, Deputy?"

Jake nodded, one short jerk of his head. "I've done my time."

"Why'd you quit? You scared?" Carpenter took a puff on his cigar and grinned.

"Scared. And wiser. My pa died in the Black Gold collapse in '72. I was trapped in the mine for several days before they got me out."

"I heard about that. Rough break for everybody." Carpenter shook his head. "Look, Deputy, I run a clean mine, even work alongside my men in a pinch. The kid could have been nosing around where he didn't belong for all I know." He glanced at the black hole leading into the bowels of the earth, a challenging look on his face. "You're welcome to go down the shaft yourself and take a look."

Jake broke out in a cold sweat. "Another time."

"I don't blame you. Sometimes I have to force myself to go down. Makes me appreciate my men every time I do."

Two men Jake recognized pushed a cart out the entrance. Good men, they wouldn't work in a place that treated kids like animals.

"Hey, Carpenter, we're shorthanded today," one of them called out. "Ol' Skinner didn't show up again."

"Skinner in that jail of yours?" The mine owner snubbed out his cigar and squinted at Jake.

"Yep. Sorry about that."

"Don't reckon he'll ever learn." He headed toward the mine entrance. "Nice to meet you, Deputy. Is there anything else I can do for you?"

"Not today."

The men disappeared into the mine, and Jake mounted his horse. He'd rather face down a drunk miner with a pistol than go into that black hole. He was a coward, plain and simple. What kind of lawman couldn't face his fears for the safety of the people he protected?

If he was man enough for the job, he'd turn around and descend that shaft with Carpenter and his crew.

Instead, he rode away. He couldn't do it.

Not today.

And maybe not ever.

✳   ✳   ✳

Livy sponged the boy's face. How small and delicate he looked now that all the grime had been washed away. He was a beautiful child with a head full of dark-red curls. She patted the cool cloth against his forehead, careful not to press too hard against the bruises. How could anyone treat a little boy so horribly?

Lord, heal this child. Save his hand, his life. And protect the other children that we haven't found. And help me to convince Luke and the others to come here for their safety.

Mrs. Brooks stepped inside the room, a stack of fresh linens in her arms. "Any change?"

Livy shook her head. "Every so often he mumbles something about gloves and somebody named Jesse, but that's it."

"Poor tyke. I'll spell you soon as I get supper on the table. I'd rather Mary and the others not see him until he's better."

"If he gets better," Livy whispered.

"Have faith, Livy. God has brought him this far." Mrs. Brooks rested her hand against his forehead, then his chest. "He feels cooler. I believe the fever has broken."

"Praise the Lord."

The boy moaned but didn't wake while they changed the sheets and put a fresh nightshirt on him. When they were done, he slept without thrashing about, looking as peaceful as Gracie taking an afternoon nap. Except for the cuts and bruises on his face.

Tears of thankfulness misted Livy's eyes.

Mrs. Brooks tilted her head, a frown on her face. "Those red curls look familiar, but for the life of me, I can't place him."

"Jessica has red hair." Livy shot a glance at Mrs. Brooks. "You don't think this could be her brother, Bobby?"

"Maybe." Mrs. Brooks bit her lip.

Livy blinked back the tears and wrung out the cloth once again. Jessica had stopped asking for her brother. If this was Bobby, it would be cruel to let her see him and then have death snatch him away hours or days after they had been reunited.

❋　　❋　　❋

"Grady, get in here."

Grady lumbered into the office, and Victor slammed the

door behind the hulking giant, shutting out the clamor of sewing machines.

"I told you to get rid of that kid."

"I did." Grady's wide, flat features looked confused.

Victor didn't know if Grady came with a few loose marbles rattling around in his brain or if one too many rounds in the boxing ring had knocked the sense right out of him.

"Then why is he over at the orphanage, living a life of luxury? As soon as he realizes we can't touch him, he'll spill the beans about this place, and that sheriff and his deputy will be all over us."

"I thought he was dead, boss."

"Well, he's not, and those boys that got away from us found him and took him to the orphanage."

"Sorry, boss."

Sorry? That's all the imbecile could say?

Victor raked a hand through his hair. His carefully laid plans were falling apart because of a bunch of dim-witted idiots. He'd picked Butch and Grady for their size and intimidation, not because of their brains. His first mistake.

The hum of sewing machines vibrated through the walls. The glove factory was his first endeavor outside of his father's well-oiled machine in Chicago, and he'd turned a hefty profit until now. If those kids hadn't started stealing from the merchants and caused the deputy to ask questions, he'd have been sitting pretty for a long time. But they were forcing him to take action.

What would his brother do? Cut his losses. That's what.

They'd move the children, and then they'd destroy the building.

✳   ✳   ✳

Billy Johansen squirmed like a bug caught in a jug of syrup.

Martha slapped her hands against her hips. "Now hold on, Jake. You can't come in here and accuse my Billy of being involved with that riffraff from shantytown."

Jake ignored the boy's mother, his attention focused on Billy. Lavinia's older sister had always run roughshod over the rest of them, even back when they'd been children in school. He could easily see that Billy had inherited her overbearing ways. Martha's timid husband, Clarence, looked on, not saying a word.

"Billy, you were seen with one of the thieves. It's only going to be a matter of time before they're caught. It'll go a lot easier on you if you tell me what you know now."

Martha huffed.

"Will I go to jail?" Billy asked, the first sign of fear or admission he'd shown.

"It depends on whether you've stolen anything. Have you?"

Billy shook his head. "No, sir."

"Well, then, if you're telling the truth, you don't have anything to worry about. Who's stealing from the merchants?"

"I've listened to enough of this." Martha stomped forward, putting herself between Jake and Billy. "Jake, you should be ashamed of yourself, accusing a child of thievery. Why, it's the most ridiculous thing I've ever heard."

Jake almost laughed. Didn't it occur to Martha that the entire town seemed intent on accusing a bunch of street kids who didn't have anyone to defend them—save Livy— of thieving? "Martha, I'm not accusing Billy of any wrong-doing. I've been told he was seen with one of the thieves."

"Well, it sounds like you think he's guilty of something, and—"

"Hush, Martha." Clarence spoke up, his deep voice at odds with his quiet manner.

Dead silence filled the room.

Martha's jaw dropped open and she sputtered, "But, Clarence—"

"I told you to hush." Clarence turned to his son. "Billy, go ahead and tell Jake what you know. Even your mother can't get you out of this one."

Billy paled and looked toward the floor. "Will," he whispered.

"Will McIver?" Jake asked.

Billy nodded, his expression downright miserable.

✳   ✳   ✳

Jake left the Johansens', planning to head straight to Sam's, not liking what he must do one bit. Not only had Will started drinking and gambling, but he'd added stealing to his vices. It all fell into place now. Will needed money to support his gambling habit. Jake should've realized Will wouldn't have that kind of money the night he'd hauled him out of Lucky's. But he'd been so focused on finding the kid drunk and on what that would do to his parents that thoughts of where Will had gotten that much money hadn't even crossed his mind.

Halfway to the mercantile, he changed his mind and stepped into Judge Parker's quarters.

An hour later, Jake found Sam alone in the store, all his cronies having gone home or to Nellie's for the noon meal.

Thankful for the absence of prying eyes and ears, Jake rubbed a hand over his jaw. "I've got some bad news, Sam."

Sam's body went rigid. "It's Will, isn't it?"

"Yes."

"What is it?" A muscle jumped in Sam's clenched jaw. "Just tell me straight."

Jake hated being the bearer of bad news to his friends and neighbors. But as deputy, he didn't have a choice. He took a deep breath. "I think Will's been stealing to support his gambling and drinking."

Sam turned away, shoulders slumped. "I should have seen it. Who else would have known where that watch was or even my sister-in-law's jewelry?"

Jake gripped his friend's shoulder. "If anybody should have recognized the signs, it should have been me. Don't blame yourself. You raised him right, Sam. It's not your fault."

"I reckon you're going to need to take him in." Sam turned to face Jake.

"I'm sorry, Sam. Where is he?"

"At home. Sleeping off another drunk, I suppose." Sam bowed his head and took a deep, cleansing breath, then untied the apron from around his waist and threw it on the counter. "I'll lock up and go with you. Sally's going to need me there."

"Before we go, there's something else you need to know."

Sam eyed him, the look on his face telling Jake nothing could be worse than the news he'd already brought.

"I've already talked to Judge Parker."

"And?"

"Since Will is so young and this is his first offense, Judge Parker wants to sentence him to a few months in jail at night and let him work off his debts with the merchants during the day."

A spark of hope ignited Sam's features. "Do you think it will do any good?"

"Maybe. If we can get him away from the crowd he's been running around with, we might be able to save him from himself."

Sam swiped at the tears swimming in his eyes. "I'm willing to do whatever it takes if it will help him stop drinking and gambling."

"I'll keep a close eye on him."

"Thank you, Jake." Sam flipped the Closed sign over.

CHAPTER TWENTY-THREE

LIVY OPENED THE DOOR to find Jake standing on the porch. He stepped inside. "How's the boy?"

"Better." She smiled. "His fever broke about an hour ago. He's still asleep, though."

"That's good."

He slumped into a kitchen chair. Livy watched him as she finished wiping down the table. She slid into a chair and touched his arm. "Jake, what's wrong?"

"I arrested Will McIver this afternoon." A worried frown creased his brow. "You were right. Will's the one who's been stealing from the merchants, not the street kids."

"Oh no." She hadn't wanted to be right, not if it meant the thief was another kid. "Do Mr. and Mrs. McIver know?"

"They know." Jake nodded, his expression grim.

"What's going to happen now?"

"Judge Parker's going to go light on him, give him a chance to turn around. Maybe this will be a wake-up call."

Livy rested her hand on his arm. "I'll pray that it is."

His gaze flickered over her face and softened. Livy's heart hitched in her chest. He gave her a lopsided grin. "I'm sorry I was so hardheaded about the street kids."

"You couldn't know. No one did."

"But you believed in them."

Livy shrugged. "It's not like street kids to put themselves in the limelight like that."

"Livy, come quick," Mrs. Brooks called from the other room. "He's awake."

Livy tossed the dishcloth on the table and headed toward the bedroom, Jake close on her heels. She slowed, glancing at him. "Don't scare him."

Jake scowled. "Give me some credit, won't you? I won't bite the kid."

Livy eased into the room and found Mrs. Brooks smiling at the boy. Cautious eyes stared back at her, shifted to land on Livy, and quickly jumped to Jake and the badge on his shirt.

Livy's heart squeezed in dismay at the way the boy's thin frame shrank against the feather tick, as if he wanted to disappear under the covers until they all went away.

"Hello." Livy injected a friendly, soothing tone into her voice. "I'm Livy O'Brien. This is Mrs. Brooks and Deputy Russell."

A quick flick of his eyes at Jake confirmed that the boy was more terrified of him than anything.

Livy stepped between the two, forming a barrier. "It's all

right. You're not in any trouble, and the deputy is not going to arrest you for anything. We want to help you, okay?"

He stared at her, silent. No way did he believe her. Livy sat on the edge of the bed. He tried to scoot away, but pain contorted his features. Instinctively Livy reached out a hand, and he froze, looking like a mouse being stalked by a cat.

She dropped her hand to her lap, all too aware of the caution that thrummed beneath his rib cage. Should he trust her? Should he tell a tall tale and try to somehow worm his way out of here? Should he play on their sympathies? Or should he keep his mouth shut?

"Bobby?"

His gaze ricocheted to Livy; his mouth opened, then snapped shut, forming a thin line.

"Your name is Bobby, isn't it?"

He dropped his eyes to the quilt covering his legs. Finally he nodded, the movement so slight Livy almost missed it.

"How are you feeling?"

"Okay," he mumbled.

Livy glanced at Mrs. Brooks. "Maybe we need to send for the doctor now that he's awake."

"I'll send Mary or one of the boys for him." Mrs. Brooks left the room.

"Bobby?" Jake stepped forward. "I know you're feeling pretty rough, but we really do want to help you and the other children. To do that, we need some information."

Bobby kept his gaze centered on the quilt, not moving, not making eye contact, not answering. Livy knew that look. He'd stay that way for a long, long time, simply out of fear.

"Bobby, I want you to look at me."

Her firm tone encouraged the boy to obey. She didn't want him to be afraid of her, but she needed him to listen to what she had to say. Green eyes filled with defiance met hers. She leaned closer, everything else fading into the background as she attempted to connect with this scared little boy who reminded her of herself.

"Bobby, I know what you're going through. I've been there. Maybe not the exact circumstances, but when I was a kid, I ran from the coppers more times that I can count." She shifted on the bed and caught a glimpse of Jake in the mirror atop the dresser. Should she reveal more? He wouldn't like what he heard. But she had to reach Bobby. She forged ahead. "And sometimes I got caught."

He remained focused on her, and she knew she'd snagged his interest.

"I'd get away from the cops and go right back to life on the streets. But one day something changed. I lost my sister and then got really sick, like you. Mrs. Brooks took me in and took care of me. She never judged me for what I'd done. She accepted me and loved me."

"I had a sister." Bobby looked down.

"What happened?"

"We got separated when we got here." Bobby's chin trembled. "I don't know what happened to her."

Livy tilted his chin up. "Bobby, what would you say if I told you your sister is here with us? She's doing fine."

"Jessie's here?" His eyes widened.

"If her full name is Jessica. Would you like to see her?"

"Yes. Please." An excited shine replaced the despair in

Bobby's eyes, and he bobbed his head, his shaggy red hair flopping over his forehead.

"Mr. Jake can bring her in here." Livy met Jake's gaze in the mirror. "She's asleep, but under the circumstances, I don't think Bobby can wait until morning."

Jake carried the sleeping child in and placed her in the crook of Bobby's good arm. She sighed and snuggled close. Bobby's gaze riveted on his sleeping sister's rosy cheeks and sweet-scented hair.

"Bobby, we'd like to take care of the other children just like we've been taking care of Jessica. But we can't if you don't tell us where they are."

The sweet moment turned sour as the color drained from Bobby's face. "I . . . I thank you, ma'am, for taking care of my sister, but I don't know nothing."

Livy bit her lip. If she didn't get through to this boy, more children would be in danger. Jake put a hand on her shoulder, and she looked up. He stepped forward. "Bobby, if you don't tell us, what's going to stop them from getting rid of the next kid who gets hurt or the next one who's too young to work?"

His eyes grew wide again. "Butch got rid of a little girl a few weeks ago."

"A toddler? About a year old?"

"Yes." Tears swam in his eyes. "The boss said she was too little, and Butch took her. Her sister cried and cried. Until Grady whipped her and made her stop. She still cries at night when she thinks nobody's listening."

"The baby's here. Luke found her and brought her to Miss Livy. Just like he brought Jessica."

Bobby's head jerked up. "Luke? His brother is at the factory too."

"He told us." Jake hunkered down. "I need you to tell me which factory. I'll take care of the rest."

Bobby closed his eyes and hugged Jessica close. "The glove factory."

✳   ✳   ✳

The doctor arrived and shooed them out. Livy confronted Jake in the kitchen. "Gibbons runs the glove factory."

"I should have known." Jake jerked on his coat. "He's been a thorn in my side ever since he got here."

"You're going over there, aren't you?"

He slanted her a look. "What if I am?"

"I'm going with you."

"No, you're not."

"You need my help."

"You're wrong there. I don't need your help."

Livy glared at him. "How do you intend to get in?"

"I'll find a way."

"What're you going to do? Break a window or kick down a door?"

He crossed his arms. "If I have to."

"For your information, Gibbons has bars on the windows, and they're too high up to see into. And there are only two doors, both padlocked."

His eyes narrowed. "And how do you know all this?"

"It's my job to know these things." She looked away. "Or it used to be."

"And what was your job, Livy?" He moved closer, green

290

eyes flashing. "Maybe it's time you told me the truth about yourself. You weren't just a poor little street kid Mrs. Brooks took in, were you?"

"You're right. I wasn't. Before Mrs. Brooks saved my life, I was one of the best lock pickers in Chicago."

"Not to mention an ace pickpocket too, right?"

Livy nodded. Might as well have it all out in the open. He was bound to find out sooner or later. Maybe if he knew the whole truth, he'd stop looking at her in a way that made her think about becoming a wife and a mother to little dark-haired babies who looked just like Andy.

He speared her with a suspicious look. "That first day I met you. Those boys did steal my watch, didn't they?"

Livy raised her chin. "Yes. And I put it back, and you were none the wiser."

His disgusted look twisted in her heart like one of the wires she used to pick locks. She hadn't wanted to hurt him, but she couldn't change her past, no matter how much she wanted to. "I'm sorry. I never meant to mislead you or anyone else. My past is behind me."

He took a step toward her. "Is it, Livy? Is it really?"

Livy looked away, unable to bear the censure in his eyes any longer. "I know you don't believe me, but Mrs. Brooks didn't just save my life when she took me in. She led me to Jesus Christ and taught me that what I was doing was wrong."

"How do you justify what you did all those years?"

The hot sting of tears gathered in her eyes. He still didn't understand how children abandoned on the streets suffered, not even after seeing Bobby at death's door, and then hearing that same child struggle with identifying the men who'd almost killed him.

"I didn't know any better. All I knew was that I was freezing, my stomach was empty, and my sister had bled to death in a filthy alley right before my eyes, taking her babe with her. I wanted to eat, to live. That's all that mattered." She wanted to shake him. He knew nothing—*nothing*—about what she'd been through. She jabbed at his chest, unable to check the tears squeezing out the corners of her eyes. "Don't talk to me about justifying my actions until you've walked barefoot through the snow or fought the dogs for bones to throw in a pot to have a little something to eat."

When she stopped, the only sound was her harsh breathing filling the room. Jake stared at her, suffocating her with his silence. Was he repulsed by what she'd told him? It didn't matter what he thought anymore. All that mattered was saving the children on the streets of Chestnut and in the hands of that monster Gibbons.

If telling the truth about her past opened people's eyes to the plight of these kids, then she'd tell the world.

Jake turned away, gripping the windowsill until his knuckles turned white. "Was it that bad?"

She closed her eyes and took a deep breath, then opened her eyes again. "It was worse—much worse. I . . . I don't have words to describe it."

He glanced at her, a hint of compassion now in his gaze. "Can you give me another chance? I promise to listen to you, to Luke, and to the others this time."

She pushed the memories to the back of her mind and

swiped at the tears on her cheeks. "I'll give you another chance on one condition."

"What?"

"That you take me with you to the glove factory."

✳   ✳   ✳

"Would you hurry up already?"

Livy shot Jake a look filled with daggers, and he clamped his lips together. She pressed her ear against the lock, a long, thin wire in her hand. The temperature, already below freezing, kept dropping. It seemed like they'd crouched in the shadows for hours, but it couldn't have been more than a few minutes.

A click later, Livy threw a triumphant look in his direction. The lock popped open, and they slipped inside the darkened building. Once the door shut behind them, Jake lit a lantern and pulled the shutters low so that only a sliver of light illuminated the room. The light revealed an office, small and cluttered, with barred windows set high in the walls.

Livy hurried to a desk in the corner and pulled out a drawer. "I tried to get a job here not long after Mrs. Brooks and I arrived in Chestnut, but Gibbons said they weren't hiring. He must have been using child labor the whole time."

Quickly they searched the office, finding precious little about employees but plenty of orders and invoices detailing the various buyers the factory dealt with.

"Funny that Gibbons would have such good records of his customers but nothing on his employees," Jake said.

They moved on to the factory floor. Other than the office, the building consisted of one huge room filled to the brim with machines and stacks of leather goods piled high. Row after row of sewing machines, packed close together, didn't leave much room to maneuver. The stench of unwashed bodies and refuse permeated the place.

Jake's stomach churned. He didn't like the looks of this, not one bit. They rummaged around some more. Livy moved away, and Jake raised the lantern, trying to see what had caught her attention.

"Give me a little more light. Nobody knows we're here anyway."

Jake turned the lantern higher and followed Livy. Haphazard piles of foul-smelling blankets ran the length of the rear wall. He spotted small boxes and crates here and there, separating the pallets.

Livy's gaze shimmered in the lantern light. "Looks like the kids were living in here."

"Where are they now, then?" Jake wanted to punch someone, namely, Victor Gibbons. If Bobby had worked in this dump, then Gibbons didn't care a fig about what happened to any of his workers, no matter what he said.

"I don't know." She riffled through a box and held up a wooden horse, missing two legs. Another box revealed a small sliver of a mirror and a tattered children's book.

Jake picked up a shirt, small and threadbare. "What do you think?"

"Definitely a child's." Livy frowned.

"But without the children, there's not any proof."

"There's Bobby."

Jake laughed, a harsh sound in the cavernous building. "One street kid's word against a man like Victor Gibbons? It'll never fly."

"It might if people saw the condition of this place."

They headed toward the front door, Jake holding the lantern high so they wouldn't trip over anything.

Livy grabbed his arm. "What's that smell?"

Jake sniffed. Dread snaked through him. "Smoke." He grabbed Livy's hand. "Come on."

He wouldn't have thought twice about the smell of burning coal since the scent hung over Chestnut most of the year. But woodsmoke? They hurried toward the front door. Jake tried it, but it wouldn't budge.

"It's stuck," Livy said.

Jake shook the knob again. "No, it's locked. Someone's locked us in from the outside."

His gaze caught and held Livy's in the flickering light of the lantern. "They're going to torch the building."

❋   ❋   ❋

Livy froze. She'd seen what fire could do to a building, reducing it to ashes in minutes. The fear of fire had hovered over the slums of Chicago like a dark cloud, striking terror into the hearts of all.

Lord, please help us.

"We've got to get out of here." Jake lifted the shades on the lantern all the way and exposed the darkest corners.

Livy's frantic gaze swept the factory: the high, barred windows, the padlocked doors. Jake ran to the rear of the building, his shadow dancing against the walls. He checked the back door, but like the front, it must have been locked from the outside. The light bobbed as he raced back to her side. Livy clutched her stomach and focused on his tense face, illuminated by the lantern and the light from the fire.

Oh, Lord, help us. Please, Lord, get us out of here. I don't want to die. Please.

"Come on." Jake pulled her through the doorway separating the office from the sweatshop and slammed the door behind them. "That'll buy us a little time."

Livy's gaze darted around the office before she broke free of Jake's hold and raced to the locked door. She pounded against the wood. "Help! Somebody, help! Please get us out of here!"

Jake wrapped his arms around her from behind, capturing her fluttering hands against her waist. She stilled, willing her pounding heart to slow.

"Save your breath. There's nobody close enough to hear," he whispered.

She closed her eyes and shuddered against him, trying not to scream, trying not to run to the corner and huddle in a ball against the onslaught of fire that would surely come.

"We're going to make it. Okay?"

She took a deep breath and nodded. He sounded so sure, so confident. She could almost believe he was right.

He kissed the top of her head and let her go. Shoving a desk chair underneath the window, he climbed onto the chair, grabbed the bars, and shook them.

Smoke curled under the door, drifting in sluggish curls toward them. Livy shivered. How harmless the smoke looked, but how deadly it would be when it wrapped itself around them and completely took over until they couldn't breathe. She backed toward the corner. They were going to die. Right here in this room. Tonight.

The smoke would kill them long before the fire consumed their bodies.

Through a fog of fear as thick as the smoke slithering under the door, Livy watched Jake. He found a metal rod and pried against the bars, using the iron as a lever, trying to create an opening big enough to escape through. Sweat beaded and rolled down his face.

A whimper gurgled up her throat.

Lord, we need You now more than we've ever needed You. Please, Lord.

Jake stopped, lowering the heavy iron rod from the window. "It's no use. The bars are bolted tight against the frame."

Livy slid down the wall into a puddle.

Oh, God. Oh, God. Have mercy.

Jake hurried across the room, hunkered down, and grabbed her by the shoulders. His eyes, their green depths fierce in the flickering light, stunned her. "We will make it, Livy. Don't give up."

Livy shook her head. There was no need for words.

Desperate time stood still.

"Please don't cry, Livy."

The air left Livy in a rush, leaving a desperate feeling of yearning inside. Tears tracked down her cheeks. With shaking hands, she traced his features, her fingers lingering on his cheekbones, the stubble along his jaw, and finally, his lips.

Jake hauled her to him, covering her mouth with his in a burning kiss that rivaled the fire raging out of control not thirty feet away. All too soon, he jerked away, rested his forehead against hers, and gazed long and deep into her eyes. He didn't say another word, but his expression glowed with a passion that seared her to the core.

A passion they would never have a chance to explore.

CHAPTER TWENTY-FOUR

JAKE HELD LIVY TIGHT AGAINST HIM. He loved her, and he'd give anything to see her safe. If possible, he'd die to save her. "Lord, help us. If there's a way out, show me."

The smoke grew thick. The roar of the fire gained momentum with each passing moment. Livy slumped against him and coughed. She'd given up. His heart lurched. She couldn't die. He'd beat a hole in the door first. His gaze darted to the only escape route.

The door.

"Come on. Head down. Crawl."

He half dragged, half pulled her across the room. He caught a whiff of blessedly cold air. He pushed her to the crack between the door and the floor. Livy scooted close, sucking the oxygen in. Jake cocooned her with his body. Breathing. Wishing. Hoping. Praying.

God, did You bring us this far to let us die? Is this the end for us? What about Ma and my brother and sisters? Who'll take care of them? And Mrs. Brooks and the orphans? They need Livy.

He blinked against the acrid smell of smoke, tears forming in his eyes. He focused on a hinge, shining black against the wooden door. He stared at the gap between the hinge and the door, his brain foggy and disoriented.

Suddenly the significance of the crack became clear.

He scuttled across the floor and grabbed the iron bar. Using brute force, he shoved the end of the shaft into the space and pried.

God, give me strength. Do it. Do it now.

A nail moved, screeching against the wood. Adrenaline surged through Jake's body, and he wedged the bar even tighter. Pressing his back against the floor, he used the leverage to force the hinge to give way, groaning with the effort.

Three more tries, and the nails popped out.

"Livy," he rasped, "we're free."

She responded with a moan.

He snaked an arm around her waist and pulled her away from the door. She clawed at him, trying to get closer to the air. He blocked her and used the bar to pry the door away from the frame.

A swoosh of fresh air slapped him in the face.

He scooted Livy's small frame toward the opening. "Go."

She crawled out, her movements sluggish.

Jake wedged his shoulders between the heavy door and

the frame, forcing his way through. He paused, breathing in, regaining his strength to push on to freedom.

Livy stumbled toward the frozen creek.

"No. Not that way."

She ignored him or simply didn't hear him in her haste to get as far away from the burning building as she could. Jake strained to get through the opening he'd created, his body acting as a crowbar. He heard the nails on the top hinge screeching against the wood.

The door gave way and crashed against the foundation. Jake cleared the opening, chased by billows of smoke. He gulped in life-giving air, trying to see where Livy had gone. He stood, lumbering away from the building in the direction he'd last seen her.

"Livy!" His voice was no more than a croak.

A shout from behind him spurred him on. He had no way of knowing who'd spotted him, but if it was Gibbons's men, they'd shoot first and ask questions later.

He cleared the line of trees and staggered along the edge of the creek toward an alley leading into shantytown, searching for Livy. The sound of breaking ice and a gasping scream galvanized him forward.

Oh, God, help me find her before it's too late.

He found her more from the sound of thrashing than from sight. He grabbed for her and missed. On his second try he managed to tangle one hand in her sodden skirt and haul her out of the water. She lay in his arms as limp as the corn-husk doll they'd made together. A shot rang out behind them as he ducked into an alley.

The dragon in Jake's lungs clawed to get out, but he

fought the urge to cough. His and Livy's lives depended on silence. He glanced at the unconscious woman in his arms. *Oh, Lord, please save her life. I've just found her. I can't lose her now. We need Your help, Lord.*

His heart ripped in two. There wasn't time to stop and give her his coat. She needed someplace safe and warm and out of harm's way. Now. And he knew just the place.

Emma's.

He staggered across the street, stumbled along behind half a dozen shacks, and zigzagged his way to the café, hoping and praying he'd lost their pursuers. He banged on Emma's back door.

No response.

He pounded the wood again. When Emma didn't answer, he started fumbling with the buttons on his coat with one hand, holding Livy tight against him with the other.

Finally a feeble light filtered through the crack at the bottom of the door, but Emma didn't answer.

"Emma, it's Jake Russell. I've got Livy out here and she needs help."

"Livy, are you there?" Emma asked through the door.

"She's unconscious. Please, Emma."

Emma swung open the door, her eyes going wide when she saw Livy's limp body, her wet clothes already stiffening from the cold. She grabbed for them and hauled them inside. "Oh, my goodness. Get in here, now."

Without any wasted motion, Emma jerked a curtain aside and pointed to a rumpled bed. Jake deposited Livy on the covers. Emma shoved him out of the small space and yanked the tattered curtain shut. "Stoke the fire."

The fire grew hot, the minutes long. Jake raked one hand through his hair, scattering the smell of woodsmoke through the room. Rustling sounds of Emma undressing Livy filled the tiny living quarters. A moan sounded, and Jake stopped himself short of ripping the curtain open. "Emma?"

"She's coming around." She pushed the curtain back. Livy lay on the bed, wrapped securely in a quilt. "Move her to my rocker, close to the fire."

Jake did as she instructed. Emma knelt and started rubbing warmth into Livy's feet. Jake did the same with her hands, cold as blocks of ice.

Shouts reverberated off the walls, and the clatter of boots rushing over the boards in front of Emma's shattered the silence. Jake heard shouts of fire. The whole town would turn out, not only to save the building but to keep the fire from spreading.

Jake started coughing. His eyes watered, and he thought he'd cough his lungs up. Emma handed him a glass of water.

Emma's gaze centered on Jake. When he recovered, she asked, "What is it? What's wrong?"

"The glove factory's on fire."

"Oh no." Alarm caught and held her features. "The whole town could burn."

He shook his head. "There's no wind tonight, and it's far enough away from the other buildings that it shouldn't spread."

"Are you sure?" Her voice trembled.

"Yes. But a healthy dose of prayer won't hurt."

"Amen to that." Her gaze swung between him and Livy, still shivering beneath the mountain of blankets and quilts

Emma had wrapped around her. He could see the questions in her eyes, but she didn't voice them.

She cupped Livy's face in one hand. "Livy, dear, can you hear me?"

Livy opened her eyes, staring at Emma. "Cold. So cold."

"I know. We'll have you warmed up before long."

Jake saw alarm cross Livy's features, and she started up in the rocker. "Jake?"

"I'm here." He gathered her in his arms and held her close.

"I thought—" she broke off.

"Shhh. It's all right. I'm alive. We both are, thank the Lord."

Livy went limp, buried her head against his chest, and cried.

"I'll make a pot of coffee. It'll warm you both up." Emma retreated to the kitchen.

Jake took a deep breath and smoothed Livy's damp hair back, thankful he could hold her, touch her, that she wasn't at the bottom of the creek, lifeless and forever lost to him.

He caressed her face, and she leaned into his touch. Her gaze softened and warmed.

"Livy, I'm sorry. I shouldn't have let you go with me tonight."

"You didn't have a choice."

Jake shook his head. "Yes, I did. I put your life on the line, and you almost got killed. Twice. If you had died, I would never forgive myself."

"No. I wanted to go." Her eyes glowed with conviction. "You couldn't have stopped me."

He sighed, his eyes focused on hers. "I've got to go help fight the fire and see if Gibbons's men are still around. Promise me you'll stay here."

"Jake, I'll go—"

"No. It's too dangerous. I need to help, but if you're there, I'll be worried about you getting hurt. Please?"

"All right. But only because Emma took my clothes."

He leaned over and kissed her. Her mouth twitched. He eased back a fraction of an inch, an answering smile tugging at his lips. "What?"

"You're cold."

"You are too." He leaned forward, his lips barely touching hers as he whispered, "That's why I'm kissing you. I figured it would warm us both up."

And he was right.

∗　　∗　　∗

An orange glow lit the sky.

Victor carefully tied his tie, then jerked the knot out and let the silk hang free around his neck. A distraught businessman wouldn't be immaculately dressed when he arrived on the scene of his business going up in flames.

He took his time saddling his horse, mounted, and rode a quarter mile before spurring the animal forward. It also wouldn't look good to arrive at a sedate pace.

The flames shot higher, and he smiled grimly. Torching the building was a small price to pay to keep from being caught up in a scandal. He'd come out of this fresh as a newly laundered shirt; then he'd take the insurance money from the building and start over.

Losing his workers would be a little harder to absorb, but it couldn't be helped. His deeds done in the dark of night were being pulled out into the daylight, and the citizens of Chestnut wouldn't turn a blind eye as those in Chicago had.

But no matter. Everything would turn out fine. With the building reduced to ashes and no children to step forward, they had nothing to hang on him.

Not one blessed thing.

His family would be proud.

*   *   *

Jake gulped down two cups of Emma's coffee before giving Livy a peck on the cheek. "Stay here. As soon as the fire is out, I'll take you back to the orphanage." He glanced at Emma. "That is, if Emma can scrounge up some dry clothes for you."

Emma nodded. "I'm sure I can find something."

Livy cupped his cheek. "Be careful."

"I will." He winked at her.

Jake let himself out and hurried toward the glove factory. How much of it had been destroyed? He'd gotten Livy to safety, and she'd promised she wouldn't follow him. He could rest easy on that score. He'd make sure the men had the fire under control, then hoof it back to Emma's.

And then he'd find Gibbons and get some answers.

The closer he got to the fire, the louder the yelling became. He sprinted forward, his bruised lungs burning from the effort. When he broke through the trees, he breathed a sigh.

The men shouted over the roar of the hungry flames to bring more water. The rear section of the factory was gone. The office where they'd been trapped still stood but was engulfed in flames. The men had formed a bucket brigade to the creek, breaking the ice so they could keep the fire contained. The factory's seclusion had contributed to its being able to operate as a sweatshop without anybody knowing about it, but its aloofness turned into a blessing while it burned.

Jake cringed at the number of times he'd ridden by and viewed the half-concealed building from a distance, not bothering to check on the factory or the workers. But there hadn't been any hint of anything illegal until Will set things in motion with his thievery. By trying to flush out the street kids, Jake had uncovered a nest of vipers in their midst.

Sheriff Carter approached him, face grim. "Somebody must have left a lamp burning or something. I haven't seen Gibbons, but he's gonna be mad as a hornet."

Jake tried to suppress the hacking cough that bubbled out of his lungs.

The sheriff glanced sharply at him. "What happened to you? You get downwind of that smoke?"

"You might say that."

Jake outlined everything leading up to the glove factory's burning. "As soon as it's daylight, we need to send a telegraph to Chicago. We might need some help."

Sheriff Carter nodded. "What do you think Gibbons will do? You think he'll run?"

"Maybe not. He probably thinks Livy and I died in the fire, if he even knows we were there in the first place. And if I can keep it that way, we might have a chance of catching him."

Soon the bucket brigade slowed to a crawl as the exhausted firefighters realized the building couldn't be salvaged and the flames no longer threatened their homes and businesses. Discussion broke out speculating on the cause of the fire.

Jake stood in the shadows, studying the crowd. Were the

men who'd locked him and Livy inside still around? He didn't know what they looked like, but he had a gut feeling he'd know them if he saw them. He remembered the three goons who'd flanked Gibbons at the rail yard. Probably more of the same.

Pounding hooves sounded on the road leading to the glove factory. Victor Gibbons galloped into view.

Dismounting, he let loose a string of curse words, then bellowed, "What happened here?"

Sheriff Carter stepped forward. "Nobody knows, Mr. Gibbons. Maybe you can tell us."

"Me?" the factory owner blustered. "I just now arrived. Somebody destroyed my factory, Sheriff, and I expect you and that deputy of yours to catch the culprits. Probably some of those street kids who've been stealing everybody blind."

Jake eased out of the shadows, close behind Gibbons, his hand resting on the butt of his gun. "Gibbons, you're under arrest."

Gibbons swung around. "My glove factory is burning to the ground, and you're arresting me? What in the world for?"

"For endangerment of children and attempted murder of an officer of the law," Jake said.

"I don't know what you're talking about." He gathered up the reins of his horse and started to mount. "If you've got anything to say, you can say it to my lawyer."

"I wouldn't if I were you." Sheriff Carter pressed his pistol against Gibbons's backbone.

The factory owner lowered his boot to the ground. The sheriff wasted no time slapping a pair of handcuffs on him.

"I want my lawyer." Gibbons glared at Jake.

"You can contact a lawyer in the morning." Sheriff Carter prodded him. "Now start walking."

Jake took up the reins of the horse and followed, keeping a careful eye out for Gibbons's hired men. He wouldn't put it past them to try to rescue their boss before they got to the jail.

Gibbons cursed all the way down Main Street. As Jake locked the cell door, the prisoner sat on the cot, cold gaze trained on Jake. "You're going to wish you'd never tangled with me. You don't have a drop of proof, and when my lawyer is done with you, you'll never work in law enforcement again."

Jake leaned his forearms against the cell. "I'm not as concerned with that as I am the lives of the children you had working for you. Where are they?"

Gibbons lay on the cot, his hands folded behind his head. "What children? I told you before, I don't hire kids."

You don't hire them; you just buy them like pieces of machinery.

Jake turned on his heel, strode into the front office, and slammed the door.

Sheriff Carter glanced at the closed door. "He's right, you know. We don't have a smidgen of evidence, especially now that the glove factory is gone."

"There's a bunch of kids out there somewhere who can identify Gibbons as the man who treated them like slaves—or worse."

"If they're still alive." Sheriff Carter poured himself a cup of hours-old coffee and eased into his chair with a grunt. "I'm going to send a telegraph to Chicago bright and early in the morning. I've got an old friend who might be able to give us a hand."

Jake rubbed a weary hand across his face. "Will you be all right for a while, Sheriff? I need to go check on Livy."

"Go ahead. I've got a pot of coffee and a shotgun if any of Gibbons's fellers show up."

Jake hurried across Main Street and cut down an alley. He crossed Second Street, his thoughts on where those children might be. They couldn't have gone far. He thought of Luke and gave a slight nod. If anybody could find them, Luke could. He'd get Livy safely back to the orphanage and see if he could find the boy.

A grim wave of disquiet wove through his gut. After what he'd seen tonight, he wouldn't put it past Gibbons and his men to do whatever it took to silence those kids.

He'd almost made it to Emma's when a shout pulled him up short. It sounded like Luke. Breaking into a jog, he headed down an alley, listening for the sound again.

"Let me go," Luke yelled.

Jake skidded around a corner and saw one of Gibbons's hired guns wrap a beefy hand around the boy's neck. Another boy dashed forward and swung a length of two-by-four. The wood cracked against the man's back, but he swatted the boy away like a pesky fly.

Lungs burning, Jake plowed into the fray. He took the man down. But before he could reach for his gun, the man jumped up, balancing on the balls of his feet.

Jake rolled and scrambled to his feet. His assailant threw a punch, but Jake sidestepped, letting the blow glance off his bicep. He planted his left boot and threw a right cross. Contact! Jake's knuckles screamed as bone met bone.

Taking a step to advance on his opponent, he walked into

a jab. Pain streaked across his chin. Air whooshed from his lungs as another blow landed in his gut.

Adrenaline pushed harder. Jake swung at the man, missing with another right cross but hitting the target with a left uppercut to his chin.

Wham!

The middle of Jake's spine burned with white-hot pain. He pivoted to face a second attacker, blocking the next blow.

"Aaarrrghhh!"

Through blurred vision, he saw Luke come in swinging, the two-by-four gripped in both hands.

He tried to yell for Luke to get away, to go for help, but all his energy focused on anticipating the wicked uppercuts coming toward him.

He couldn't tell what the men looked like in the dark, other than that both were big, beefy men with fists of iron, much like those he'd seen with Gibbons. He didn't doubt they'd kill him and the boys if they could.

His fist made contact, and one of his attackers went down like a felled oak.

Luke and his friends rushed the remaining thug, boards and sticks flying in every direction. Jake ducked.

Two fists exploded in his face, and Livy flashed across his befuddled mind.

Lord, please don't let them find Livy.

CHAPTER TWENTY-FIVE

"You're falling in love with him, aren't you?"

The first light of dawn streaked across the sky; the miners would troop through the door soon. Since neither Emma nor Livy could sleep, they'd cooked breakfast and peeled and cut up the vegetables for half a dozen meat pies for the evening meal. They'd even baked three blackberry cobblers. The savory aromas of cobbler and baking bread filled the café.

"I don't know. I'm worried sick about him." The knife slipped and nicked Livy's finger. She wiped the blood on the voluminous brown work dress Emma had lent her. She bit her lip and slanted a look at her employer.

Emma snorted, rolling out biscuits faster than Georgie could devour tea cakes. "Well, I'm worried about him too, but that doesn't mean I'm in *love* with him."

Livy smiled, her face softening. "Strange as it may seem, Emma, I do love him." She smiled, her hands falling to her lap, her chores forgotten. "From the beginning I liked him, but I was afraid. Afraid of men, afraid of marriage, of having babies, and afraid of someone finding out about my past."

Emma threw her a glance. "Most of us have pasts we're not proud of."

"I know, but Jake's a sheriff's deputy, and his family are pillars of the community. I'm just a pickpocket from—"

"Don't say that. You've been redeemed by the blood of the Lamb. Your sins are washed away, never to be remembered. God's given you a new life and a passion to help children who don't have anybody else. If Jake—or anybody else in this town—can't see that, they're dumber than a lump of coal. And trust me, Jake's not dumb."

"His attitude toward the street kids *has* changed, especially since Luke brought Bobby to the orphanage. I think he realizes they don't choose to live on the streets, that all they really want is to survive and for people to care about them."

Emma's hands stilled, and she nodded. "Isn't that what we all want?"

Livy smiled. "Yes."

They worked in silence, Livy glancing out the window every few minutes. Still no sign of Jake. What could've happened? It'd been hours since he left. She finished cutting up a chunk of beef and dumped it in the pot to boil. She looked around. Breakfast was ready and waiting, and everything they could prepare ahead of time for the evening meal was finished.

She couldn't wait any longer or she'd go crazy. "Emma,

I need to go look for Jake or at least see if Sheriff Carter has seen him."

"Do you think you should? You breathed in a lot of smoke, and that tumble in the creek didn't help matters."

"I'll be fine." Livy didn't tell her that her lungs still felt like fire and she hadn't completely warmed up, but she couldn't stop worrying about Jake.

Emma tipped her head toward the door. "I'll manage by myself. Take my coat. It's mighty cold out there."

"Thanks, Emma." Livy hugged the woman, thankful she'd found Emma. Not only had she given her an income that helped out at the orphanage, she'd been a lifesaver last night.

Livy hurried toward Main Street. Merchants were opening their businesses and getting ready for the day, some standing in clusters and talking about the excitement of the night before. She slipped past, in a hurry to get to the jail. She shook her head at the irony.

McIver swept the boardwalk in front of his store.

"Morning, Mr. McIver. Have you seen Jake?"

His broom stilled, and he shook his head. "Not since he arrested Gibbons last night."

Livy gasped. "Gibbons is in jail?"

"Yep." He jerked his head in that direction. "Jake might still be there. I haven't seen him or Sheriff Carter this morning."

"Thank you." Livy rushed across the street, trying to keep the hem of Emma's dress and coat from becoming coated with mud. Had Gibbons resisted? Had Jake been hurt? Fear mounted as she turned the knob.

Sheriff Carter looked up when she stepped inside, his

double-barrel shotgun lying at the ready across his desk. His hand fell away from the weapon. "Morning, Miss O'Brien."

"Good morning, Sheriff. Have you seen Jake?"

He mopped his pasty-white brow with a damp handkerchief. "He left about three hours ago to escort you back to the orphanage. You haven't seen him?"

Apprehension pooled in Livy's stomach. "He never showed up at Emma's."

"Don't worry yourself, girl. Jake can take care of himself."

"Mr. McIver hasn't seen him either. Something's happened to him. I just know it."

Sheriff Carter scrunched up his face as if he might be thinking the same thing. "It doesn't look right." He glanced at the cells behind him. "Miss O'Brien, can you do me a favor?"

"Yes, sir."

He grabbed two pieces of paper off his desk. "I can't leave our guest alone, but I need to send these telegraphs to Chicago. Can you run over to the post office and do that for me?"

"Got it. Anything else?"

"Could you ask McIver to head on over here? He'll stand watch while I take a look-see around for ol' Jake."

"Yes, sir." Livy stopped, her hand on the knob. "You feeling all right, Sheriff?"

A grimace of pain crossed his face. "Just a little twinge. I'll be fine. Now, go on, girl."

Livy scurried away. She gave Mr. McIver the sheriff's message and hurried to the post office. After giving the postmaster the messages, she checked at the boardinghouse. Miss Nellie hadn't seen hide nor hair of Jake all night. Livy thanked her and left. She stood on the boardwalk, trying to decide where to look next.

Panic clawed at her. Gibbons's men wouldn't think twice about killing Jake and throwing his body down a mine shaft or dumping him through a hole in the icy creek. If he'd run into those men, she'd probably never see him again. In desperation, she headed to shantytown. A lot of people had been out and about last night, helping fight the fire. Surely someone had seen something.

The temperature had risen, and the snow melted, dripping from the roofs in slow, steady streams. Livy slogged through the slush, keeping to the boardwalk as much as possible, but this part of town didn't have many walkways, unlike Chicago's cobblestone streets. She grew more fearful with every step, with every person she asked about Jake. No one remembered seeing him, not since he and Sheriff Carter had hauled Gibbons off to jail in the wee hours of the morning.

She turned down another alley, hoping against hope she'd find him. *Lord, let him be alive. Please.*

A half-grown boy who looked like Luke darted down the street ahead of her. Livy hiked up her skirts and broke into a run.

"Luke!" she shouted.

They almost collided at the end of the alley.

"I've been looking for you," Luke said.

"Have you seen Jake? I can't find him anywhere."

"He's in a bad way." He grabbed her hand. "Come on."

Livy jerked him to a stop. "Has he been shot?" *Oh, Lord, please, not that.*

"No. Just beat to within an inch of his life."

Her heart lurched with fear. She'd known something had gone wrong, or he would've kept his promise and come back to Emma's last night. *Oh, Lord Jesus, please keep him alive; please don't let him die.*

"Take me to him."

✳   ✳   ✳

Victor Gibbons stared at the ceiling, hands clasped behind his head. Frustration welled inside his gut. It galled that he'd had to send for his brother's lawyer to get him out of this mess.

If it hadn't been for that McIver kid getting the town all riled up, none of this would have happened. Then that deputy and that nosy little lady from the orphanage had decided to snoop around when Butch and Grady torched the factory. Bad timing, to say the least. It would have been better if they'd died in the fire.

But they couldn't prove a thing.

Grady and Butch had stashed those kids in an abandoned mine. Nobody would think to look for them there. Once Jimmy Sharp took care of them, the only person who could identify him would be that kid named Bobby. No jury would convict him of any wrongdoing on the word of one street kid.

It would be easy to start over somewhere else. As soon as he got out of here, they'd regroup in a bigger town, a little closer to Chicago—but not so close that his brother could tell him how to run his business.

He smiled. Maybe this would all work out after all.

✳ ✳ ✳

Jake came to with a start. He felt like he'd fallen down a mine shaft and hit rock bottom. A wave of panic washed over him at the thought of being trapped in a mine. He stifled a groan and concentrated on the scents and sounds around him. The musty smell of old blankets and rotting wood permeated the air along with the pungent odor of burning coal, its fire barely keeping the cold at bay.

Not a mine. At least he could be thankful for that.

He opened his eyes and stared at the remains of an old shack. One wall had collapsed, but the rest looked fairly stable. He turned his head and came face-to-face with a group of dirty, bedraggled boys ringed in a semicircle on the other side of a tiny fire, all eyes trained on him. He didn't even try to guess their ages. A couple were as big as Luke—he scanned the half-dozen or so faces for the boy and didn't see him—and some were smaller, as small as Georgie. His heart twisted at the gaunt faces and hollow eyes gazing back at him in the dim light.

He blinked. How had he gotten here?

It all came back with a rush. The fire, arresting Gibbons, going after Livy, the fight.

What if they'd found Livy? And where was Luke?

Daylight filtered through the cracks and crevices of the dilapidated building. Several hours had passed since he'd left her at Emma's.

He struggled to sit up, breaking into a cold sweat with the effort. It felt like a knife stabbed through his chest with every movement, every breath. The smaller boys scrambled to their feet and retreated behind the older ones. Two of them brandished iron pipes and threw nervous glances at each other. Jake eased up against the wall, waiting for the pain to subside before he tried again.

"How'd I get here?" His voice sounded like the roar of a bear after a long winter of hibernation.

They didn't seem inclined to answer.

"Do I look like I'm any danger to you? I couldn't catch a turtle in my condition, let alone one of you boys." He studied the boys wielding pipes. One of them looked familiar. Jake caught his eye. "You brought Bobby to the orphanage, didn't you?"

The boy glanced at his companions before giving a cautious nod. "How's he doing?"

"He's going to be all right." He inched into a better sitting position, gasping with the effort. He looked toward the boy who'd answered. "Last thing I remember, two big guys were getting the best of me. What happened?"

"You knocked Grady out; I got in a pretty solid lick to Butch's head." The boy grinned. "Shook the ground when he fell."

Jake returned the grin, but it quickly turned into a grimace of pain.

A fit of coughing took his breath away, and he hugged his torso with one hand, groaning with the effort to keep from coughing up his lungs. The boys watched silently until he regained his breath.

"Where's Luke?"

"He said something about going for help."

A thump sounded, then two more. A boy pushed aside

a crate and crawled through an opening into the makeshift living quarters, stopping when he saw that Jake was awake. "Luke's coming."

Luke crawled inside, followed by a woman. She stood and shook out the mud-spattered cloak she wore, the hem covered in filth. Then she threw back her hood, revealing a mass of reddish-brown curls.

Jake's heart pounded. "Livy?" he rasped.

Her blue gaze collided with his and a smile flew across her face. She hurried to his side, knelt, and threw her arms around his neck. "You're alive."

Jake almost passed out from the pain when she hugged him, but he didn't want the boys to think he couldn't take it. He winked at them. Several grinned.

He'd broken the ice with them. Ignoring the throbbing in his ribs, he wrapped an arm around Livy and pulled her close, breathing in the intoxicating scent of her hair, reveling in having her next to him.

Thank You, Lord.

She pulled away, her hands fluttering over him. She touched his face, her fingers gentle. "Are you hurt?"

"I'll live. I think."

Luke hunkered in front of the fire, holding out his hands for warmth. "I think you've got some broken ribs."

Tears filled Livy's eyes. "Oh."

"I'm fine. Really. There's nothing that won't heal with time." He let himself drown in her eyes. "I'm glad you're all right. I was worried about you."

"Not as worried as I've been."

Jake struggled to stand, his aching body protesting. "Luke,

I've got to get back to the jail. Sheriff Carter will need me. No telling what Gibbons's men might do."

"Think you can make it?"

"Pretty sure."

Jake led Livy to the opening, but she turned back.

"I wish you'd come to the orphanage." Her plea included all the boys. "You're all welcome. You know that. I've told Luke part of my story, but you boys need to hear it as well. I lived on the streets of Chicago for years. I did a lot of things I'm not proud of, but when I met Mrs. Brooks, my life changed. She led me to Jesus and taught me that stealing was wrong. She's not like the others. She's good and kind and loving."

"We'll talk about it, Miss Livy, but we can't promise anything." Luke poked at the fire.

Livy touched his shoulder. "We'll be there when you decide to come, day or night."

Luke nodded and turned to Jake. "I need to ask you something."

"Shoot."

"Did . . ." His lips trembled. "Did any kids die in the fire?"

"No, thank the Lord. Why do you ask?"

"My little brother was there. The boss, the one you call Gibbons, shipped him here in one of those crates."

Fingers of pain that had nothing to do with his bruised ribs and tortured lungs clutched Jake's chest as he recalled Gibbons's railcar and precious machinery. Had children been in those crates?

Dear Lord, no.

He cleared his throat and gripped Luke's shoulder. "They weren't there, but we're going to find them."

∗ ∗ ∗

Jake left Livy at the orphanage before heading back to the jail.

He limped to the doorway leading to the cells in the back and leaned against the doorjamb, trying not to wince. "Well, Gibbons, your men didn't finish the job this time either. I'm going to find a way to nail your hide to the wall."

Gibbons gave him a bored look. "You can try, Deputy. But like I said, you don't have any proof."

Jake turned away, and the prisoner called out, "Hey, Sheriff, you sent for my lawyer, didn't you? A man's entitled to legal counsel."

"Yeah, I sent for him," Sheriff Carter hollered, then muttered under his breath. "Not that it'll do any good, you good-for-nothing snake."

Abner McIver skidded into the jail. "Hey, Mr. Jake, Mr. Stillman asked if you could come see him."

Jake flipped the boy a nickel. "Thanks, Abner."

The boy grinned. "You're welcome."

Jake made his way to the bank, where he approached the nearest teller. "Mr. Stillman in?"

"Yes, sir. Go right on in."

The banker's office looked about as cluttered as Jake's desk at the jail. They shook hands and Stillman gestured to a chair. "Thanks for coming over."

Jake held his breath and carefully lowered himself into the roomy leather chair. Stillman eyed him over his spectacles. "You all right?"

"I'll be fine in a week or two." He winced, inching to a more comfortable position. "Abner said you wanted to see me? Is it about the mine?"

"Yes."

Jake sighed and closed his eyes. "What is it this time? Brown sell out? Or has the new owner upped his offer?"

Stillman laughed softly. "Both, actually."

Jake cracked open one eye. "What?"

He waited for the familiar ache, the worry that plagued him knowing control of the mine where his father, Seamus's sons and brothers, Emma's husband, and others had died. But it didn't come, only a weary realization that there was nothing he could do about it. "Why? Not that it matters, I reckon."

"Brown didn't say." Stillman leaned back in his chair. "So where do we go from here? As it stands, there are now two owners, you and—" he riffled through some papers on his desk—"somebody named J. T. MacPherson. You can either sell your shares to MacPherson or agree to operate the mine with him. With fifty-fifty ownership, you're at a stalemate."

Jake leaned his head against the high back of the leather chair, trying to think. He could sell the shares he owned and easily pay off the loan against the farm. But could he do that knowing that MacPherson planned to reopen the mine? Could he live with himself knowing that any day, the whistle might blow, and dozens of men might die because of him?

He couldn't. "There's nothing else to be said, Mr. Stillman. I won't open that mine back up, and I won't take money for my shares knowing the new owner plans to open that death trap up again."

"I see." Mr. Stillman folded his hands together on his

desk. "Jake, I understand your dilemma, but there's your family to think of. If I have to, I'll call in that loan, sell the shares, and settle the debt myself."

Jake eased to his feet, clutching his cracked ribs with one hand. "You do what you have to, then. But put the farm in Ma's name. I don't deserve it."

✳   ✳   ✳

Luke took a deep breath and knocked on the door.

"You sure about this, Luke?" The others fidgeted behind him.

"No."

But he'd follow through.

He didn't remember the last time he'd had a bath. His clothes hung on him in rags, and his shoes were falling apart. The others were in just as bad a shape as he was. Some were worse. They couldn't battle the cold much longer, especially the younger ones. If it didn't work out, they could take off anytime they pleased. From what he'd seen, Miss Livy didn't keep anybody under lock and key.

When she opened the door, he almost bolted.

"Luke." She smiled. "Come in."

They filed in, Luke leading the way. The others bunched together close to the door, unsure about becoming part of the orphanage family. Mrs. Brooks stood at the stove, a wide smile on her face.

"Are you here to stay?" Livy grasped him by the shoulders.

Luke glanced at the others, then nodded. "If you'll have us."

"Of course we'll have you."

And she hugged him to her, dirty, stinking clothes and all.

CHAPTER TWENTY-SIX

JAKE SPOTTED THE STRANGER a stone's throw from the jail.

His gaze narrowed. No, not a stranger. He'd seen the man at the train station the day he'd inspected Gibbons's railcar.

The man limped toward him, dressed in a suit and a wool overcoat with a cane clasped in his right hand. They met at the jail. A jagged scar raced down one side of the man's face. A pair of pale-blue eyes flickered to the sign over the door and back to Jake.

"Afternoon. What can I do for you?"

"Jimmy Sharp. Victor Gibbons's lawyer."

Jake jerked his head toward the door. "Come on in, then. He's inside."

Sharp insisted on seeing his client alone. Sheriff Carter

gave them ten minutes. Twenty minutes later, Sharp came out, his gaze spearing Jake before settling on Sheriff Carter. "I need to see the judge about making bail."

He was soft-spoken, but Jake could sense the steel that lay beneath the words. Maybe such steel made the man a good lawyer. But if Gibbons was guilty of everything Jake suspected him of, Sharp would have a hard time proving his client innocent.

Sheriff Carter shuffled some paperwork. "You'll have to wait. Judge Parker won't be back until Monday."

The lawyer stared at them, his eyes cold and calculating. "I'll be back on Monday, then."

He turned to leave, and the door opened. A tall man, whipcord thin, stepped inside. The lawyer and the newcomer squared off immediately, the tension so thick, it rippled through the jail like an unexpected blizzard. The newcomer pulled his coat back to reveal a six-gun strapped to his leg. "Sharp, what are you doing here?"

"Meeting with my client." The lawyer didn't even try to hide his disdain for the other man. "You got a problem with that, *Detective* Schmidt?"

"Not as long as you don't do anything illegal while you're here."

"Move aside, then, and let me pass."

The detective stared him down for a long moment and finally stepped to the side. "I'll be watching you, Sharp."

The lawyer laughed. "You do that."

After Sharp left, Sheriff Carter shuffled toward the hatchet-faced detective and pumped his hand in a hearty handshake. "Smitty, it's good to see you." He turned to Jake.

"I'd like you to meet my right-hand man, Jake Russell. Don't know what I'd do without him."

The detective's shrewd gaze raked Jake from head to toe and back again. One corner of his mouth turned up in a half smile. "Looks like you came close to finding out."

Sheriff Carter laughed. "It'll take more than a couple of Gibbons's goons to get rid of Jake."

The smile faded faster than snow on a hot day. "Gibbons? As in Victor Gibbons?"

"You know him?"

"Know him? His brother's one of the smoothest operators out of Chicago. Took over from their father. I've been trying to pin something on the Gibbons family for years."

"Sharp's his lawyer."

Smitty grunted. "Figures. Two peas in a pod."

"That you, Smitty?" Gibbons called out.

"Yeah." Smitty moved to where he could see the prisoner and leaned his shoulder against the doorjamb. "Well, Gibbons, looks like we've got you this time."

"'Fraid not, Smitty." Gibbons laughed. "Like I told the deputy out there, they don't have a shred of evidence against me."

✻ ✻ ✻

Busy didn't even begin to describe Emma's Place on Saturday night. The miners sat shoulder to shoulder, lingering longer than usual, eating and rehashing the fire from the night before. Livy kept their coffee cups full and her ears open.

"I heard Gibbons was using young'uns for labor. Brought 'em in from Chicago and made 'em work day and night. Treated 'em like slaves, he did."

"How'd he get away with that? Seems like somebody would have talked."

"They worked, ate, and slept in the factory." The miner snorted. "Well, mostly worked. I don't think they got much food or sleep. Nobody knew they were there except for Gibbons and his crew."

"Gibbons better hope he stays in jail. He might have an accident if he finds his way back to shantytown again, if you get my drift."

A low growl of agreement ringed the table.

"What happened to them kids? They didn't die in the fire, did they?"

"No. Sheriff Carter said nobody was in there. Nobody knows where they are."

The miners kept eating. They were probably trying to wrap their minds around the possibility that Gibbons had silenced the children forever. She'd known some cruel men, but that kind of brutality went beyond her worst imaginings.

Please, Lord, let them be alive.

She hurried to the kitchen to grab two more pots of coffee. She turned away from the stove, both hands full, and spotted Jimmy Sharp at the door. Her knees almost buckled. She retreated behind the curtain separating the kitchen from the eating establishment before he saw her.

What was he doing in Chestnut? She could think of only one reason.

Gibbons might not have the guts to kill a passel of kids, but Jimmy Sharp wouldn't think twice about it. She'd heard horror stories of how he got rid of his enemies by tying weights to their feet and dumping them into the Chicago River.

He hid behind his position as a lawyer, but he was one of the most vicious crime bosses in Chicago. She couldn't take the chance he might recognize her. He'd been in court a number of times when she'd been brought before the judge.

"Mary, could you pour the rest of the coffee? I'll wash dishes for a while."

Mary grinned and reached for a towel. "Be glad to. I'm purely sick and tired of washing dishes."

Livy stayed behind the curtain, washed dishes, and kept an eye on Sharp. His presence in Chestnut couldn't be an accident, and she intended to find out exactly why he'd come to town. She followed him when he left the café, keeping to the shadows as he crossed the street and headed down one alley after another. He stopped in front of a saloon. Livy melded with the shadows as he looked to the left and to the right, then limped into a narrow alley between the saloon and a saddle shop. Livy darted down an adjacent garbage-strewn alley. At the other end, she spotted the glow of a cigarette and heard low voices. She eased forward and crouched between two crates, careful not to make a sound.

Sharp stood with two men, his sparse frame small compared to their hulking stances. Livy shivered. Sharp's lean build had led many in Chicago to underestimate him. And most hadn't lived to tell about their lapse in judgment.

"What do you want us to do with all them young'uns? Just leave 'em in the mine?"

Fear mixed with thankfulness clutched Livy. At least the children were still alive. For how long was anybody's guess.

"Blow up the mine." Sharp's unemotional voice came out colder than an Illinois winter. "As far as most folks know, it's closed because of that explosion a couple of years ago."

"And then what?"

"Get out of town. As soon as I spring Gibbons, we'll cut our losses here. Chestnut's too small to do business without drawing attention to ourselves. I told Victor that, but he wouldn't listen."

The men separated, Sharp heading back the way he'd come, the two men going in the opposite direction. Livy waited a full five minutes before leaving her hiding place. She followed the path the goons took, choosing the lesser of two evils, in her rush to get back to Main Street.

Livy burst into the jail, winded from running the entire distance from shantytown. Jake jumped to his feet, the pained look on his face clearly showing he'd moved too fast for his bruised and battered body. She didn't see Sheriff Carter.

"What's wrong?"

"Jimmy Sharp's in town."

"The lawyer? He came by here earlier today." He gestured toward the cells. "Spent some time with Gibbons."

Livy snorted. "He may be a lawyer, but he's a crook and a murderer first. I overheard him telling Gibbons's men to blow up a mine." Tears filled her eyes. "And those kids are in the mine. They're going to shut them up for good and then get out of town."

He grabbed her arms. "Which mine?"

"He said something about an explosion a couple of years ago. How many mine accidents has Chestnut had?"

"Only one." Jake's jaw hardened. "The Black Gold mine.

The mine was so unstable after the explosion that we boarded up the entrance."

"We've got to stop them."

✳   ✳   ✳

Jake eyed Livy as he tried to decide on the best course of action. Making a snap decision, he propelled her toward the door. "Go to the boardinghouse, and tell Harvey and Smitty to meet me at the mine. Harvey knows the way. Oh, and tell Miss Nellie to send Sam here to the jail. If Sharp's as dangerous as you say, I don't want to leave Sheriff Carter alone."

"Be careful." Livy's hand rested against his shirt, the heat of her palm branding his heart.

He hauled her into his arms and hugged her tight, ignoring the pain in his ribs. "You too. Now go."

As she hurried to the door, he called out, "You stay with Miss Nellie, you hear?" He thought she nodded but couldn't be sure. As soon as she'd gone, he went to the cot where Sheriff Carter dozed. "Sheriff, something's come up. I've got to go."

"What is it?" Sheriff Carter struggled to a sitting position, pulled on his boots, and followed Jake into the office.

Jake shut the door to the cells and outlined Sharp's plans as quickly as possible.

The sheriff reached for his gun belt. "I'll go. You've already tangled with these fellers once."

"It's a tough trek out to that mine." Jake caught and held the sheriff's gaze.

Sheriff Carter's eyes blazed. "I know it, but you need my help if we're going to save those kids."

"Smitty's meeting me at the mine. And I've sent for McIver to come here to the jail."

"Good. McIver can take care of Gibbons." The sheriff grabbed a shotgun and filled his pockets with shells. "Saddle a couple of horses. We'll ride part of the way."

*　　*　　*

Jake crouched in the shadows near the Black Gold mine, his entire body aching. He ignored the pain. A bunch of kids' lives were at stake, which meant more than a few bruises and broken ribs.

Sheriff Carter hunkered down near him, his labored breathing loud in the silence. They'd left the horses and walked the last half mile. The sheriff shouldn't have come, but as sheriff, he felt responsible for those kids. Jake could understand his determination to do whatever it took to save them.

Gibbons's thugs were nowhere to be seen, but the boards had been ripped from the entrance, so they'd been here and might still be inside.

Simply looking at the gaping black hole made him break out in a cold sweat. He knew this mine as well as anybody alive other than Gus. It boasted more twists and turns than poison on an oak tree. If those kids were to survive, he'd have to find them and lead them out. But could he force himself to go inside?

He didn't have a choice, did he?

Two men who looked like the two he'd tangled with the night before came out of the entrance, pouring a stream of black powder on the ground. In a matter of minutes, they'd strike a match and blow the entrance.

Where were Smitty and Harvey? They couldn't wait any longer.

The sheriff tapped Jake on the shoulder and motioned for him to track around behind the men. Jake slid silently through the underbrush, easing closer. In position, he waited for Sheriff Carter to make the next move.

A match flared, and Jake's heart leapt. They were out of time. What was taking the sheriff so long?

Sheriff Carter stepped into the open, his shotgun trained on the men. "Put your hands in the air. You're under arrest."

The man with the match dropped the flame to the black powder and went for his gun. A sizzling stream of fire zigzagged like lightning toward the entrance to the mine. Jake dove for the black powder line in the rocky sand. Before he hit the ground, he saw Sheriff Carter's eyes go wide, one hand clutching his chest as he staggered backward. The double-barreled shotgun fell from his limp fingers.

Oh, God, no!

Jake's body severed the line of powder as the blaze sputtered toward him. Praying he'd done all he could to stop the path of the flame, he rolled and came up with gun in hand.

Too late.

He stared into the emotionless face of the man who held a pistol against the sheriff's pasty-white temple. Jake sought the sheriff's pain-glazed eyes.

"Don't worry 'bout me, Jake. Do what you gotta do."

"Shut up, old man." The one with the gun pinned Jake with a hard look. "Toss your gun over here."

Jake hesitated.

The man cocked his pistol. "Do it. Now."

The thug would blow the sheriff's head off without any more thought than he'd give to squashing a bug. Jake tossed his gun on the ground. The second man palmed it and pressed it into the small of Jake's back.

Sheriff Carter clutched his chest and groaned. Jake surged toward him only to be jerked back. "Can't you see he's dying?"

The man let go of the sheriff's collar, and he slumped to the ground in a heap, unmoving. "No different than if I'd shot him, I reckon." He leveled the cocked gun at Jake. "You just don't know when to quit, do you? Well, this time there won't be no coming back."

Jake squinted at the thug, intent on finally getting a good look at him. A wide face, scarred and battered, with a mis-shapen nose. The face of a prizefighter. Jake winced. No wonder his fist packed the power of a sledgehammer.

So this is it, Lord? I'm going to die? Leaving Ma, Tommy, and the girls to fend for themselves. And the kids in the mine. Even if I can't get to them, send someone else. They don't deserve this. And Livy.

Oh, Lord, Livy.

His heart shattered into a million pieces. He'd hoped to ask her to marry him, to have children with her, to grow old together. But it would never happen.

"No, don't shoot," the second man said. "I've got a better idea. Throw him in the mine with the others. He can enjoy a long, slow death if the explosion doesn't get him first."

A grin slashed across the wide face of the prizefighter, and he laughed, a low, guttural sound that left Jake in no doubt he relished killing. "Now, why didn't I think of that?"

Jake tried to jerk away as the prizefighter slammed the

pistol against his temple. They grabbed him by the arms and hauled him into the mine. Jake fought to remain conscious, his only thought to save Sheriff Carter and the kids.

He came to inside the shaft and lurched to his feet, holding on to the damp rock walls. How long had they been gone? If he headed out the entrance, they'd shoot or set off the powder with him right on top of it.

Making a quick decision, he turned and staggered deeper into the mine to get as far away from the explosion as he could.

Save us all, Lord.

*   *   *

Harvey led the way, Detective Schmidt and Livy following. They crashed through the underbrush of a winding, overgrown trail leading to the abandoned mine. The men had tried to get her to wait in town, but she couldn't, not knowing if Jake and the children were all right. She felt a twinge of remorse. Jake had told her to stay with Miss Nellie. The Bible said she was to submit to her husband, but they weren't married yet. She vowed she'd do what he said once he popped the question.

"It's up ahead, around the bend from Gus's cabin." Harvey panted, his face ruddy from the exertion of climbing the steep hillside.

Smitty put a hand on Harvey's arm. "Let's go slow from here on out. Remember, there are two men, possibly three, working for Gibbons and Sharp. Trust me, they won't hesitate to kill us if they get the chance."

Harvey nodded and fell back, letting Smitty take the lead.

Moments later, Harvey tapped the detective on the arm and pointed. The opening of the mine yawned before them, a dark hole leading to a pitch-black interior.

Livy shivered, aching for the children.

They'd endured a brutal life in Chicago; then Gibbons had made it even more horrible by enslaving them to work in the glove factory before dumping them in the mine like rotten garbage. Gibbons might be in jail, but with Sharp making the decisions now, they didn't stand a chance.

Smitty hissed, "Get down."

Livy and Harvey didn't have to be told twice. They ducked low while Smitty crept forward. Livy strained to see what drew his attention. Jake? Or Gibbons's men? Sharp?

"Stop!"

She jumped as Smitty yelled and took off running.

The next few seconds were a blur. Smitty crashed through the underbrush toward two men silhouetted in the clearing. A line of flame shot toward the mine.

Livy's horrified gaze tracked the sizzling path of the flame. "No!"

CHAPTER TWENTY-SEVEN

THE ROAR OF SMITTY'S GUN and the rocks and dust that spewed out of the mine drowned out her scream.

Stunned, Livy stared at the entrance to the mine, paralyzed. They'd done it. They'd blown up the mine, sealing dozens of children inside. And Jake? Where was he? He'd said he'd meet Smitty and Harvey here. Had they killed him? She fisted her hand against her mouth.

She'd know. Wouldn't she?

Her gaze slashed toward Schmidt and the two men. She fought her way through the underbrush on rubbery legs. One lay on the ground, not moving. The other stood, holding his shoulder, blood oozing through his fingers. Schmidt leveled his gun at the one still standing.

"Where's Russell?" His tone left no doubt that if he didn't get an answer, the man better prepare to meet his Maker.

The man jerked his head toward the mine and gave a short bark of laughter. "Probably dead by now. We threw him on top of the explosives."

Livy's legs gave way, and she slumped to her knees. Pain like she'd never felt, not even when her sister died, knifed through her. *Jake. Oh, Jake. I've just found you. Please don't leave me so soon. I love you. Oh, Lord, not Jake. Please, Lord.*

She'd never planned on falling in love, but he'd stolen her heart with his crooked smile, the twinkle in his eyes, and the way he'd made corn-husk dolls for the girls and carved farm animals for the boys.

Lost in her grief, she scarcely heard the blaring of the alarms calling all able-bodied men to the mines. Shouts rose as men arrived and took up shovels. Was there any hope they could save Jake and the children? She wanted to believe, but her heart wouldn't let her.

Her hope had blown up with the mine.

Schmidt lifted her to her feet. He held out a black muffler, the one she'd given Jake. "Miss O'Brien, Harvey and I are taking these two to jail. Why don't you come along with us? There's nothing you can do here."

Livy clutched the knit scarf, holding on to this small piece of wool that had touched him. A scent of bay rum clung to the soft material. Jake's scent. "No. I want to stay. In case . . ." Her voice broke. "In case they . . . find him."

The detective patted her awkwardly on the shoulder. "All right. I'll be back shortly, so don't try to head back to town alone. Okay?"

Livy nodded. She wouldn't leave the mine until they'd found Jake and those children, dead or alive.

✳ ✳ ✳

Jake couldn't breathe.

Coal-black darkness surrounded him, and an oppressive weight pinned him down. He could feel the cool dampness of the mine, the smell of dirt and unmined coal unlike anything aboveground.

He clawed his way to full consciousness. He had to get to the others, see if they were safe. "Pa?" he rasped. "Thorndike? Seamus?"

No one answered.

He struggled to remember. There'd been an explosion. Where were the others? Had he alone been spared to face a slow, agonizing death, buried alive?

His heart pounded. His mother had begged them not to buy shares in the mine, but Jake and his father knew they could make a killing if they owned their own mine. They'd be able to make their own rules and keep all the profit to boot. They hadn't banked on tragedy.

His mind slammed back to the present.

The thugs. The kids. The explosion meant to kill them all. Sheriff Carter.

Jake moved, and the rubble on top of him shifted. He struggled to his knees, bracing his hand against the jagged dirt-and-rock walls. Tears gathered in his eyes and slid down his cheeks. "Oh, Lord Jesus, help me. I don't want to die, not like this. It would have been better if they'd shot me."

The thought of never seeing the light of day closed in on

him, and fear bubbled up as strong as he'd felt two years ago. What were the odds of being rescued twice in one lifetime? He doubled over, his forehead pressed to the ground.

"Please, Lord," he whispered. He stayed still, reining in his fear. Years-old training kicked in. *Breathe slowly. Conserve energy. Don't panic.*

"With God all things are possible."

Jake stilled, the pounding in his heart slowing, the fear subsiding as he grasped at the lifeline. "Lord, what are You trying to tell me?"

The truth rolled over him in slow waves, clearing the fog in his brain. If he'd lived through the explosion, those children would have. And they'd be terrified. They wouldn't even have hope of being rescued. A hope he could offer them if he could find them. If his presence brought them comfort, so be it.

"For such a time as this."

Jake took a deep breath, stood on shaky legs, and started inching his way deeper into the bowels of the mine.

❋　　❋　　❋

"There's a body here! Somebody bring a lantern."

Livy scrambled over rocks and debris, hoping and praying they'd found Jake. *Please let him be alive, Lord. Please.*

"It's Sheriff Carter."

Men crowded around.

"Is he dead?"

"He's still breathing, barely. I don't see any injuries, either. A couple of you guys hitch up a wagon and get him to the doctor."

Livy watched the men ease the sheriff into the wagon. *Lord, where will it end?* Sheriff Carter was supposed to be back at the jail. Not here. She bowed her head and prayed for the sheriff, for Jake, for the children, and for the men risking their lives to get into the mine.

The rescuers carted load after load of rocks and dirt away, trying to clear the opening obliterated in the explosion. Some men brought wheelbarrows and more picks and spades to help the work go faster. Word circulated among the rescuers that Jake and the children were trapped inside, and more men showed up, some coming straight from working in other mines to help.

Livy wanted to help dig, but her limbs had turned to jelly. She'd never been afraid of much of anything. She wanted to pitch in and do whatever needed doing, but the thought of losing Jake paralyzed her to the point that she could only sit and stare at the rubble. She closed her eyes and tried to let God's peace waft over her. That's all she could do. She was too drained to pray, too fearful.

After a while, she felt a stirring at her side and opened her eyes. Gus watched the commotion. He threw a shy glance her way. "What happened?"

"Some bad men blew up the mine. Several children and Jake are inside."

"Mr. Jake?" Gus's voice trembled. "And some kids?"

"Yes." Livy patted his arm. Dear, sweet Gus. Such a tender heart filled with compassion.

"What were they doing in there?" A confused look crossed his face. "It's been closed for a long time."

"A man named Gibbons brought the kids here to work

for him in the glove factory, but when Jake started asking questions, he moved them to the mine to keep Jake from finding them."

"They'll never get in that way." Gus shook his head. Dirt and rocks from the entire hillside covered the opening to the mine.

His observation hit her square in the chest. "There's no hope, then."

Oh, God. Oh, God.

"There's another way." Gus motioned for her to follow him.

"Oh, Gus." Livy sighed. The old man didn't know what he was talking about.

"Come on. I'll show you."

Livy followed simply because she didn't know what else to do. He led her down the hill and around the bend to a shack. He opened the door to the stable attached to the side of the cabin. Little Bit stared at her from the stall. How could Little Bit help get Jake and the kids out? Maybe Gus thought the donkey could help haul the debris away. It would take a hundred donkeys to clear the entrance to the mine.

"Gus, I appreciate you trying to help, but—"

"Look." He motioned her forward, moved aside a stack of crates, then a cobbled-together barrier revealing an opening in the side of the hill.

Livy peered at the black hole, hope tickling the edges of her heart. "Where does this lead to?"

"The Black Gold mine." Gus grinned, as excited as a child on Christmas morning.

Hope became a full-fledged giggle. "Can you lead the way to the old mine?"

He nodded.

Livy threw her arms around him. "Oh, Gus, thank you, thank you, thank you. We've got to tell Smitty."

* * *

"For such a time as this."

Jake stumbled forward in the dark, his only thought to find the children and comfort them. His hands, scratched and bleeding, tracked along the rough rock walls searching for a cache of emergency supplies.

The miners stashed torches and lanterns all through the mines for emergencies. He kept moving until his hands felt a depression in the rock. His questing fingers located the carefully wrapped provisions lashed against the rock shelf.

For such a time as this.

* * *

"Please."

McIver and Smitty looked at each other, and Livy knew they weren't going to let her go.

"Please take me with you. The children will be frightened enough as it is. I grew up on the streets of Chicago. I *know* what they've been through."

A wiry young man stepped forward, miner's hat in hand. Determination glinted in his hard gaze. "I'm from Chicago too. I'm going in."

Four more miners stepped forward, tough men looking like they'd fight anyone who dared tell them they couldn't go after Jake and the children.

"All right. Grab a lantern and line up." Smitty stabbed a

finger at Livy. "And you, young lady, stay right by my side and do everything I tell you to."

Livy scrambled into line. "Yes, sir."

They eased into the mine, Gus leading the way, humming as he moved forward. Smitty sandwiched himself and Livy in the middle of the pack. The miners carried lanterns to light the way.

Livy tamped down the surge of panic rising in her throat as soon as they entered the darkness. She'd been in some tight spots, but she'd never been underground before. She didn't know what she expected, but the coolness and the dank smell surprised her. And complete darkness so thick she could almost reach out and touch it.

The only light came from the lanterns the miners held high. She shivered. How could these men work like this day in and day out, living their lives underground?

Gus turned left, then right, then left again until Livy's head spun with confusion. She looked back at Smitty, his face illuminated by the flickering light. "I hope he knows where he's going."

Smitty clenched his jaw, looking none too happy to be underground. "I do too. Otherwise, Jake and those young'uns might not be the only ones lost in this mine tonight."

✳   ✳   ✳

Thankful for the lantern he'd found stashed among the emergency supplies, Jake kept moving, searching for the children. His thoughts cleared, and memories long suppressed clamored for his attention. There were two or three logical places to stash the children. But he wouldn't take any chances. He'd search every nook and cranny, just to be sure.

Systematically, he went from right to left, moving from one tunnel to the next, not leaving any area untouched. He slowed when he reached the scene of the explosion two years ago. He paused, forcing himself to look at the collapsed shaft to his right. The entire thing had imploded on itself, sealing everyone inside fifty feet below the surface of the mine.

He broke out in a cold sweat, not wanting to check the area, but the children's safety demanded he leave no stone unturned. He climbed over the rubble. He'd gone another fifty feet before shifting rock and dirt blocked his way. He held the lantern high. The collapse wasn't new, so tonight's explosion hadn't triggered it. The children couldn't be in this part of the mine. Jake turned away, thankful he didn't have to go down that particular tunnel and face the demons of his past.

Tunnels branched off in several directions. He took an opening on his immediate right. If memory served, it wouldn't take long to search this area. There were a few more places he figured Gibbons might have left the kids, and he was anxious to check them.

He went down four more dead ends before staggering into a hollowed-out place half the size of the office at the jail. Fifteen or twenty boys and girls stared at him, their faces gaunt, eyes sunken in their heads. Silent. Scared out of their wits. Cold. And hungry.

Someone coughed, the sound loud in the stillness.

Jake lifted the lantern high so they could see his face. "I'm Jake Russell. I'm here to help you."

To break the ice, he told them about Bobby, Jessica, and the little girl Luke had left at the orphanage.

Then he met Luke's little brother, Mark.

✳   ✳   ✳

After what seemed like an eternity, the tunnel widened, allowing them to fan out. Livy breathed easier in the open space. Ore carts that hadn't been used in over two years sat silent. Broken ax handles lay inside one cart, a man's tattered coat draped over the edge of another.

One of the miners pointed to a pile of rubble. "There's the shaft that collapsed two years ago." His gaze sought and found Livy's in the lamplight. "Jake Russell and Seamus O'Leary were the only two to survive. Rescuers pulled 'em out ten days later."

Livy swallowed hard against the lump that formed in her throat. *Oh, Jake. And you were willing to risk your life to save the children?*

Gus led them down another tunnel, moving single file again. A murmur, a ripple of excitement—*something*—coursed through the men in front of Livy. She strained to see over or around them.

A single light cast from a mining lamp shone in the distance.

✳   ✳   ✳

The children stirred, the older ones moving quietly to shield the younger. Jake calmed them. "It's all right. They're here to rescue us. Trust me, okay?"

"Will they take me to Luke?" A fragile hope tinged Mark's voice.

"Yes." Jake hugged the child to him. "As soon as we get out of here, we'll go find Luke."

Seventeen pairs of eyes trained on him, filled with trust he didn't deserve. He'd been their only hope, their only lifeline to cling to. Tears stung his eyes. *Lord, help me to be worthy of such trust.*

"Jake!"

His head jerked up at the sound of Livy's voice.

Livy? Here? He stumbled to his feet and caught her as she launched herself into his arms. He wrapped his arms around her tight, not sure he'd ever let her go.

"Oh, Jake, I thought I'd lost you for good this time."

"I guess I'm a lot like that cat of yours. Got nine lives, it seems."

She grimaced. "You're fast using them up, Jake Russell."

He hugged her close, marveling that he had another chance to hold her. Hot tears stung his eyes, and he rested his head on the top of her head. "We lost Sheriff Carter."

She lifted her head, her eyes shining. "No, he's alive. They took him to Doc Valentine."

Jake's heart swelled with gratitude. God had abundantly blessed all of them.

A cough reminded him they weren't alone. Reluctantly he loosened his hold on Livy and motioned toward the children huddled behind him.

"I've got some friends here I want you to meet."

CHAPTER TWENTY-EIGHT

MRS. BROOKS TOOK LUKE by the shoulders. "They've found the children."

"Where? Is Mark with them?" Luke's heart slammed against his rib cage. "Is he alive?"

He needed to go to him. Now. Mark was just a little kid. He'd be scared, and it had been so long since they'd seen each other. They had a home now, a home with Mrs. Brooks and the other children.

He couldn't wait to tell Mark. His little brother would be so happy.

"In one of the mines. Word just came that they're out of the mine and headed this way."

"I've got to go to him." Luke ran to the door but turned back. Hot tears stung his eyes. "If it's okay with you, that is?"

Mrs. Brooks smiled. "Of course it is. Go to your brother."

Luke grinned and was out the door like a shot. He ran toward the mines, feeling like he could fly. His steps faltered. What if Mark wasn't with the other kids?

Please, God. Please let him be all right.

Long before he got to the mines, he saw the lights. It looked like half the town had shown up. Then he saw a group headed toward him, the lights from behind blinding him to their faces. Some of the figures were tall, others small.

And some were being carried by the others.

They neared, and he spotted Mr. Jake and Miss Livy. Mr. Jake carried a child. When he saw Luke, he said something.

The child lifted his head, and Luke saw his brother in the shifting lantern light.

"Luke." A huge smile split Mark's face. He scrambled from Mr. Jake's arms.

Luke ran forward and scooped his brother up. Mark's thin arms wrapped around his neck.

Luke hugged him tight, blinking back tears.

He'd finally found Mark.

*   *   *

Livy bustled about the kitchen, giving instructions, keeping everyone busy. The orphanage overflowed with children. She glanced at the girls they'd rescued from the mine, and her heart twisted with compassion. They'd need a lot of tender love and care to get over what they'd been through. But with God's grace, they'd make it.

She smiled at a girl named Clara. Clara's eyes were still

red-rimmed from crying. Crying for joy because she'd been reunited with her baby sister, Hannah.

"Here." She handed the girl a bowl. "Peel these potatoes. Georgie, run upstairs and help Mrs. Brooks."

Mark stuck to Luke like glue. Luke didn't let on, but Livy had spotted tears shimmering in his eyes when he thought no one was looking. Mark and Clara weren't the only ones who'd cried buckets of tears the last few days. She'd cried her share.

They weren't rolling in food, and certainly not money, but the townspeople had pitched in, bringing what they could spare to help out. More than one had apologized for not realizing the need was so great.

Thank You, Jesus, for taking care of these boys and girls, for helping us find them, and for allowing Sheriff Carter to live, and for keeping Jake safe, and . . .

She smiled. Her prayer of thanks was a mile long. She'd been blessed so abundantly this Christmas. More than she'd ever thought possible. God had fulfilled the desires of her heart with a home and a family, and she'd fallen in love with the most wonderful man on earth. She didn't know what might happen next, but no matter what, God wouldn't let her down.

The kitchen door opened, letting in a blast of cold air.

"Seth, shut that door. I'm having a hard enough time keeping the house warm as it is."

"Yes, ma'am." The door banged shut.

Livy whirled at the sound of Jake's voice, her face growing warm at the sight of him. "I'm sorry, Jake. I thought you were Seth. The boys have been running in and out of the house all day."

Jake dodged Seth and Georgie as they raced through the kitchen, three boys from the mine following at a more sedate pace. They smiled shyly when they saw him. Jake glanced back at Livy. "Looks like you and Mrs. Brooks have your hands full."

"We wouldn't have it any other way." She smiled, then sobered. "How's Sheriff Carter?"

"Chomping at the bit to get back to the jail, but Doc's keeping him on a tight rein." He grinned. "And I think he's enjoying Mrs. Brooks's visits as well."

"They're a matched pair, if I've ever seen one. Have you arrested Sharp yet?"

He shook his head. "No. Smitty and I have searched everywhere, and he's nowhere to be found. We figure he skipped town as soon as he heard we'd found the children and arrested Butch and Grady. We probably won't have to worry about him anymore."

"Praise the Lord. We don't need his kind here in Chestnut, that's for sure."

Jake snagged a biscuit from the stove. Livy swatted his hand, and he grabbed for hers, rubbing his thumb along the soft tissue of her palm. Livy shivered at the touch.

"I'm going to see Gus. Want to ride along? I imagine Mrs. Brooks and the girls can handle things for an hour or so."

"Oh, I couldn't. There's so much to do."

She glanced around the busy kitchen, at the girls pretending to be engrossed in their work. Little sneaks. Not a peep could be heard out of any of them, they were so engrossed in Jake and Livy's conversation.

"I'll not take no for an answer. Right, girls?"

"Yes, sir." Giggles erupted from their audience.

She couldn't resist the teasing glint in his eyes or the snickers from the girls. She reached for her cloak. "All right. Mary, tell Mrs. Brooks I'll be back in a little while."

"Yes, ma'am."

The sun shone bright and cheerful after so many dreary days of snow-laden clouds. Livy smiled, soaking up the warmth.

Jake helped her into a wagon, climbed up, and headed toward town. He motioned to the wagon bed, where two straight-back chairs lay. "Those are for Gus."

Livy smiled. "He'll be so happy."

Jake reached for a burlap sack at his feet. "And these are for the boys. I didn't want to take them inside. I was afraid Georgie's curiosity would get the best of him."

Livy opened the sack and pulled out a wooden horse, the intricate carving revealing how much time and effort Jake had put into this one piece. "Oh, Jake, it's perfect."

"It's a good thing I made so many pieces to begin with. I finished two more this morning, so I think there's enough to go around."

"Thank you. You'll come over on Christmas Eve, won't you? I want you there when they open their presents."

"I wouldn't miss it." His eyes twinkled, making Livy wonder what he had in mind.

As they neared the middle of town, a commotion broke out on the other side of the jail, close to the barbershop. Shopkeepers swarmed out of their businesses heading that way. Jake pulled the wagon up short and set the brake.

"Wait here," he said, jumping down and hurrying toward the crowd.

Livy didn't hesitate. She hiked her skirts, jumped out of the wagon, and took off after him, pushing her way through the throng. She came to a screeching halt when she saw the source of the noise. Smitty pulled Jimmy Sharp toward the jail, the lawyer cursing a blue streak and fighting against the handcuffs chaffing his wrists.

"Come on, Sharp. You've managed to get out of more than one scrape in Chicago, but not here. Gibbons and his boys are singing like canaries in there, so I don't think you're going to worm your way out of this one."

Sharp jerked against the handcuffs. Smitty yanked him back around, and the lawyer came face-to-face with Livy. His sudden stillness caught Smitty's attention, and the detective stopped. A sardonic grin split Sharp's face.

"Well, if it isn't Miss Livy O'Brien." He cut his gaze back to Smitty. "Hey, Detective, if you want to make the headlines in the *Chicago Tribune*, she's the one you should arrest."

Smitty turned Sharp toward the jail. "Aw, shut up, Sharp. I've heard about all of your jawing I can stand. I'll let you and Gibbons cuss at each other for a while."

"You don't want to hear about Light-Fingered Livy O'Brien? The best lock picker in Chicago?" Sharp leveled a shrewd gaze in her direction. "I wondered where you'd gotten off to. Haven't seen you around the last couple of years. I'd think a little hole-in-the-wall like Chestnut would be slim pickings for the likes of you."

Detective Schmidt squinted at Sharp, then turned to Livy, his gaze assessing her. "Miss O'Brien, is that true? Not that I'd expect you to admit it if you are Light-Fingered Livy."

Mr. McIver and the Huff sisters stared at her, their faces

cold and unreadable. Reverend Warren looked shocked—and disappointed.

All Livy's hopes and dreams came crashing down around her. No matter how far she ran, she couldn't outrun her past. It nipped at her heels, ready to snare her at any moment. She squared her shoulders. She couldn't lie about her past, not if her Christian faith meant anything at all.

"Yes, sir. It's true."

She dropped her head. She couldn't offer a defense for her past, only that she'd been forgiven by a higher power than the courts of Chicago. Yes, God, in His infinite mercy forgave her, but now she'd have to go back to the city and face her punishment, whatever it might be.

"Well, aren't you going to arrest her?" Sharp jeered. "Don't tell me the mighty Detective Nate Schmidt is going soft."

Livy looked up and could see the indecision on Smitty's face. He wanted to give her the benefit of the doubt, but the evidence—and her own admission—didn't give him any choice.

Jake stepped in front of her, pushing her behind him. "Smitty, Miss O'Brien has been an upstanding citizen since she came to Chestnut."

Tears filled Livy's eyes, spilling over to plop in the mud at her feet. Jake believed in her. He believed in her goodness. Even if Smitty took her back to Chicago, she'd tuck that belief into her heart.

"If it hadn't been for her, we wouldn't have caught Gibbons and Sharp here and those goons of his." Sam McIver scratched his head. "Isn't there some way to pardon her since she's done so much for Chestnut?"

Miss Janie sidled up to Livy and tucked an arm around her waist.

Smitty glanced at Mr. McIver, then at Jake, a calculating look on his face. "I'll see what I can do. Snagging Sharp and Gibbons is a pretty good trade-off for giving Livy O'Brien her walking papers." His gaze caught Livy's, and she thought he winked. "You're free to go, Miss O'Brien. Just don't leave town, you hear. It wouldn't look too good, you know."

Livy nodded, giddy with relief. "I wouldn't dream of it, Smitty."

❊   ❊   ❊

Jake tapped on Mr. Stillman's open door. The banker looked up from the papers strewn over his desk. He stood and reached out a hand. "Jake. Good to see you."

"Mr. Stillman."

"How you feeling?"

"Better." Jake rested a hand against his chest. "As long as I don't breathe, I make it fine."

"Glad you're on the mend. It's hard to believe Gibbons pulled off such a thing in Chestnut." Stillman shook his head. "And I was one of the ones who went out of my way to get him to open up a factory here."

"Don't blame yourself, Mr. Stillman. You couldn't have known he planned to use child labor."

"Maybe not, but I do feel partly responsible for those poor kids. You can rest assured they'll be taken care of." He folded his hands on his desk and peered at Jake over his spectacles. "Now, what can I do for you today?"

"I've decided to keep my shares in the mine."

"What about that explosion? It destroyed the entrance."

"The entrance behind Gus's cabin is at a lower point. It'll actually work better than the original entrance. And while I was down there, I realized that most of the mine is still stable."

Stillman gave him a shrewd look. "Is that the only reason you changed your mind?"

Jake leaned forward. "MacPherson is going to reopen that mine. And until I know what kind of man we're dealing with, I plan to be right there to make sure it's the safest mine this side of Chicago."

Stillman grinned. "Being stuck in that mine again must have addled your brain. You sure you want to go through with this?"

"As sure as I've ever been."

CHAPTER TWENTY-NINE

THE ORPHANAGE BLAZED with light on Christmas Eve. The girls were thrilled with their corn-husk dolls, and the boys galloped their wooden horses around the parlor, filling the room with joy and laughter. Livy kept an eye on the children they'd rescued from the mines. They weren't as rambunctious as Seth and Georgie, but she figured it would only be a matter of time before they whooped and hollered with the rest of the children.

A knock sounded at the door, and she wove through the crowded room to answer it. Who could that be? It seemed the entire town had already been by to offer them Christmas cheer. She shifted a platter of cookies to her left hand and opened the door to find Smitty and Lavinia MacKinnion. The shock of seeing the two of them together almost made her drop the cookies.

Miss MacKinnion smiled. "Good evening, Miss O'Brien. Detective Schmidt graciously offered to escort me over so I could bring the children some sweets for Christmas." Her smile faltered and uncertainty clouded her eyes. "That is, if you don't mind."

"Of course not." Livy took the bag of candy Lavinia held out and glanced at Smitty. "I thought you'd gone back to Chicago."

His gaze flickered toward Lavinia, and a flush stole over his long, thin face. "I decided to come back for a few days until Sheriff Carter gets back on his feet."

"That's wonderful. Jake sure could use a hand."

Livy held the door wide and ushered them into the front room, unable to keep from staring as the two made their way to Mrs. Brooks's side. She shook her head as she placed the cookies on the table, already groaning with food. Miss MacKinnion and Smitty? Who would have ever thought it?

She turned toward the kitchen.

Jake's lazy gaze met hers across the sea of children milling about the room. He gave her a lopsided smile. Warmth that had nothing to do with the overheated room surged through her. She'd barely seen him in the last couple of days. He'd gone with Smitty to take Sharp, Gibbons, and the rest of his goons to Chicago, and she'd been helping get all the children settled in at the orphanage. There'd been no time for anything else.

He moved, making his way toward her, his green-eyed gaze intent on hers. Livy held her breath. When he reached her side, he didn't even pause. He laced his fingers in hers and led her from the room. Her heart pounded so loud, she feared the entire gathering heard it.

He pulled her into the privacy of the kitchen, shut the door, and looped his arms around her waist. She shivered at his touch and rested her hands on his shoulders.

Sighing, she traced a cut along his jaw. The bruises were fading, the cuts healing. Her heart flipped alarmingly at the thought that she'd almost lost him.

Thank You, Lord, for keeping him safe.

A tiny smile kicked up one side of his mouth. "Light-Fingered Livy O'Brien, huh?"

Livy swatted his arm, her face flaming. "I'll never hear the end of that, will I?"

"Nope. Probably not."

Jake sobered, tilting her chin, his eyes capturing and holding hers. "Livy, I don't care who you were before you came to Chestnut. I know who you are now, and that's the Livy O'Brien I love."

"I love you, too." Livy's breath hitched, and she couldn't hold the tears at bay. "I never dreamed I would fall in love or that anyone would ever love me back."

Jake cupped her face in both hands, wiping away her tears with his thumbs. Then he drew her forward, tilting her face to meet his. His kiss melted her heart and left her longing for more.

He rested his forehead against hers, and she let herself drown in the soft, tender look in his green eyes.

"You stole my heart the first day I met you," he whispered. "Will you marry me?"

"Yes. Oh yes."

Her fingers, light as a butterfly's touch, tangled themselves in his hair and pulled him to her.

Acknowledgments

I'M IN AWE OF THE AMAZING TEAM at Tyndale House who can take a lump of coal in the form of a manuscript and turn it into a beautiful work of art worthy of publication. The acquisitions team, editing, marketing, sales, administration—the list goes on and on. Each of you adds sparkle to this book, and I thank you for your individual touch. Special thanks to Jan Stob, senior acquisitions editor, for welcoming me into the Tyndale family. It's been a joy to work with you all.

Even though romantic-suspense author Robin Caroll doesn't read historicals as a general rule, she's willing to suffer anything for a friend, and she's got an awesome eye for burrowing deeper into a character's motivation and conflict. I owe many, many parts of *Stealing Jake* to her plotting expertise, but especially Luke's gut-wrenching life story. Thank you. For everything.

In the early stages of plotting this manuscript, Tracey Bateman suggested I move this story from Wyoming Territory to a rough Illinois town on the outskirts of Chicago. It made all the difference! Thanks, Tracey. Special thanks to the Seekers: encouragement, critiques, brainstorming, the totally hilarious titling sessions, hand holding, pity parties limited to twenty-four hours, and ecstatically happy parties in Seekerville. Almost every one of you read part or all of *Stealing Jake* at one time or another, some more than once. To some of the best friends—nay, *sisters*—a girl can have: Mary, Julie, Janet, Debby, Missy, Tina, Audra, Ruth, Myra, Sandra, Glynna, Camy, Cheryl, and Cara. Leave no woman behind.

American Christian Fiction Writers (ACFW) is my home away from home throughout the year and even more so every September at the annual conference. I can't imagine not having all of you in my life. What a blessing the loops, chapters, contests, and conference are. If it takes a village, ACFW is a shining city built on a hill.

Thanks to my agent, Steve Laube, a man immersed in the publishing industry. When he speaks, I listen. I might not always understand, but I definitely listen!

I owe a huge debt of thanks to my extended family, who always believed in me, and to my husband, Iran, and my sons, Sean and Darin. The three of you put up with a lot of quick meals and a house that wasn't always spotless to let me pursue my dream. I couldn't ask for a better husband and children to share my life with.

I don't know how my Lord and Savior, Jesus Christ, and my heavenly Father decide these things, but I'm honored that storytelling is the gift I was born with. It seems trite to thank You for that, but it's one of the most treasured gifts I've ever received. I can't imagine wanting to do anything else.

Discussion Questions

1. Luke's pickpocketing escapades force him to leave Chicago, and from there, things get rough for him. In what ways have any of your bad decisions cost you dearly?

2. Both Livy and Jake are facing severe money problems. Can you relate to the way they handle their problems? How?

3. When Livy doubts God's provision of food, the sheriff happens to come by with a wagonload of supplies from a cart accident. Why is it often difficult in lean times to have faith in God's provision? How have you seen Philippians 4:19 play out in your life?

4. Current news stories are rampant with adults who misuse and abuse children, like the kidnapped street kids in the sweatshops of Chicago. How has the United States made strides in protecting the innocent since the late 1800s? What about third-world countries? Can you think of specific cases you've heard of? How can you be involved to help them?

5. Livy tries to hide her past from Jake. Was she right to keep her past a secret? How could Jake have encouraged Livy to trust him more? In your experience do people tend to turn away from a person's difficult past or appreciate their transparency? What factors in a person's story or personality might cause those reactions?

6. Livy rescues people because she once needed to be rescued. Even if you haven't had a similar need in your own past, do you feel the same inner nudging to reach out to others? How do you cultivate and act out that motivation?

7. Have you ever failed to speak up about an issue due to a fear of feeling discomfort or for your own self-protection? What resulted from that experience? If you could relive that moment, would you have the courage to say something?

8. Is there something in your past that has prevented you from moving on in the present, or do you know someone who seems stuck because of a past hurt? What would it take to heal a trauma like that? Would you need to repeat the experience to finally move on from it?

9. In chapter 25, Emma says, "Most of us have pasts we're not proud of." In what ways do you see this as a true statement? How is Emma wrong? Have you been misjudged or have you ever judged someone for something they did in the past but have been forgiven for? What happened as a result?

10. Livy is a defender of the weak (the street kids) while the town folks, even some of the well-meaning Christians, want them gone from their town. Can you think of any time in which you or someone you respect judged someone wrongly? How can we be more like Christ, who is the ultimate defender of the weak?

11. Livy refers to herself as "just a pickpocket from Chicago." Do you ever attach a label like that to yourself or to someone else? What keeps you from identifying yourself and others as redeemed by Christ?

12. The miners work underground in darkness and difficult circumstances, day in and day out. How do you respond when asked to work in difficult circumstances?

13. Will McIver resorts to stealing to support his gambling and drinking habit. Eventually his misdeeds catch up with him and he's forced to pay for his crimes. Considering the situation, does he receive an appropriate punishment? How easy would it have been for Will to let the blame fall on someone he knew rather than on the faceless street kids?

14. Does Jake and Livy's love story develop at a steady pace? Can you see these two falling in love and making a life for themselves and the children in the orphanage? Did the ending leave you with a satisfied smile that all would be well with their future?

TURN THE PAGE FOR A PREVIEW OF ANOTHER NOVEL BY PAM HILLMAN.

"(Hillman is) gifted with a true talent for vivid imagery, heart-tugging romance, and a feel for the Old West that will jingle your spurs."

Julie Lessman,
author of the Daughters of Boston series

★ AVAILABLE IN STORES AND ONLINE ★

CHAPTER ONE

Seth Malone was dead?

Leaving his brother, Buck, to care for the horses, Slade Donovan followed the daughter into the house. She'd swept her golden-brown hair to the top of her head and twisted it into a serene coil. A few curls escaped the loose bun and flirted with the stand-up lace of her white shirtwaist. She sure looked dressed up out here in the middle of nowhere.

Then he remembered the empty streets and the handful of wagons still gathered around the church when they'd passed through Wisdom at noon. He snorted under his breath. Under other circumstances, a woman like Mariah Malone wouldn't even deem him worthy to wipe her dainty boots on, let alone agree to talk to him in private. He couldn't count the times the girls from the "right" side of town had snubbed their noses at him, their starched pinafores in sharp contrast to his torn, patched clothes. At least his younger brother and sisters hadn't been treated like outcasts. He'd made sure of that.

He trailed the Malone woman down the hall, catching a

glimpse of a sitting room with worn but polished furniture on his right, a tidy kitchen on his left. A water stain from a leaky roof marred the faded wallpaper at the end of the wide hallway. While neat and clean, the house and outbuildings looked run-down. He scowled. Surely Seth Malone could have kept the place in better repair with his ill-gotten gain.

Miss Malone led the way into a small office that smelled of leather, ink, and turpentine. She turned, and he caught a glimpse of eyes the color of deep-brown leather polished to a shine. The state of affairs around the house slid into the dark recesses of his mind as he regarded the slender young woman before him.

"Mr. Donovan," she began, "I take it you received my letter."

He nodded but kept silent. Uneasiness wormed its way into his gut. Did Miss Malone have brothers or other family to turn to? Who was in charge of the ranch?

"I'm sorry for what my father did. I wish it had never happened." She toyed with a granite paperweight, the distress on her face tugging at his conscience.

He wished it had never happened too. Would his father have given up if Seth Malone hadn't taken off with all the gold? Would they have had a better life—a ranch of their own maybe, instead of a dilapidated shack on the edge of Galveston—if his father hadn't needed to fight the demons from the bullet lodged in his head?

He wanted to ask all the questions that had plagued him over the years, questions his father had shouted during his drunken rages. Instead, he asked another question, one he'd asked himself many times over the last several months. "Why did you send that letter?"

Pain turned her eyes to ebony. "My father wanted to ask forgiveness for what he had done, but by that time he was unable to write the letter himself. I didn't know Mr. Donovan had a family or that he'd died." She shrugged, the pity on her face unmistakable.

Slade clenched his jaw. He didn't want her pity. He'd had enough of that to last a lifetime.

She strolled to the window, arms hugging her waist. She looked too slight to have ever done a day's work. She'd probably been pampered all her life, while his own mother and sisters struggled for survival.

"I hoped Mr. Donovan might write while my father was still alive, and they could resolve their differences." Her soft voice wafted on the still air. "I prayed he might forgive Papa. And that Papa could forgive himself."

"Forgiveness is too little, too late," Slade gritted out, satisfaction welling within him when her back stiffened and her shoulders squared.

She turned, regarding him with caution. "I'm willing to make restitution for what my father did."

"Restitution?"

"A few hundred head of cattle should be sufficient."

"A few hundred?" Surely she didn't think a handful of cattle would make up for what her father had done.

"What more do you want? I've already apologized. What good will it do to keep the bitterness alive?"

"It's not bitterness I want, Miss Malone. It's the land."

"The land?" Her eyes widened.

He nodded, a stiff, curt jerk of his head. "All of it."

"Only a portion of the land should go to your family, if any. Half of that gold belonged to my father." Two spots of angry color bloomed in her cheeks, and her eyes sparked like sun off brown bottle glass. "And besides, he worked the land all these years and made this ranch into something."

Slade frowned. What did she mean, half of the gold belonged to her father? Disgust filled him. Either the woman was a good actress, or Malone had lied to his family even on his deathbed.

"All of it."

She blinked, and for a moment, he thought she might give in. Then she lifted her chin. "And if I refuse?"

"One trip to the sheriff with your letter and the wanted poster from twenty-five years ago would convince any law-abiding judge that this ranch belongs to me and my family." He paused. "As well as the deed to the gold mine in California that has my father's name on it—not your father's."

"What deed?" She glared at him, suspicion glinting in her eyes. "And what wanted poster?"

Did she really not know the truth? Slade pulled out the papers and handed them to her, watching as she read the proof that gave him the right to the land they stood on.

All color left her face as she read, and Slade braced himself in case she fainted clean away. If he'd had any doubt that she didn't know the full story, her reaction to the wanted poster proved otherwise.

"It says . . ." Her voice wavered. "It says Papa shot your father. Left him for dead. I don't believe it. It . . . it's a mistake." She sank into the nearest chair, the starch wilted out of her. The condemning poster fluttered to the floor.

A sudden desire to give in swept over him. He could accept her offer of a few hundred head, walk out the door, and ride away, leaving her on the land that legally, morally, belonged to him. To his mother.

No! He wanted Seth Malone to pay for turning his father into a drunk and making his mother old before her time. But Seth Malone was dead, and this woman wouldn't cheat him of his revenge.

No matter how innocent she looked, no matter how her eyes filled with tears as she begged for forgiveness, he wouldn't give it to her. Forgiveness wouldn't put food on the table or clothes on his mother's and sisters' backs.

"No mistake." He hunkered down so he could see her face. "You have a right to defend your father's memory, I reckon. But I'll stick by what I said. The deed is legal. And that letter will stand up in court as well. You've got a decision to make, ma'am. Either you sign this ranch over to me, or I'll go to the sheriff."

Silence hung heavy between them until a faint noise drew Slade's attention to the doorway.

An old woman stood there, a walking stick clasped in her right hand. Her piercing dark gaze swung from Mariah to him. He stood to his full height.

"Grandma." Mariah launched herself from the chair and hurried to the woman's side.

The frail-looking woman's penetrating stare never left Slade's face.

He held out his hand for the deed. Silence reigned as Mariah handed it over.

"I'll give you an hour to decide." He gave them a curt nod and strode from the room.

About the Author

Christian Booksellers Association bestselling author PAM HILLMAN writes inspirational fiction set in the turbulent times of the American West and the Gilded Age. Her novels have won or been finalists in the Inspirational Reader's Choice, the EPIC eBook Awards, and the International Digital Awards.

Pam is the assistant director and financial officer of American Christian Fiction Writers. She lives in Mississippi with her husband and family and loves to hear from her readers. Visit her website at www.pamhillman.com.